THE NORTHERN CHILD

ASHLEY CULLEN

To Mima

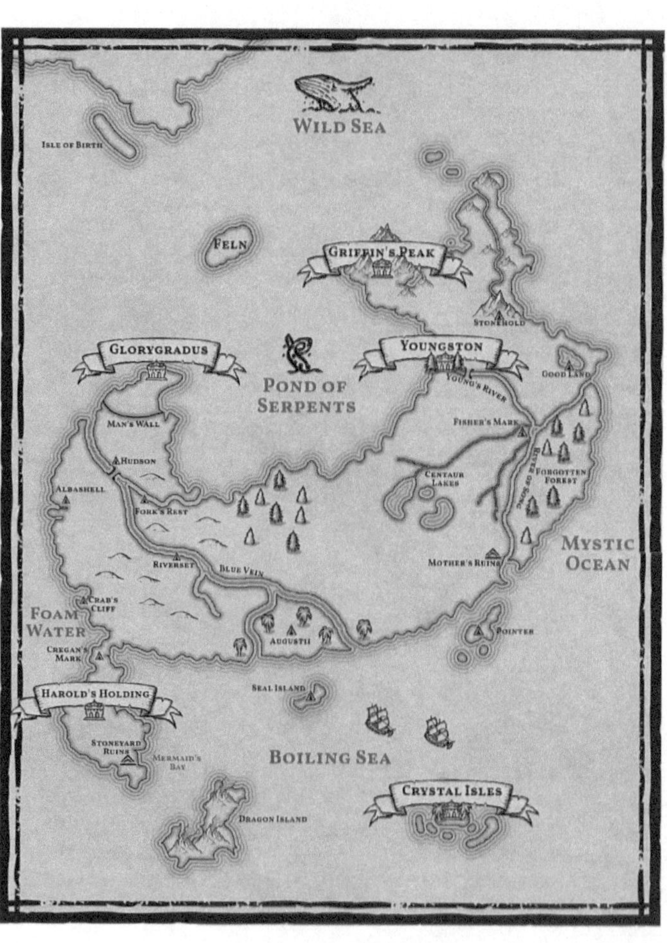

WILD SEA
ISLE OF BIRTH
FELN
GRIFFIN'S PEAK
STONEHOLD
GLORYGRADUS
POND OF SERPENTS
YOUNGSTON
YOUNG'S RIVER
GOOD LAND
MAN'S WALL
FISHER'S MARK
HUDSON
CENTAUR LAKES
FORGOTTEN FOREST
ALBASHELL
RIVER OF BLOOD
FORK'S REST
RIVERSET
BLUE VEIN
MOTHER'S RUINS
MYSTIC OCEAN
CRAB'S CLIFF
FOAM WATER
AUGUSTII
POINTER
CREGAN'S MARK
SEAL ISLAND
HAROLD'S HOLDING
STONEYARD RUINS
MERMAID'S BAY
BOILING SEA
CRYSTAL ISLES
DRAGON ISLAND

The Start of a Song

Autumn kissed the dying leaves with shades of yellow, red, and brown. The air ran crisp and smelled of plant decay. Winter was coming. As the nymph sat beneath the giant pine branches of the First Tree, they knew that this winter would be different.

Because they heard a song.

It was quiet at first. The wind loved to sing, and the trees loved to join. Often, they sang of the seasons changing. But last night, faint and unsteady as a wolf cub's howl, the wind crooned a song that had not blown through the land for generations. *Northern Child...*it whispered.

The nymph had been waiting for it.

The nymph placed a delicate green hand against the rough bark of the First Tree. The wind kissed their cheek. They had never left this forest, and asked the First Tree for good luck. A pine needle fell from the branches and skimmed their arm. *Go on.*

With a nod, the nymph pulled their cloak tight around their body. It was time to go. They would not make the same mistake twice. They would not watch their world burn again.

*Northern Child...*the wind cried.

The nymph turned and followed it.

BOOK I

BIRTH

One

Griffin's Peak

The boy stared at the dragon's egg from the crack between the wooden door and the rough stone wall. The glow from the torches shimmered on its black shell, like moonlight against the still water of a pond. This morning, he'd been a normal boy living in the shadows with his brothers.

But that was before.

I need to sleep. His hands were sweating. He wanted to storm into Stone Teeth's chamber and take it. With a shuddering sigh, he turned his back on it and walked away. The other lads were headed for bed. They clapped him on the back. Soon they'd all be rich! All thanks to him.

It's different now. With a pit of uncertainty, he knew his life was about to change. He thought back to the morning. It started like any other, with a blow to the face.

It's cold. The boy shivered, tugging the ragged animal fur tighter over his thin frame. Chilled air licked his cheeks and bit his nose. Cuddling further into the blanket, he willed sleep to find him again.

"Oi!" A rough sack smacked him.

The boy sprang up, rubbing furiously at his violated jaw. His pale hand closed over a meager pillow, ready to attack the one who'd assaulted him.

"Sleepin' on the job, Crow?" Laughed a gaunt young lad. His wiry body shook with laughter beneath a loose stained jerkin lined with matted fur. In his hand was a worn leather sack that Crow guessed was filled with flakes of flint.

"On the job?" Crow grumbled. "Most the boys are still sleepin'." Relieving the pillow from his fist, he rose from the cool stone floor and stretched. Black hair sat atop his head like the ruffled feathers of a raven. He ran a hand through it, trying to smooth it down, but had no luck. "I hope a griffin plucks you off a cliff."

"Ain't enough meat on him for the griffins to eat." A passing boy snipped.

Crow glanced around to see that most boys were still sleeping despite the activity around them. *They'll get shaken awake soon enough.* Torches were jammed into the rigid mountain walls, feathering the room in a dull orange glow. Mouse, a small boy with ashy gray hair, was lighting them as he did every morning. Sleeping sacks littered the floor like a grungy goat-skin carpet. Boys from all ages slept buried under the sacks' thin embrace. Some sat up and yawned as they awoke for the day's dig.

Bones plucked at a bug crawling in his fur collar. "We're startin' a new tunnel today. Stone Teeth will toss us off the mountain if we don't show up early to pick it clean."

Bones ran a hand through his short blond hair. His face was as sharp as his wits, his eyes brown and full of private jokes. Like Crow, he was one of the few boys dropped off to the Underground Lads before he was five winters old. Now fourteen, the Lads were all they knew. Crow had no recollection of his life before.

The Underground Lads kept the boys off the streets, where they'd likely resort to thieving and begging for coin. Crow was put to work, provided a place to sleep, and offered two meals a day. But most of all, the Lads offered him brotherhood.

"A new tunnel..." Crow followed Bones out of the packed cavern. "How did you know we're leaving the other one?" The rough stairs to the dining hall chilled the undersides of Crow's feet.

"Because I know everything." Bones glided down to the wooden door awaiting their arrival. Bright light leaked through the cracked wood. The thin boy wrenched it open, and sunlight bathed the hall in a white glow. Crow had to shield his eyes from the sudden influx. It always took him longer to adjust to such brightness. *Stupid blue eyes.* He blinked away the irritation. They were more sensitive than the others.

The dining hall was practically empty for now. The morning sun blazed through the windows, illuminating the far rock wall. Outside the fogged glass stood the mountains surrounding the kingdom of Griffin's Peak, the snow-capped summits reflecting the daylight. Wooden tables crowded the room, only a few held a portion of boys for breakfast. The air smelled like baking bread and boiled eggs. Bones and Crow waited near the hot stone oven filling the hall with thick heat and smoke.

A round young man, white as a ghost, hovered over the roaring flames and blackened stone top. Red hair stuck to his forehead with grease. With a frown, he handed Bones and Crow their dishes; two boiled eggs and a heel of brown bread slathered in snow apple jam.

"You need any more kitchen boys?" Bones snickered once his food was securely in his grasp. "Stone Teeth wouldn't force me into the tunnels if I didn't fit."

"Piss off." Pudge, the red-headed boy, replied with little passion. At this point, quips from Bones were as common as mice in the sleeping room.

"I bet if Pudge cut half his blubber away, you could make yourself a new coat." Crow observed. He sat on a splintered bench before shoving a large bit of bread into his mouth. The jam was tart.

"It's been a while since I got a new one." Bones agreed.

The boys continued to eat the rest of their breakfast in silence. The hall slowly grew louder with chatter and laughter. Crow sighed as he peeled open a rubbery boiled egg. Although the days of the Underground Lads were long and hard, it was impossible to imagine where he'd be without them. Yet sometimes, Crow felt disconnected from the others. All the boys remembered their lives before. Some even remembered their old names. But not him. He'd always been Crow, a nameless boy with nameless parents. *But Bones is like me,* he thought, chewing the slippery egg white. Ultimately, all the boys were stitched together by abandonment, dead parents, or worse. Crow ate meals every day and had a place to return to every night. He'd stay in the Lads until he was grown, then he'd head out into the mines.

Sometimes the thought left a bad taste in his mouth, but mining was all he knew. Crow forced the rest of the bread into his mouth, willing himself to think of something else.

"Alright." Bones stood up, relieving Crow from his thoughts. "Let's go before everyone gets the jump on us."

The wind was the first thing to greet them as they left the shelter of the dining hall. It whipped Crow's hair from his eyes and pulled loose his clothing. Griffin's Peak was always cold and windy. *"A man from*

Glorygradus or the Isles would be blown right off the cliffs." Stone Teeth had laughed at them once. *"But Mother Vitania made us of tougher stuff, sturdy as rock."*

The mountains loomed around them, taller than the legendary pines of the Forgotten Forest, cutting into the horizon like crooked teeth. The sun bounced off of the white peaks in blinding silver light. Houses, inns and shops were carved into the mountain walls honeycombing the slopes. While another kingdom like Glorygradus was said to spread far and wide, Griffin's Peak spread up and up and up. Narrow stone pathways connected a tavern to a blacksmith, a home to an alchemist. They bandaged large cracks and fissures that ended in deadly drops. The White Water split the kingdom in two, running down the mountains of the Peak as angry white mist and roaring water.

Wooden bridges were already clogged with miners ready to begin the day. Crow looked up to the sky. Up there, the Griffin's Roost stood guard over them all, the keep that dominated the summit of the Great Claw. The home of the king. Thick ropes crisscrossed the kingdom's sky holding wooden baskets swinging in the wind. The rope crawled across the kingdom in a web, carrying different goods to portions of the city much faster than a man could.

Got to hold on tight today, Crow reflected as the wind tore at his clothes. The Underground Lads was little more than a hole dug into the base at the bottom of the Great Claw, conveniently placed where the wooden baskets started and ended their journey. Large wheeled gears turned in an endless rotation from the White Water's current, pushing the ropes endlessly around Griffin's Peak's sky. The baskets made the perfect transportation for skinny boys on their way to the upper tunnels.

Crow liked to make his jump at a sheltered platform built beside the calming river. The baskets started close to the ground before beginning the long climb up to the summits. The boys had to jump into them at just the right moment, and Crow and Bones were the most practiced.

"Maybe I'll keep a jewel for myself this time." Bones grinned. Running forward, his long limbs gracefully cleared the ground as he jumped up. His thin arms shot out and grabbed the ropes that ran from the basket's corners and secured it to the thick moving line. Once Bones's feet made purchase in the box, it lurched forward with newly added weight before finally settling.

"If you can even find one!" Crow called after him. With a running leap, Crow jumped into the next. The wind whistled in his ears and swayed the basket as it ascended further into the air.

Crow whooped, his cheers ripping away into the wind. This was the best part of his day.

With the sun shining off of the fresh snow and the wind ruffling his hair, Crow could almost pretend he was flying. *Like a griffin,* he imagined. He'd only ever seen one once, two winters ago, and it was so far away that it appeared no larger than an eagle. According to Stone Teeth, they used to be everywhere, but they fled once the feln appeared to rip the land apart.

The basket jolted as it traveled across the jagged edge of a cliff face. It was still too early yet, but soon it would be filled with iron and flint from men and women with dirt-crusted faces.

Portions of the kingdom rose up to meet him before falling away as he left the mountain's side. Crow felt the freezing mist from the White Water lightly kiss his cheeks and fingers. Wooden hovels littered the slopes beneath him like unsightly wasp nests. As he ascended, the homes shifted from wood to stone, and the people milling about in the early morning got plumper in their bright-colored clothes.

Crow climbed higher still, and soon nobles were traded out for knights in shining armor that reflected in the morning sun. The knights of court could be seen sparring with the danger of falling to their deaths off unforgiving cliff edges. City guards and soldiers began to descend into the squalor below, and performers grasped for a high-born lord or lady's attention. *It's a different world up here.*

Then the Roost rose, momentarily blotting out the sun. Massive stone griffins sat carved into the Great Claw's face hundreds of feet high. An arched doorway gilded in gold stood between them, dwarfed by the guarding statues. It was said the castle was engraved into the mountain during the Conquering Age, when the first men braved the Pond of Serpents. All the children of the Peak knew of Arthur Thunderborn, who harnessed the power of lightning and claimed the Great Claw in the name of men.

Eventually the Roost fell away; and Crow remained above them all.

The cart took a sharp right, and he had to grasp the rope to keep from flying out. Where he headed now was less settled, spattered with wooden platforms jammed into the rock to process findings from the caves. A stark black ribbon tied to a stick and thrust into the crevassed mountainside told Crow where they needed to be. *There's where we'll be diggin' today.* Stone Teeth always left before dawn to mark the spot.

Bones braced ahead of him to jump out. The baskets made no stops, so timing was everything. Countless boys fell to their deaths due to a poorly executed leap. Bones seized the opportunity when the box grazed the rocky slope, and landed swiftly on his feet. Crow followed suit.

The wind was stronger up here; it threatened to push him off the side of the summit with every gust. The other Lads would catch up soon, but for now they were alone.

Bones stood at the platform's edge, a thin pole against the ripping winds. Crow never understood how the other boy could be so sturdy. Bones stared down at the Roost through the lines of ropes and baskets. It was smaller than Crow's hand up here.

"Taller than all of them." Bones said. "My parents could be one of those slugs down there and I'd never know." Fluffing his fox collar, he turned. "Bet my father's the king. He screwed some wedded noble lady and dropped me off to the Lads to keep it hush."

"The king's got red hair." Crow rolled his eyes. "If anything, Pudge is his son."

Crow bumped Bones on the shoulder to make him feel better. Bones was stubborn, and got caught up in his head more than Crow sometimes. He showed up early to every dig, dragging Crow with him in hopes of finding something grand. He had dreams of traveling around Frukjera, from Youngston to Glorygradus. They fantasized about wandering the world as children. But that was before Shadow disappeared.

That bad taste rose in Crow's throat again.

One day, at the end of a dig, Bones and Crow stood on a platform much like this one. "At least we're not eatin' a bunch of pebbles like Picker had to." Crow had said. "We've got a home."

"This ain't no home. They'll throw us out once we're too big."

"Then we'll join the others." Crow urged. "We've got brothers here."

"Please." Bones glared. "Even you don't believe that, Crow. You and I both know, we're not like the rest of them."

"We're exactly like the rest of them." Crow didn't talk to Bones for two days afterwards.

Bones smirked now, lightly pushing Crow away and entering the tunnel. "My hair could be red." He said. "But it's so dirty no one can tell." He laughed, vanishing into the darkness. Crow ran after him.

A few fatty lanterns were already hanging on the walls, casting sharp shadows where the uneven rock receded and stuck out like frozen waves. *Looks promising.* Crow thought, picking up a pickaxe from the pile thrown lazily against the wall. The tools were worn with heavy use, stained with dirt and rusting. The perk of being first to a dig meant being first pick of the axes. Bones and Crow grabbed the best ones.

"Ha! Look who we got showin' up!" A great voice bellowed. "Bone's n Crow, gettin' first sniff o' the place? Just blew her open yesterday! Ha!"

The leader of the Underground Lads stood in the fire light; cheeks stained with soot. A black leather shirt stretched across his thick chest, synched into a large belt heavy with tools. His tree trunk arms were crossed over his chest. He appeared comically massive in the narrow tunnel. Yellow hair fell to his broad shoulders in matted curls. An equally yellow beard framed his smiling mouth, which earned him his name. Mouse liked to snicker that Mother Vitania got lazy when making Stone Teeth, throwing a handful of pebbles into his mouth instead of giving him proper teeth.

"You know it." Bones smiled back. "Think I'll find some gems and keep them for myself today."

"You do that, boy, and I'll throw you off the side of the mountain me self. Ha!" Stone Teeth grabbed some flint from his belt. "This is a promising one, boys. There are natural tunnels all through here. Small Red only needed to blow in an entrance. Ha! I lit the one over there." He motioned to the right, where a dull glow of lanterns shone through the stone archway. "It splits into two smaller ones, figure both o' you could take one, don't seem to go deep. I'd rush in before the other Lads get here."

"Sounds like a plan." Bones swung his pickaxe over his shoulder.

The tunnel broke into two, as Stone Teeth had said. Both were narrow, with one large enough to stand in. The other was a low black hole that needed to be crawled through.

"I'm takin' the right." Bones said immediately, already shoving past Crow. "No crawlin' for me today."

"You never crawl *any* day." Crow smirked, grabbing the closest lantern off the wall. He saw bloody knees in his future, but Crow would have chosen this hole anyway. He liked the challenge and the dark.

Once he squeezed into the entrance it opened into a taller passage. Crow shimmied in and stood. The cave hugged his sides like a frightened child. He wanted to see how deep it went, and get the feel and the layout of the thing before looking for potential findings. He didn't mind the jagged rocks or the sharp shadows. Crow liked searching the tunnels, observing quietly the story that the rocks told. He smiled, recalling the first time he'd explored a tunnel alone. No more than six winters old, Crow had screamed and shouted in protest.

"Don't make me!" He wailed, clinging to Shadow's legs. The older boy had deep brown skin and warm brown eyes. He used to teach all the young ones how to properly find treasures, and he became one of Crow's closest brothers.

"We've all done it." Shadow said as he wrenched Crow off his leg. "Besides, all good jewels are always in the smaller holes. Don't you want to find good jewels?"

"What about the cave-feln?" The stories passed around the Underground Lads always depicted monsters in the dark eating little boys.

Shadow knelt, ruffling Crow's thick black hair. "All the feln got chased away to their island long ago. There are no monsters in that hole. The only monsters you got to worry about," Shadow pointed with his thumb over his shoulders, back behind them to the cave's entrance, "are out there."

Crow took a deep breath, facing the black hole with eyes fogged from tears. Then, he began to dig. That day he'd come out with a basket of emeralds, and the cook had given him fried bacon in celebration.

Now, the air stank of burning fat from the lantern and everything was dark.

The cavern before him yawned open into a giant pocket, so large that darkness swallowed the lantern's light. *How deep does this go?* Crow wondered hesitantly. Too many boys had gone missing in the mountains, only for search parties to find passages that ended in sheer trenches and underground rivers. Just last moon's turn, Snitch crawled into a cave and never came out. Crow listened for any hint of running water, or echoes that would uncover empty pits.

Nothing.

Edging forward, Crow kept his eyes on the ground, careful not to step into any sudden holes. *The floor's smooth,* too smooth for a natural cavern floor. Crow knelt and brushed his knuckles against the granite ground. *This's flattened.* There was no doubt about it. Not even the floor of their sleeping room was as smooth as this. He held out his lantern and stood back up.

A moment of excitement flashed through his mind. Perhaps he'd come across a secret room, sealed away by ancient men to hide treasures and runes. Jewels or magic spells. *Even the Thunderborn's staff,* Crow thought with boyish exhilaration as he continued to inch forward. The floor continued with little interruption. No indication of walls or ceiling kissed the edge of Crow's firelight.

"Hello!" Crow called, listening to how his voice bounced off the walls. *There's an echo, but nothing too big.* The flame flickered against something carved into the floor. Crow bent down and stretched his arm to let light pour over the crevasses and lines.

"Dragons." Crow's eyes grew wide with wonder. He crawled forward on his hands and knees, curiosity spurring him on. Two large feathered serpents were carved into the floor. Their long necks were looped and staring into the cavern as if urging Crow to crawl further in. Each feather was dug into the granite in painstaking detail. Their wings were folded like a bird's. Intricate snowflakes clustered and filled the space between the dragons' thin limbs. Crow's breath snuck between his lips in a puff of frozen air.

The carvings seemed to be leading him deeper, like something was waiting for him at the end of this long picture.

Crow stopped. His fingers were red from the cold stone floor. *Bones needs to see this.*

It took Crow only a few minutes to reach the narrow tunnel from whence he came. The cave had come alive with other boys, and Crow nearly crashed into Mouse on his way out.

"What's the rush?" The small boy asked.

"Where's Bones? There's a room in here." Crow pulled Mouse close. "I think it's got treasure or something."

"For real?" Mouse stared at Crow skeptically. "Stone Tooth just found this cave."

"Yeah, it's old stuff. *Magic* stuff." Crow insisted. "*Dragons* are dug into the floor."

The small boy's eyes widened. "Dragons!" He yelled, causing the others to stop and stare. *Maybe I should've told Bones first.*

"What's this I hear about dragons?" Bones emerged from his tunnel and dusted himself off with his free hand, lantern clutched in the other. Crow told him what he'd found.

It didn't take much convincing to gain followers. Soon, a line of boys was squeezing through the narrow tunnel, with Bones in front and Crow behind. Multiple torches and lanterns flickered off the wall, shadows danced against jagged surfaces. Boys spilled from the crack and faced the cavern with quiet excitement.

The lanterns made it easier to see. Faded walls drank up as much fire as they dared. The height of the space remained a mystery as their light concentrated on the intricate carvings on the floor. The boys moved forward eagerly, yet cautiously, not forgetting the tricks of mountain caves. Crow followed Bones with pride. *I found this place, and now we get to share the treasure.* What could possibly be in here? Unicorn horns? Dragon teeth? Ancient runes?

The end of the hall was now in sight. The dragons on the floor clawed at something that lay before them. The firelight seemed to shrink, and goose bumps riddled Crow's arms as a chill ran through the group. Hesitation hit a few of the younger ones. "What if this is a lair of the feln?" Puke—a small pale lad—asked. Others nodded. For a moment, Crow's enthusiasm faltered. He knew the feln were far away, but what was this strange place? Why was it so cold?

"It's not." Bones answered. "The feln never made nothing like this." He waved his flickering torch at the ground, then to the wall before them.

The snowflakes on the ground clustered and eventually piled from carving to sculpture, building against the tall granite slab behind them. Two stone dragons relieved into the slab bent their necks to stare at something nestled into the stone snowflake nest. As the boys approached, a shine from the nest caught the torchlight and glimmered.

"Treasure!" The boys exclaimed, all shoving one another to get a closer look. The small ones were trampled and pushed to the back. Bones and Crow elbowed their way to the front, where sharp snowflakes jabbed into their torsos. The nest reached Crow's chest. The jostling continued until Bones waved his lantern around, threatening to set hair on fire.

"Piss off! We can all take a look!" He shouted. "It's big, isn't it?" Bringing the fire down to the object, the flame nearly died. A hush fell over the group.

"It looks like a polished rock." Crow said. Tucked in like a bird's egg, was an oval stone the size of Crow's head. Pitch black it was, with a scaled polished surface that warped the reflection of the Underground Lads as they stared at it. The light bounced off of it like rippling water.

Something deep inside Crow urged him to reach out and touch it.

"Is it some kind of jewel?" Mouse asked. "I've never seen a thing like it."

"Me neither." Bones marveled. With a thin hand, he touched it—only to instantly rip his hand away with a curse. "It's bloody cold!" He seethed, shaking his hand like he'd been burned.

"What do you mean—*ouch*!" Mouse squealed, sucking his finger.

"No way it's that bad." Crow said in disbelief.

"Come on then," Bones urged, "you touch it."

"Touch it."

"Touch it!" The others chanted.

"You scared?" Puke squeaked from the back.

"I'm not scared! I'm just smarter than all of you." Crow saw his reflection in the stone. "Maybe it's some kind of ice..." His blue eyes stood out starkly on the rippling black surface. *It's like a moving thing, like the rippling of a puddle.* He had to inspect it closer.

"I've never touched ice like that." Bones insisted. "Go on. Or are you goin' to let Puke call you scared?"

Without an answer, Crow placed his palm against the stone. It felt cool under his skin. Thin but incredibly strong.

"It's...fine." Crow said. "You all girls or something?" He wiggled the thing free and picked it up with both hands. "Look at it."

With a hard expression, Bones reached for it again.

"Ha!" Stone Teeth boomed.

Everyone turned.

The large man was at the end of the hall. Crow was surprised he'd managed to fit through the cracks. "Is this where my crew ran off to?" He yelled, striding forward carrying a torch as long and thick as Crow's arm. "I'll have you all eating goat hooves tonight, unless you each got your weight in gold!"

"We found somethin'!" Mouse retorted.

Stone Teeth waved the torch, clearing the boys out of the way between himself and Crow. A serious expression set on the man's face; his eyes only flickered to the dragons on the wall briefly before settling on the thing in Crow's possession. Crow held it tighter to his chest. Stone Teeth stretched a meaty hand out to grab it.

"*Ha!*" He gasped, snatching his arm away. "That's one cold piece o' work!" Leaning down, he inspected it, dragging a finger across his hairy chin.

"For some reason Crow's the only one who can hold it." Puke said.

"That so?" Stone Teeth took his eyes from it for the first time. "Where'd you find it?"

"In there." Crow gestured behind him. "Is it worth somethin'?"

Crow's question hung in the air as Stone Teeth inspected the floor, the frosted nest, and finally the sculpture relieved into the wall. "Too cold, aye." Stone Teeth mumbled. "She was right..." The large man turned; his face white as snow. He then grabbed a pickaxe from one of the boys and swung it down onto the stone's surface. Crow screamed like he'd been struck, and nearly dropped the stone from the force.

It didn't break! His eyes bulged in astonishment. The axe glanced off harmlessly, leaving not even a scratch.

"You may want to hold onto it a bit longer, boy." Stone Teeth clapped him on the shoulder. "If I'm right, we need to take it to the Roost. What you have, son, is a dragon's egg."

The boys exploded in excited chanting and pushing, wanting to see the egg in a new light. Grubby hands grabbed for it only to dart away in pain. Crow's heart hammered with the same passion, yet he felt frozen in place as he clutched the egg to his chest. Looking at Bones, the excitement in his gut faltered.

Bones stared at Crow frowning, jealousy burning in his eyes.

Two

The Roost

The Roost dominated the sky. Crow had never been so close to it. He realized the sheer scale of it was incomprehensible until he stood beneath the griffins' shadows. He'd always viewed it from afar, on the cliff faces and mountain trails. From here, the legends seemed truer than fiction about the castle's creation. *How could men build a place like this?* He wondered.

The late autumn sun hung low above. Despite the approaching evening, the yard remained clogged with lords, farmers, shopkeepers, beggars, traveling knights, city watchmen and priestesses. All waited for a chance to hold company with the king. King Arthur Arrowhead only held court once every moon's turn, when the moon rose full into the night. Requests, grievances, praise and enquiries must all be made by sun down.

Stone Teeth had held company with the king before. "Good man has one hell of a stone up his hole, ha!" He'd said. As the leader of the Lads, he requested food, equipment, and reported findings. Boring stuff. But regardless, the stories about the people of court were always fun to hear. Plus, it was exciting to know a man who met with the king. *And now, I'm goin' to.*

Crow tightened his grip on the strapped satchel slung across his chest. The stone, or egg as they referred to it, felt heavy against his shoulder. Days had passed since Crow found it. Further exploration of the chamber provided more carvings of snow and dragons, but no other eggs were found. Empty rooms and tunnels were explored for a time, but they had nothing to offer. Two boys were lost in the endless mazes, and Stone Teeth thought it best to ditch the territory altogether. Stone Teeth kept the egg in his chambers for safekeeping. Rumors speculated on whether or not it would hatch. Bones was quick to lay them to rest. *"Dragons don't come from the mountains."* He retorted. *"They live in the south."*

Bones, Crow frowned. The boy had been in a sour mood ever since the egg appeared. He no longer woke Crow to accompany him early to the mountains. He sat quietly at their meals, and worked harder and longer than usual. The message was clear, he was angry that Crow could handle the egg and he could not. Bones's cool demeanor left Crow in a nasty mood too. *Such a stupid thing to be mad about.* Soon enough, the egg would be gone, and hopefully it was worth a pretty penny.

Yet, Crow looked down at the dirty satchel cradling his treasure, biting his lip. "You think King Arthur's goin' to give us a lot of gold for this?" Crow tugged at the strap.

"Hard to say." Stone Teeth said. "Don't see why not. It's a rare egg you got there, boy. Ha! A dragon's egg in the mountain! Cold as sin. Never thought I'd see one."

"Why not just take it to the Jeweler's Den?" That's what they usually did with their findings

"An egg's no jewel! The lack of sunlight's made you dim. Besides, this one here's different. You ever seen any dragons up in these mountains? You see any flames drawn in that cellar?"

"No." Crow admitted.

"Aye. I've seen dragon eggs before. They're traded up from Harold's Holding where they deal with the buggers all the time. They never hatch once men take 'em, but they're pretty. Hot to the touch, they are. This one, though, I've got a mind to believe we got an ice dragon's egg. Ha!"

Crow raised his eyebrows. He'd only heard stories of the fierce fire-breathing beasts that dominated the southwestern coast. Impossible to tame, the dragons ruled most of Mermaid's Bay. Dragon Island remained untouched by men, ancient nymphs or even the feln. Shadow and Stone Teeth used to share tales of brave heroes who tried to ride the dragons, only to end in fire and blood.

"I thought ice dragons weren't real." Crow said.

"Most people don't." Stone Teeth confirmed. "But there's a kernel of truth in many stories, even ones made to scare children."

"Should I start worryin' about cave-feln?" Crow raised a brow.

"Ha!" Stone Teeth bellowed. He scratched his chin. "Once you've been around as long as I, lad, you'll learn that the world's a stranger place than you thought."

"But if this is an ice dragon's egg," Crow nearly whispered, "why are we givin' it to the king?" Crow didn't want to give it away. "If it's so rare, we could take it to the markets." He added quickly.

"It's a piece o' history, boy! There's more to life than coin! Besides, those chambers ought to be given to the king. Escavatin' stuff like that isn't our job. Let the king lose his own men among the mountain caves. I need my lads."

Crow peaked at the egg again. Could it really hold a creature thought to be myth? Crow reached for it. He wanted to see the black shell in the sunlight. His hand wrapped around its rough surface. *Cold.* Before he could lift it from the satchel, Stone Teeth slapped him upside the head. Crow dropped it, nearly keeling off balance as it sunk back into the bag's embrace.

"What was that for?" Crow hissed.

"Don't you go takin' it out now." He admonished. "These folks don't need to see it."

It was true. The Roost remained clogged with the people of court. Crow had never seen such a mix of folks together. From the ropes that crossed the Peak's sky, segregation hung over the kingdom like an invisible wall. But here, merchants and miners, nobles and beggars, all of them tolerated the presence of the other. Granted, most kept to their respective groups, but seeing them all packed together was still a rare sight. Among them, Crow spotted a few knights in mismatched armor. They wore no colors, nor arms to tell which king they served. The knights of the Arrowheads wore crested helms adorned with the arrowhead of their king. Crow didn't know much about the banners from the other royal families, but not one of these knights seemed to belong to anyone. *Foot knights.*

The presence of such knights wasn't anything special. Crow would often see them wandering the Planks. But *these* in particular, these were—

"Women." Crow blurted with wonder.

A group of them stood huddled together, murmuring among themselves. They seemed maybe ten winters older than Crow, an age that most women had a babe in their belly. He'd never seen women dressed in armor this way, with strong arms protectively clasping the hilts of damaged weapons. *They stand like men.* The tallest and broadest of the group met his eyes. Her skin was deep and golden, her straight black hair chopped roughly at the jawline. The woman's dark sharp eyes scrutinized him.

"What are you looking at, boy?" She spat.

Crow quickly looked away, clutching the satchel closer. Stone Teeth roared with laughter, slapping Crow on the back.

"Starin' at the wrong ladies, lad. Ha!"

"I didn't know women could be knights." Crow muttered.

"Aye." Stone Teeth nodded. "There are a few. They'll find no work here, though. King Arthur's too much o' a religious man. They'd best get back to the road."

"We're not here for petty work." The woman said. She stood tall as Stone Teeth, with a two-handed longsword strapped to her back. It was a nice sword, Crow noticed, with a silver unicorn rearing at the pommel.

"We carry a message from Good Land." Another said. Her ratty blond hair was tied in two tight braids down her skull. "Duke Milfred has concerning news for the king."

"And he sent women? I imagine it can't be that important." Stone Teeth laughed.

"We don't need to answer to this fool." The woman with the sword said. "The road from Good Land to Griffin's Peak isn't what it used to be. You'd be begging us for protection before the moon rose." They walked away to join their other companion.

"Foot knights always think they're more important than they really are." Stone Teeth grumbled to Crow, watching the women's backs. "That's why you always see them drinking the taverns dry in the Planks. The dukes and kings don't want 'em, so they think the common man does."

Stone Teeth told the truth of it. Most of the foot knights that Crow saw were involved in street brawls or bloody vigilante business.

"What man would fight a woman?" Crow shook his head.

"Men that don't fear the Mother's wrath." Stone Teeth shrugged. "You'll find a lot of them as you get older, boy."

The sun dipped below the jagged horizon as Crow and Stone Teeth were ushered into the long hall. They were among the last to speak, and a day of standing had taken a toll on Crow's shoulders and legs. He was ready to throw the stupid egg at King Arthur's feet if it meant a warm plate of food and a comfortable place to sit. But upon entering the great golden doors, a new buzz of excitement returned strength to his bones. *I'm in a castle.*

Banners as long as ships hung from an impossibly-high ceiling. They were red as blood emblazoned with the gray arrow of the royal family. Great crystal clusters covered the top of the hall like stars, causing light from the decorative torches to dance and sparkle like sunlight on the sea. Relieved into the stone walls were tremendous scenes of Arthur Thunderborn wielding lightning and griffins taking flight. The epic carvings followed Crow and Stone Teeth as they drew closer to the throne. The chair of the Roost looked like it'd burst through the floor in an act of the Mother, jutting violently upwards on a jagged stone untouched by a chisel. It wasn't ornate or lavish, yet it held a definite air of power. The throne loomed above any noble, peasant or Underground Lad who entered its domain.

Upon the ancient throne sat King Arthur Arrowhead. His red hair and beard burst from his head like wild flames. His limbs were thick bands of muscle, reined in behind his simple gray doublet. A belt of rubies synched across his waist, and on his head rested the crown of Griffin's Peak; gold hammered in the shape of feathers crusted with gemstones of ruby, sapphire, and emerald. Crow had only ever seen the king from miles high, when he was tucked on precarious cliff sides with the other boys as they watched courtly celebrations from afar. King Arthur looked no different than the other tiny people from that height.

But now, King Arthur sat above them all.

His son, named Arthur as well, sat to his right in one of the smaller seats for council. If Crow could remember correctly, the heir was close to the same age as him, although the prince already had a hint of a red beard along his jaw and could probably snap Crow's arm like a twig. A few more council members were present, but Crow knew not their names.

"You stand before Your Highness Arthur Arrowhead, king of Griffin's Peak and ruler of the Ridge." Sir Maxwell Tryke, the king's champion, boomed. Crow knew him from spied tourneys and stories from Stone Teeth. The knight was in charge of King Arthur's royal guard. He wore heavy-plated steel, polished to a shining silver with the arrowhead of the king melded into the breastplate. He looked like a knight from the songs, a handsome man with a strong jaw and long blonde hair. "Please bring forth your queries and thanks for the time bestowed unto you today."

Stone Teeth bowed, and Crow followed suit, the satchel swinging away from his thin frame. He would have stayed stooped forever if Stone Teeth hadn't wrenched him back straight. It earned a few small chuckles from the council.

"To what pleasure do we owe the Underground Lads today?" The king asked.

Crow looked to Stone Teeth for direction. He'd thought of standing before the king and recounting his story multiple times over the past few days, but now that he was here, words failed him. *Too many eyes on me,* he thought. Arthur II narrowed his eyes at Crow's continued silence. The scrutiny was intolerable. Crow wiped the sweat from his hands on his trousers.

"Stone Teeth says we dug up a dragon's egg." Crow blurted. He was about to reach in and grab the egg for them to see, but hesitated. *Don't. Don't touch it.* Instead, Crow cradled the bottom of the satchel in one hand, pulling the cloth away with the other to expose the rippling black shell to the hall. He was careful not to touch it with his bare hands.

"Straight to it." Stone Teeth mumbled. The leader of the Lads then recounted the events that transpired in the egg's finding. The king listened. "Not a bloody soul can touch it." Stone Teeth said, making eye contact with Crow only for a moment before returning his attention to the king.

The council met them with skepticism.

"Dragons don't live in the mountains." One snipped.

But their apprehension died in their throats as Maxwell Tryke was asked to bring the egg to the king. His reaction was identical to all the others when he placed a naked hand upon the surface. Crow held back a smirk. Not even the king's champion had the power to hold the egg.

Arthur II shot up from his council seat, eyes fierce with want.

"Bring the thing here." King Arthur said. Reluctance stayed Crow's feet, but with an encouraging look from Stone Teeth, he began his ascent to the throne.

"We don't know what kind of trickery this could be." A councilman protested.

"Aye." Another agreed. "A product of dark magic."

"Proof of ice dragons on Frukjera has never been found."

"End this charade," a plump woman spat, "we have other urgencies of court. The disturbing women from Good Land—"

King Arthur raised his hand and the protests ceased. By now, Crow was at his feet. A part of Crow, deep in his chest, wanted nothing more than to stuff the egg back in his satchel. *I don't want the king to take it.* He realized. Yet there he stood, presenting it to the king regardless.

And to Crow's surprise, King Arthur Arrowhead, in all his strength and wealth, could not stand the chill. Thrice he tried; his palm was blue with frost before he gave in. The council erupted in murmurs of magic, feln and tricks. Arthur II would have flattened Crow if it weren't for a stern look from his father.

Examining his recovering palm, King Arthur said, "A curious gift you bring me. Boy," he suddenly looked to Crow, "tell me again where this stone was found."

The cool air wafted against Crow's skin, and the sky purpled as the sun finally hid beneath the mountains. Crow's right eye was already beginning to swell shut from the welt blooming on the side of his face. Stone Teeth stalked in front of him, so angry that women risked falling off the pathways to get out of the large man's way. Crow followed him at a distance, ashamed.

Why'd I do that? Why? His mind screamed. Crow was a passive boy, content to watch and listen, exploring the darkness, lost in his dreams. *I should have let him take the stupid egg.*

Yet, when the king thanked them for the egg and ordered it be taken away, Crow pulled the satchel back to his chest. It was a strange horror that gripped him. His entire existence hinged on this strange stone. He was nothing before he found it, and would be nothing after it was ripped from him. Crow clung to it like the last piece of bread before a famine. "You're not meant to have it." He spat, fire in his chest.

Retreating from the throne, Crow slung the bag over his shoulder. "*We f*ound it. Why should you get to keep it? What have you done for me?"

His small tantrum only lasted a few minutes, if even that long. Through shouts from the council and a grab from Sir Tryke, the satchel was seized from him, but not before Crow punched and spat at Sir Tryke's armored body. Stone Teeth's meaty hand met the side of Crow's head and shocked him into silence. Crow was allowed to leave the Roost unpunished by the king's grace, but the Lads would receive no compensation.

"I ought to throw you to the griffins." Stone Teeth growled. "Felt like I was dealin' with Bones back there! I always took you for one of the brighter boys!"

"I'm sorry!" Crow shouted. He was angry that Stone Teeth had hit him, but he was even angrier that he'd acted like such a child. He kicked a rock off the side of a cliff. "I—why can't anyone touch it? We could've got money from the Jeweler's Den; the king didn't give us nothing! He doesn't care about us. I was just lookin' out for us."

"Is that so?" Stone Teeth turned. "And would you have cried like a sucklin' babe once the trader took it away too?"

"I'm no babe!" Crow seethed. Anger spread through his bruising face, hot and humiliating. "Why can't King Arthur hold it? Why can't *you* hold it? Or Bones? Or Mouse, Picker, Pudge? Why should *I* give it away when it feels like it was meant for me?" Crow stopped walking, stamping his feet into the ground. He knew he was being childish, but he felt like a piece of him had been ripped away. The only piece that made him interesting.

Stone Teeth grabbed him by the shoulders. "Listen, boy," he muttered, "it doesn't matter. Don't go searchin' for answers either because you won't find any. That kind of thing will drive a man mad. You're an Underground Lad, and tomorrow, you'll return to the tunnels and do your duty. And, Crow, you hear me now?"

"I—yes."

"Good. Should some pretty lookin' lass or anyone come askin' you about some egg, you know nothin', we gave it to the king." He looked directly into Crow's eyes. "And you sure as Vitania's grace couldn't hold it. Do you understand me?"

Crow blinked. *Who would ask? Who would know?* "But the other boys know..."

"I said, you understand, boy?" Stone Teeth's fingers bit into his shoulders.

"Yes." Crow stammered. "I understand."

Although he didn't. Not at all.

THREE

THE PLANKS

The dining hall was packed, warmed by excited bodies and torches lining the rough walls. The late autumn night swallowed the sun as a full moon waxed behind mountain peaks. Everyone banged on the tables, urging Crow to speak of his time with the king. Even Pudge left the cooking fires to hear about the treasure the Underground Lads would receive in exchange for a rare dragon's egg.

When Crow recounted with a nervous voice that they'd get nothing, the hall exploded in uproar.

"What a scam!"

"Screw the king!"

"Why'd you have to act like a babe and get our gold taken away!"

"Stone Teeth should've gone alone!"

"I'll give you another black eye to match!"

Crow's ears burned as he sat down. The shredded goat, roasted potatoes and boiled peas sat on his plate untouched. He stared at his food, allowing the jabs to rip through the air. He'd do anything to disappear.

Stone Teeth's strange warning still hung over him. All the boys knew he could hold the egg, and now they hated him. Should anyone come asking, they'd surely give him up. *My loyal brothers,* he thought bitterly.

"Can't believe the king isn't givin' us anything." Bones said beside him. The thin boy's mood seemed to have perked since they gave the egg away, which irritated Crow to no end. "But I think women knights are even more unbelievable. What kind of man would fight a woman?" He snickered.

"Don't know." Crow mumbled.

"Shame the king's goin' to take the tunnels from us. Probably hopes he can find more of those eggs. Maybe they'll find Snapper and Ash hoardin' them in there."

"If Snapper and Ash can touch 'em." Crow said, staring at his cooling food. "Sir Tryke couldn't. Not even King Arthur." He noticed Bones sour a bit, which egged him on. "Only me. I guess I'm special." Not that Crow actually felt special. *That'll make him mad,* Crow knew. "More special than the *king.* I guess I'm more special than you—"

"Special as in Clunk special, who used to bang pebbles together and wet himself in the corner." Bones seethed.

"Maybe Clunk could have touched it too. Guess we won't know; too bad you weren't chosen."

Bones sat up and puffed out his chest. "Chosen, ha!" He slapped the table, earning a few glances from the boys nearby. "It is too bad, isn't it? I wouldn't have ended up cryin' to the king! I wouldn't wait for Stone Teeth to tell me what to do like some little kid. I wouldn't even give it up. Our Mother, a chance fell into your hands and you blew it! The egg was *wasted* on you. It should've been me!" He jabbed a boney finger at Crow's chest. Crow smacked it away. Most boys were quiet now, watching with bated breath.

"You've been pissin' me off ever since we found it!" Crow shouted. "Actin' like a jealous little girl because you can't hold it."

"Because it's not fair! You never get up early for digs, I do! You never made plans to get out of here, I did. You used to follow Shadow 'round like a stray dog; then when he disappeared, started followin' me around. You hide away from everyone like you've got something interesting about you, but you gave away the only thing that made you special!"

Crow picked up his plate and smashed it into Bones's stupid face. Boys howled, banging the tables and shouting for a fight. Peas squished into Bones's hair, and the fat from the shredded meat dribbled down his pointed face. Standing, Crow shoved himself away from the table.

"Thinkin' you're better than everyone else doesn't make you interesting, either." He spat. Tears began pooling and burning his swollen eye. Before the others humiliated him for crying, he spun and ran out of the Underground Lads and into the cold. The wind ran through his hair like icy fingers. His rough spun woolen shirt did little to protect him from the night's chill, but he didn't mind. The shame and anger from before were enough to keep him warm.

The basket swung lazily in the mountain breeze as it carried Crow high into the moonlit sky. Griffin's Peak was lit from beneath him; fire from hearth and home pocked the vales and cliffs like stars. The narrow passages held drunken men and women lurching from one tavern to the next, shady figures clinging to the shadows and the watchful city guard. Crow watched them all with little interest before turning his gaze to the sky.

That's when he saw it.

Against the pale circle of the moon, impossibly far away, a griffin soared. Its graceful feathered wings clung to the wind as it passed through the starry sky. Crow could cover it with the tip of his thumb, but there was no mistaking it. He lurched forward in the basket as he tried to get a better look. His eyes were fixed on the griffin before it disappeared behind a jagged summit. He waited for the creature to return. After a few minutes, Crow relaxed and shifted his attention to the coming cliffs.

Maybe when Bones was done fussing, Crow would tell him what he saw. Rubbing his swollen eye, Crow frowned. The thought of the others dampened his mood again.

The worst of it was, Bones was right. Why had he been able to hold the egg? He wasn't very interesting at all. He didn't spend his days hatching escape plans, or preparing for a life of adventure outside the Peak. He didn't even remember who his parents were. He spent the day lost in thought, in the dark, watching the world around him. It was true that he wanted to be more than an orphan of the Underground Lads, but he never did anything about it. Crow groaned, preparing to jump.

The rough stone scraped the bottoms of his feet as he landed precariously on the cliff's edge. King Arthur's knights hadn't claimed the cave yet from the look of it. The tunnel's mouth gaped at him, black and menacing. But Crow wasn't afraid of the dark. He sat down, staring at the black gash in the mountain's side. The wind pulled at his hair and clothes, inviting him inside.

Crow remembered standing in the mouth of a hole much like this one, on some other slope honeycombed with thousands of them. Shadow was with him, Bones too. The other boys were milling about, finishing the morning's dig and loading the cart with a meager supply of iron. Crow was eleven winters old.

"The Champion's Melee is today." Shadow said.

"It is?" Crow asked. "How do you know?"

"Some miner was talkin' about it on our way up this morning." Shadow replied.

The Champion's Melee happened every spring. Knights from all over the Ridge and even some of the other kingdoms performed an unmounted fight for the king and his people. The winner won gold and glory.

"I think it's dumb that the Champion's Melee isn't to the death anymore." Bones said.

"It's a waste of soldiers." Crow rolled his eyes. "Kings always need soldiers to fight their wars."

"There hasn't been a Petty War in winters." Bones shrugged. "I say we bring back the blood!"

"I've been scouting," Shadow said, "and found a nice ledge with a whole view of the Roost's yard. Figured me, you two and a few other Lads could take the afternoon and watch."

"Stone Teeth'll have our heads." Crow mumbled.

"Screw Stone Teeth." Bones insisted. "Let's do it!"

And they did. Shadow, Bones, Picker, Beak, Pebbles, and Crow huddled onto a narrow overhang to watch the melee from afar. They could make out the small figures of King Arthur and his two sons, along with Sir Maxwell Tryke in his shining armor, sitting on a gray and red pavilion with the best view of the fight. Trumpets roared and knights clashed together in combat. Steel sang and men shouted in rage. In the end, a slender knight from the Crystal Isles was the last standing. He held up his spear in victory as the boys cheered.

"That's going to be us." Crow told Bones as they followed Shadow on the descent. "We can be knights and win a bunch of gold from the king to travel the world!"

"I'm goin' to fight with a spear like the champion today." Bones beamed. "What'll be your weapon?"

"A sword." Crow slashed at the air. "As long as one of us wins, we can share the gold. But the winner gets to decide where to go."

"If I win, we're seein' Man's Wall around Glorygradus." Bones decided.

"I want to see the Isles, where Shadow's from." Crow said, remembering the stories of water clear as glass and fish of colors he'd never seen.

Excitement bubbled through Crow's veins as they continued to fantasize about their weapons and armor. Over the next few days, Crow and Bones would practice dueling each other with sticks and pickaxes when the older Lads' backs were turned. But as they wore on, and the excitement of the melee faded, so did their ambition. The play-fighting stopped and the digging continued as before.

Crow sighed. The night air grew cold, and the full moon hid behind a wispy cloud. The memory left him hollow. How excited he'd been. If he'd dug up a dragon's egg back then, would he hand it over to Stone Teeth and the king so easily? *I miss Shadow.* He rubbed at his swollen eye.

His breath puffed from his lips like a ghost. Movement from inside the tunnel caught his eye. Crow shot up, squinting into the dark. *There!* Again, a small shadow flickered close to the entrance, sticking to the wall. Daring a glance behind him, Crow noted that no baskets were approaching. It would be minutes before he could grab the next one. He turned back to the tunnel.

A petite figure stood at the entrance. Shadowed by the overhang, Crow could barely make out the figure's details.

"Who are you?" He called, wondering if it was one of the lost boys from a few days ago. When he received no answer, Crow took a brave step forward. "Snapper? Ash? The king's men are taking this cave soon. They won't want any boys wanderin' in it."

The figure stepped shyly from the cave. Wind roared past Crow, threatening to push him entirely off the mountain. The figure wore a black cloak with a large hood that shadowed their face beneath it. Soft black gloves and socks covered their hands and feet. Whoever it was must have been young. Even under the cloak Crow could tell they were slight, an inch or two shorter than himself. A satchel snapped in the wind. The clouds parted, and the full moon's light glinted off of the object held within.

"The egg." Crow took another step forward. The figure flinched, ready to flee. "How'd you get it? We took it to King Arthur." He knew this wasn't a different one. It was the same egg he'd held. He knew it as sure as he knew anything. "It's mine." He said, the words spilling from his mouth.

The figure turned to flee but Crow was on them in an instant. They crashed to the ground together. Despite Crow's thin frame, it took him little time to gain the upper hand. He pinned the figure down and the egg rolled from the satchel. Crow dove for it. His hands wrapped around the cool exterior as he rolled away from the mystery child, panting heavily. He stopped just a few feet from the ledge, clutching the egg to his chest.

His heart pounded against the strong shell. Crow sat up with his prize held protectively in his grasp. The stranger was staring at him. They both sat on the ground in silence, still as stone.

The cloaked figure brought up their hands and removed their hood. Crow nearly dropped the egg.

Because, in front of him, sat a nymph.

Crow had never seen one before. No one had. No one alive anyway. Yet, he knew without question that a nymph sat across from him now. Drawings of nymphs adorned the pages of Stone Teeth's few history books. The little forest creatures disappeared hundreds of winters ago, after the feln lost the war and the last unicorn was killed. That's what Crow was told, at least.

It looked strange, like a person, but feral in an animalistic way. The nymph's jaw was soft, reaching a delicate point at a tiny chin. The nose was sloped and pointed like a small fish hook. Impossibly large eyes stared back at him, rimmed with pale long lashes and irises greener than any plant Crow had ever seen, even at night. The nymph's ears were long and pointed, and their skin was strangest of all. Pastel green in the moonlight, with a spattering of golden freckles covering their face and neck. Pale yellow hair sat atop their head like a bird's nest, light as sunlight.

"Northern Child..." The nymph whispered. Their voice sounded like a song, too high for that of a man, and too low for that of a woman. It was somewhere in between, oddly beautiful.

"You speak Frukjeran?" Was all Crow could manage. The nymph nodded.

Both sat in silence, swallowing each other in disbelief. Surely this was a dream. Crow looked down to his hands holding the egg. *Ten fingers,* he counted, glancing up to the creature again.

"Nymphs are supposed to be dead." Crow said.

"Not dead. Just gone." The nymph said quietly. Their eyes were huge, much larger than a normal person's. Crow could get lost in their strangeness.

"After the feln invaded and the last unicorn died, all the nymphs went away." Crow parroted. Stone Teeth was fond of history, and most of what Crow knew came from him. The nymphs used to be all over Frukjera, before men and even before the feln came to rip the land apart. They worshipped strange gods and unicorns. Stone Teeth said they lived among the trees and sang magical songs. *What would Stone Teeth think of this?* What would anyone? None of the Lads would believe him.

"Tell me." The nymph said. "Was it you who found winter's young?"

"Winter's young?"

The nymph motioned to the egg in Crow's grasp.

"This? Stone Teeth said this was an egg. An ice dragon, since normal dragons don't live up here..." The nymph seemed to ponder this for a moment. Was Stone Teeth wrong? Was it not an egg, but something else?

"Ice dragon." The other repeated. "Yes. Was it you then, who found the ice dragon's egg?"

"Maybe." Crow remembered Stone Teeth's warning. "*And you sure as Vitania's grace couldn't hold it.*" Well, so much for that. Crow was staring at the egg in his lap, then he looked up and narrowed his eyes. "Wait. How'd you get this? King Arthur took it."

"It was not his to take."

The statement hung in the air.

"Our Mother." Crow cursed. "Did you...steal it?" The stone in his grasp was much heavier than before.

"I suppose." The nymph said. "Although, as I said, it was not his."

The cool black shell rippled; Crow bit his lip.

He didn't know what to do. If King Arthur found out, he'd surely hang him for a thief. If Stone Teeth found out, he'd probably kick him out of the Lads. Honestly, Crow didn't know which fate was worse. "King Arthur will kill us if he found out you stole it." *Us?* There was a line being drawn here, a line Crow was about to cross. Once he crossed it, there was no going back. "What were you thinking?" He angrily stood up. "The king knows who dug it up. He will come for the Lads and me when he notices it's gone!"

"It is not his." The nymph repeated.

"You *stole* it. We're goin' to be in trouble."

The nymph didn't seem to understand. "No one saw me. I am simply bringing the ice dragon to where it belongs."

Crow stared at the other in disbelief. There was no way he was about to deal with this alone. Even if he wanted to, he couldn't leave the egg here. The nymph would just take it and the king would come looking for him anyway.

He could tell the king the truth. Leave now and get back to his life before.

That bad taste again.

"I need help." Crow knew someone who would readily help, had dreamed of a moment like this his whole life.

Hopefully Bones wasn't too angry with him.

It took a while to convince the nymph that Crow had to return to the Underground Lads. It took even longer to convince them to jump into one of the moving baskets.

"How'd you even get up here?" Crow asked them.

"I climbed." They replied.

"Well, we're not climbing." Crow decided. It would take them three times as long to reach their destination. In the end, the nymph relented, and Crow found himself descending into the kingdom with a dragon's egg and a creature that was meant to be dead long ago. In that time, he'd learned the nymph's name.

The Arms that Reach for the Sky and Turn Shades of Green and Gold, in Frukjeran at least. It was the closest translation their languages allowed. Crow opted to call them Tree. It was close enough.

Tree had donned the hood of their cloak, concealing their features as they clung to the rope. Tree gave the satchel back to Crow so that he could hold onto the egg. The nymph refused to take it back at all, insisting that Crow must look after it now.

"I don't know how you got this out of the Roost." Crow shook his head. "I heard it's impossible to storm."

"It is?"

Crow nodded. "During the Gold War, when the Arrowheads beat the Yarlworths, it was only 'cause some servants threw open the doors from the inside and let 'em in. They would never have been able to break in otherwise."

"The Gold War?"

"Yeah. The Yarlworths were the first kings of the Peak. But after a few tough winters, they ran out of gold. Everyone starved. I heard folks even started eatin' each other." Crow paused for dramatic effect, but it was impossible to read Tree's expression under the shadow of their hood. "The Arrowheads were a powerful family of warriors, and promised to kill the king and give his gold back to the people. As the Yarlworths lost, they retreated into the Roost, and it was impossible to get them out. So, the servants opened the doors for the Arrowheads and betrayed their king."

"A bloody tale."

"Yeah." Crow laughed. "There's a song about it. The new King Garth had the servants executed for treason even though they helped him win the throne." Crow lowered his voice conspiratorially. "Some say they then cooked the Yarlworths and ate them at the victory feast."

"Is that in the song?"

"No way. If a king's man heard you say that, he'd cut out your tongue." The wind ran chill fingers through Crow's hair. "But if the servants didn't open the gates, the Arrowheads wouldn't have gotten to the Yarlworths. The Roost can't be stormed."

"Can't be stormed, maybe." Tree admitted. "But we have been hiding from men in their stone houses for many winters. Men see what they wish to see."

"How many nymphs are left?" Crow asked.

"Few." Tree replied. "I have not seen another since the feln were driven to their island. Most of us followed the unicorns. The land you call Frukjera has little for us now."

"What? How many winters old are you? You've seen a feln?" The ugly beasts who ransacked Frukjera before men arrived. Generations had passed since one stepped foot on the mainland. They were forbidden.

"I live as long as the trees." Tree replied.

"Wow." Crow leaned back in the basket. There were trees in the Forgotten Forest said to be hundreds of winters old. It was the oldest and most preserved forest on the continent. "What keeps you here, if all the nymphs are gone?"

Tree was quiet, everything hidden beneath the shadow of their cloak. The wind tugged at it, but seemed unable to rip it from their face, like some sort of strange force kept it in place.

"A song." Tree finally said.

The basket grazed against a sharp cliff's edge, Crow steadied himself and looked ahead.

The lights caught his eye first.

Torches clustered together like a swarm of lantern flies. They were at the entrance to the Underground Lads. Crow recognized the colors of the castle guard. Swords hung at their sides. It was still dark, but the light of the fires was enough for Crow to see Stone Teeth's shock of yellow hair among the metal helmets. His heart dropped to his stomach in an instant.

"We need to get off." He hissed, more aware than ever of the basket's movement toward the drop point.

They were still clinging to a thin outcrop of rock. The path wound down to the jostled wooden hovels, taverns and shops that squished against the mountain's base like narrow rock and timber growths. *The Planks,* the people called it. Crow knew if they were going to avoid the guards, they'd need to jump now with the cover of alleys and shops between them. Returning to the Lads with the stolen egg wasn't an option. Even if he gave it up, what would become of him? Also, what would they do to Tree? *Tree would probably tell them the egg belongs to me.* And if Stone Teeth was to be believed, that's the last thing Crow wanted.

They escaped easily despite the narrow landing. Tree followed after him quickly, watching the empty basket continue its long descent.

"Those torches far down there," Crow explained, "they're the castle guards, probably sent by King Arthur since you stole this." He gestured to the heavy satchel at his side. "Thieves who get caught get their hands crushed by stone. But—but thieves who steal from the king..." Crow swallowed. "Hung."

"Your people have harsh laws." Tree commented. "We must not let them kill you, Northern Child."

This is the second time they've called me that, Crow wanted to ask what it meant.

"Where shall we go?" Tree asked.

"Down there." Crow pointed to the cluster of the lower city. "Until they go away. Hopefully they won't look twice at some kids in the alley." The darkness would cover them. *"The only monsters you got to worry about are the ones out there,"* Shadow's words reminded him.

The trail down into the Planks was easy enough. They came upon a few beggars but were left alone. Eventually the outcropping widened enough for easy walking. Stone and wooden bridges patched cracks and falls. Planked docks hung over cliff edges; their wooden supports rooted into the ever-sloping stone beneath them. Crudely built homes with straw shutters began to clutter the mountain face. The wooden shops and taverns were erected precariously on thin platforms; bridges and steep paths connected everything in a narrow maze of rock and wood. Some shops were stacked so close together that Crow could hop onto their roofs and travel the Planks without ever touching the ground.

They spotted gray birds sitting on thatched ceilings, speckling homes with white droppings. Rats squealed and cats watched them from thin alleys. Crow could hear the drunken singing of men and women pouring from a tavern not too far off.

> *"And Wanda, O' Wanda,*
> *The maid a queen to be,*
> *Wanda, O' Wanda,*
> *The queen who ruled the Peak!"*

"That song's *'Wanda the Wonder'.*" Crow whispered to Tree. A favorite of Stone Teeth's.

Glowing firelight filled a few windows with a warm luminosity. The streets were more populous here despite the hour. Crow couldn't read the signs on the doors, but he did recognize the tavern when they came upon it. Its twin doors were wide open, spilling yellow light onto the street. Men and women sat inside on crowded tables, all dirty and laughing and drinking. No one paid them any mind.

For a moment, Crow saw his brothers in their dirt-smudged faces, drinking after a hard day of work only to get up at dawn and do it again. He saw Mouse, Puke, Pebble, even Bones, clashing ale heavy mugs together after a day in the mines. But he never saw himself.

"What are we goin' to do?" Crow turned to Tree; whose features remained a mystery despite the glow of the tavern. "I can't go back home if they're lookin' for me. I don't have anywhere to go. I've never even left Griffin's Peak before." He glanced at the egg in his satchel. Hate filled his chest. *If I'd never found this...*grabbing the stone, as if to smash it, Crow was suddenly dragged into a dark lane beside the tavern by Tree.

He heard the clink of armor before he saw them. Two of King Arthur's own knights walked side by side, red cloaks streaming. One pulled aside a drunken woman. "Have you seen a boy running around here? He's got black hair and eyes of light blue."

"Tons o' boys like that." The woman slurred.

"He'd potentially be carrying a stone."

"Not seen any with no stone." She hissed. They let her go.

"How's it possible that an orphan boy stole into the Roost? Seems like it could be one of those slimy councilmen to me." One of the knights muttered.

"Aye. But the king insisted the boy may have something to do with it." The other replied. "It was a strange stone they received."

"It must be, for King Arthur to be so upset at its disappearance."

"Between this and the news from Good Land..."

"It's a strange time. We should continue. The boy could be any-where."

Crow waited until they left before allowing himself to breathe.

"Do not blame the ice dragon." Tree whispered. "It is greed that endangers you now."

Greed. Crow thought bitterly. If there were knights in the Planks looking for him, they shouldn't stay put for long. "We need to get goin'." Crow struggled to find courage. "If we can dodge the guards, maybe we can get help from Bones." Taking a deep breath, Crow left the shadows of the lane.

Light bounced off of her silver unicorn pommel like a star. The rest of her longsword was slung behind her broad shoulders. The woman foot knight from the Roost stood before them; muscled arms crossed in front of her armored chest.

"Still staring, boy? I would keep my eyes down if I were you. They are mighty blue."

FOUR

GRIFFIN'S PEAK

"What does the king want with a small orphaned boy?" The woman continued.

Crow glared at her. She was the same height as Stone Teeth, impossibly tall and muscled. "I'm nearly a man." He spat.

"An orphaned nearly-man, then." Her gaze shifted from the satchel at Crow's side to Tree, who stood partially behind Crow like a silent shadow. Instinctively, Crow placed a protective hand over the bag to shield the egg from view. *We could run,* he thought, *and hope this woman can't catch us.* It might cause a scene. Was it worth the risk? Crow could lie and tell her the king wasn't after him...but that probably wouldn't work. She recognized him from earlier. Looking her up and down, Crow observed her battered armor, greasy chopped hair and dirty face. The only treasure she owned seemed to be the longsword on her back. *She's staying in the Planks.* If King Arthur gave her anything for her travels, it wasn't enough for a nice place to stay.

"They'll find no work here." Stone Teeth had said.

"You're from Good Land." Crow remembered. Good Land was a stronghold of the Ridge; the vast scope of eastern territory that the Arrowheads ruled. "You serve...the duke." Crow couldn't remember his name. Good Land was far from here.

"Duke Milfred Keefe." The woman straightened.

"You carried a message from him." Crow's heart pounded in his chest. Every instinct told him to run. "Did the king listen to it?"

"Tell me, boy," She spat impatiently, "what is it the king wants with the likes of you?"

"I don't know. I'm just tryin' to get home to the Lads." Crow tried. He looked about nervously. The streets were empty.

"And who's this?" The woman raised a dark brow at Tree. "And what have you got there?" She elevated her arm and grabbed the pommel of her sword. "I don't sympathize with thieves."

No, Crow braced to run.

But Tree suddenly stepped in front of him. "He is no thief." The nymph declared. They pulled back their hood, the light from the tavern splashing their exotic features. "He shall not be harmed."

The woman's arm dropped. "Impossible." She gasped, staggering back as though she'd been struck. Tree donned their hood once more as two men lurched passed smelling of ale. The three of them stood gaping at each other in silence as drunken singing continued through the night.

"O' Wanda! O' Wanda!"

"I'm no thief, like Tree said." Crow confessed. The little nymph's reveal gave him confidence. "The king is looking for this." He showed her the bag at his side. "Tree's the one that took it. But—but they don't really understand how this stuff works. And now King Arthur's after me." He told her about the egg and how it seemed frozen to the touch, leaving out the fact that he could touch it. The words spilled from his mouth like vomit. *Maybe I shouldn't be tellin' her all this.* But he needed help.

"A nymph..." the woman whispered, as though the rest of Crow's story didn't matter. "How?"

"You have seen the tides shifting." Tree said from the shadows of their cloak. "The world is not as it once was. This meeting tonight was sung by the gods."

The woman scrutinized them with eyes sharp and hard. Crow remained poised, ready to leap into the darkness at any moment. The swollen side of his face burned, and the egg at his side felt like it weighed the same as a boulder. There must be something special about this woman...*sung by the gods.*

"Come." She eventually said, her voice shaky as she tried to hide her nerves. "I don't want to be seen conspiring with a wanted child. I am staying at the Fat Goat not too far from here."

"How can we trust you—" Crow began.

"Our thanks." Tree nodded, following the woman.

Narrowing his eyes, Crow trailed after the pair. He had no choice. The Underground Lads was probably still clogged with city guards. *Maybe they'll be gone by morning,* he hoped. Bones would love to hear about what happened tonight.

The Fat Goat wasn't far, as the woman said. Carefully, the trio traipsed through the Planks, opting for narrow passages and rickety bridges in favor of the main streets. Guards marched down from the mountaintops, hands on their swords and red cloaks billowing in the chill air. Looking for a single boy, they didn't seem interested in their small group. Crow kept his head down regardless, jealous of Tree's cloak. Cats watched them pass, eyes shining in the firelight.

"Good, keep your head down." The woman said. "I don't know if the guards have alerted the inn-keep."

The inn was nearly empty. A great firepit in the middle of the room warmed a pot of bubbling stew. Two men stood over it. Their hair was matted and clothes tattered; Crow noticed one had a rusted knife hanging by his side. Wooden tables and benches held similar lots, each keeping to themselves or the mugs in their hands. Scratched short swords, damaged shields, and dented helmets adorned the rickety furniture. The head of a white goat was mounted on the rock wall, and under it were two doorways. A wooden staircase in the corner led up to the second story. Crow could hear footsteps up there, and spied a woman staring at them over the railing eating a fresh snow apple.

One of the doors under the goat burst open, and a stout woman holding two horns of thick brown ale tumbled out. The woman's hair was wiry as straw, and she gave the trio a once over before saying, "We don't take beggars, miss. Tell 'em to piss off and join the Lads down the mountain. There'll be no food for them here." She handed the ale to the men at the fire.

"They've eaten." The foot knight said. "I couldn't stand to see them on the street on a cold night like this." Her lie sounded almost believable. The inn-keep sniffed.

"This is why I don't understand you women. Our hearts are too fragile for such work. Aye, then, I'll expect a penny for each in the morn."

They climbed the stairs, each plank bending under their weight, save for Tree's. The girl who'd been eating the snow apple turned. She eyed them up and down, tucking a bushy piece of blond hair behind her ear. She was short, eye level with Crow, but her arms were wired with muscle, and her thin blue gown clung to her torso and suggested no softness. *She's familiar.* Crow thought, rubbing his swollen eye.

"Jade," She said, addressing her taller companion, "you go out to buy a mule and come back with some children."

"You were at the Roost." Crow blurted. "With the blonde braids."

"Bring Kath to my room." Jade said. "You'll want to hear this."

Crow must admit, a room full of women foot knights, a nymph and an ice dragon's egg was never a place he thought he'd find himself. The room was simple, barely large enough to fit all of them. There was a straw mattress in the corner and a plain wooden chest at its end. Crow and Tree sat on the bed, the straw itched his legs, but it was softer than the rock floor Crow usually slept on. The three women stood, arms crossed, expressions hidden under masks hard as stone.

After relaying his story and tugging off Tree's hood to prove he wasn't a liar, Crow had learned their names.

There was Lady Jade, who had brought them here. She didn't offer Crow much of an introduction. She was from Good Land, and kept it at that.

The blonde one, Lady Gretchen, was the nicest. She came from Youngston across the river, she said, where Queen Charlotte II gave her and her twin sister their knighthood. Her sister died in a centaur raid two winters ago, and Gretchen left the Roam, traveling between Good Land, Stone Hold and Griffin's Peak ever since.

Lady Kath was the youngest, though she scared Crow the most. Her frame was thin, like a boy, and her smirking face reminded Crow of Bones—all sharp edges and secret wit. She said that her hair was all chopped off, so no one could grab it. Her skull was lumpy, and a large scar ran from the tip of her right ear to the corner of her thin lips. "I'd say you should see the other man's face, but it's gone." She laughed. Stone Hold was her place of birth, but the duchess of Augustii in the south had knighted her.

None of them knew what to make of Crow's story. Tree had shocked them, even rendering Lady Gretchen to the floor. "A ghost from the past." She'd murmured.

"Surely the king should know of this." Kath said.

"King Arthur mocked us." Lady Jade spat. "We carried Duke Milfred's plea, and the king waved us off. He doesn't think of us as proper knights. He wants the boy and his strange stone, aye. But my father told me stories of the nymphs. They were wiser than men." She pointed to Tree. "We all thought them dead, yet here one stands to defend this boy before my sword."

"You folk from Good Land have always been superstitious." Kath smirked. All eyes remained on Tree, drinking in the sight of them. Crow turned. In the firelight, the nymph's green skin shone like the dark needles of pines. Their features were sloped and delicate, yet those eyes held such age that they made Crow uncomfortable. *They've got to help us,* he hoped.

The egg felt cold in his lap. After his retelling, he'd looked to Tree and abandoned Stone Teeth's warning, showing the egg's strangeness. He watched as each woman failed to lay a hand upon the shell. Tree had refused to even try despite the urging of the knights.

"We should go to Glorygradus." Gretchen said. "The Historian's Guild might know what to make of this. The Ridge has nothing close to the West's records."

"Glorygradus is a world away." Crow chimed in. He needed to get back to the Lads once it was safe. He had to tell his brothers of what happened. They had to see it to believe him.

"Unless we hire a ship." Kath suggested. "It's just a hop across the Pond of Serpents."

"We don't have the money." Jade said.

"I'm not goin' across the Pond." Crow stood. He would not be talked over by women. Not over this. "Half the ships that sail across don't come back. My brother, Shadow, sailed after getting kicked from the Lads. Stone Teeth brought us word that the ship never made it to port." Shadow had saved bits of all his findings to get to Glorygradus as a cabin boy. "He told us he needed to see the world. A winter came and went before Stone Teeth found out that his ship never docked." Tears threatened creep down his face. Crow rubbed at his eyes furiously.

Gretchen stood; her eyes soft. "He does have the truth of it. The Pond of Serpents doesn't get its name from false legends. However, Crow—was it? King Arthur wants you and that egg. You are not safe here if you want to keep it."

"It is not the king's choice." Tree said from their place on the bed. It was the first time they spoke in a long while. "This egg is born of ice."

"There have never been ice dragons recorded on Frukjera." Lady Jade said.

"Man's memory is short."

"It doesn't matter." She continued. "There are none now. The nature of the egg is strange, but what purpose does it serve? The winters have turned it to stone."

"Well," Tree tilted their head, "to hatch, of course."

"To hatch?" Crow gasped, nearly dropping the thing. "You mean a baby ice dragon's goin' to come out of it?"

"It is an egg, so yes." Tree replied.

"But," he stared at the shell, all black and rigid and gleaming, "dragon eggs never hatch for men. Even if they did, dragons in the south can't be tamed. They burn and eat everything. Not even kings conquered them."

"That is because they are not here to be tamed. The seasons cannot be tamed. You do not conquer summer or autumn or winter. You live alongside them. Your people are very fond of conquering things, it seems." Tree shook their head. "There is a song, taught to us long ago by the unicorns." Tree hushed, and the room fell silent.

Then the nymph began to sing.

Their voice rang through the air like soft summer bells, in a tune mellow and sad. The nymphic language was like nothing Crow had ever heard. Words were impossible to distinguish, rather, the song was an endless stream of melody, rising and falling and brushing the ears like falling snow. As the song continued, the torches and candles shrank, and their shadows shifted and danced to the endless string of song. *It's beautiful,* Crow thought, just as he felt a pulse beneath the egg's shell. Staring in shock, Crow felt like something was writhing inside, coiling, clawing...

Tree's song stopped.

The flames rose, Crow blinked his surprise away, and the strange movement in the egg ceased.

"That was the song that has kept me here. It may have kept others too, but I have not seen them. The unicorns sang of a Northern Child, who would wake winter's young again." Tree said.

Kath blew out a puff of air. "Our Mother." She whispered, leaning against the timber wall.

"You suppose I'm this Northern Child?" Crow wrinkled his brow. "You kept callin' me that earlier." He'd dreamed of something like this happening, secretly in the tunnels where no one could hear his imaginings. Wild adventures filled his head as he dug gold for the nobles of the Peak. But he'd never let them leave his mind. It was dumb to hope for such a fantastical thing. Crow felt anxiety gnaw at his belly. "What am I supposed to do?" He looked to Tree. "Hatch the egg, then what?"

"I do not know."

"But you said the *unicorns* were singin' about this. Did they mention anything else? What's the point of hatchin' an ice dragon?"

"The gods reveal what they wish."

"I must say," Jade broke in, "you need a plan. You cannot stay here. Call it what you will, but the king will not let theft from inside the Roost go unpunished. "

"Maybe Tree could sing to him." Kath sniggered.

"He's sending the city guard to look for the boy." Gretchen said. "It's only a matter of time before we're found. If we're to help, the first thing we should do is leave."

Crow's heart sank. He felt the control slipping away. "My brothers...I should tell them. I'm an Underground Lad. I've never left the kingdom. They're all I've known."

Tree stood from their perch on the mattress. They planted a delicate gloved hand atop Crow's. Crow pulled away uncomfortably, but he caught the other's eyes. Their green depths were so sad, so sad and full of understanding. He had to look away.

"There comes a time when one must leave all they have ever known." Tree murmured.

Deep in Crow's soul, he knew it was true. Maybe he always knew. Crow stared at the ground, willing the tears that crept through his lids away. He didn't want to look like a child in front of everyone.

"Do you know when this egg will supposedly hatch?" Jade asked, alleviating some of the attention from Crow.

"It will not hatch here." Tree said. "Dragon eggs are not like those of other creatures. One as ancient as this will require the gods. We must bring it...I do not know what your people call it...to the forest I am from. The forest echoed with ocean song, along the eastern coast."

"The Forgotten Forest." Jade said immediately. "Just south of Good Land. We have many legends of its ancient magic. It is unmanned to this day."

"Yes," Gretchen agreed, "along the Mystic Ocean, I remember. We passed it while sailing the River of Song."

Crow's life as he knew it was fading before his eyes. There would be no staying here. How could he? The guards were already searching the Underground Lads and would surely start to knock on doors and turn over every rock until he was found. It was suspicious at this point that he wasn't with the others. *I won't get to say goodbye.* He wished Bones could be here.

"Crow," Tree said, "you are the Northern Child. Will you wake winter's young?"

He could feel the coiling and twisting again beneath the shell for a moment. This was it. "I don't think I have a choice." He mumbled, but staring at the egg in his lap, he knew even if things were different and the king wasn't looking for him, he wanted it to hatch. "Yes."

"We'll accompany you to the Forgotten Forest." Jade decided. "The road is not as safe as it once was. You'll need arms at your side."

"I've only seen one dragon in my life." Kath said. "From far away over the sea. I'd like to see this ice dragon."

"Singers will write about this day." Gretchen sighed. "I can feel it."

"We leave tonight." Jade said. "Under cover of darkness."

Crow's reflection stared back at him from the shell's polished surface. He gritted his teeth, and shoved the egg back into his bag. "Then let's get goin'. I don't want to change my mind."

Clouds rolled in from the north, blanketing the night sky in a thick layer of black. The stars and moon were gone, swallowing Griffin's Peak in shadows. It was as if Mother Vitania herself were keeping them safe.

The Planks were quiet. Even the drunks had hobbled home. Cats ruled the streets now, staring at the five of them from rooftops and porches. Gretchen gave Crow one of her cloaks. It was heavy wool and green as pine needles. He was thankful for its warmth. A hood made him feel safer, but it didn't shadow his face quite as well as Tree's strange black one. Meanwhile, the three knights donned their armor: Lady Jade's was heavy steel, dark and dented plate, her longsword strapped over her shoulder, pommel sweet and silver. Gretchen's was much the same but for an old battle-axe chained to her side. Kath wore tough leather, brown and cracked and studded. She favored a dagger on her belt and an oak bow on her back. Each of them *clinked clinked clinked* as they walked. Crow and Tree sounded like ghosts in comparison, whispering against the rocky paths.

As they descended toward the gate, the Planks fell in favor of steep ugly sharp rock, too slanted to build anything but stairs. The cats had followed them like small black shadows. *Probably just looking for food,* Crow's stomach growled. He thought of the shredded goat waiting for him back at the Lads. The boys should all be asleep by now, cuddled in their furs. Crow knew it was just over this ridge, he could see the empty baskets and ropes crisscrossing above him, slowly crawling towards his home. He was thankful they wouldn't pass it.

The gate loomed ahead, large and granite, the iron door hung down from great thick chains. Massive torches hung on either side of the archway. They were always lit, a beacon for those entering the narrow mouth of the city. Crow had heard that Griffin's Peak was one of the few kingdoms without a wall. The mountains did all the work. The city only needed a front gate, its granite wall long enough to reach out to the deep cliffs that swooped up into the summits that held Griffin's Peak in its valley.

As Crow had feared, the gate was swarmed. The iron door remained open, and a collection of guards stood under the orange light of the great flames. This hour of night meant no traffic, so they couldn't sneak through using a crowd.

Jade halted while they were still far enough to get out of sight. A cat skidded between her feet. "How many do you count?"

"Seven." Kath said. "I'm surprised there isn't more." She grasped her bow. "I can take out two or three before they come for us."

"No." Gretchen stepped forward. "Bloodshed will put a bigger target on us."

"She's right." Jade confirmed, turning to Crow. "Do you know another way out?"

"No." Crow shifted the satchel strap further up his shoulder. "I've never left before."

"What of you?" She regarded Tree.

"I came through this gate." They said, a gray tabby sat at their feet. "This is the gate we shall leave. We have friends."

Turning, Crow saw a pack of alley cats sitting behind them, whipping their tails and flickering their ears. *Mother, there must be twenty.* Tree knelt, and whispered into the tabby's ear. Crow couldn't hear what the nymph said, but he guessed it was a song.

The tabby mewed and trotted ahead; the great hoard of alley cats followed. They were a wave of gray, black and brown as they trotted forward, eventually breaking into a run for the gate. Tree followed, their cloak billowing as they ran. Jade gripped her sword in both hands and unsheathed it. The steel was smooth, sharp, and ready to bite flesh, should it need to. With their weapons ready, the knights followed. Crow wished he had a weapon of his own as he trailed behind.

The cats reached the guards first. The men drew their swords, alarmed and confused. Then the cats attacked, hissing, spitting, and jumping for their faces. They swarmed around armored legs and crashed against plated backs like water against a cliff face. Yelling, the guards swiped at the animals with their blades, but the cats were too quick, darting away and twisting in the air. Some managed to knock one or two of the men over. Claws scratched at their eyes. As Crow drew closer, he heard curses over the yowling and hissing.

A brown cat climbed the red cloak of a city guard. The man grabbed it by the scruff and sent it flying through the air. "Light them!" One guard yelled, shaking a cat from his leg and reaching an unlit torch towards the ones hanging on the gate.

The cats spat and climbed where they could, shifting like a furry plague coming from the shadows to swallow them whole.

"Oi!" A guard screamed, slashing at three or four, he'd spotted their group running for it. Crow could now feel the fire against his face, bathing it in sweat and light. A cat climbed onto the guard's back and bit the exposed flesh between his helm and collar. "Grab them!" He yelled, wrenching the beast off. "It's the boy! Don't let them pass!"

They were nearing the archway now. Crow spied the intricate carvings of Arthur Thunderborn flickering in the shadows from the great fires. His pace quickened to keep up with the others. Tree was well ahead of them now, dancing beneath the arched gate with feet light as feathers. He heard the groaning of chains as another guard from atop the wall grabbed the winch. The gate squealed as it rose.

Then an arrow whizzed through the air, sinking into the man's neck. He made no sound as he reached for his throat and fell. The gate fell with him. Kath nocked another arrow while she ran.

The cats were still attacking, more had come running from the Planks to join. Crow ran through the mess and spotted a few lying on the ground, bloody and still.

Finally, they reached the arch. Crow was the last under the passage when a fist grabbed his green cloak. Crow nearly choked as the guard wrenched him to a halt. He grabbed the guard's hand at the wrist, trying to twist it away. Cats climbed his captor's back and bit at his neck, but went ignored. The guard's eyes were wild in the firelight. "Not today boy—ah!" In a splash of red, his hand separated from his wrist. Crow felt bile sliding up his throat. He hunched over and spewed onto the ground. Lady Jade stood over him, her sword gleaming in the light. No sooner did he finish that another guard was scrambling for them. The man's eyes were bleeding from deep gouges.

Jade dragged Crow under the gateway, and he nearly fell with the weight of the egg swinging wildly at his side. He followed her with aching legs full of panicked energy. The path slowly swallowed them, and the torches' heat of Griffin's Peak faded behind their backs. Crow could hear the shouts of the city guard along with the wailing of cats. And above that, the keening of the man with one hand. He wanted to look back. He wanted one last glimpse at the only home he'd ever known.

I can't. His legs carried him on. *I can't look back. Forward. Only forward now.* Tears ran down his face, blurring the dark road ahead. His home was lost. And so was he.

FIVE

THE HIGH ROAD

Crow knelt beside the stream as long as he dared, filling his skin with fresh mountain water. His legs screamed as he stood up again. *At least my feet stopped hurting,* he thought, twisting the skin shut. His feet went numb yesterday. They were like lifeless stones hanging on the end of his legs. Meanwhile, his arms felt like limp string, and the satchel's strap had dug an angry red rash along his collarbones.

It'd been two days and two nights since they'd fled the Peak. As the sun rose on the third day, Crow felt what little strength he had left fading. But they dared not stop. Surely the king sent riders after them, and outrunning a mounted man would be impossible. *We can't even stop to eat,* Crow's stomach rumbled. Bits of tough goat jerky were shared among the group to eat while they walked. Tree refused it; they would not eat the flesh of another creature.

"We must stay off the main road." Jade said wisely as they'd fled. "It will take us longer, but the mountain paths will cover us."

They split off into the woods, north and away from the road that would take them directly to Stone Hold. The heavily trafficked roads of the Ridge cut through the mountains like cobbled scars, and made traversing the vast territory less treacherous. Crow's group broke further up into the pine-covered slopes. The tracks up here were little thicker than game trails, and rock slides often interrupted their path, which meant they had to climb northward to get around the loose ground. The pines grew thicker the farther they went, until the main road completely disappeared from view.

"Do you know where we're goin'?" Crow had asked that first night, worried they'd get swallowed into the wilderness never to return.

"We're looping back east." Gretchen said. "Kath has traveled this way before."

"We just need the sky." Kath assured. But pine and clouds obscured it.

The night passed in stumbles and hurried over-the-shoulder looks. When the sun rose, Crow was surprised to find they were actually heading east as Kath said.

The second day was hard, but the thought of thundering hooves and the city guards kept them going. The autumn air was crisp, pine needles filled the forest with a clean sweet smell. Crow marveled at the unbroken undergrowth, but fear gave him little time to stop and appreciate the wild. The egg was heavy at his side, and he began carrying it in his hands to relieve some pressure from his shoulders.

They'd found a small hunter's shack that afternoon. It appeared abandoned, with brown needles littering the rotten timber floor. "Maybe we can stay in there." Crow said. "There could be food."

"No." Jade insisted. "We are still too close, and someone might stop in." And so, they continued. Crow glared at her back the whole time.

The second night was clear; stars peeked at them from above the trees. Crow was gnawing on a tough strip of jerky, wishfully thinking of what Pudge would be serving for dinner. *I shouldn't have made fun of him so much,* Crow thought as he chewed the salty meat. His legs ached, and blisters calloused the sides of his feet.

"I'm surprised we haven't come across anyone." Kath said. "This path is less traveled, but usually there's a hunter or a few foot knights about."

"You think it's happening up here too?" Gretchen asked.

"Could be."

It was true; they hadn't crossed paths with anyone. A few spotted deer darted from the undergrowth, and Kath had killed a hare that now hung from her belt...but other than that, no one. *The road is not as it once was,* Jade had said. Crow wondered what that meant. Bandits, mountain cats, griffins coming farther south? He was too tired to ask, instead, letting the questions float about in his head.

The only one who didn't seem to be slowing was Tree. They looked like a little black ghoul gliding through the trees. They'd occasionally pluck weeds from the ground and eat them. Crow would watch with mild interest. One time Tree offered Crow a handful of acorns, but Crow wasn't hungry enough to try them.

Then it was the third day.

The water skin leaked a few cold drops as Crow handed it off to Gretchen.

"I don't know how much longer I can go." He confessed. It was meant to be a thought, but the words passed through his lips. Crow wanted to fall into the stream and float to the Forgotten Forest if possible.

"Me too." Kath said. "We should stop soon; we can't continue like this much longer. They should've caught us by now." The trees were breaking, and the slopes leveled out to graceful valleys covered in a thin layer of grass and stones. Squat stone hovels pocked the green valleys, smoke rose from most of them. The soil was too thin to grow proper crops here, so most small farms held herds of goats.

The animals stood out stark white against the countryside. Faded blue mountains chopped up the horizon.

"Any of these folks could report us to the king." Jade protested.

Crow glared at her, rubbing his bruised eye. It had healed decent enough the last two days. "I won't make it." He said. His legs could barely walk beneath his weight. "Besides, what if King Arthur never sent riders out this way, how would anyone know?"

"I bet the king's put a handsome reward out for a thieving boy." She retorted. "Since you're so tired, turn yourself in to one of these farmers here. They can wheel you back to Griffin's Peak in their milk carts."

"I didn't kill no one. *You* cut a man's hand off."

"Anyone." Jade's tone was cool.

"What?"

"'I didn't kill *'anyone'*, were you lot never taught how to speak?"

Crow was about to haul the egg over his head and smash it against Jade's stupid face.

"Hey," Gretchen pointed, "look up there."

A little way down their path sat a low built cobbled stable. Horses grazed inside wooden pastures cut from thick pinewood. It covered a lot of land, the nearest farm appeared no more than a speck higher up the slope. The stable must have been a quarter mile from them, and with every step Crow saw more horses.

"We'd make much better time with a horse." Kath said.

"Are you suggesting we steal one?" Jade hissed.

"We have enough coin for two horses, maybe." Gretchen said. "We don't need to steal."

"We should stop." Kath said.

"Nymph," Jade turned to Tree, "what do you think?"

"Their name's Tree." Crow spat.

"The forest is not going anywhere. We need energy for our journey."

A wooden cabin stood sentry before the stable and its pastures. As they approached, Crow saw smoke rising from its chimney. A worn statue of Mother Vitania was erected before the door, reaching no higher than Crow's waist. Moss crept up her stone skirts, and her face was so worn that only a stump of a nose remained.

"Religious." Kath noted.

It was a welcomed sight. "Hospitality's important to the Mother." Crow explained to Tree. Asking for a place to rest was worth the gamble.

No one was tending the horses or pasture as they approached. Jade knocked on the door with an armor-clad fist. Crow heard the shift of a lock, and the old wooden door creaked open. A small faded elderly man stood in the doorway. Wrinkles etched his sun-weathered face, and his bald head was as smooth as a chicken's egg. Other than that, the man seemed in good shape. Despite his small stature, he held himself well, and his eyes were gray and sharp.

He balked at the sight of women in armor.

"Welcome...travelers." He said, eyes darting between Jade, Gretchen and Kath. He barely noticed Crow and Tree at all. "What brings you to my door?"

"Rest, good man." Gretchen replied. "We have our own provisions, and can offer you coin. All we ask is for a place to rest our heads tonight. The barn would do just fine if you have an empty stall."

The old man raised a gray brow, eyes finally resting on Crow and Tree's shadowed forms. Crow bit his lip, hoping King Arthur hadn't sent riders this way. "Where are you headed?"

"Youngston." Jade answered. "We had business in Griffin's Peak."

"I'm surprised you're taking the high road."

"The main road is not what it used to be." Jade replied easily. Crow was surprised by how clever she was. "We decided we'd be safer taking a less traveled route."

The old man nodded in understanding, much to Crow's relief. "Aye, it's true." He said sadly. He opened his door wider and stepped to the side. "Come in, there isn't much space, but you must be hungry. I have salted carrot and onion strew boiling over the fire."

Garrett, the old man's name was, had a small yet cozy home. A mountain cat's skin carpeted the middle of the splintered wooden floor. Leather bridles and hempen rope hung on the walls between shelves packed with moth eaten books. A stone hearth at the far end held a cast iron pot that bubbled with stew. Shoved against the left wall was a simple wooden table and a collection of stools, under which a trap door lay which Crow guessed led to the cellar. Kath offered the hare at her belt, skinning and tossing chunks into the stew with her dagger. The smell that filled Garett's home was enough to set Crow's mouth to watering. There weren't enough stools, so Gretchen and Jade took the floor. Crow sat on the stool with a groan. His feet pulsed painfully as he put the satchel down between them, and his shoulders sang at the sweet respite of its weight. Tree sat beside him; they were nursing a bowl of boiled broth poured for them before Kath added the hare. They brought it up to their shadowed face, and slurped delicately.

Crow snatched up his clay bowl and could hardly wait for the stew to cool. The rabbit grease pooled on top of the broth, burning his tongue as he swallowed it. He barely felt it. The carrot and onion were soft, and the meat tender. The five of them slurped down their stew with not a word. Garrett watched them from his chair at the fire, nursing a bowl for himself.

"Thank you for your kindness." Gretchen said between mouthfuls. Crow nodded as an afterthought.

"All of Vitania's children are welcome under my roof."

Crow glanced at Tree. *Do they count?* He wondered.

"There haven't been many travelers on the high roads of late. Not even hunters." Garret said. "Winter is coming and the forest is ripe with deer coming down from the north. It's been a lonely season."

Jade nodded gravely, wiping grease from her mouth. "The main roads are much the same. Folks have been vanishing. Corpses have been found left in cold blood with their throats slit and belongings stolen. A few moons back my companions and I stumbled across an entire escort."

Corpses, Crow's eyes widened. He never knew the roads of the Ridge to be dangerous. Stone Teeth occasionally took to the smaller villages to look for recruits and had only come back once or twice with a tale of danger. Even Lads who had traveled to Griffin's Peak complained that it was hunger and cold that almost did them in. Picker was the only one to have a thief pull a knife on him. Even Shadow, who came all the way from the Crystal Isles, only had good things to say about the travelers he'd met.

"My son," Garrett whispered, staring into his bowl, "he was traveling to Youngston to visit my daughter, Wanda. In Youngston, she found work in a pot studio. She made these bowls we're using. When she left, she told me she'd write me every fortnight. I've kept every letter for the past two winters. Only, I haven't received a letter from her in three moons now. My son went to go check on her because I'm too old for the journey, and the horses need tending to anyway. He took one of our stallions for a swift trip." He took a shaky slurp of stew. "The stallion returned, and my son did not.

"The Stone Hold guards found him at the bank of Young's River, right by the bridge. They said the stallion came running in from that way. I've sold a lot of horses up there and they knew the mark. I had to bury my boy out back, just behind the barn. Craek was a handsome lad," his voice broke, "whoever did for him poked him full of holes. He fought, he did, the horse too…the beast still has the scratches to show for it." Garrett's wrinkled hands clutched his bowl so tightly Crow thought he might break it. "It's a cruel thing for a father to bury his son."

"Our sympathy." Jade murmured.

"He's with our Mother now." Gretchen said.

Garrett nodded. "That he is. You said you were headed to Youngston. Please, check on my Wanda. She has long brown hair and eyes as green as grass. She works at the Potter's Craft. Please tell her to write me. Tell her I worry for her."

We're not going to Youngston, Crow wanted to say. He wondered if his parents were alive, and if they thought of him this way. He chewed on a carrot, staring into the foggy broth of his stew. It'd been a while since he thought about them.

"We will." Kath said.

Garrett walked them out to the barn. He apologized for not having enough room in his home, but the stable floor was relatively clean and padded with layers of straw. He left them that evening after offering them a loaf of brown bread and butter. The travelers ate it gratefully, Crow already felt his strength returning with some rest and food in his belly. An oil lamp rested beside them on a bale of hay, leaving a faint glow in the fading evening light.

"We shouldn't have lied about findin' his daughter." Crow murmured, staring at the egg in his lap. He'd taken it out of the satchel and watched how the lamplight played across its black shell.

"We shouldn't have." Kath agreed. "But we told the man we're headed that way. If men from Griffin's Peak come questioning him, it's all the better that they head in the wrong direction."

"His daughter should know he wants to hear from her." Crow said. "I used to wonder if my parents would ever come for me. Bones and me, we were left at the Lads 'fore we knew our parents. Sometimes we'd pretend our father was the king, other times a champion. I would always hear my other brothers talk about their mothers and fathers. Some of them died, some of them were drunks who left them on the road one day. But all of them had memories of them at least." Crow furrowed his brows, hand running across the egg's exterior. "In my dreams, I started imagining my parents as farmers, miners, inn keeps...whatever. That made it worse for some reason. And then, I don't know when, I stopped thinkin' of them at all. If they really cared, I thought, they'd come for me, or send someone to see me. Waitin' for my parents was stupid, I didn't want to be like Bones and wait for something that wouldn't come. The Underground Lads were my family, even though I didn't like them sometimes.

"Wanda should know, if she's alright. She should know her father's tryin' to reach her. I'd want to know."

"My father beat me bloody until I put a knife in his side." Kath grinned. "I would have traded the world for a man like Garrett to be my father once."

"My mother taught my sister and me how to braid our hair." Gretchen sighed. "'No nasty man can grab ya' now,' she'd say. A fever took her from us when we were young."

Jade said nothing; she just sat with her longsword in her lap, polishing the silver pommel with a frown. Crow looked to Tree, who'd finally put down their hood.

"Do nymphs have parents?" He asked.

"No. We are raised by the land." Tree said. "But I have always found the relationship between kin quite beautiful."

"Not mine." Kath snorted.

"Probably not." Tree allowed. "Although...interesting maybe." They shared a quick laugh, all but Jade who continued to clean her blade.

"After we hatch the egg," Crow determined, "once it's safe, we'll go."

"Aye, Crow," Kath yawned, leaning back against the hay bale, "we'll go."

And Crow marveled that his first instinct wasn't to return home.

Scrape

Crow rolled over, drawing his cloak tighter around himself. He could feel the straw poking through the woolen fabric, tickling his skin. *Sleep, get back to sleep,* his body began to relax again, thoughts drifting...drifting...

Scrape.

Grumbling, Crow reached over his head, squeezing his ears with his elbows.

Scrape. Scrape.

Springing up, Crow searched the dark stable for whatever had woke him. He didn't remember falling asleep, but he wished to return to his heavy dreamless slumber. Crow narrowed his eyes. Lady Jade sat against a corner, running a smooth rock along her great sword's edge. "Oi," he hissed, "why you doin' that right now? It woke me up."

"The sound of a sharpening blade is the most comforting thing in the world." Jade answered, at normal volume. "They think so." She motioned to Kath and Gretchen, who lay asleep in the straw as if dead.

Crow rolled his eyes and flopped back over, bunching his cloak around his head. It was too late now, though, his dreamless sleep had passed him. As he closed his eyes, his mind wandered to the danger behind them, the odd crimes that plagued their journey, and the limbo of his future. Crow opened his eyes angrily. Tree wasn't sleeping either; the little nymph was sitting across from him, picking at the straw.

"Do nymphs not sleep?" Crow whispered, sitting up once more.

"Of course, we sleep." Tree replied, blinking.

"Oh."

Scrape.

"But it is hard sleeping so far from trees and the stars." Tree admitted. "It is not comforting to be isolated from the land. I never understood why men found it necessary."

"What about when it gets cold? Don't you need to keep warm?"

"I sleep in the trees, close to the gods."

"Even in winter?"

"Even in winter."

Crow frowned. "That sounds horrible."

"It is not the best." Tree smiled. "But winter does not last."

"You said before that most nymphs left Frukjera, and only a few stayed behind."

"Yes."

"So, are you lonely?" Crow wondered.

Scrape.

"Lonely?"

Crow nodded. "I've always been surrounded by others. Not a day went by when I was by myself. Everyone knew me and I knew everyone." Now, these four strangers were all he had. "How do you deal with it?"

"I see." Tree said. "Nymphs...we are not like other creatures. Man, feln, wolf, centaurs...all have the desire to be surrounded by their kind." Tree leaned forward. "I used to hear the howl of a lone wolf in the forest, and it was so sad. *Join me*' it cried, *'I am here.*' I'd never experienced sadness like that." Tree pursed their lips. "Even when nymphs were here, we did not band together like wolves or men. We came together to sing for the passing of seasons, but for the most part we lived among everything except ourselves. My neighbors are tree and river and bird and deer. We find our own company in our world."

Jade's stone had gone quiet.

"But," Tree whispered, their eyes far away, "When that lone wolf found his pack, and his voice joined the others, I listened. And a part of me wanted it too."

Six

The High Road

"Why are you called Crow?" Kath asked, reining up beside Crow and Tree.

After a night of rest and a modest breakfast of boiled greens and goat marrow from Garrett, Crow felt as rested as he was like to get. Jade offered the man four coppers for allowing them to stay the night, and one silver piece for any horses he was willing to give them. Much to Crow's surprise, the old man parted with three. After viewing them it was easy to see why.

Kath and Gretchen rode a massive black draft, twice as tall as Tree at the shoulder and thicker than a bull. White fur speckled its nose and hooves. "He's too old to work on the farm, but will get you from one town to the next so long as you don't lather him up." The draft was large enough to carry both of the smaller women. Gretchen took off her heavy mail and wore her leather underclothes to reduce the weight. Jade also opted to remove her armor, slinging it over her horse's rear.

Jade's horse was only a little younger, a slim painted mare that pinned her ears and bucked any horse that wandered too close. She'd given Garret many foals over the winters. "She's done," Garrett laughed, "the last three stallions I sent to her nearly got torn to pieces." *Seems fitting,* Crow thought as he watched Lady Jade upon her back.

Crow and Tree shared the back of a donkey. Crow was embarrassed at first; the dusty brown donkey was only half the size of Kath and Gretchen's ride. But as they disembarked, Crow started to grow attached to the creature. He'd never ridden before, and the fact that they didn't have a saddle and only a pair of roped reins made it even trickier. But the donkey was sure footed, took its time, and didn't spook as much as the other horses. Crow wondered if Tree had anything to do with it. The nymph sat in front of him, patting the donkey's neck and whispering to it every once in a while. "Little Traveler", Tree called it.

"We can't thank you enough for your hospitality." Gretchen had said as she mounted to leave.

"No need, the fact that you'll check on my Wanda is thanks enough."

Crow frowned. *After. After I hatch this egg, we'll look for her.*

They decided to continue on the high road towards Stone Hold. The gentle slopes started to rise again; rocky cliff faces jutted vertically from the ground, surrounding them in a stone forest. Pines ate up the sky once more. The high road was more established here. Game trails widened to gravel paths. They climbed out of the valley and rode along the mountain's edge. Trees clung to the soil above them to their left, and to their right the path dropped off just a few paces away. Over the edge, the main road ran parallel to them. Crow even glimpsed it a few times, the possibility of King Arthur's guard not far from his thoughts.

The journey felt easier with sleep, food in their bellies, and horses.

"Well?" Kath pushed. "Crow, like the bird? That's pretty strange."

"In the Underground Lads our old names mean nothin'. Our brothers name us something new. I don't know if I had a name before, I was too young." Crow explained. "I'm called Crow 'cause my hair's so dark." He reached up and patted down the tangled mess with one hand. It stuck out wildly. "Our names are based off stuff we notice. Bones is really skinny, Shadow was from the Crystal Isles and had dark skin, Mouse is small—"

"Creative." Lady Jade sneered. Crow glared at her. *I know what we'd call you,* he thought. He could hear Bones now: *"Wide Wench"* he'd snicker. Crow smiled, wondering what Bones thought of his disappearance. Was he still mad?

"Are there any girls in the Underground Lads?" Gretchen asked.

"No." Crow frowned.

"Why not?"

"I don't know." Crow furrowed his brows. "Digging's not for girls to do. It's hard and you got to work all day. The tunnels are no place for a girl."

Jade snorted and Kath laughed.

"Men," Kath sniggered, "you pray to a goddess who birthed the world but act like women are frail creatures needed to be coddled. Mother Vitania should come down from the sky and slap some sense into you."

"I second." Jade agreed.

"Third." Gretchen clapped.

"All creatures are equal." Tree piped in. Crow flushed in embarrassment.

"I think girls are equal." Crow added quickly. "Mother Vitania made sons for protection."

"That's how you know men made the *Written Word*." Gretchen sighed, patting the axe at her side. "This's the only protector I need. And most of the time, I need it *because* of men."

Crow thought of the guard who grabbed him at the gate of Griffin's Peak, the screech the man made as Jade separated his hand from his wrist. He eyed her blade. What would the Lads think when they found out he needed women to protect him? What did they think even happened to him? The city guard had been at the Lads' door searching for him that night. Crow wished he could write a letter to them, but he didn't know how. Stone Teeth would love to hear nymphs still roamed Frukjera. The rest of the boys couldn't read anyway, but Stone Teeth would fill them in.

King Arthur must still be searching for him. They were lucky they hadn't been caught yet. The truth was, Crow didn't know when he'd be able to return to Griffin's Peak, if he could at all. *I'm goin' to be like Shadow, leave and never return.* Except Shadow was probably at the bottom of the Pond of Serpents with the rest of the ship he'd boarded. He hoped he wouldn't end up like that.

The pommel of Jade's blade glinted in the sunlight, bringing Crow back from his thoughts. The unicorn shown brilliant in the sun, rearing and polished mirror-clean. Kath caught him staring. "Admiring Lady Jade's sword? Not bad for a foot knight, right?"

"Where'd you get it?" Crow asked.

"It was my grandfather's." Jade replied with a curt nod. "Passed down to my father, then to me."

"The unicorn is quite lovely." Tree said from in front of him. Jade seemed pleased to hear it.

"Aye. My grandfather was champion to Duke Garth Keefe, the duke of Good Land at the time." She said. Crow nearly slid off his donkey. A duke's champion wasn't as important as a kings', but it was impressive nonetheless. "He would accompany the duke to Lake Nagishim to hunt white deer and wolves." Jade spoke with a proud tone, sitting up straight and smiling. "Many winters ago, they were out for a hunt on the summer solstice. Across the water, a great white unicorn parted from the trees of the Forgotten Forest. My grandfather had spotted it and showed the duke. Duke Garth was said to have wept from its beauty, and claimed it was a blessing on the Keefe legacy. He gifted my grandfather the sword the next week, and changed his arms from a rising sun to a white unicorn on a purple field. He barred access to the Forgotten Forest from men, save for the Arrowheads should they ever visit."

"He was right to count himself blessed." Tree said. "Unicorns do not show themselves without reason."

"When my grandfather died, he gave the sword to my father, who became the champion to Duke Harold." Jade frowned.

"Is your father still the champion?" Crow asked.

"No. He died a few winters before Duke Harold did." She turned to look at Crow from her painted mare. "There is no such thing as an old knight. No old *brave* knights, anyway. 'Die with a blade in your hands and another in your belly', he told me. 'Such is our duty.'"

"Was it one of the Petty Wars that killed him?" Crow pressed. There hadn't been a war since Crow was born, but the royals were known to get ambitious and call their armies to seize more territory.

"No." Jade spat.

"Look at us," Kath laughed, "a pack of orphans."

"*'The girls of spring danced in the grass,'*" Gretchen sang, her voice surprisingly soft and sweet, "*'the boys of summer climbed in the trees. No parents for the children ruled by the night, save for the moon with her light so bright, so bright.'*"

Vitania's Children, Crow liked this song. A lot of the boys would sing it. Kath took up the second verse, and even Crow found himself humming along. Tree's legs swung delicately to the melody. The sun warmed Crow's head, Little Traveler moved steadily beneath him, and he smiled.

They camped the night a small way off the road and into the trees. Tree set a fire as Crow gave water from his skin to the horses. Crow was amazed that the animals didn't run away. Instead, the strange herd gnawed at the grass around camp. "They know we will keep them safe." Tree said, their green skin shining in the flame light.

They shared some crushed acorns and hard jerky. Crow's legs were sore from riding all day, but it was still better than the pain of walking for three days straight. The autumn nights were getting cooler, but the fire helped keep the worst chills away. Snug in his lap was the egg, cold and black and mysterious. Sometimes, when Crow placed his hand on the shell, it felt like something was moving inside. Coiling, thumping, sometimes in his head he could hear a thin *hiss*.

He wondered if it would hatch soon. They hadn't even reached Stone Hold yet, and Crow knew the Forgotten Forest was even further than that.

Taking turns to sleep made the night pass slowly, but eventually Tree shook Crow awake. The sun peaked through the gold and orange leaves. Extinguishing the fire and preparing the horses, the group was back on the road. They spotted their first traveler within an hour. Crow pulled up his cloak and kept his head down, the hunter paid them little more than a glance. Then the road became even more crowded. Women with carts of chickens and carrots rolled by, men leading cows and carrying pickaxes, even a few armored men.

"We're getting closer now." Jade said. "The road will take a sharp right down this slope and connect into Stone Hold."

Crow's heart fluttered. He'd never seen another city outside of Griffin's Peak, even if it was much smaller. He sat straighter on his donkey.

"We'll split off from you." Gretchen said. "Kath and I can go ahead and make sure the town's not overrun with guards. I'd rather ride through Stone Hold than run up to Wrath River and find a way across."

Jade nodded. "We'll wait here."

The sun was at its highest in the sky when Gretchen and Kath rode ahead. Crow sat against the mossy trunk of an oak tree, petting Little Traveler as it nibbled at the grass beside him. Jade was close by, sharpening her blade. Tree sat on a low branch, looking like a small ghostly shadow.

"The egg grows restless." Tree said. Jade looked up from her sword. Crow stared at the satchel lying in the grass next to him. He moved the flap aside and looked at the egg's shell.

"Sometimes I think somethin's moving inside." Crow confessed. "I can feel it under the shell."

"It senses that we grow closer to the forest every day."

Lady Jade stared at the egg uneasily as she sharpened her weapon. "If I hadn't touched it myself, I wouldn't believe it would be capable of hatching. But in Good Land, we hold the history of nymphs in high regard...what little is known anyway. If I could tell my grandfather, he would weep."

Crow pursed his lips, running a hand across the black shell. He remembered the odd room he'd found it in, the strange pull he felt, and how Stone Teeth brought a pickaxe down on it without a scratch. That felt like winters ago, but it'd only been a few days.

"Have you ever seen a dragon?" He asked both of them, but before they could reply, a pack of foot knights rode past. Crow quickly tugged the satchel's flap over the egg, and Jade stood up, holding her great sword.

The knights didn't regard her. "We should be heading to Youngston." One said atop a chestnut stallion. It was a nice horse for a foot knight. "There'll be good coin there, I reckon, if we can find a way in."

"King Arthur will be calling on men." Another answered on a thin white mule. "There's no way he'll let an attack like this stand. Youngston is the Peak's sister kingdom, to do nothing would show weakness. We'll find more gold and glory with the king." They continued riding, voices fading in the autumn day.

"Attack?" Crow blinked. "On Youngston?"

Gretchen and Kath rode up on their black draft shortly after. "It's safe." Kath said, breathless, her scar twisting in a grin. "The last thing anyone is talking about is a missing boy with a weird rock."

"It's Youngston." Gretchen said. "Youngston is under siege."

Seven

Stone Hold

Stone Hold stood at the base of Mother's Guard, a great mountain that shot up from the rocky valley to block the mouth of Wrath River roaring down from the northeast. A squat round stone castle raised in the city's middle, all surrounded by a thick gray wall. Taverns, inns and an open marketplace swarmed the castle like stone beetles. The keep was encased in a second rock wall, taller than the first. The outer gate was open, despite the news, and from it flew the red and gray flag of the Arrowheads along with the sigil of the duke: four white pebbles on a red field.

It's not so different from home, Crow thought as he watched the children run from one alley to another. Mother's Guard covered the village in shadow, and Crow noticed that there weren't as many people cluttering the streets as the Peak. Men and women huddled together inside shops and homes, faces pale and whispering to each other. Eventually, the streets grew too narrow to ride so they had to find a place to drop the animals. An inn on the main street held a tiny yard filled with four other horses. Crow patted Little Traveler before walking away.

"What're we doing here?" He asked.

"We need more supplies." Jade said.

"We also need to find out what's happening in Youngston." Gretchen added.

"You think it's a Petty War?" Crow asked.

"The last one was twenty winters ago. We are due for another." Jade allowed. "But Youngston has little to offer. If Griffin's Peak isn't attacking, I don't know who it would be."

It was true. Crow had been lucky that another war hadn't struck yet. The most recent incident he knew of was when Shadow told him that Seal Island tried to break ties with the Crystal Isles before Shadow joined the Lads. *Who could put Youngston under siege?* Glorygradus was at the other side of Frukjera, the Crystal Isles lay far to the south, and Harold's Holding seemed a whole world away.

Walking between stone homes and winding paths, they eventually reached the middle of Stone Hold, where the second wall wrapped around the city's stout keep. In comparison to the Roost, Stone Hold's castle was a peasant's hovel. Two guards stood on either side of an iron barred gate. Just the sight of them made Crow uneasy, so he kept his cloak clasped tightly around his head.

The markets were in the shadow of the castle gates. A ring of smiths, taverns, apothecaries and traders circled the cobbled square. There were also a dozen wooden stalls, but most were empty. A hunter hung fresh butchered elk and rabbits, shouting for villagers to spare a look at his wares. Another man displayed daggers with jewel-crusted hilts; Kath seemed particularly interested in them.

"Fish! Salted fish! Fish from Young's River! Salted bass, black carp, and river snake! All cured! Bass, black carp, and river snake! Bundled sweet reeds!" The man stood beside a wooden cart filled with salted fillets and greens. A mini horse stood next to him, asleep despite the market noise. Silver fish scales were sewn into his jerkin, making him shine in the autumn afternoon. The man took one look at them and yelled, "Great for travel! Cured and filling!"

Crow guided them in the trader's direction. "He might know somethin'."

Tree seemed more interested in the mini horse than the fisherman's wares, giving the small beast a pat. The river fish were filleted and smoked, their pink and white meat looked tough as leather. It'd be a welcome change from goat. *I've never had river snake.* Crow thought, eying the coiled piece of muscle. The skin was flaky and dry. A pile of them lay together between wrapped sweet reeds, purple berries and boiled acorns.

"All young lads should eat a good river snake." The trader said, his deep brown eyes looked Crow up and down. "It's all muscle." He slapped Crow's boney shoulder. "Will make you grow big and strong!"

"You said you caught these from Young's River?" Jade asked. "Did you hear about what's going on in the Roam?"

"Aye." The trader nodded solemnly. "I keep to the Ridge's side of the bridge, it's been quiet—especially with the danger on the road lately. A few nights past, I was pulling some reeds, and my old Betsy was grazing beside me. Seemed a peaceful afternoon when a hunter from the Roam told me Youngston was under attack. 'They closed their gates. Any riders that try to escape are slaughtered,' he told me. I thought it could be centaurs since they always run a mess of the Roam...but then I never knew centaurs to lay a kingdom under siege. The hunter told me much the same. I wondered if the Arrowheads finally attacked, but apparently ships left Youngston's port to ask the Peak for help...so it can't be them."

"Then who surrounded Youngston?" The question came from Tree. The fisherman frowned at them, wary of their shadowed figure.

"Don't know." He admitted. "From what I heard, those who got close enough to find out saw no arms, most have only seen the smoke. Those who got too close, well…" He shook his head. "I've heard nothing more than that. And now the centaurs have grown bold with Youngston's power locked behind its wall. Fisher's Mark has locked its gates as well. Young's River will be crawlin' with people trying to get out of the Roam soon enough. Where do you travel to?"

"Griffin's Peak." Jade lied.

"It'd be wise to take the high road, which is a long journey." He motioned to his selection. "A group like you needs some proper food."

"We'll take a snake." Jade decided. "A few strips of smoked black carp, and a bundle of sweet reeds."

Jade also bought a leather pouch to pack their provisions. As time passed, Crow grew less anxious of getting recognized. The people of Stone Hold kept to their business, the news of Youngston filling the air with uneasy energy.

Jade showed her sword to a crafter, Kath haggled the price of fletching feathers, and Gretchen kept to herself, silent and still. Crow found Tree admiring some jewelry from a woman's wooden stall.

"Men have such exquisite craftmanship." The little nymph said. Laid out was a simple necklace of thin silver and gold chain, a few ruby crusted rings, and a bracelet of copper wire with sapphire charms. Crow wondered if he'd dug any of these jewels, only for them to end up here.

"Off with you." The woman spat. "Make way for the people with coin."

"We'd find jewels like that in the Lads." Crow told Tree as they scampered off. "Then Stone Teeth would sell them to the Jeweler's Den, and they'd end up on rich folks' fingers."

"Did you learn how to make such jewelry?"

"No." Crow admitted. "Only find it."

"I would like to learn such magic. Men have always fascinated me with their skill of crafting. Even the feln, too, I suppose."

"It's not magic, it's trade." Crow paused. "What kind of stuff did the feln make?"

"Much of the same as men, though cruder by some degree. They forged more weapons than anything else. Their tools were used for burning and killing."

"Did nymphs ever make weapons?" Crow looked at Jade's sword.

"No. A lot of creatures find a sort of beauty in violence, men and feln are not the only ones. But we nymphs do not quite understand it. We do not build tools for the purpose of harm."

"When me and Bones would play knights, I always dreamt of havin' a cool weapon like Lady Jade's." He held out his arm as if he were holding a blade. "We'd fight bandits and enemies of the Peak." A cold flash ran through his arm like a bolt of frozen lightning. It sparked deep through the bone in a flash. Crow immediately grabbed the satchel out of instinct. He could feel the egg's cool shell through the fabric. And a twisting, pushing, stretching force.

"You feel it." Tree murmured, face in shadow. Crow's mouth was dry, and the egg stilled. Letting it go, he let out a shaky breath.

"Will there be a war?" He asked, suddenly thinking of Youngston.

"There will be something."

Kath, Jade, and Gretchen returned to them with some more supplies. Jade had gotten her hands on powdered willow root, and Kath a whole bundle of trimmed feathers.

"We should water the horses and be on our way." Jade said. "We're lucky no one's looking for you here, but I do not wish to spend the night. We'll camp off the road."

They made sure the horses had water and hay before brushing them off. Crow had never groomed a horse before, so Kath taught him where to stand and which brush to use. The brushes were worn and dusted, but they were able to get off the worst of the mud caked into the horses' fur. Crow had the most trouble digging rocks out of Little Traveler's feet. Tree murmured in the donkey's ear so Crow wouldn't get kicked in the face. He was sweating by the time he'd finished grooming.

Gretchen was donning her heavy armor over her leather tunic. Crow watched curiously as she struggled to clasp on her shoulder plates.

"I'm going to Youngston." She said.

"It's under siege." Crow balked. "It's the opposite way of the Forgotten Forest. After we hatch—"

"Not we. Me. I'm going to Youngston alone."

Crow looked at Jade and Kath with wide eyes. They hardly looked surprised. Kath pursed her lips and Jade frowned. "You should take a horse." Jade said.

"No, it'll only make me easier to spot. On foot will work for me."

"Then take some food." Kath offered. "A little thing like you won't need much." She smirked.

"I've got more muscle than you." Gretchen smiled. "But, aye, I will take some of that salted fish."

"How're you going to get in?" Crow shook his head.

"I'm from Youngston, I'll figure it out. Queen Charlotte knighted my sister and me when she was just a girl. I cannot stand by as my home stands without. I will offer them my axe and defend my kingdom."

Her home. Would Crow do the same thing for Griffin's Peak? He had to admit he held no love for the king, but if he could, he'd want to protect the Underground Lads.

When they reached the gate, Gretchen took a few supplies, coin, and a rusted knife. She attached them all to her belt.

"It's an honorable thing you're doing." Jade said, patting her on the back in an awkward goodbye. Kath hugged her.

"It was a pleasure riding with you. Whoever's outside of Youngston's gates will flee at the sight of you." Kath said.

"May the gods bless your journey." Tree said. Gretchen smiled.

"It's been an honor to witness nymphs still among us." She replied before turning to Crow. The boy bit his lip awkwardly. He was surprised that he didn't want Gretchen to go. *I wish Jade were leaving instead.* "Be brave and keep that cloak nice for me." She patted Crow's shoulder. "I wish I could stick around to see what's planned for you. I hope to hear a song of it."

They mounted their horses, Tree shared the old draft with Kath this time, and they said their last goodbyes before splitting where the road took a southern turn. Crow suddenly reined up and turned Little Traveler to face Gretchen's receding form.

"Lady Gretchen!" He called. "Find Wanda! In Youngston! Find Wanda and write to that old man! Let him know his Wanda is safe!" He could feel her smile from Little Traveler's back.

"I will!" She replied. "I will find her for him, and I will find her for you! Be brave, Crow!" Then she turned to continue north.

Crow watched her go. "I will be brave." He murmured.

As Stone Hold faded behind them, so did Crow's fear of King Arthur. Surely, he'd be busy with the siege of Youngston. Beyond Stone Hold, the Ridge began to flatten. Large mountains dominated the sky behind them, fading blue against their northern backdrop in exchange for rolling hills to the south. The soil grew richer and dark with oaks, maples, and hickories sprouting from the land in great orange and golden hues. He'd never seen the sky so big. It seemed to go on forever. The air felt thicker too, each breath felt heavy enough to make him sick.

They stuck to the main road. It was the quickest, and the trouble in the Roam gave them the confidence they needed to take it. Crow kept his hood up and made sure not to look too long upon the faces of folk wandering by. Small cabins dotted the road, along with tiny villages that didn't even have their own walls. They passed two inns, one of which Kath said she'd killed a thief a few winters back. Hunters wandered by with arrows and carcasses hanging from their shoulders. Foot knights in rusted armor made japes that they were headed the wrong way, and one family with an old mule even asked them for an escort to Stone Hold. "The coin would have been welcome." Jade sighed as they continued. "But I'm hoping to reach the Forgotten Forest before winter."

"How much farther is it?" Crow asked.

"We'll reach the junction of Young's River and the River of Song within another day and a half." Kath replied. "If we're lucky, we can grab a boat down the river for a way, and hop off along the forest's edge. I'd say three days would be a good guess."

"Three days." Crow slumped on Little Traveler's back.

"The world will see ice dragons once again." Tree said from the draft. "It cannot be rushed."

"Do you know much of ice dragons?" Jade asked.

"Only as much as the songs have sung." Tree said. "They are considered the children of winter, as dragons of fire are the children of summer. Long ago, before man or feln, they flew over this land's northern skies as dragons do in the south. Some of our people prayed to them much like the unicorns. They would breathe great winds of ice that would turn water hard as stone. The ancient nymphs and unicorns travelled across lakes and rivers this way. There is a song about a unicorn who roamed from what you call Griffin's Peak to what is now your Glorygradus across the great pond. An ice dragon flew above and made the ice so thick that not even a creature of the sea could pierce through."

"Where did the dragons go?" Crow asked, enraptured.

"Away." Tree answered simply. "The gods do not give their secrets to mortals, and the dragons seemed to hear a song from another land that called to them stronger."

"But not the dragons to the south." Jade frowned.

"No." Tree agreed. "The summer dragons do not concern themselves with lands far from their island."

"The cave I found had carvings of snowflakes and dragons." Crow said. "The room seemed as big as a dining hall. It was *made*, with a floor smooth as marble. I'd never seen a natural tunnel like that. Someone carved it. I thought it was somethin' to do with Arthur Thunderborn. Only, if the ice dragons went away before men, then who made that room? Was it the nymphs?"

"It was not." Tree replied. "We do not alter the land in such ways. How familiar are you with men's history?"

"Stone Teeth liked history. Shadow too." Crow shrugged. "All I know comes from them."

"Tell me, how is it that men came to this land?"

"We traveled across the Wild Sea." Jade answered. "From the Isle of Birth. Men landed on the northwestern shore, where Glorygradus stands today."

"Men are from the north, and that is where the dragons flew. The song of the Northern Child has been sung before. Something called them there."

"The early men sailed to Frukjera. There is nothing in the north." Jade said.

"What are you suggesting?" Kath raised a brow at Tree.

"Surely if there was a man who tamed a dragon before, the histories would note of him." Jade insisted.

"Just as the histories note that nymphs have not disappeared?" Tree replied.

"If that's true," Kath cut in, "why do you care about the Northern Child? Where do nymphs fit in if the Northern Child is about a man and a dragon?"

"I do not know." Tree answered after a pause. "I listen to the songs, and I do what I can. I believe there is a reason for me to help you, but the gods do not deign to share all of their wisdom." Tree stared back at Crow with their shadowed eyes. Like Crow held the key to their future.

Crow frowned. "Even if I am this Northern Child, I don't know what I'm supposed to do."

"Just have faith." Tree said. "You are here for a reason."

Crow wished he could believe them.

That night, Crow dreamed of winter.

Winter in Griffin's Peak was harsh. The world turned white from wild blizzards, and wind threatened to toss men hundreds of feet to their deaths. But this was different. *Peaceful,* he thought. His feet were buried in white fluffy snow and clusters of snowflakes fell gently from the cloud-blanketed sky. Oddly, he felt no chill, and walked through the snow as if it were soft fur. *Where am I?* He wondered.

Ruins rose around him. Grand stone arches and crumbled buildings stood as frozen relics beneath piles of snow. Trees asleep from the cold broke through foundations of abandoned homes. *This used to be a powerful place,* Crow knew with a strange certainty; statues as tall as castles stood sentry over their ruined kingdom, broken yet noble. They were shaped as naked women with long flowing hair, men clad in stone armor holding up weapons that had long crumbled away, and *dragons.* As he continued, he saw the remains of a temple for Vitania; its spier reached toward the sky, a moon was carved above the arched doorway. Crow continued. *I need to keep walking,* he thought.

"I'm sorry." The voice was quiet, faint as the wind. "My beautiful boy. Northern Child."

Crow spun around, but no one was there. The stone ruins stared back him; their quiet beauty now sinister. Crow swallowed.

"My beautiful boy." The quiet sobbing came from his right. "Oh, oh, oh..." Crow turned again, and this time he wasn't alone.

A wall of snow encased him. No. Not snow. It moved; feathers white as winter. A dragon impossibly large curled around him, its feathers shown like diamonds in the sun. Hard black scales hid under the wavering plumage like shadows. Horns clear as ice spiraled from the beast's head, as tall as himself. A long serpent neck bent towards a woman huddled on the ground. A black cowl hid her face from him. "My boy." She whispered, voice strangely far despite her closeness. The dragon turned its great head towards Crow. *The eyes are blue, like mine.* Despite its pointed teeth and massive size, he was not afraid of the creature. He reached out to touch it.

But then the dragon swung its great head back towards the woman, opened its giant mouth, and sent forward a swirl of frozen breath to kill her.

Crow sat up with a scream. His skin was slick with sweat. Leaves crunched beneath his damp palms, and the fire had burned down to embers. They were camped off the road in a wooded area. *A dream.* He panted, shakily running his hand through his hair. The egg lay next to him safe in its satchel.

They'd decided to rest under a thick cluster of oak trees. Tree slept across a low branch, Jade against the tree's base, the horses stood grazing in the dark. Kath sat across from the fire; her face lit dimly by the orange glow. She had been fletching some arrows before Crow started awake.

"Nightmare?" She smirked, returning to her business. Crow nodded, laying back down. But he knew sleep wouldn't come again. He couldn't forget the woman's shrouded face, her strange cries. *"My boy."*

"Jade!" Kath hissed, and Crow was up again. Kath stood beyond the fire; an arrow pointed off into the trees. Jade was up too, unsheathing her great sword. Tree sprung awake. Their green skin glowed dully against the fire's embers. Kath stamped out the light despite the blindness it caused them. *It's always safer in the dark,* Crow knew. Grabbing his satchel, Crow slung it around his shoulder and stood. A twig snapped close by to the north. *A rabbit,* he hoped, *or a fox.*

But that hope was dashed as Crow's eyes adjusted to the darkness. He heard another shuffle of leaves. A shadowed head peeked from behind the trunk of a thick maple. "Show yourself!" Kath let an arrow fly in warning. It buried itself deep into the wood. "State your business!"

Jade's mare whinnied from behind. Crow spun to see three men approaching them from the south. As they grew closer, Crow caught the sheen of metal in the moonlight. Two of the men held short swords, and one a dagger. Lady Jade turned on them, but Kath kept her stance on the one behind the tree in case he had a bow. The horses snorted and pawed the ground.

"How 'bout *you* state *your* business?" One of the men said. He had on a ragged chain link shift and two different pairs of boots.

"If it's gold you want, best move on." Jade said, she wore her tough leather underclothes, but her armor was at the base of an oak with everything else. "We don't have any, and copper isn't worth bloodying yourselves for." That made the men laugh.

"Bloody ourselves? Four o' us against two women and two children? I'd say you don't know your situation."

"Besides," said the man with the dagger, "it ain't gold we want, though I'll be takin' that sword of yours."

"We heard from the guards of the Peak that King Arthur's lookin' for a boy with a magic rock. Some said he'd been traveling with a couple of women." Despite the dark, Crow saw the whites of their eyes reflecting in the starlight. They looked at Crow and the satchel he carried. "We know what it's like to be wanted by some lord or other. Give us the rock and that sword of yours, and we'll be on our way."

"No." Crow said. "It's mine."

"Bold talk for a lad without a weapon."

Crow wished he had one just then.

"Step off." Kath said with her back still turned. "Or you're dead men."

"We need horses too." The third man muttered.

"Alright," the daggered one shrugged, "may Mother Vitania forgive us for murderin' some daughters."

The man in the chain link shift rushed forward, his sword held high above his head. Crow braced, ready to fight with nothing.

Jade cut off the man's attack as quick as a cat. He raised his sword at her, but she caught the stroke with ease, shoving his weapon aside before lunging for his right. Quick, too, he shuffled out of the way and drove for her middle. Jade dodged him easily. Meanwhile, Kath spun, letting loose her arrow at the knee of the man with the dagger, it skidded off his plated pants but was enough for him to hesitate. Just as Kath nocked another arrow, one whizzed by Crow's ear and nearly knocked him from his feet. Kath twisted back around and loosed with a curse. Crow assumed she missed.

I can't do anything, he thought helplessly as Jade brought her sword down in a deadly diagonal slice. The man's shift parted like butter, and her sword dug deep into his collarbone. He was down. Even Tree was able to join the fray. Crow heard a bizarre song from within the horses and suddenly the beasts raced forward, driving at the bandit with the dagger. The bandit screamed and thrust at the animals to scare them off, but the giant draft bulled him over. Large hoofs stomped over his body, and Crow heard a sickening *crunch.* Jade was pulling her sword from the man's belly and Kath whooped as her arrow landed its mark. There was only one bandit left, and he'd just reached Crow.

Crow fell away as the man's sword slashed where he'd been. He fell to the ground, and the egg rolled away. Crow desperately wished he had a weapon. His heart pounded in his ears. The only sound in the entire world. He rolled as the man's sword bit the ground.

"The real monsters are out there." Crow would not disappear like Shadow. He could not die here.

Roaring, he wrapped his arms around the man's legs and brought him down. The man dropped his sword in the fall, and to Crow's surprise, they were close to the same size. However, Crow was a wiry child, and the man was thickly muscled. They wrestled for a moment, and it didn't take long for the bandit to end up on top. Grasping for anything, Crow's hands reached for the egg that had fallen to his side. He wrapped his hands around the cool shell just as the man wrapped his meaty hands around his throat. Crow brought up the egg with all his strength and smashed it against the bandit's skull. It sent him to the ground.

Seizing the moment, Crow flipped on top of him, bringing the black stone down on the other's face. Crow still heard nothing but his own heart as he brought the egg down again and again and again. Something wet and warm covered his fingers, making the egg slippery. "It's mine!" He yelled.

Tree pulled him off. The bandit's leg twitched one last time. The man's face was nothing more than a red ruin, unrecognizable. As the madness left Crow's veins, he felt his dinner rise. He swallowed it back down. Kath, Jade, Tree, and even the horses were staring at him. A man lay dead to the north, two arrows jutting out of his corpse. Another was trampled and twisted, and the one Lady Jade fought was lying in a puddle of his own blood. Then, there was...

Crow dropped the egg on the ground. He stared at the man's red pulpy face.

"Was he your first?" Kath asked, kicking the bandit's foot.

"My first?" Crow looked down at his blood-soaked hands. He picked up the egg again and wiped the shell with his cloak. It remained smooth and undamaged.

"If the king sent out a reward for you, then expect to kill more." Jade said sternly. "We cannot sit here wide-eyed all night. And now you got blood all over your cloak. Get up. We must move from this."

Kath stripped the trampled corpse of his tough leather shirt. She threw it in Crow's direction. "Leave the cloak." She told him. Crow looked to Tree, who gave him a sympathetic look and pulled up their hood.

"None of our hands are clean here." They said.

"Should we bury them?" Crow asked no one.

"No." Jade buckled on her armor. Crow glared at her, wishing she'd run off to Youngston instead of Gretchen. Pulling the shirt over his head, he ditched the cloak and grabbed back up the egg and satchel. *So much for keepin' it nice for her.* Crow released a deep shaky breath before returning to the man he'd killed. He covered the face with his bloody cloak and unbuckled the man's sword belt. It sagged a bit around his waist even at the tightest knot, but it would serve. He grabbed the sword from the dirt and sheathed it awkwardly. Jade nodded her approval.

Kath stole a few coppers from the men and took the archer's arrows. Jade grabbed one of their daggers, mumbled it would be worth a trade. She was in a particularly bitter mood, Crow noticed. "She hates killing rogues." Kath whispered. "It's never an honorable fight. Her father and grandfather fought for the duke, in wars. All we do is murder vagabonds on the road. It's insulting for the real 'knightly' lot."

First light started to color the autumn sky as they mounted up. Crow felt almost naked without his cloak, but the leather shirt was long sleeved and warm enough, although a little big. Little Traveler was anxious to be on the way, the horses didn't like the smell of blood.

"We should teach you how to properly use that sword." Lady Jade said as she gathered her mare. "You should know how to fight, especially if men will be coming after us."

Crow remembered playfighting with Bones. Their imaginary weapons would clang together as they shouted curses and taunts. He'd dreamed of wild adventures in which he and Bones killed bandits and save some innocent town folk. Bones, Mouse, Ash, and Picker often played bandits and guardsmen. *"You're dead!"* Crow would yell, pretending to stab down into Ash's belly with a stick. *"My guts!"* Ash would scream. *"Ah! They're everywhere!"*

Crow set his mouth in a bitter frown. *I want to learn how to fight. If I can't be an Underground Lad anymore, I will be a knight.* It was the first time, he realized, that a future outside of the mines was tangible for him.

"Teach me." He agreed, remembering Jade's speed and the ease in which she slid her sword across the bandit's shoulder. "Teach me how to fight like you."

A hint of a rare smile touched Jade's lips.

They rode off into the morning gloom, leaving the corpses behind.

EIGHT

THE RIVERSIDE

The group lost their taste for the main road. Instead, they struck south through the woods. It made the journey longer, much to Crow's dismay, but he felt safer among the trees and with a sword at his side. Wet leaves littered the ground like a golden carpet, causing their horses to tread carefully. Little Traveler nearly tripped over a hidden root and Crow almost slid from the donkey's back. They passed through a small village where the folk shared wary expressions, guarding their hovels with pitchforks and hoes. Other than that, the only company they held were the empty hunting cabins within the forest.

The night was crisp and freezing. Crow's breath puffed from him in steaming clouds. They stayed in one of the empty shacks to avoid catching a chill. Crow swept out the dead leaves, Tree collected acorns, Jade gathered firewood and Kath kept watch for wanderers. Long spears of black shadows covered the forest floor as the sun sank to the west. Jade stoked a fire outside and they settled around it, eating salted fish and sweet reeds. Crow's hunger never left him long. His stomach felt flatter than before, and his arms seemed a little thinner too. He frowned. *I probably look like Bones.* Tree placed a few pine needles in one of Jade's tin cups and set their water near the fire. They nursed it once it was steaming.

Jade suddenly stood up, picking up two long sticks. She threw one at Crow, smacking him in the shoulder. "What was that for?" Crow hissed.

"You told me you wanted to learn how to fight. You might want to learn how to catch first." Crow glared at her, wrapping his hand around the stick and standing.

"What are we supposed to do with sticks? I got a *sword.*"

"As do I, but the edges aren't blunt. And, as much as it may seem, I do not wish to kill you...most of the time. Before you take up a blade, you must master this." She held the stick at its base.

"Come, Tree," Kath said to the nymph, "let's move to the shack, they need space."

Crow stared at the piece of wood in his hand, thinking of the pickaxes he'd held. "Yeah, alright." He said, wrapping his other hand around the base.

"One hand." Jade chastised.

"But it's heavy." Crow felt it drop.

"It's a stick, boy." Jade spat. "The sword you carry is heavier, and one handed. What's your dominant?"

"My right."

"Then we will start with your left." She tossed her own stick from side to side. "My father always said a man should fight equally well with both."

"Too bad you're a woman." Crow teased.

"And you're just a boy. Come, let's make a man of you."

They trained as the fire grew dim. Crow's left arm felt like a limp weed by the end. He was so sore that he could hardly sleep. Bruises were already welting beneath his shirt, his fingers were swollen and red from where Jade had wacked them, and he nearly cried when he sank to the floor of the hunter's cabin to sleep. Jade's method of teaching felt more like an excuse to beat him. But after a couple of brutal rounds, Jade told Crow what he did wrong, repeating the motions, slower each time so he knew when to block, move aside, and prod offense.

"I couldn't even defend myself once." He complained, panting.

"And you won't. Not tonight and not tomorrow. But eventually, you will." She said. "These sticks are good, keep yours on you."

And so, his stick lay next to his sword on the floor. Crow stared at it as he tried to ignore the pain. He hadn't been this sore in winters. The long days digging in the Underground Lads had hardened his body, but that was nothing in comparison to Lady Jade. He felt a fire inside him. He'd wield the sword eventually, and he'd be the best.

That night, he dreamed of the man he'd killed.

Crow shot up. Sweat covered his body despite the chill. He quietly got up and restarted the fire outside of the shack. "I wonder if I'll ever sleep again." He whispered to the flames.

Tree greeted him at dawn, and camp was packed up. Crow didn't say anything about the night before, but the deep circles under his eyes told the others enough. Hopping onto Little Traveler's back nearly killed him. "My legs are goin' to fall off." He said to the donkey.

A thin layer of frost blanketed the ground and started to melt in the morning sun. Crow wondered where he would go when winter hit. He remembered huddling with his brothers on cold winter nights and hot stews thick with goat marrow and soft onions. There would be no stews for him here, though. They ate on the road, munching on crushed acorns and smoked fish. It was a bitter breakfast, but Crow could feel energy returning to him.

The second night of training went as terrible as the first, and this time Crow actually did cry when he lay down near the fire. *It can't get much worse than this,* he reasoned, staring at the satchel next to him.

The egg's black shell rippled like a quiet lake. He placed a hand on it and tried to sleep. He dreamed of dragons with feathers white and gray as a blizzard. He sat on the great beast's back and watched as the dragon raised villages to the ground.

That morning, Tree offered Crow a bundle of leaves and root paste they'd collected the night before. "For your aches." The nymph said. Crow was horrified he'd been heard, but as Tree applied the paste and leaves to his bruises, he actually felt better.

"Must be some sort of nymph magic." Crow marveled.

"The world takes care of its children." Tree then went on to explain which plants had healing properties. Tree didn't know the correct word in Frukjeran for some of them, though. Crow listened intently, enjoying the soft chime of Tree's voice.

By midday, the forest began to thin. A small game trail led them to a dirt road. More folk appeared. Most were hunters and fishermen. "You're going the wrong way." One of them said. "Best to head north, Youngston's under siege and Fisher's Mark has closed its gates." Families passed with packs on their backs, cows, pigs, chickens and dogs. Tree kept their cloak up and Crow missed his own disguise as well. But he had little to fear of people from the Roam. Still, he kept a hand on his sword for comfort.

Eventually, plains of grass swallowed the trees. The tall stalks seemed to go on forever. A sea of green and yellows. The mountains dwindled to blue humps far to the north. All he'd ever known was squished across the horizon. The ruined face of the man he'd killed flashed in his mind and he quickly turned. He tasted bile. Suddenly he didn't want to see the mountains ever again.

It didn't take them long to spot the river.

It was wider than any river Crow had seen before. The water was fast and green, Crow could hear its roar from here, as if it was some great slithering beast.

"Young's River." Kath said.

"Will we see the bridge?" Crow asked. He'd heard it was one of the largest ever built, a beautiful tribute to men's conquest that connected the Roam to the Ridge.

"No. It's miles and miles north, near Youngston itself." Kath said.

As the roaring of Young's River grew closer, they spotted a two-storied wooden structure on its shore. An inn with a large smoking chimney and sprawling porch. A lazy paddock was built beside it, nearly filled to the brim with horses and cattle. A dock on tall stilts hovered over the river. Four boats were tied in. Men stood about the porch and docks with drinks in their hands.

"The Riverside." Jade said. "Looks quite busy."

"Must be filled with people fleeing the Roam." Kath guessed.

"Is it safe to stop?" Crow asked, anxious after their run in with brigands.

"If they're from the Roam, then yes." Jade said. She nodded at the pole boats tied to the docks. "If we could catch a ride down the river, we would reach the forest much quicker."

"You think it's worth the risk?" Kath raised an eyebrow.

"We shall find out. We should rest the horses anyway. It's been a while since they've had proper grain." Jade decided.

Crow made sure the satchel was sealed and close to his side as they reined up to the stable. A thin stable girl with hair as yellow as straw took the animals from them. She seemed delighted by Jade and Kath. "Are you knights, ladies?"

"Aye." Kath nodded, her shaved head and scarred face didn't seem to intimidate the girl like it had Crow.

"I only seen one other lady knight in these parts. It was winters ago, but I remember she used an axe to keep the wolves off our chickens that season. She used it better than any man I ever saw." Her smile was gap toothed. "We're packed 'cause of Fisher's Mark is closed off, but you'll find a hot meal and ale inside."

Tree kept close to Crow's side as they padded along the planked porch. Crow kept a hand on his sword. But they received little enough attention.

The Riverside's ale flowed like water and meals were tossed out to every packed table. A bear skin sat before a large hearth at the end of the long hall. The great fire had a few iron pots hanging over it with boiling broth filled with game that hunters brought themselves. The wooden tables were massed with all different types of people. There were farmers, families, tradesmen and even a few ladies dressed in simple yet elegant gowns. They all shared a table here. Those who hadn't brought their own food were dining on river bass covered in mashed peas and roasted potatoes. Crow's mouth watered.

They found a seat close to the door and shoved their way onto a bench. It wasn't long before a stout man with yellow hair like the stable girl's brought them ale. Crow took a sip and nearly spat it out. "It tastes like wet bread." He'd always assumed it tasted great by the way Stone Teeth and miners from the Peak would quaff it down.

"Not a fan?" Kath laughed.

"They don't got water here?" Crow sighed, taking another sip and forcing it down with a large gulp.

"They don't *have* water here." Jade corrected. "The water from Young's River will make you sick, it's not as pure as the streams from the mountains." She took a long gulp from her horn. "You'll learn to appreciate a good ale in time."

Crow narrowed his eyes and took another swig. He turned to Tree, who sat with their mug between their gloved hands. "What do you think of it?"

"It is quite strong." Tree coughed, but they drank some more. "Yet strangely savory."

"Strong?" Kath hooted. "This is practically water in comparison to the great stuff."

Surprisingly, though, the more Crow drank the less he hated it. He would hardly call it *good*, though. His mug was almost gone by the time the yellow haired man came back. Jade gave him two coppers each for a meal and another cup. Crow's head was swimming when the keep brought them more. His face felt warm too.

"I believe this drink is growing on me." Tree giggled; their laugh sounded like tinkling bells. The nymph began to hum as their horn was filled again. Jade took the mug from them before they could drink any more.

Their food came hot from the kitchens. The river bass was baked and flaky with a thick pea sauce steaming on top of it. The potatoes were golden and crisp, but the inside was fluffy as a fox's fur.

"A meal fit for kings." Crow laughed, wiping the grease from his fingers. It was the first proper food he'd had in days.

"Now there's a mighty sword." A small thick man with a red bald head and brown rough spun wool tunic squeezed into the bench next to Lady Jade.

"Aye. Mighty sword for a mighty woman." Another man took his seat beside Crow. This man was almost the opposite of his companion, tall and lanky with a hooked nose and greasy brown hair. "Haven't seen a sword as fine as that in a long while."

"Thank you." Jade said suspiciously. "It's been in my family for generations."

"To family." The bald one said, offering his mug for a clash. It was Kath who raised hers in reply. They drank.

"Name's Paul." The bald man said. "And this skinny one here is Greg."

"What is it you want?" Jade asked.

"Suspicious, this one." Paul laughed.

"We know foot knights when we see 'em." Greg said. "Though," he looked Crow and Tree up and down, "not many women, or children as young as them." Crow sat up a little straighter at that.

"Most are headed north now. King Arthur is going to be calling men to the Peak soon." Paul said.

"And how do you know we're not headin' there?" Crow asked, placing a hand on the pommel of his sword. Paul and Greg regarded him shortly and laughed, turning to Jade.

"The lad's right." Jade plucked a flaky piece of bass into her mouth. "We could be headed north."

"True enough." Paul shrugged. "But, see, we're headed south along Young's River, all the way to Crescent Bay. Greg and me are river men. We 've been poling Young's River from Youngston to Crescent Bay since we could walk. Never had a problem in all the winters of my life."

"The river isn't what it used to be." Greg said. "Not long ago a man was found dead near the bridge of Youngston. We've seen a few corpses float by. And now Youngston's under attack, so Fisher's Mark is closed."

"You need protection." Kath guessed.

"We do." Paul nodded. "And we're desperate enough to take on some women and children for it. We don't carry no treasure worth stealin', but these days...you just never know when you'll need a good sword about you."

"We'll pay for your service." Greg added.

Crow turned to Tree, who had grabbed their mug back from Jade. Taking the river would mean a quicker voyage, and one that would require far less walking. Jade was chatting with Kath about the proposition. Crow frowned, looking to Tree again. "They don't even ask us." He said to the nymph. "Actin' like we're babes along for the ride. I mean," he lowered his voice, "aren't you older than all of us?"

"Yes." Tree nodded, rocking back and forth. "But in the ways of men, I am younger than you."

"What do you think of these men?" He whispered. "Will they help us? You knew Jade would help us back in the Planks."

Tree laughed. "The gods sing what they sing."

Tree and their stupid mysteries, Crow rolled his eyes before turning back to Greg and Paul.

"Here's the deal." Kath proposed. "You'll not need to pay us. We will only ride with you part of the way. We wish to be dropped off on the edge of the Forgotten Forest, shortly after Young's River merges to the River of Song."

"The Forgotten Forest? Why on Vitania's grace would you want to go there?" Paul laughed.

"Do we have a deal?" Jade asked.

"Aye." Paul rubbed his chin. "Haven't heard much trouble coming from down there anyway."

"I'll drink to that." Greg raised his cup. "We're leavin' at first light. Paul 'n me are sleeping in our boat. We have an extra room if you don't mind squeezing together. The inn's filled to the brim, you won't find no room here, and even the stables are taken."

"What about our horses?" Crow asked.

"Sorry, lad," Paul frowned, "we've got no room for such."

Crow didn't realize how attached to Little Traveler he'd become until they sold him for some coppers to a family pulling a cart of carrots. "You take care of him." He told them. "He's loyal and will serve you well."

Jade's mare sold for a silver piece to a foot knight, and the draft went to a hunter for two fresh rabbits and three bulbs of garlic. Crow wished they could return them to Garrett. *I wonder if Gretchen will make it to Youngston and find Wanda.* He hoped that she did.

And so, their little group dwindled once again as they loaded their belongings onto Paul and Greg's boat.

The boat was lightwood, planked and kept in good condition. Crow thought it was pretty big for a river boat. But he could only compare it to the slim canoes that fit in the mountain streams. It was wide and flat, with two long poles held against the small rails. When they traveled down river, the current did most of the work. They didn't need to use the oars and sails so much until they made the long crawl back up. A small wooden cabin popped out of its top toward the back. Corn, flour, and potatoes inhabited the barrels below decks. The cabin had two rooms; one was more of a closet. The floor held just enough space for a wide mattress stuffed with rags. It was too small to hold the lot of them. However, they'd make do.

Crow stood on deck, watching as the sun hung above the horizon. The sky was all pinks and oranges and yellows, and larger than he'd ever seen. Here against the river, not even trees shielded them. *It's an ocean in the sky.* He thought of Shadow standing on the deck of some trading cog, looking up at the sky with hopes of adventure.

Did you get to see the sky so big? He wondered.

A sharp *thwap* tore Crow from his revere. Spinning around, he came faced with Jade holding a great wooden stick. "What was that for?" Crow spat, rubbing his back. His own stick still hung at his side tucked next to his sword.

"Practice."

"Right now?" Crow motioned around him. "We're on a boat."

"We are." Jade agreed. "Limited space. A good place to learn."

Crow could already feel his body screaming in pain. He unbuckled his sword belt and handed it to Kath. He gave the satchel over to Tree carefully. The boat shifted under each step because of the river's current. Paul and Greg came out from their cabin to enjoy the show much to Crow's horror. Even a few men from the inn came to laugh as Jade's stick came crashing down on his fingers, knees and elbows. One savage blow nearly knocked him into the river. It was dark by the time their dance ended, torches burned in the night and most of the folk from the porch disappeared for the warmth inside.

Crow lay upon the deck panting and staring at the stars. The others had retreated to their cabins, save for Tree, who waited for Crow with the satchel around their small shoulders.

"I feel like I'll never get better." He sighed in frustration. "Lady Jade's too hard on me." Tree offered Crow a hand, he took it, arms wailing as he stood up. "You got any more of those healing plants?"

"I am afraid not." Tree said, giving Crow the egg.

"Not even diggin' tunnels hurt this bad." Crow complained.

"It is because your body knows how to dig tunnels. It does not know how to fight."

"I guess." Crow frowned. "Shadow taught me how to dig. I don't remember it ever hurtin' so much. But I do remember bein' scared of the dark. He taught me that the dark is our friend."

"This Shadow seemed wise."

"He was." Crow murmured. "You would've liked him."

That night Crow hardly slept. The cabin was cramped, and only Kath fit on the mattress. His body ached against the hard-planked floor and he found himself missing the dirt of the woods. When he closed his eyes, he'd see the man's ruined face and snap back awake.

He managed to get a few hours in, though, because he awoke to footsteps outside, and the sound of Paul and Greg laughing. Jade and Kath were gone, but Tree remained asleep looking like a small black shadow curled in the corner.

Young's River was misting in the morning air. The green water crawled south, tugging at the boat's rope.

"Just in time, lad." Paul said. "Come, help me unleash her." Paul hopped onto the Riverside's dock and untied the knot, tossing loops of rope at Crow so it didn't fall into the water. The rope was heavier than Crow thought. As he caught the last of it, the boat began to drag down the river. Paul vaulted from the dock onto the deck, lurching the boat from side to side. The two men took up their long thin poles and used them to keep steady and shift towards the middle of the river. They knew the river like their own mothers they said. The two men moved the boat to their will with ease.

Much to Crow's excitement, the river carried them smoothly. Flat fields of grazing cows, wheat and corn blanketed the countryside. *It's the Roam*. Crow marveled as he beheld the western bank. The eastern side didn't look much different. Tall grasses of reeds and lion tails hugged the river's edge. They passed a few fishermen and one hunter cleaning a buck, turning the dark waters red. A fishing skiff passed by, traveling north with four men at its oars.

"How's she fair?" Greg called.

"Watch yourself at the crossing." One man called back. "Keep your swords about!"

"The crossing?" Crow asked.

"Where the river splits into four, 'round Fisher's Mark." Greg explained. "It's as I thought, sure to be some trouble 'round there. We'll reach it by nightfall."

They ate the last of their salted fish that morning, graciously accepting some dark red apples from Paul. They were much sweeter than the tart snow apples from Griffin's Peak, and softer too. Tree came out of the cabin only to hang on the side of the boat. Holding their head, the nymph grew sick and spewed over the edge. Their cloaked form made Paul and Greg uneasy.

"The river's calm today." Paul boasted to Tree. "You must be a sensitive one."

"I prefer dirt beneath my feet." Tree hiccupped.

The two men raised their brows at that, but Kath quickly gained their attention by asking about their travels.

Clouds rolled in as the day wore on, blanketing the sky in a thick sheet of gray. Tree had returned to the cabin, and Jade stood along the deck watching the scenery change with Kath. The fields of crops and farms slowly disappeared, replaced by uninterrupted leagues of prairie. Grasses of different colors and thickness grew tall as men. There wasn't a hovel to be seen on the west bank, or even a hunter's rest for that matter.

"It's so empty." Crow said.

"Aye." Paul nodded. "A large portion of the Roam still belongs to the centaurs."

"Do you think we'll see any?" Crow asked. He'd heard countless stories of the savage raids the half-men carried out. Songs were sung of the great knights and kings who slew them. Besides the dragons of the south, centaurs were the only other creatures that never bent to men's conquest. Or even the feln's.

"Maybe." Paul shrugged. "They don't come close to the river much, though. There's a collection of lakes, deep into the plains, where the herds are the thickest. I've only seen a few over the years. A small boat like this isn't much o' a bother. But I hear some of the larger ones have trouble."

"One of our old companions had a sister killed by a centaur." Kath said.

"My father died in the War of the Herds when King Quent went off to try and put an end to them." Greg stuck a pole out and poked a boulder. "Such a stupid war that was. Fisher's Mark nearly revolted."

Crow had never heard of such a war. "The king of Youngston went to war with the centaurs?"

"He tried to." Paul laughed.

"A selfish king." Greg dared say. "The centaurs rarely fell on Youngston. It's got tall oak walls and an army of well-trained men. But King Quent was thirsty for conquest. The Roam's only got one other stronghold, when most other kings got at least three."

"He wanted those lakes." Paul explained. "There's a group of three of them, larger than any lake on the continent."

"Behind manned walls, herds died by the hundreds when they dared attack." Greg shook his head. "But in the open field, each cen-taur is a mounted soldier, twice as powerful and twice as savage. King Quent marched all them men to war and not a quarter returned, not even the king himself. He's probably rotting away in some field along with my father, a burial fit for a Young."

"You speak this way of your king?" Jade raised her brows.

Greg laughed and spread his hands. "This is my king." He said of the river. "And this," he motioned to the boat, "is my queen."

"They provide more for us than any so-called king ever has." Paul shrugged.

Such words could get your tongue cut out in Griffin's Peak, al-though in the tunnels Crow and his brothers could whisper what they wanted with not a worry that anyone would hear. *The river's the same for them, safe.*

"You think the Young's will ever conquer the centaurs?" Crow asked.

"No." Greg said. "If there's anything you'll learn quick in life, lad, it's that men can't rule the world."

The night was black. Clouds shrouded the starlight behind their thick dark layers. Kath and Jade lit two oiled lanterns and hung them off hooks from the cabin's small overhang. The water was a current of black ink, dragging them through a sea of dark grass. Somewhere far off, Crow heard a wolf howl. He wondered how Tree was doing. The little nymph had retreated to the cabin long ago, only emerging to heave into the water. "Please call to me once we have reached the forest." They'd mumbled on their way back inside.

In the night, it was hard to see anything beyond their bubble of light. If they reached the forest, Crow wasn't sure they'd even know.

Down-stream a light—like a star landed upon the ground—shown orange in the gloom. It appeared no larger than Crow's pinky nail at this distance. He stood, squinting into the night.

"Fisher's Mark." Paul said. "We'll be upon the Jumping Trout soon enough and tie up for the night."

As they drew closer, the floating light broke up into millions of tiny stars, lanterns and torches and streetlights. Fisher's Mark was still half a mile down the river when they pulled up to the Jumping Trout on the western bank. There was only one other boat at the dock, and the inn's large wooden wrap-around porch was empty. Not a single torch shined through the dark shuttered windows. Only the splash of water hitting their boat filled the air.

"Odd, the hour isn't very late." Greg frowned. "There should be a fire in the hearth at least."

"Is it wise to stop?" Jade asked.

"It's wise not to test the river at night." Paul said. "Come, let's see what's amiss."

Paul and Kath jumped onto the dock together, and Crow helped with tossing the rope while Greg brought the boat into place. Lady Jade fetched Tree, who seemed grateful that they'd made a landing. However, their relief did not last long. Once the boat was secured, Tree said, "This is a haunted place."

The group fingered their weapons as they approached the other boat. It was smaller than Paul and Greg's, holding fishnets and thin woven rope. The cabin was empty and big enough to fit two men lying side by side.

"We should keep going." Crow said, fear getting the better of him. His sword felt slick in his sweaty palm.

"This place could just be abandoned." Kath assured, though she had an arrow ready. "Maybe after hearing the news, everyone fled behind the walls of Fisher's Mark."

The wood creaked underfoot. Tree held a lantern from their boat, giving the group enough light to guide the way. It wasn't the dark that scared Crow. It was the silence. He remembered the bursting life from the Riverside.

Jade pounded a mailed fist against the wooden doors; her great sword unsheathed. Pushing the door open, they were met with blackness and a rank odor. "Light the torches." Jade instructed at once, and Crow tugged the torches from their place on either side of the door and stuck them in the oil lamp. "Our Mother..." Paul gasped.

Five men lay sprawled across the floor in pools of blood.

"Kath, with me, we'll check the beds. Crow, you stay here with the others. Keep your sword up." The boy did as he was told, staring at the bodies with wide eyes. *They've been dead a while,* the smell hit his nostrils rancid and rotten. The blood had seeped deep into the wood, and one of the bodies was bloated beyond recognition. A deep gash opened up the man's throat to the bone. *And that one was a fisherman,* the other body was slumped against the wall, holding a red ruin of a stomach. He was wearing a silver scaled shirt that reminded Crow of the trader in Stone Hold. Only one of the corpses wore armor. A butcher's knife buried into his exposed neck spelled the end for him.

Can't tell who he fought for. The armor was thick heavy iron, stained soot black and oily in appearance. The helm was crestless and crude with a chunky visor. *A foot knight maybe?*

"Two more dead in the rooms." Lady Jade said. "They fought hard." She frowned.

"Otherwise, the place is empty." Kath said.

"Who could be responsible for such butchery?" Paul gaped, his head nearly purple from anger and grief.

"Centaurs?" Crow wondered.

"No." To everyone's surprise, it was Tree who answered. "These are troubling times, indeed." Bending down, they pulled the helm from the man.

Except it wasn't a man at all. The face looked close to that of a man, but the milky white skin, open red eyes, pointed fangs, and long pointed ears that parted matted white hair told of another creature.

"A feln," Tree said.

Nine

The Jumping Trout

"How could this be?" Paul knelt before the creature's body. "Good Mother...feln don't leave their island."

"One hasn't been seen since the banishment." Jade marveled. The feln melted into the sea and never came back. They were more of an ugly myth.

Crow eyed the butcher knife lodged in the feln's pale neck. "It attacked." Crow decided. "That man over there has a sliced throat, the other a ruined belly. One of 'em probably used the knife because it was all they had. If there were other feln, they might have left after this one died."

"An observant lad." Greg said.

"The feln were a gluttonous lot." Kath crossed her arms and frowned. "But why are they here now? They haven't left their island in two hundred winters. Has some king decided conquest on their ugly land? There hasn't been blood between us in generations."

Tree held the helmet. "A bear may sleep all winter, but it will inevitably wake up."

Crow frowned.

"We've learned a grave truth tonight." Jade said. "The violence on the roads, the murders..."

"Youngston." Kath murmured. "Good Mother..."

"Not many kings would bother to assault Youngston from land." Jade's voice was faint, but Crow thought he heard fear. "But perhaps it's not a *king* who has laid siege to Youngston."

The room reeked of bloated bodies and fear.

After much debate they decided to stay in the Jumping Trout for the night. They dragged the bodies out and into the river. "Young's River gives us life." Paul insisted. "And if these men grew up along the shore, they'd want to be laid to rest in it." Crow thought of the corpses they left behind from the Ridge, how they'd be rotting in the open air much like these men. *They were goin' to kill us,* he told himself. They said a quick prayer to Mother Vitania for the men and then dumped the feln in the grass. The rivermen refused to spoil the waters with a godless creature. "Let those who pass know what happened here." Greg said.

Crow found Tree with the feln as the others dragged the last man into the water. Tree placed the helmet down beside the corpse. Their cloak swung lazily in the night wind. They looked like the shade of death, come to collect the dead feln's soul. If feln even had souls. Crow walked to stand beside Tree, staring down at the ugly thing's face. The feln were here before men arrived and began the extinction of the nymphs and the unicorns. Men came to Frukjera to settle from the north and clashed with the feln. Forests burned, kingdoms rose and fell within lifetimes, and the unicorns and nymphs slipped further into mystery as their world soaked in blood around them. In the end, the five kingdoms of men prevailed, and ran the feln from the continent.

"What're you thinking?" Crow asked.

"That the gods were right to ask me to stay." Tree replied.

"It'll come to war." Crow knew. A larger war than they'd ever seen.

"My people are passive creatures; the gods plan what they plan, and we stand by and watch. We never partook in war before."

"You think this has to do with the ice dragon?" Crow had to admit the timing couldn't be a mere coincidence. Maybe these gods Tree sang to were real.

"It has everything to do with the ice dragon." Tree whispered. Crow put a hand on the nymph's shoulder. "When I heard the song of the Northern Child rise again on the winds," Tree continued, "I left my forest. We have made a mistake by allowing such violence to run rampant here."

"It'll be violent again." Crow said.

"Yes." Tree agreed quietly. "But this time, I will not watch my world burn." And to Crow's surprise, Tree kicked the corpse on the ground. "I will not stand and do nothing again."

Inside, Jade and Crow kept their swords close as Kath started a fire in the hearth and spit her fresh rabbits. She had garlic from their trade at the Riverside, and crushed it with the flat of her dagger, stuffing it underneath the rabbit's skin. Soon, the rank smell of death dissolved under sizzling fat and roasting herbs. But Crow found his appetite small despite the enticing aroma. In fact, everyone seemed reluctant to eat their share after their discovery. The fatty meat melted on Crow's tongue, and garlic filled his mouth with savor, but the food might as well have been made of sand. He forced down every bite. Even Jade wasn't particularly savage during training that night. Crow almost managed to land a blow.

"You're improving quickly." Kath told him as he settled for sleep. They picked the room closest to the dining hall, with a straw bed large enough for six. Kath and Tree were taking the first watch.

"Don't feel like I am." Crow admitted.

"You are." Kath said. "You may not be landing blows or blocking, but I can see it in how you carry yourself." She smiled.

Crow slept on the edge of the mattress, holding the cold egg to his chest inside its cloth case. He dreamt of a white dragon hatching. Its feathers spattered with dark red blood. When he tried to clean the baby off, he realized the red was coming from his hands, blood ran down his fingers thick and warm. When he looked up, a man with a ruined face lunged at him, grabbing his shoulders—

Screaming, he woke to darkness and Kath and Tree. "Since you're up, it's your watch now." Kath whispered, shaking Jade awake.

Crow sat in silence, his dream haunting him. Jade silently sharpened her blade; the *scrape scrape scrape* was their only company until dawn.

That morning, they boiled the rabbit bones in water with the rest of the garlic and threw in some sweet reeds. The broth was oily and filled Crow's stomach with warmth in preparation for the chill autumn day. The days and nights were growing colder. *Not as cold or windy as the Peak,* Crow thought thankfully. But winter was definitely close at hand. It was common to wake up to frost-hardened grass.

The sky was slate gray as they walked out onto the docks; the two riverboats tugged lazily at their ropes. Lady Jade walked toward them, her hands on her broad armored hips. "We will follow you through Fisher's Mark on this smaller fishing boat. It'll be good for us to have our own transport along the River of Song."

"Aye." Paul nodded, "let's hook her up to us, so we don't get separated."

Kath rode with the rivermen for better protection, while Tree, Crow and Jade manned the narrower fishing skiff. Tree wasn't very excited about the prospect of traveling the river again, and it didn't take long for them to retire to the tiny cabin. Their boat followed Greg and Paul smoothly enough, which Crow was thankful for. His arms would have fallen off if he had to row down the stream.

Fisher's Mark grew before them, a great wooden and stone island with a tall timber keep at its center. The wall was a thick ring of stone, moss slicked its face like a slimy green carpet. The city stood at a junction of rivers coming together, appearing to float atop the churning green waters. "Young's River splits into five smaller veins: one east to Good Land, two west, and one large vein that continues as the River of Song. Fisher's Mark sits between the two western streams, surrounded by river on three sides." Jade pointed to where smoke rose into the clouded sky. "The river is usually clustered with boats this way." Jade frowned. As they drew closer, Crow saw men upon the walls with crossbows. Green and brown flags flapped in the gentle river breeze.

"We have news of the Jumping Trout!" Paul called up to the guards once they were beneath the tall walls.

"What of it?" A man yelled down.

"We spotted feln! On our Mother Vitania, feln!" Paul cried. As they crawled beneath the battlements, one of the guards ran off and grabbed a few others. They poked their heads over the wall.

"Pull up your boats, good folk! We must have words!"

Fisher's Mark had a large port at the river crossing, where all five veins connected as one. The great wooden platforms were notably empty. Only a few boats were tied in, some even big enough for a crow's nest. The gate that accessed the port was drawn closed.

Tree emerged from the cabin to see what was going on, and Crow frowned. "We can't stop." He said. "We need to reach the forest, and who knows how long they'll keep us for questioning."

"No." Jade collected the rope as Paul and Greg poled them in. "I don't want to waste any more time." She agreed.

Kath helped the two men pull into port. "We'll leave you here." She said. "We've got to keep going. Thank you for your service."

Greg nodded. "It was a pleasure." He smiled at Crow. "Keep workin' on those sword skills, boy. Show these ladies how men can fight." Jade rolled her eyes at that as their skiff lurched with Kath's added weight.

"May Vitania protect you on your journey to the forest." Paul frowned. "We hope you find whatever you seek."

Then, Tree pulled down their hood. It had been so long, Crow forgot how green the nymph's skin appeared, with freckles gold as amber. He forgot their delicate beauty and strangeness.

The gate to Fisher's Mark screamed as it was wrenched open, but Paul and Greg paid it no mind. Paul's head nearly turned purple from shock. Greg almost stepped off into the water.

"May the river protect you in her swift current." Tree said. They raised up their voice in a high note, and the current suddenly dragged their boat away from port as the guards from Fisher's Mark appeared under the arched gate.

"My sorrow rides with the wind, my ghosts are my last lovers," Paul's voice was loud and smooth and deep, carrying across the waters as he watched them go. Crow raised his eyebrows in surprise.

"He's got a proper singer's voice." Crow said.

"I will remember you in the foam of the sea as you fade from me. This song is my lament, for I am the last."

His song was melancholy, and as they floated away, his words drifted off. Paul and Greg never turned from them, even as the city guard reached their boat. They were little taller than Crow's thumb in the distance.

"A beautiful song." Tree said. "What is it called?"

"The Last of the Unicorns." Jade replied.

They rode through the crossing. Jade and Kath took up their oars and kept them on course through the rivers' intersection. "That way's Good Land." Kath said, pointing to the vein that stretched east. Fisher's Mark faded behind them, a drum of wood and stone closed from the world. *Will Paul and Greg tell the guards 'bout Tree?* It surprised Crow that the nymph decided to relieve their disguise.

Even now, Tree kept their hood down. They stayed at the side of the boat, clinging to it as it lurched this way and that. But they seemed stronger than before. "I can feel the forest." They explained. "Can you feel the pull, Crow?"

"I don't know." Crow frowned, holding the satchel close to his side. He felt nothing. He stared down through the bag's opening, at the cold shell. Crow worried his lip as he gazed at it. What if nothing happened? What if this had all been for nothing? At the moment, the egg seemed as lifeless as the boulders jutting up from the stream. *It has to hatch.* Crow had felt something moving inside, coiling, twisting, reaching for him. Something had to come from this.

"There she is," Kath hooted, "the Forgotten Forest."

On the eastern bank, the tall, yellowed grass led to gold and orange trees standing guard. "They're huge!" Crow gaped. Oaks with trunks three times as thick as Lady Jade stood holding massive branches reaching out over the river; brown leaves floated down like rain. Pine trees stood like green spears reaching into the sky as tall as the mountains of the Ridge, and maples red as sunset pushed through the canopy of yellows and oranges. The sea of grass was replaced by a sea of trees. The trees of the Peak had been tall spindly things, finding what purchase they could in the rocky soil, but these looked like they'd been here for thousands of winters. The air was thick and fresh.

Tree stood from the rail of the boat, a smile adorning their thin lips. Their hair was the same golden color as the leaves littering the air. Crow inhaled, taking in the deep crisp scent of the woods.

They rowed down the river until the forest threatened to engulf the eastern shore. Eventually, they found an outcropping of gray boulders that came out far enough to work as a landing site. Kath and Jade brought them in, and Crow hopped onto the slick rock, holding one end of the hempen rope as Jade and Kath pushed the oars down into the mud and brought the boat bumping up against the stone. It took all their strength to heave the skiff out of the water and onto the bank.

They took up their gear. "We should mark a path back to the boat." Crow said as he started for the dense wood.

"It is fine." Tree said. "The trees will remember." The nymph seemed especially chipper. *They're home.* For the hundredth time, Crow wondered when he'd return to Griffin's Peak and the thin mountain air.

The light of the day seemed to shrink as they entered the shady embrace of the Forgotten Forest. "In all my winters living so close," Jade said, "I've never entered this place."

"Me either." Kath said. "I sailed along this river a couple of times, and every time I think, *'there's a forest that holds everything and nothing.'* I never considered myself a believer in magic, but something about this place feels too pure for me." She smiled a toothy grin. "And here I am, with my blood-soaked hands. It almost feels wrong."

A chill breeze pulled at Crow's rough leather clothes, as if inviting him in further. Crow knew what Kath meant. The very air felt alive here, buzzing with energy. The trees felt like they were watching them with bated breath. *Who are you?* They asked.

"It will be tonight." Tree said, leaves falling in their hair. "Tonight, Frukjera will hear the song of ice dragons."

TEN

THE FORGOTTEN FOREST

"This's the forest your grandfather saw the unicorn?" Crow asked as he traipsed across a carpet of pine needles and fallen leaves.

"Aye." Jade nodded. "It's strange to be here. The people of Good Land are forbidden."

It feels forbidden. Though it looked no different from any other wood, save perhaps for the exceptional height of the trees, there was an air of foreboding. At one point, a doe crossed their path, her brown coat blended perfectly with the endless sea of tree bark. She looked at each of them, flickering her ear at Tree. She walked beside them a few paces before stepping away.

Crow had never seen a deer so calm. He voiced as much to Tree.

"Because men do not hunt here." Tree explained. "She fears wolves and bears. Maybe she would fear you if I were not here too."

"Are there other nymphs here?" Kath asked curiously. Tree shook their head.

"I am the last in this wood. I do not know if there are others in Frukjera."

The Forgotten Forest was bursting with life. Crow had never seen so much game. Fat red squirrels dug among the ground for their last harvest. Rabbits burst from every bush, an owl hooted at them from a low branch, bucks rubbed their antlers against tall pines, and a pair of foxes nearly tripped Jade. Kath had her hand on her bow, almost blown away by the amount of prey.

"I can't even bring myself to shoot one." She confessed. "Not here."

"When did you get so soft?" Jade jested.

"Show me a man and I'll fill him with arrows." Kath smirked. "But animals are cute. I feel more remorse for shooting a hare than a knight."

"I would ask that you refrain from hunting the creatures here." Tree said. "They are my companions. The wolves are too noble to listen, but the lives here are not for men to take."

"Then we won't take them. You have my word." Kath promised.

The clouds burnt away as the day grew late, but the forest floor remained a shadow underneath the fall canopy. A chill fell upon them as the sky darkened. Crow caught himself shivering and missing the thick green cloak that Gretchen gave him. He hoped she was okay. He hoped the feln had not captured her.

"Where're we goin'?" Crow asked, keeping his arms crossed tightly to his chest.

"Men would call it the First Tree." Tree replied.

As they walked, night arrived. Stars twinkled beyond the leaves in a moonless sky. Crow's eyes slowly adjusted, but it was still hard to see. Despite this, Tree seemed to know exactly where they were. Tree led them through patches of berries, a field littered with pinecones, and trees and trees and trees. Just as Crow's feet began to hurt, Tree stopped. "We are here."

It was hard to see at first, but the trees parted to a circular clearing, allowing enough starlight to illuminate the field.

The trees of the Forgotten Forest were weeds compared to the monster rooted in the middle of the clearing. It was a giant red wooded pine, with a trunk thick enough for six riders to pass beneath side-by-side. Thrusting into the sky like a mountain, its limbs could support all four of them for miles and miles up. Crow heard countless creatures living among its branches. He'd never seen such a grand tree in all his winters.

"Our Mother." Jade whispered, staring up. The top was impossible to see.

Tree knelt on the edge of the clearing. Not even leaves fell on the soft grass here. "We must ask permission before we walk here. This is an ancient and proud life before us."

Crow got to his knees, placing the satchel on the ground beside him. He thought of Bones sniggering, *"you're kneelin' to a tree like it's some kind of king."* But it didn't feel strange. It would feel wrong to walk up to it as if it were a common pine. *It is a king. A king of the forest.*

Tree peeled off their gloves and stuck them in a hidden pocket of their cloak. Placing their pale green palms against the grass, they closed their eyes and sang a few high notes in the mysterious song of the nymphs. Their voice rang through the wood, high as a bird call and climbing higher with each note, until it broke off into sudden quiet. Crow stared at them as silence followed.

A light breeze picked up, rustling the leaves of the trees around the group and pulling at their clothes. "We may approach." Tree said, standing. "Every forest has a First Tree." They explained, walking into the clearing. "Some have been killed, others have been standing for generations. Our people have always done magic beneath such trees. We need their wisdom, and the gods will listen to their songs loudest. Northern Child, bring forth the egg."

Jade and Kath exchanged a look, and watched as Crow drew the cool stone from his satchel. His heart thumped nervously in his chest, and his hands were sweating despite the chill. *If I really am this Northern Child, I guess this is where I'll find out.* Darkness enveloped the egg's shell, drinking up any light the stars provided. The shell felt thin as paper, inside something was pulling for him. His stomach felt giddy and sick and dreadful. *Everything will change.* They sat around the egg; Crow placed it in the middle of them as Tree instructed. His hands shook.

"Do we just stare at it all night?" Kath asked.

"No." Tree shook their head. "The Northern Child must give his life's warmth to thaw winter's young."

The egg needed his blood. Tree assured him that a small cut across the palm would be enough. Kath handed over her dagger and a rag. "It's sharp." She assured. *Be brave.* Crow swallowed as he pressed his hand against the cold steel. The dagger was sharp as Kath said, and bit into his flesh cold and solid. Tears sprung to his eyes, but he tried to ignore them as his blood gushed hot from his hand. He brought it down on the egg's black shell, and it seemed hot as fire. Crow whipped his hand away with a cry of pain—as if he'd been burned. The wound on his hand steamed with clotted blood. The red dribbled across the egg's surface, looking nearly as black in the darkness.

Crow's eyes glued to the steaming wound on his hand. His heart threatened to jump up his throat.

Then Tree sang.

The Song of Life, Tree told him later.

Tree's voice bounced through the trees like a fiddler's flute, a child's laugh, a mother's cry; it somehow embodied them all. Words were indistinguishable, as they always were in nymph, but the feeling was so magnetic that Crow found himself understanding the song's meaning. Tree was pleading to the gods, to the trees, to the stars, pleading for life. Pleading to autumn for winter to come. The wind picked up once more, and the trees began to sing along to the swelling song as they shook their leaves in the frozen air. The world was electric. *This is it!* Crow exhaled, feeling his breath pulled from his lungs as the song built up and up and up. Crow had never wanted anything so badly in all his life. Tree bellowed one final note and a *CRACK* boomed across the forest loud as thunder.

The great shell split.

Out poured a long serpent neck- slimy and covered in red goo. *It's black,* was Crow's first thought. The tiny dragon was still. Its bulbous eyes closed. *It's...* "Dead." Crow's heart sank.

The dragon lay half out of the cracked egg, small and frail. It seemed still as stone. As fragile as a baby bird. Crow reached forward and waved a hand above its tiny head. Nothing.

The disappointment was almost too much to bear. Crow slumped under the weight, staring at the little creature with tear fogged eyes. The air was smothering. Crow's hands shook as he reached out to cup the dragon's head. It was limp. Crow inhaled sharply; his voice strangled. "This can't be it."

Tree looked exhausted from the song. The nymph watched the creature with eyes wide with sadness. "But..." they whispered, sounding more like a child than ever, "...I heard the songs."

Jade stood up, her hands on her hips. "How could this be? We stole from the king of Griffin's Peak." Her anger flared. "And this is what we have to show for it?"

"Jade—" Kath frowned.

"We *killed* for this." The foot knight said. "Am I supposed to sit here and find out it was for—" She stopped and fell to her knees. Her dark eyes were wide and staring back among the trees.

Crow sniffled. He didn't realize he'd been crying. He could have stared at the dragon's corpse all night. But the silence was too loud.

Everyone was looking behind him. Crow turned, dropping the dead dragon's head.

The white of its coat glowed against the night. Its hooves crunched against the dead leaves as it parted from the cover of the forest and into the clearing. Cloven hooves.

The unicorn's platinum mane danced lightly on the wind like spun silver. Its horn was shining and as long as Crow's arm, deadly and beautiful. The very sight of the great white beast took his breath away. From everything he'd seen in his life, from glimpses of griffins, nymphs, and feln, this...*this*...a legend come to life.

Tree cried out, kneeling and sobbing as the creature walked toward them with a graceful gate. The unicorn's eyes were two flecks of molten gold; it stopped just a few paces from Crow, flicking its great silken silvery tail. *Bow,* something told him, and he did.

Crow knelt, facing the ground for what felt like several minutes. His body shook from shock. He didn't know what to think. *Bow. Bow. Bow.* He felt a tap on the shoulder, lighter than the weight of a bird but stronger than steel.

Then the vision hit him.

Flashes of light pierced before his eyes: he saw clear blue water, a deck beneath his feet, a dragon of black scales and white plumage roaring and taking wind, a girl with skin white as snow and eyes piercing blue, a second dragon gray as a storm...the images threatened to blind him. Crow was floored by them, feeling the cold wet grass smack his face as he fell beneath their weight. The visions continued: he saw Jade's bright sword in his hands, smoke against a river wide as the sea, and finally a wall of white stone. *Man's Wall,* he knew at once. Crow reached out to touch the limestone. When his hand connected, he plunged into black.

He woke to something wet and soft against his cheeks. *Cold,* he thought as another fleck melted against his skin, then another and another and another. Man's Wall still splayed behind his eyelids. He'd never seen the great structure, but it was legendary across all of Frukjera. The wall reminded him of Shadow, how his brother worked so hard to see it.

The unicorn, he suddenly remembered.

Someone called his name.

"Crow." Lady Jade.

Crow cracked his eyes open. *It's snowing.* The stars were hidden beneath a layer of clouds, small fluffy flakes floated down to the clearing floor. His breath puffed out from his lips; he watched it dissolve in a wisp of smoke into the night. Jade's stern frown appeared against the cloud-covered sky. "He's awake." She said, and Lady Kath showed up too.

Crow stared at them blankly before slowly sitting up. His head spun, and Man's Wall faded. "Is it—is the unicorn still here?" He asked, taking a moment to look across the clearing. The grass was covered in a thin layer of snow.

"No." Jade replied. "It walked off after you collapsed."

"But the drag—" A hiss cut Kath's voice short.

Tree came forward with tentative steps; in their grasp they held a small, coiled creature like a swaddled babe. A thin neck peeked up from the nymph's arms, large blue eyes found Crow's. The tiny dragon wailed, exposing needle-sharp teeth. The dragon flapped small leathern wings at the snow, reaching for Crow like a child would its mother. Without hesitation, Crow grabbed for it. Falling clumsily into his arm, the dragon felt light as a bird, with scales smooth and cold. Its two tiny wings acted as arms as it clung to Crow's leather shirt, its long hind legs scrambled for purchase in his arms, and its scaled tail lashed wildly against his belly. Crow's heart swelled with relief. "Alive." He gasped. "Alive." He cradled the dragon and laughed.

"The unicorn gave her life." Tree said. "I thought they all left us, but..." just the thought of it brought tears to Tree's big green eyes. "You truly are the Northern Child." They bowed.

"I watched with my own eyes as the unicorn knighted you." Jade said. She stood, unsheathed her giant sword from its scabbard and laid it at Crow's feet. "I-I believe we have been brought to you for a reason. Wherever this journey takes us, I will swear my sword to you and use it to defend you, and this ice dragon." She graced him with a rare smile.

"Aye." Kath pounded her chest and placed her bow before them. "And me."

Crow stared at the foot knights, the weight of their words heavy in his stomach. *It's different now.* He looked down at the dragon in his grasp and found strength in her blue eyes. "I was meant to find that tunnel." Crow said, finding certainty in his words that he hadn't felt in a long while. "The unicorn showed me Glorygradus." He said. "I think it wants me to go there."

"Then that is where you must go." Tree said.

"We will accompany you." Kath promised.

Relief flushed through Crow's body. He was glad he wouldn't be continuing this journey alone. *I lost my brothers,* the only family he'd ever had. He stared at the faces before him; Jade with her hard expression, Kath like she held a secret jape, and Tree with their deep sad eyes. He wished Lady Gretchen could have been here, Bones too. *If he could see me now,* maybe this was his new family. The dragon hissed in his arms. Crow smiled.

"How'll we hide her?" Jade asked.

"We will not." Tree said. "It is time for Frukjera to know that the Northern Child has returned."

"What a pretty song it'll be." Kath smiled. The implications were huge. Crow's entire existence had been in darkness, his very name long forgotten with his parents. Soon, the whole world would know of the boy with the dragon.

"What will you name her?" Jade asked, grabbing her sword back up.

The dragon had coiled her tail tightly around his arm. She had two nubs atop her tiny head where great horns would eventually grow. Crow thought she'd be white, like the dragon in his dreams, but her scales were pitch black. Black as oil, black as night, black as a

"Shadow."

ELEVEN

THE FORGOTTEN FOREST

The chill had settled deep beneath Crow's leather clothes, through his thin skin and deep into his bones. It was getting colder. He crunched through the stiff leaves and frosted floor. The snow from the night of Shadow's hatching never stuck, but the days grew colder and darker with each passing sunset. Compared to the Peak, early winter in the Forgotten Forest was mild, the trees sheltered them from the worst of the frigid winds, and their night fires kept the frozen temperatures at bay. But it was getting harder to keep warm. If they wanted to avoid the worst of winter's cruel season, they'd have to keep heading south.

In Crow's satchel, which used to hold Shadow's egg, he carried large clumps of dried moss. Tree showed him how it could keep him warm if he shoved it beneath his underclothes. For the most part, it worked. It itched like a thousand cave spiders, though. Crow patted his full bag; he'd need it tonight. At first light, they would leave the Forgotten Forest behind, find the old fishing skiff from the Jumping Trout and sail it down the River of Song.

The forest had been kind to them. The wood was ripe with food. They ate bright red berries, tart but pleasing, large yellow mushrooms that were as filling as goat meat, and countless crunchy roots as hardy as potatoes and carrots when boiled. Tree showed them everything.

"Food grows everywhere here." Crow marveled. Food free of coin. True to their word, they hadn't hunted for game; with their bellies always full the thought never crossed their minds. As he walked, Crow passed a large flat-topped mushroom clinging to an oak. *A plate shroom, it can be roasted over flame and eaten charred.* It fascinated him that so much food existed in the forest. He remembered his old brother, Picker, who had eaten mud before he joined the Lads out of desperation. *If we learned about all these plants, we'd never go hungry.* The harvest the forest provided was enough to keep Lady Jade, Lady Kath, Tree and Crow well from hunger. But, Shadow had no taste for roots, mushrooms or berries.

Just thinking of the little ice dragon quickened Crow's pace. He didn't like being away from her for long. Shadow seemed so fragile, like a gangly featherless baby bird. She curled up on Crow's chest at night and followed at his heels or sat upon his shoulders during the day. She took a quick liking to Tree, which was no surprise, but was still cautious of Jade and Kath.

Crow fiercely loved her.

"Shouldn't we feed her?" Crow asked Tree one day. "I don't know what dragons to the south eat, but it's probably not mushrooms."

"The dragons in the south eat everything." Lady Jade said, sharpening her blade. "Which is why Harold's Holding is underground to this day."

Tree nodded. "A dragon cannot be treated like other animals. She will not eat anything dead placed at her lap; she must oversee her own food. Placing a dead animal before a dragon is insulting."

The dragon only ate what she hunted. Despite her small gangly size, Shadow found her own prey in the mice and chipmunks carelessly roaming the forest's floor. She reminded Crow of the prowling alley cats from the Planks, sticking to the shadows and waiting for prey to wander by. Once she caught them, she'd twist their tiny necks with her razor-sharp teeth. Using her hind talons, she'd hold the carcass to the ground and rip into it like the hawks of the Peak.

I wonder when she'll breath ice, Crow thought. Shadow was only a few days old, and Crow knew nothing of how dragons matured. Besides the coolness of her scales, Crow guessed it would be impossible to tell Shadow apart from the common fire-breathing dragons to the south.

He heard a familiar wail and hiss, and approached the camp huddled just beyond this band of hollies. Kath and Jade were piling sticks for their fire tonight. Jade's heavy armor was cleaned and laying against the trunk of a tree. Shadow stood on top of the polished steel, flapping and wailing at Crow when she spotted him. Tree sat beside her, rubbing the dirt off of a twisted gnarled purple root. Crow recognized it. *That one heals,* though he couldn't remember the name.

"I got moss." He announced, dropping his bag. He fell to the floor with it, staring up at the sky. The little dragon ran for him, finding a comfortable spot in his lap. Crow smiled and ran a hand down her back. Lady Jade scoffed as she dumped the rest of their kindling.

"I hope you're not too tired from your gardening. We must train tonight." She said.

Crow's arms ached at the notion, but each training session seemed to hurt a little less.

As the sun sunk below the trees, they woke a fire. The orange flashed against Shadow's black scales like a rippling ocean of lava. Crow settled with a charred honey mushroom covered in crushed bird berries. Shadow tolerated the flames to sit at his side. She hissed at pieces of ash that floated too close.

"Tomorrow, we sail." Kath said between mouthfuls of food. "You remember where we left the skiff, Tree?'

"Yes." Tree replied, their tone a little odd. "Well, the trees do."

"So long as we find it." Kath shrugged.

"I'll miss it here." Crow sighed, patting Shadow's head. Their safety ended when they left the trees. Their safety and secrecy. "Will people believe you're an ice dragon?" He whispered to her. She curled by his side. Regardless, a boy with a dragon hatchling would be enough to write a song about. Men had stolen dragon eggs for centuries in hopes to tame one and conquer the sky. But the eggs never hatched, and only a fool would try and steal a baby from a dragon's nest. Once Crow left the Forgotten Forest, would word reach back to Griffin's Peak about a boy and a dragon? *Will Bones and Stone Teeth and the rest know it's me?*

"Do any men know the Northern Child's song?" Crow asked.

"Perhaps they did, long ago." Tree replied. "Some could still know, but men have short memories."

They finished up, and Crow and Jade prepared for their nightly dance. Shadow didn't seem to appreciate Jade's training methods, whenever she'd land a harsh blow, the dragon would hiss and flap at the wind. Only Tree's calming hums kept the baby dragon from rushing at Lady Jade's ankles. This time, Jade only landed hits on him twice, the least amount yet. Jade seemed approving but didn't say much. "You would have lost your left arm and been stabbed in the belly tonight. You're getting smarter." She simply said.

Crow pursed his lips but basked in the small compliment.

The nightmare woke him before dawn. It was the bandits again, the man whose face he'd smashed with Shadow's egg. Crow was digging in a tunnel, smashing his pickaxe against a sparkling vein of rock. Suddenly, the bandit was there, leering at Crow where the stone should have been, and before Crow could stop—he brought the axe down hard between the man's eyes.

With a start, Crow's eyes snapped open. Shadow was staring at him with a tilted head. Slowly sitting up, he rubbed the sleep from his eyes. It was still dark, but the sky was turning a bruised blue. He might as well stay awake. It had been a few days since the man he'd killed plagued his dreams. Crow wondered if he'd ever be able to sleep in peace again. Did everyone dream of all the people they've killed? Maybe the nightmares returned because today, once the sun rose, he'd leave their shaded sanctuary for Glorygradus. The image of Man's Wall still burned bright in his memory. The other fleeting images that the unicorn had shown him were already fading from his mind, but the sparkling limestone wall of Glorygradus remained clear as a mountain stream.

Tree was also awake, much to Crow's surprise. The little nymph had slept more soundly than ever since they arrived in the forest. Tree poked at the fire's embers with a long stick, acknowledging Crow with a nod.

"Nightmare?" Tree asked.

"Yeah." Crow muttered, running a hand down his face.

"Do you wish to talk about it?"

Crow bit his lip.

"You do not need to," Tree added.

"No—no, it's okay." Crow didn't want to bother them with it.

"I get nightmares too." Tree whispered. The embers blazed in the reflection of their big eyes.

"You do?"

Tree nodded. "I was here at the end of the Age of Blood." Tree whispered. "I listened to the trees wail as they burned. I heard the unicorns die one by one, and I watched my people disappear into the sea. I dream of it often, the suffering we all felt. And in my dreams, I do the same thing I did back then."

"And what was that?" Crow whispered.

"Nothing."

Crow stood up and sat down next to Tree. Tree stiffened. They sat in silence as the sky lightened.

Shadow ran off to find some small creature to eat, while the four of them ate a collection of forest berries and nuts. Packing didn't take long. Lady Jade donned her armor, Crow strapped on his sword belt and pulled the moss from his tough leather top, and Tree wore their black cloak but kept the hood down. It was nice not having to lug the egg everywhere. But now Crow found his neck constricted by Shadow perched on his shoulders. She liked to sit on him like a scaly scarf.

They found the boat quickly with Tree's guidance. The sunlight that shimmered off of the River of Song nearly blinded Crow when their group broke from the thicket. Shadow stood and flapped her wings, roaring at the water. Crow felt naked without the protection of bark around him. The shadows of the trees reminded him of the safeness he'd felt in the dark mountain caves.

The rocky outcropping was wet from the river's spraying current, but otherwise, the boat was as they'd left it.

"Which way is it from here?" Crow asked as he, Kath and Jade started to push the boat into the stream.

"We'll continue down the river." Jade said. "If we can hire a trader at Crescent Bay, we can head west along the Green Coast, and back up to Glorygradus." The foot knight frowned. "It's a long journey, but the Roam is full of centaurs, and with Youngston under siege from the feln..."

"It'll be best to avoid the conflict as much as we can." Kath said.

Jade stayed on the rock to push them into the river.

Tree made no move to join them.

"Hey!" Crow said. "We're leavin'. Come on."

"I served my purpose to you." Tree replied, their eyes deep and downcast. "I have delivered winter's young to the Northern Child and sang Shadow back to life. My part in this song is done." Tree frowned. "My place is here, in the forest of my birth."

Crow stared at the nymph in disbelief. He thought of Bones, the other Lads, and Stone Teeth, who all now seemed part of another life. Would Tree be the next one he left behind?

"Are you saying you don't want to join us?" Jade asked.

"Tree," Kath said, "you have to come with us, you're the only one Shadow likes beside Crow." Her tone didn't lighten up Tree's mood. Shadow hissed, idly flapping at the air.

"My journey has come to an end—"

"No." Crow decided. "It hasn't." Crow stomped to the back edge of the boat, closest to shore. "This is *my* journey. I'm the Northern Child, and I say you still gotta come with us." Jade stared at him in quiet surprise. "Unless," Crow amended, "if you want to stay in your home, I'm not goin' to make you leave." He thought of the loss that weighed on him the night he'd fled from Griffin's Peak. "You don't need a reason to stay with us. We want you here. Shadow wants you here. My old brothers are gone, and I don't even know if I can ever go back to them."

Tree traveled with him since the start, even if it was just for a short time before Jade found them in the Planks. *They stood up for me.* "You left the Forgotten Forest." Crow said. "You heard the song, and you decided to leave everything behind and follow it." Crow held out his hand. "You could have done nothing." He added quietly. Tree flinched.

"You're a wanderer like the rest of us." Kath smirked. "Your place was here in this forest once, but not anymore. You can't say no to our leader, now, can you?"

Leader.

"You must teach this one how to care for a dragon." Jade added, her tone feigning boredom. "He'll kill it before the moon grows full." Crow glared at her, but the comment made Tree laugh.

"Perhaps," Tree said, their green eyes brighter than before, "it would be wise to counsel the Northern Child with such knowledge."

Relief started to uncoil in Crow's chest. "It'll be better than spendin' your time listening to wolves howling all night."

"Yes." Tree agreed, seeming relieved as well. Shadow wailed, lashing her tail excitedly. Walking to the edge of the slick rock, Tree took Crow's hand and leapt onto the deck.

"We sail for Crescent Bay." Jade said, pushing the skiff from the shore and hopping on board. Leaving the Forgotten Forest behind, they sailed south down the River of Song, and back into the world.

TWELVE

THE RIVER OF SONG

Large trees hugged the western bank; their twisted gnarled roots buried deep into the river's edge, but the eastern shore was the opposite. Tall golden grass stretched on forever, not a single village or hunter's hut interrupted the endless plain. Crow was thankful they hadn't run into any fishermen or hunters yet. He knew once they got to the bay, Shadow's—and Tree's for that matter—existence would be known, and he was glad he had time to prepare.

The dragon stuck to Crow's shoulders while they sailed the river. She wasn't keen on running water; spitting and hissing each time a splash dared seep into the wooden deck. Even Tree received poor treatment from her. Crow's neck ached from her constricting tail, and despite his affection towards her, he was tempted to toss her into the cabin and lock the door.

Shadow's attitude changed when she learned that fish lived under the surface.

They had been traveling for a few hours when a small silver fish jumped out of the water and flopped onto the boat. "A gift from the gods." Tree said in surprise as Shadow leapt from Crow's shoulders and fell awkwardly to the ground—she still didn't know how to fly. The dragon's neck darted at the small fish like a striking snake, and soon she was ripping into its white flesh. From then onward, Shadow ditched Crow's shoulders for the edges of the boat, watching the water in unbroken concentration.

The sky darkened, so they pulled the skiff up onto a grassy bank. The tall stalks of grass reached up to Crow's knees. "It's not as cold as the woods." Crow said, clearing grass with his sword.

"The cold won't reach here for another moon." Jade answered.

They didn't build a fire out of caution. "This is centaur country." Kath warned. Her words hung in the air ominously. Crow dined on packed dried red berries, pine nuts and snake mushrooms in silence.

Even under the light of the stars, Shadow was nearly invisible. Crow reached out to her, stroking her scales. He could feel her presence, like an extra sense deep inside of him. He always knew where she was, and though she was only a few days old, he couldn't remember what it was like not having her around.

Jade's blade scraped against her scabbard. "Come." She said. "Let's train."

"You're usin' your sword?" Crow balked.

"*Using,* aye." Jade said. "You will block all of my attacks tonight, or you will bleed. It is time you knew the true weight of steel in your hand."

Shadow felt Crow's nerves. She hissed at Jade, thrashing her tail in distaste. The foot knight ignored her, and before Crow could reply, Jade ran at him.

Crow barely whipped his sword up before Jade came down on him. He managed to push her aside and stumble back. He didn't know how long their dance lasted, it could have been minutes or hours. His heart pounded in his ears as he caught swipe after swipe, wading through tall grass like it was water. Her sword caught his upper arm and sliced through the leather of his sleeve. Crow cut away before the cold steel could kiss his skin. Sweat ran down his sides like ice water. He never managed an offensive strike, but in the end, Crow had blocked every blow.

Falling into the grass, he stared up at the starry sky. "You could've *killed* me." He panted.

"But I didn't. Though, I came close a few times."

Crow would have glared at Jade if he had the energy to raise his head.

"You should be proud." Jade admitted. "You defended yourself well. I wouldn't have used my sword on you if I thought you weren't ready."

Crow wasn't so sure about that, but he took the compliment and her offered hand.

The morning was calm. The river carried them downstream at a steady pace, and still not another boat was seen. The trees on the western bank shrunk and then disappeared, replaced with more rolling hills of grass. Crow thought he felt the sun's rays more than the day before, and almost felt hot as they crawled down the stream. The grass grew thick and green on either side of them. *We're outrunning autumn.* Jade and Tree navigated the river for the first part of the day. It was smooth as a looking glass, even Tree didn't feel as sick as usual. When the sun hung highest in the sky, they passed the duty on to Crow and Kath. Jade and Tree retired to the cabin; both exhausted from a night on guard for centaur herds.

Crow dipped his oar awkwardly into the river, thankful that the current did most of the work. Shadow was basking in the sun, her long wings outstretched and soaking the warming rays. Kath mirrored Crow, sticking an oar in the water to steer the skiff further towards the middle of the river.

"I'm surprised we haven't run into anyone yet." Kath said. "I've traveled this river a couple of times, and this far south usually holds boats trading from Crescent Bay."

"Fisher's Mark is closed." Crow shrugged. "They've got nowhere to trade to." Unless they wanted to make the journey to Youngston. And even then, Youngston was under attack. Crow wondered what they would find in the bay.

"Still, the warmer waters are an attraction for fishermen. There are usually a lot of them traveling the River of Song anyway."

Crow frowned, feeling the weight of his sword on his belt. "Do you think feln could be..." He let the question fall, afraid of the answer. If the feln decided to come south with an army, if they were truly going to war with men, they could be sailing into the mouth of the beast.

"I suppose." Kath shrugged. "I don't know how many there are, but if they're up by Youngston, I'd assume this far south should be safe. Although," She grinned, "the world isn't what I assumed it was; with nymphs and baby ice dragons and unicorns...now feln coming off their island..." She shook her head. "I'm probably wrong."

"They'll kill us."

"Or us them."

Crow's anxiety stayed coiled in his belly. Lady Jade and Kath were not good sources of comfort. His training made him feel a little better. Crow thought he was good enough with a sword to hold his own against an unskilled enemy. *Could I do it again though?* He wondered. *Can I kill someone?* The man he'd pummeled to death still haunted his sleep.

"Do you ever get over it?" Crow blurted.

Kath raised an eyebrow at him in question.

"Killin'—*killing* I mean." Crow sighed. "I still dream of the man from the Ridge. His face is all caved in, and he's always reaching for me."

"Your first." Kath nodded. "You'll never forget the first man you kill. The rest will blend together, though, depending on how many you must. Whether that's better or worse is up to you." Kath brought her oar out of the water and rested it across her lap. "I'm not the right woman to ask for advice. Killing was never hard for me."

"You still remember, though, your first man?"

"Aye." She replied gravely. "He was my father." Crow's eyes widened; he remembered her sharing that she'd stuck a dagger in her father's side. "My mother ran off when I was young." Kath continued. "I don't remember her. I couldn't tell you what she looked like. But I remember every line in my father's face. He was a nasty man, a roaring drunk who took out his anger on his little girl. I will spare you the details, but I would often go to sleep as sore as a training soldier. I did love him for a time, when I was really young, despite what he did to me. He was the only family I had, after all.

"But as I grew older, I resented him. When I was seven winters old, I ran away. There's no Underground Lads for little girls like me, so it didn't take long for him to find me a few miles from home. He beat me so bloody that night, I thought he'd kill me for sure." Strangely, Kath smiled. "He should have.

"At eight winters old, I ran again. This time I cut my hair short and made it two days before I was found again. As I lay on the floor that night, I realized I would not escape him. Many moons came and went, and I endured his abuse in silence, each day more resolved in what I had to do. Our Mother said men should never lay a hand on their daughters, so not even the fear of divine punishment could stop me. I was on our Mother's side.

"When he had drunk himself to sleep one night, I stole away a dagger that he'd kept in his bedside chest." Kath's eyes were far away, buried in the memory of her telling. "I slid it into his side, between his ribs. His skin parted so easily; I remember. He opened his eyes in terror and stared into mine with shock. I twisted the knife as he died. It was so quick. He didn't scream, or curse me, or even grab me. He just died, one moment his eyes were full of anger and the next they were black with death. I almost wished it took longer.

"I left that night and camped on the road. I found a group of hunters headed to Youngston and laid before their fire. That night was the best sleep I'd ever had in my eight winters of life. I had bought my freedom for the price of one drunk man's life." Kath dipped the oar back into the water. "A price I'd happily pay again."

Thirteen

Mother's Ruins

Crow's head pounded. *It hurts,* he thought as he woke. There would be a welt on the side of his head soon, its pain had dragged him back from blackness. He wondered if he had the strength to open his eyes.

There was grass beneath him, slick and wet from his soaked clothes. The River of Song roared at his feet, cold water splashed his ankles. The air was muggy and hot, making his leather shirt stick to his skin uncomfortably. A hiss sounded in his ear. "Shadow." Crow spluttered.

Cracking open his eyes, Crow was greeted by his small black dragon, slick and wet and sitting in the glistening green grass unharmed. The sun shined like a bright white eye in the sky. Crow's head screeched in protest as he raised it. He reached for Shadow and stroked her back. Lady Jade lay panting beside him, black hair plastered to her dark forehead. Her sword was in its scabbard beside her, but her armor was gone. Water soaked her rough brown underclothes, turning them black.

"How—how long?" His words were a jumbled slur. His lips tasted of river water.

"You've only been out a few minutes." Jade said, staring at the slate blue sky.

Crow kept his hand firmly against Shadow's back. He squeezed the dragon to his chest with shaking hands. Only then did his slow wits begin to remember the others. "Tree and Kath..." the memories slammed him harder than the rushing current.

They'd been traveling down the River of Song for two nights, the ride had been smooth, their arrival at Crescent Bay predicted one more day ahead. With their supplies low, and the threat of centaurs looming, Crow looked forward to landing upon the sandy shores. His anxiety had dulled as they traveled longer and longer with no hint of people.

The sun was high in the sky when they heard the thunder. *No, not thunder,* Crow realized, *water.* The smooth blue water turned white in its wrath ahead of them. Crow and Tree dug their oars deep and into the muddy ground to slow the boat's climbing speed. When that didn't work, they tried to push themselves to the western bank, but it was too late. The river's current held them in its grip and wasn't letting go. Jade barely had enough time to take off her heavy armor and strap her sword to her back before the river turned to chaos.

Giant boulders burst through the angry river's current like stone fists. It was all they could do to avoid them, reaching out with their oars in desperation and clashing them against the stones. Tree's was the first to snap, and Crow's followed shortly after when he rammed it into a cluster of rock, wood splintering through the air as the fishing skiff spun around.

Crow desperately clung to the rail as the boat was tossed through the spray. Twice he feared they would capsize as they lurched left to right with frightening speed. Shadow roared and kept her tail locked around his wrist. She jumped and flapped her wings. Crow knew she wanted to leave the boat behind but still couldn't fly. Lady Kath sat hunkered by the cabin's door, using her weight to try and keep the boat level.

"Why didn't you warn us of rapids!" Crow shouted. She looked back at him bewildered.

"They've never been like this before!"

It was then they saw a huge outcropping of stone, more island than boulder, splitting the angry river in two. They could do nothing but hold on as the boat sprinted towards the great gray wall. Jade crouched, her thick limbs tense and ready for the inevitable collision. Tree was on the other side of the boat, and Crow could hear their wavering voice singing a desperate prayer.

The skiff caught the rock's right shoulder, sending the left side nearly vertical into the air. Crow felt Shadow rip from his arm and plunge into the raging water.

Without a second thought, he let go of the boat and fell in after her. The water met him with an icy slap.

The world was nearly black beneath the booming surface with running mud and sand. He was tossed through the current like a child's doll, tumbling through the river without a notion of up or down. Arms and legs flailing, he smacked a stone and then a branch, but the panic kept the pain away. Crow heaved a massive kick as his lungs burned.

By some miracle he burst through the surface. Unfortunately, it wasn't for long. Crow had just enough time to gulp air and gather his surroundings before he was dragged back under. He didn't see the boat, and the grass on each bank was flying by in a green blur. *Shadow,* he thought, pushed to the surface again. He could still feel her. She was alive. "Shadow!" He screeched before water filled his mouth and took him once again.

The sword on his belt might have weighed a thousand pounds; he struggled with it beneath the water, unclasping the buckle and feeling it rip away into the current. This time, he was able to surface more easily. "Shadow!" He called again; white river spray roared past. Grass and trees flew beside him. At one point, Crow reached out for a low hanging root, but the river was so strong that it wrenched him away, nearly tearing his arm from his shoulder.

I'm goin' to die, he thought. Flashes of his old brother, Shadow, rotting beneath the waves of the Pond played in front of his eyes in the muddy water. He saw himself, no more than bones floating along the river floor lost forever. Then he thought of his dragon, welcomed to the world only to be drowned out. *She can still make it.* She wasn't gone yet. He kicked at the water one last time in desperate hope. His lungs were burning, if he inhaled river water now, it would all be over.

The sun greeted him when he rose again. Hope, sudden and fierce, settled in his belly. Lady Jade was wrestling with the current, her dark eyes fixed on him. On her shoulder was Shadow, nearly strangling the woman with her tail around her neck. Luckily, Crow didn't have to battle the current to reach her. Beyond her though, Crow spotted a wall of white foam. His heart sank, and his hope wilted. A field of jagged rocks were rushing up to meet them. Should the river drag them through, they'd be sliced to ribbons

Jade ignored the imminent danger. And instead focused on swimming to the eastern bank. She crawled against the rushing water; her strong strokes edging her ever closer. Crow was dragged under again, but when he resurfaced, he saw by some miracle the knight had made it, holding onto another gnarled root. "Swim, boy!" She shouted, anger keeping her afloat. Shadow screeched.

Energy pumped through his limbs as Crow kicked at the water. The rocks grew ever closer. It was getting harder to breathe. *I'll miss my chance,* he panicked, and the river swallowed him one last time.

Crow didn't have time to orient himself. One moment his vision swam with running mud, and the next, something large and hard rushed past his head. *It hit me,* he thought, before the pain smacked him like a landslide, and he slipped from consciousness into the dark.

And now I'm here. Crow looked to his left at the small dying tree that had saved them. "Tree and Kath." He mumbled again, his head pounding. "Have they—?"

"I don't know." Jade sat up; her mood particularly sour. She turned her gaze on Crow, anger twisting her features.

"Hopefully they're still on the boat. The boat that'd we'd be on too if you didn't decide to jump like a fool."

It was Crow's turn to fix her with an icy glare. "I was rescuin' Shadow." He shot back.

"*Rescuing,* you should learn to speak properly, boy. Have you ever been taught to swim?"

Shadow tossed her tail against the ground, sensing Crow's anger.

"I pledged my sword to follow you on this journey." Jade continued. "But I will not throw my life away. Your stupidity left us stranded. We best hope they were able to dock somewhere safe along the river with all of our gear."

"Why did you jump in?" Crow growled.

"Because *I* can swim." She stood up, brushing the grass stuck to her underclothes and picking up her sword. "Can you walk?"

Crow's head threatened to split in two, but he was able to stand. He felt sorer than ever before. *I should push her into the river,* he thought bitterly. Shadow whined until he picked her up, his legs felt like they were made from stone, but he could walk. And so, they followed the river in hopes of finding Tree and Kath at the other end.

Their walk was a silent one. The endless prairie of the Roam stretched out before them uninterrupted. Crow wished he had his sword at his side. If the centaurs descended on them, it would surely spell the end of them both. They hadn't seen any yet, though, and Crow hoped to keep up the trend.

Much to his irritation, Shadow seemed to enjoy the company of Jade now. She would cry from Crow's arms and flap awkwardly for Jade's shoulders. Crow guessed the dragon had a new appreciation for the knight who saved her life. Lady Jade didn't seem to mind; she'd grab up Shadow and stroke her long scaly neck and even crack a smile from time to time. Shadow turned to look at Crow, offering him an apologetic chirp.

"Traitor." Crow muttered.

The sun began to set, and Crow's stomach growled. But without their gear, the prairie offered no food. Just grass, grass, and more grass. Crow's mouth watered at the idea of sizzling meat. The rapids had calmed, and the River of Song was smooth once more, but still they came across no sign of the boat, or Tree and Kath.

It was against the backdrop of an orange sky that the pair noticed a few clustered humped shapes against the river. "A village down here?" Crow asked, for the thousandth time wishing he had his sword.

"It used to be." Jade replied. "We're closer to Crescent Bay than I thought. If I'm not mistaken, up ahead lies Mother's Ruins."

Crow swallowed. The name had a haunting ring to it. "It's abandoned?"

"Aye. It was an old fishing village long ago when men were still conquering the east. It was too far from any kingdom of power. The Crystal Isles were far to the south, and Youngston much too far to the north. With no help from the kings and queens, the village was attacked by the feln. They killed everyone. It's an empty shell now, filled with broken homes. Even after the feln were defeated, this village remains a miserable place. Every attempt to establish it goes horribly wrong. The centaurs fall on it every time."

"You don't think there's centaurs there now, do you?"

"Hard to know. I knew a few foot knights who camped in those abandoned homes. Most are lucky to leave by dawn. The fools who stay longer come back with stories of narrowly escaping a herd." Jade said. "I've never bothered to camp there. I'd rather take my chances on the river."

"We'll be quick then." Crow resolved.

They reached Mother's Ruins by dark. Lady Jade held her sword in both hands, and Shadow was perched upon Crow's shoulder to give him courage. She didn't like this place; Crow could feel it. The village was just as Jade described it, a shell of emptiness. Many of the thatched roofs of homes had caved in long ago, only the stone walls remained. Few timbered beams still held, rotten and full of holes. Grass grew in between the narrow paths, and the prairie was slowly swallowing the village. *It's cursed.* The emptiness was haunting, but welcome for tonight. They seemed safe from centaurs and men for now. Crow's hair prickled on end; he imagined the people slaughtered here; their bones long buried in the soil.

Shadow hissed and Jade signaled them to stop. Crow plastered himself against a crumbled wall, the darkness shrouding them.

Footsteps, Crow heard the crunch of grass underfoot somewhere amongst the thin alleys. *Not centaurs,* he realized. The sound whispered against the land too softly to be hooves, whoever it was made sure they were careful. There were more than one pair. Crow looked at Jade and held up two fingers. She nodded. The steps grew closer, they were quiet and slow, moving through the ruined homes with careful speed. Eventually, Crow could hear the rustle of leather breeches.

Shadow tilted her head to the side and chirped. The steps abruptly stopped.

Crow reached up to clamp his hand over Shadow's muzzle, but then he heard a familiar voice.

"Get against the wall." Lady Kath whispered.

"It is Shadow." He heard Tree reply softly.

Crow nearly jumped out from his hiding place, relief swelling through his chest. "Kath, Tree!" Crow waved excitedly. "We're over here!"

Jade hit him in the arm. *"Shhh."* But even she couldn't keep the relieved smile from her face.

Kath and Tree appeared to their right, between two skeletal remains of a wooden structure. Tree's black cloak hung damp around their slender frame, and Kath still wore her layered leather clothes and held her bow. But she only had four arrows.

Jade kept her sword about. "We were hoping we'd find you again." She said.

"Us too." Kath nodded. "I would have taken you for dead if it weren't for this one insisting you were alive." She motioned to Tree.

"Did you tie the boat around here?" Crow asked hopefully.

"No." Kath frowned, and Tree matched her expression.

"It broke against the rocks." Tree said sadly. "We had to abandon it, or risk sinking as well."

"We lost our supplies." Kath said.

"Best keep moving then." Jade nodded, as though the blow didn't affect her.

"I don't want to stay here." Kath agreed.

Despite the late hour, they dared not camp. Instead, they made it a priority to leave Mother's Ruins behind in hopes that Crescent Bay would hold supplies and traders. *It's time for the world to know,* Crow decided. They'd find their redemption on the bay's waters, or their death.

Mother's Ruins was larger than Crow thought. Though it was hard to distinguish details in the darkness. *This must've been the center.* An empty stone fountain overgrown with weeds stood in the middle of the old market square. The statue had long crumbled away, but the waxing moons adorning the fountain's walls told Crow that it was once a tribute to Mother Vitania. The ruins in the square were especially dismal. Most of the walls were knocked down. Some of the stone was even black beneath the sprouting grass. Any wood was smashed and buried into the land, long rotted. Crow could almost see the feln running through here, lighting the square ablaze as they rode down innocent people.

"This is a sad place." Tree whispered.

"There's a song for it, you know." Kath said. "A woman escaped to the bay and later wrote *'Blood of My Bothers',* it's popular in the Crystal Isles."

"How does it go?" Tree asked. Crow was curious too; he'd never heard it.

But before Kath could raise her voice and sing the melancholy tune, a new sound in the night stopped them all in their tracks.

Clopping against the ground like the drum of death, was the song of hooves.

Fourteen

Mother's Ruins

"Hide!" Jade hissed. They ditched the town center for the safety of the narrow streets. Even Crow knew that trying to run from centaurs in the open field was a fool's dream.

The hooves slowed to a trot somewhere nearby before stopping all together. Crow heard his heart pounding between his ears. Shadow remained silent and poised on his shoulder. A rough, guttural voice barked a few clipped words in a language Crow couldn't decipher. He looked at the others. Tree's face was nearly white, Kath shifted one of her remaining arrows into her bow, and Jade's grip tightened on her sword's hilt. *Not riders.* His hope wilted. Looking to the dirt floor, he looked for something he could use as a weapon. *Nothing,* he despaired.

One of the centaurs seemed to trot off, the *clop clop clop* of its hooves fading into the night. *They're splitting up.* The other stayed quiet for a moment before easing into a slow walk. They dared not move as the sound grew closer. Crow thanked Mother Vitania that centaurs couldn't sneak as stealthily as men. By the sound of it, the beast was walking through the street outside. Hunching down into the shadows, Crow's eyes remained glued to the white light of the stars filtering through the window.

Then the light was blotted out.

A large hulking form passed before the window, thick brown hair almost black in the night, shaggy and coarse, took up the entire opening. Crow held his breath, Shadow's head snapped to attention, even she knew not to risk a single hiss. The centaur paused before the shattered window. Crow's stomach sank, hoping that the darkness would conceal them, and most of all, that the centaur wouldn't bend to peek inside.

To his relief, it continued on, and they waited for the hoofbeats to fade before shifting position.

"We're sitting targets here." Kath whispered. "We've got to move."

"We cannot outrun them." Tree worried. "Perhaps we should wait here until the centaurs leave."

"What if they don't?" Crow whispered back. "This place's big, if we stay in the dark, maybe we can sneak out." *The darkness is our friend.* "If we wait 'til daylight, they could find us easier."

Jade nodded. "Who knows how long they've been here? The night will shield us as Crow said." Her sword glinted in the starlight. "We must stay together. If one falls on us, we'll need everyone."

With one last pause to listen, they left their shelter.

Their feet whispered against the ruined ground; every scuffle of their shoes made Crow wince. Kath led their way from alley to alley, broken wall to broken wall. They skipped across wide paths, the light of the stars and moon seeming as bright as the blazing sun. Crow had no clue which direction they were headed, but Kath seemed sure of herself. She looked to the sky for reference before continuing their quiet dance. At one point, they heard the hoofs again, and they stopped short, plastering themselves against a rotten wooden frame.

Crow dared a glance. He saw the silhouette of one of the centaurs far down the path. He couldn't rip his gaze away. The torso was thick and muscled and covered in the coarse hair that covered the horse-like lower body. It reminded Crow of their old draft horse, massive and stocky with a thick layer of muscle and hair. In the centaur's grasp was a sword. The sword was a two-handed weapon, but the centaur held it in one palm like a common short sword. Crow swallowed and slunk back into the shadows. Once the beast moved on, they hurried past.

"I thought centaurs didn't have steel." Crow whispered to Jade.

"They don't smith." Jade whispered back. "A centaur with a weapon is a centaur that has successfully raided men."

There were two more close encounters: Jade almost got spotted from the shine of her weapon, and Crow had kicked loose a stone that almost cost them their hiding place. However, as the night wore on, Crow's little confidence started to bloom. "We've got to be close to getting out." He whispered to Tree.

But his hope was smashed a moment later.

Tree's cloak caught on the shard of a broken window. It pulled the little nymph to the ground as they leapt to the safety of another crumbled shop. Tree's small frame smacked against the ground, seeming as loud as a war horn. Crow ran to them without hesitation, helping them up. It didn't take long before the pounding hooves began.

When Crow looked up, he saw a centaur charging them. It wasn't the one with the sword. Instead, this one held a large club the size of a young tree.

Shadow flared up on her hind legs and hissed.

"Get out of the way, fools!" Jade yelled from the shadows. The street was straight as an arrow, and the centaur was charging at them with its club held high in the air. Snapping into action from his fear, Crow pulled Tree and dove towards the others. One thought dominated everything else: *run!*

They sprinted down cobbled walks and dirt paths, twisting this-way-and-that in hopes of losing the large centaur to quick turns and confusion. Crow's feet pounded the ground with the same rhythm of his heart, Shadow's talons dug into his shoulders like tiny knives. At one point, he nearly fell from a broken wheel sticking out of the dirt. None of this was enough to slow him, but to his despair, the thundering hooves were relentless and gaining.

"We can't outrun it!" Crow cried. No matter how many twists they made, the streets were still large enough to allow the centaur to follow. It would catch them soon. And, should they be so unlucky, the other might too.

Kath spun around, her back hitting the beaten stone wall. The centaur would round the bend any minute now. "We should make our stand here." She held an arrow taut in her bow. Jade nodded, bracing her legs and holding her sword ready. Crow glanced at Tree, who was staring at the sky. "I hope your gods can save us," Crow said. He picked up a rock and held it in a white knuckled fist. Shadow flapped her wings, her scales puffing up like the quills of a pined forest crawler.

The centaur rounded the bend.

"Make your arrows count." Jade said.

Kath nodded.

Crow held the rock high above his head. There was no room for fear anymore, only bravery.

They could see the whites of the centaur's eyes. Though its torso was the shape of a man, Crow thought it resembled more of a beast. Coarse hair covered its thick chest and arms, even its face. The club was blunt and thick, the end stained black in the darkness.

Kath released an arrow.

It sunk into the muscle of the centaur's front leg. The hit only seemed to enrage the beast. It let out an angry grunt, speeding up. Kath was down to three arrows, she lodged another in her bow. The centaur dodged the next by slamming against a wall. The stone around them shook. *Two more,* Crow's heart threatened to burst through his ribs.

Jade screamed and ran forward. She managed to duck the first deadly swipe. Her sword flashed to the centaur's flank, but the creature side-stepped away just in time. The narrowness of the alley worked in Jade's favor. It was harder for the large centaur to move about and reposition for another blow. Crow's hand shook around his stone.

Kath nocked her second-to-last arrow, and the centaur thrust its club down on the wall that Jade was against just a moment before. The hit exploded the stone into powder. Jade landed a savage slice against the centaur's withers, but she was playing a dangerous game. One hit and she'd be down.

Shadow seethed on Crow's shoulder. She was angry, and it swelled within Crow as well. "I'm done watching this." he growled, allowing Shadow's icy anger to bloom inside him. He ran forward. Shadow had no fear, and neither did he.

"Stupid boy—" Kath hissed.

Jade narrowly missed another attack; her moves beginning to slow.

Crow ran for them. He shared Shadow's mind, barely able to distinguish where he ended and she began. *Fly!* Crow thought, throwing his rock and hitting the centaur in the chest. Shadow's wings were twice as long as her thin body, and caught the air clumsily at first, but she stayed aloft. *"Fly!"*

The beast paused long enough to see the black dragon soaring through the night. Shadow's screech was loud enough to ring Crow's ears.

She fearlessly approached, snapping her head back to strike. She unlocked her jaw, and from her mouth came forth a bright blue flurry of flames. *No,* Crow realized, feeling the chill from where he stood, *not flames. Ice.* Shadow sprayed the centaur in the face. It reared, screaming as its eyes froze over from blue to black in bitter cold. Jade seized the opportunity, held her sword tightly in two hands, and thrust up with the force only battle could bring. The sharp blade bit into the centaur's belly. She pushed it through so far that it buried itself to the hilt. With a scream, she twisted the sword before wrenching it out.

The centaur fell to the ground, dead before it landed.

They had no time to celebrate the victory.

"The other would have heard us." Kath said. "We should run."

And they did.

Mother's Ruins finally seemed to fall behind them as they broke through the endless maze of ruined halls and homes. With the river to their right, and the prairie to their left, they thought they spotted the beginnings of Crescent Bay. It was still miles off, but Crow could see the faintest shimmer of the sea in the distance, growing brighter as the sun rose above them. Shadow flew with him, wings pumping in the air. *She won't need to ride with me anymore,* he wanted to smile at the sight of her.

But the danger wasn't over. The other centaur had found them.

Exhausted and in the open field, the dance for life started again.

Crow's legs burned from running, glancing over his shoulder he saw the centaur approaching them fast in the dull morning light. "It'll mow us down like weeds with that sword!" He panted. Their speed was failing.

Kath stopped, planting her feet firmly on the ground. Her bow poised and ready. They stopped with her.

"We can't fight it." Jade warned her, panting.

"I know." Kath's usual smirk was gone, her scarred face downcast and serious. Her eyes caught Jade's, and they stared at each other as long as they dared. "Make it to the Isles." She said, the pounding hooves seemed to shake the ground.

"No." Jade planted her feet, holding her sword up.

"Jade–"

"Kath." Jade frantically looked from her companion to the centaur. "You can't be serious. Not for this. We'll try together."

"We'll all die. I'll slow it down."

"I will not let–"

"Jade!" Kath ground her teeth together. "This is bigger than me." Her voice shook for the first time since Crow met her. "Let me do this for something bigger than me."

Tree grabbed onto Crow's arm. The nymph's large eyes were glassy with grief. Crow frowned and turned to Jade; the centaur's hooves pounded the ground like an earthquake. "We'll fight it together." He ripped his arm from Tree's grasp.

"Will you sing of me?" Kath asked, turning her attention back to the centaur charging for them. Her legs were locked in place, but Crow could see how they shook. Yet her arms were strong and still as stone. Jade was silent as long as she dared. She sheathed her sword and squeezed Kath's shoulder.

Crow's stomach dropped.

Jade began to move away, and grabbed Crow's arm. "Your dragon won't be able to get close without getting sliced."

"We will sing for you." Tree said. "The wind will not forget what you have done here."

"Good." Kath smiled then, and brought the string taut.

"No." Crow shook his head. "We'll fight it together. Like the other one."

"We're in the open, it has a sword." Jade whispered. Tears streaked her dirty face, but she acted like they weren't there.

"I said no." Crow prepared himself to stand his ground, he could hear the centaur's breathing now.

"Crow, don't be an idiot!" Kath yelled, her eyes never straying from her target. "Run for the bay."

"Why?" Tears blurred his vision. His resolve started to crumble. His legs betrayed him as Jade began to drag him away. Even Shadow abandoned him, and instead flew to Tree's side. She didn't have it in her to breathe ice again.

"My story ends here, boy." She let the arrow fly, it thudded into the centaur's stomach. It yelled in rage and held the sword up high, slowing a little, blood blooming down its thick fur. "Make sure it's not for nothing." And then she nocked her final arrow. Crow turned then, releasing himself from Jade's tugging. His instincts won in the end.

They ran.

Shadow cried as she flew above them. Her scream was high and as sad as a child's. Daring a final glimpse over his shoulder, he saw Lady Kath standing with her bow, like a lone statue against the plains. The centaur was almost on her, she arched her back and held her bow up to the sky, ready to shoot the final blow through the creature's skull. The sword came down on her just as she released it. Crow ripped his gaze away before he could see the end. Shadow cried again, her wails piercing the air.

They ran and ran and ran until their legs could no longer carry them.

The centaur didn't follow.

The day was warm, the sun shone high, and not a cloud marred the slate blue sky. The breeze was salty and gentle as it rustled the grass.

Before them laid the sea, sparkling in the sunlight and bluer than anything Crow had ever seen. The eastern horizon was straight and unmarred by land. The sea never ended.

Crow always wanted to see the ocean to the south. When Bones and he dreamed of traveling around Frukjera when they were young, the Crystal Isles were one of the many kingdoms they'd fantasized about the most. Shadow had filled their heads with clear blue waters, mermaids and fish the size of ships.

Now he was here, the waters sparkling like a thousand jewels, and he felt empty.

They had continued their journey in silence. The tall lush green grass from the Roam began to grow short and bristled. The River of Song crawled to their left, and for the first time in days, they came across a hunter's shack. The sea rose before them, dominating more of the horizon. A dirt path sliced through the grass until the Roam gave way for good. Swooping down in lazy hills of dunes covered in sand.

The tops of the dunes were blanketed in shrubbery brush. When they reached the top, Crescent Bay splayed out beneath them. The beach's sand was white as fresh fallen snow. The tide rolled lazily against the shore, which was shaped like a sliver of the waning moon. The air smelled of salt and rang with the cry of sea birds.

There were fishermen's shacks clustered against Crescent Bay's stilted dockside. Shadow perched on Crow's shoulder, she hissed at the men working the docks. Two boats of size were tied into the bay. One massive cog was floating far in the horizon, large black sails billowing in the breeze.

Although the bay wasn't crowded, after being isolated for so long, the beach might as well had been as populous as Griffin's Peak.

Tree stopped at Crow's side. "It's time for Frukjera to know."

Crow nodded, ready to leave the forsaken grasses behind. The grasses that took so much from them.

"Her story is over." Tree whispered.

"Aye." Jade said. "And here, ours begins."

They headed down to the beach.

FIFTEEN

CRESCENT BAY

The sun beat down on Crow's leather shirt. He felt like he was cooking inside of it. Shadow was on his shoulder, Tree stood to his right, cloak snapping in a salty breeze. Jade was to his left; her brown underclothes stained. Her sword was red with dried centaur's blood. Crow knew they'd look strange to the others. His feet were buried in the hot white sand. It was softer than anything he'd ever felt. It was harder to move in, though, the more he walked the more he seemed to slow. He felt strangely calm as they approached the men of the bay. Or maybe just numb. What could these men take from them that the centaurs didn't? With Shadow able to fly, Crow feared less for her safety, and he was oddly unconcerned for his own.

They weren't unnoticed for long.

Two boats were tied to the docks, each of an appropriate size for a small crew. One held a flag of purple cloth blowing in the wind, a white unicorn rearing in the middle. "That one's from Good Land." Jade said with a frown. "They may have heard about us." The other ship's sails were black, and the boat itself was dark stained wood. "And that's from the Isles. They stain their sails black for the Rope-Ringers." The third boat still remained out at sea, and had black sails as well. It must have belonged to the Isles.

Shadow's piercing cry brought the men running from the docks. She sat tall on Crow's shoulders. The men scrambled around them, holding short swords, scaling knives, and fishing spears. Crow eyed them warily, and Jade stood a little taller, her sword a silent warning.

"A dragon!" Someone cried, many of the men were so dirty that Crow seemed as clean as a noble in comparison. There were even a few women. "The boy's got a dragon!" They were so enraptured with the sight of a hatchling that Tree almost went unnoticed. Even though dragons were commonly seen in the sky over the Boiling Sea, a man had never successfully hatched one.

They were swarmed by a ring of salty suntanned bodies. Jade raised her blade when a hand grew too bold. Crow flinched back at their scrabbling. He wanted to slap their hands away, to scream at them until his voice disappeared. These men didn't understand what they'd been through. Shadow felt his grief. As the men drew closer, she hissed and snapped, flapping her long wings and slashing her tail through the air.

"Our Mother, a nymph as well!" A man holding a spear said. His silver scaled jerkin had patches of purple cloth sewn into the shoulders. Their eager eyes turned to Tree, who stood silent and wide-eyed. Some men fell to their knees, some pushed harder to grab a better view, and a few even asked Tree to sing.

Crow looked to Jade in bewilderment. She simply offered him a curt nod. *I have to handle this,* he knew. This was the new normal, the new existence he must bear amongst men. Their circle was stifling, suffocating. He thought of Bones and how he would revel at being in the center of it all.

Crow closed his eyes, banishing the grief for now. It threatened to overwhelm him.

"Stop!" Crow yelled. Shadow screamed at his words, and the voices of the crewmen died in their throats. His confidence quailed inside, but he tried not to let it show. He opened his eyes again. "We're lookin'—looking for a passage to the Crystal Isles. Who can take us there?"

"What do you have to offer for such a journey?" The voice came from within the crowd. The folk from Good Land stood a little straighter and parted. A man in a loose white shirt and fitted leather pants trimmed with yellow thread made his way to the front. His clothes were cleaner than those of the ragged men around him, a curved sword hung from his belt, and a sun-tanned palm rested on the pommel in a quiet threat.

"The Crystal Isles is days away, should the wind be so kind." The man continued. "I've heard rumors from the river's port town. Some strange tale of a boy running with a nymph." He regarded Tree for a moment. "While others talk of thieves fleeing Griffin's Peak with King Arthur's treasure."

Shadow hissed. Crow glared at the man.

Jade stepped forward. Despite her lack of armor, she appeared no less threatening than any of the men surrounding them. Her brandished weapon called a few crewmen to raise their fishing equipment in reply.

"We are no thieves, sir." She said. "I am Lady Jade Threu, daughter of Sir Michael Threu and Sir Garret Threu, champions to the dukes of Good Land." Her words were sharper than any sword. "The Northern Child stands before you. Chosen by the unicorns and the nymphs. On my father's grave, I have seen the unicorn choose him myself." Murmurs rippled through the crowd. "Tell me, in all of your travels, have you ever seen a man hold a dragon like this boy does?"

The captain's hand gripped the pommel of his sword. Crow held his gaze; the crowd was poised, anxious for their captain's next move. Then, the man's harsh face broke into a grin. "You see this, men?" He laughed. "A woman with spirit." Everyone seemed to relax, even Crow allowed himself a small sigh, but Jade remained still as stone. "Aye, I have heard of your father, and the sword you carry. Your family is well respected in Good Land." He frowned. "I was not aware he had a daughter. You have his look.

"But that doesn't change what I've heard about this boy." He continued. "The king has ordered the lad's return to the Peak for stealing."

"I didn't steal from the king." Crow growled, Shadow matching his tone. Crow straightened his posture. He needed these men to respect him. They could not fight this crowd off should the captain decide to seize them. More whispers hissed through the crewmen.

"I did." Tree's voice shocked the crowd into silence. Even the captain couldn't hide the twitch of his brows in surprise. For the first time in generations, men were hearing the strange voice of a creature thought to have vanished long ago. A ghost from the past come to life. "Crow is the Northern Child. He woke winter's young from stone. This king of yours wishes to possess a song which is not his."

The crowd swallowed Tree's words mostly in silence, glancing from the nymph to each other.

"You know what we want." Crow said. "And you know who we are. Who are you?"

"Grant Gills, captain of the *Swift Maid.*" Grant answered proudly. "Truth be told, I wish you no harm. But we sail for Good Land at dawn, and then to the Peak. King Arthur has called the men of the Ridge to war." He looked the three up and down. "You know of the enemies we face?"

"The feln." Crow nodded.

"What am I to tell the king's guard when they hear my men talk of you? Am I expected to tell them that we let you go and disobeyed King Arthur's orders? We hold the stories of nymphs in high regard in Good Land, as I'm sure Lady Jade could tell you." His mouth hardened. "But I will not risk the wellbeing of my crew should King Arthur investigate the rumors that will likely spread from this."

"Piss on King Arthur!" A ragged voice yelled from the crowd.

"Warmonger!"

"My king is my captain!"

"Enough!" Grant spat.

"Are you so afraid of a man hundreds of miles away?" Jade narrowed her eyes.

"If you take us, we won't follow quietly. Shadow won't fly with you." Crow warned. He hoped his voice hid the fear that thumped through his heart.

"The Arrowheads are no kings of mine." A small man pushed his way through the rabble. His skin was darker than Crow's leathers, and his clothes were silken and colored as bright as berries and flowers and colors Crow had never seen before. The man's bald head gleamed beneath the sun, golden beads hung from his oiled wiry beard and *clack clack clacked* as he swaggered. His crew followed him, each in the same loose-fitting silk of rainbow colors. To Crow's surprise, this captain was even shorter than he, but the way in which the man carried himself made him seem larger than the grizzled Captain Grant. With eyes green as the shallow sea, the man from the Crystal Isles regarded Shadow with childish excitement. "I was wondering what had kidnapped the men from their docks. You require passage to the Isles, I heard?"

Crow offered a curt nod.

"It just so happens we're sailing back there."

"What is your price?" Jade asked, though Crow knew they had no coin to offer.

"Price? Ha!" He laughed. Grant frowned at the other captain's flamboyant nature. "My wife, she's a fan of the legends of nymphs and their songs." He looked Tree up and down, and to Crow's surprise, he knelt before them. "It would be an honor to carry you upon our *Wave Song.*"

Crow traded sand for the smooth polished planked wood of a deck. The captain, Julio Wave-Song, whom the ship was named after, offered them a prized place on the boat. "We took the boy before you had a chance to catch him." Julio told Grant, who accepted the clever lie with grudging silence.

"There's a large war coming." Grant warned. "A child with a dragon running from a king makes for interesting gossip. But a man with a dragon, flying into battle, now that is worthy of a song."

Am I runnin' away? Crow felt Shadow on his shoulder, she seemed heavier than before. *I'm not,* he thought stubbornly. The unicorn had shown him Man's Wall, he had to get there. Joining any battle now would be suicide.

Regardless, the words stung. Lady Gretchen had run into the fray the moment she heard, and Kath...the memory was too fresh to dwell on.

"Tell the men of Good Land what you have seen here." Tree told them as they departed. "For the Northern Child has come, and upon his shoulders he carries no ordinary dragon, but a dragon of ice."

Sixteen

The Boiling Sea

Crow stood at the prow staring out into the open sea. The *Wave Song* was a lovely ship, large and dark with black sails ready to drink up the wind. They were given a room beside the captain's and above the crew's, a great honor. Their room was as large as the entire fishing skiff they'd sailed down on the River of Song. And the crew treated them as royals. Asking for Crow and Tree's blessings when they walked by, or for the grace of touching Shadow's black scales. The dragon didn't seem fond of them, though, and would hiss should any man forget themselves. They were fed colorful fruits that were common along the Green Coast, fruits that Crow had only seen in the trading markets of Griffin's Peak and never dreamed of tasting. The captain also feasted them on bizarre fish caught from the sea, roasted and salted and sprayed with tart lemon and orange juice. It put all the food Crow had ever eaten to shame. And Julio's wife, Francia, immediately fell in love with them.

She was even taller than Jade, with skin black as the ship's sails. Her hair was tied in long thick black braids that ran down to the base of her back. She fancied jewelry, gold hoops hung from her ears and looped around her arms and ankles. She jingled with each long stride. Though Julio was the captain of the ship, Francia was the captain of Julio, thus the true leader of the *Wave Song*.

They had sailed off days ago, the coast of Frukjera fading behind them as they journeyed southeast. Despite the awe of the open sea, the hospitality and the gifts bestowed upon them, Crow felt numb. The only time he didn't wallow was his training with Jade, which had begun again on the deck. Captain Julio offered Crow a scratched longsword and scabbard. The blade was much larger and heavier than anything Crow had ever used before. It was nice to face off with Jade using the same weapon, but he tired much faster than before.

He was also given a silky white tunic that hung loosely around his torso, and an old pair of Julio's own leggings. They were blue as the sky, but too short for his legs and ended awkwardly at the ankles. Jade preferred the clothes of the crewmen, rejecting Lady Francia's pleas for the foot knight to try her own wardrobe. Even Tree was bestowed a new cloak, this one red as forest berries with green leaf trim.

The crew loved their nightly dance, often forming a large circle to watch. Shadow, growing larger by the day, perched on the high wooden beams and tight ropes to scream down at them. Crow judged her to be the same size as a cat. She enjoyed flying beside the ship's hulking side more than perching on Crow's arm. Her ice breath had returned, and she'd spit great bouts of blue frost over the water.

The sailing had been smooth, days clear and wind steadily pushing them south. The men chalked it up to Tree. Despite the nymph's obvious sea sickness, the crew believed they must be lucky. But poor Tree spent most days in their room, drinking fresh water and pining for land. They came out at night, though, when Crow and Jade began to train.

Francia was also a constant witness to their dance. She loved to watch Lady Jade with the blade and was particularly attached to her. "If you weren't accompanying Crow, I'd have you as my champion. We need more women in the sea." She'd said. Jade seemed to enjoy

Francia's company as well, sharing stories of her father and her grand-father's service. Her closeness to the crew and Francia angered Crow. He felt alone. Tree stayed hidden in the cabin most of the time and even Shadow barely lifted his spirits. Kath haunted his dreams now, and the others didn't appear to be mourning her at all. It only made him train harder.

Tonight, they used dulled blades that were stored on the ship. Though the swords' edges weren't sharp, a swipe or stab left Crow's skin harshly bruised or broke the skin. The light clothing of the Isles held no resistance to the kiss of steel, but Crow dodged most of Jade's attacks. A few times, Crow even pressed an offensive, forcing Jade to retreat a step before she twisted back on him. The crew screamed and cheered, but it fell on deaf ears.

Their swordplay was an escape. Crow's mind grew blank as they pressed and blocked, pressed and blocked. The outside world no longer existed. All that remained was his sword and the enemy. There was no Kath, no dragon, no impending war. Only Crow and the deck beneath his shifting steps. *I can dance all night,* he'd think, arms burning and sweat beading on his brow. Tonight, they pressed so hard that the crew slowly faded under the stars. Even the captain and his wife retreated to their room, Tree ran off once again, and Shadow watched quietly from her perch. The song of steel rang through the night.

"Enough." Jade huffed, blocking a downward strike. Her hair and clothes were dark with sweat. Crow nearly dropped his sword from exhaustion.

"You've been pressing hard lately." Jade noted, slicking her hair away from her face. Nodding, Crow sheathed his sword.

Jade frowned, sensing Crow's sour mood. "Crow. I know what you're going through." She said, somewhat awkwardly. "This," she motioned to his sword, "isn't going to help."

"It seems like I'm the only one going through anything." Crow mumbled. "She was your friend too. But it's like you've forgotten her."

"What makes you think I've forgotten?" Jade's anger flared. "Just because I don't mope around like a child? Does that mean I don't care? I've known her much longer than you, boy." She spat. Glaring, Crow stomped off to sit against the rail.

Much to his irritation, Jade followed. She sat next to him; her expression sympathetic. "I'm sorry." She mumbled. "I shouldn't have said that."

Crow picked at the loose threads on the knees of his pants. Waves slapped against the ship to fill the silence.

"I feel like she's dead 'cause of me." Crow whispered.

Jade sighed, staring at the sky to avoid his eyes. Crow kept his own gaze forward, too awkward to look at her as well.

"You can't think like that." Jade said eventually.

"How else am I supposed to think of it?" He turned to her, his anger dissolving to anguish. "I know—I know we had to leave her there. But she never would've been in that field if it weren't for me."

"Lady Kath was a knight. A true knight. And a true knight chooses how and when they die." She said.

"Doesn't make it any easier." He murmured. "When we fight, I forget about her. So, if I keep fightin—"

"Aye. You'll forget for a while. But that's no way to grieve. It will not help."

"How would you know?"

"Because you're running. When I lost my father, I ran too." Jade murmured, leaning back against their wooden support. She still didn't meet his gaze. Her tough exterior seemed to crack, leaving a vulnerable young woman in its stead. *I'd forgotten,* Crow realized, feeling rotten for lashing out at her. He'd never had a father to grieve for. "I did the same as you." Jade continued. "I shielded myself with cuts and bruises, with days and nights in the yard, fighting any man willing to try me. My world was the sword in my hands, and the sword in my hands did not feel pain. If I kept fighting, maybe I wouldn't feel pain either."

"How did you make it better?" He pleaded.

"You said you lost a friend to the Pond." Jade said. "How did you make *that* better?"

Crow frowned, imagining his brother Shadow on this very boat. *He'd love to be here.* "I didn't." He confessed. "I just, it was like he wasn't really dead. There was no proof, so I pretended he wasn't." Bones had shouted off the summit of a mountain for an entire day, his grief echoing across the valleys. Crow went back to work, pretending nothing had happened. "I still think of him, though. Time made it better, I guess."

Jade nodded. "When my father died, and it came time for the Keefes to pick a new champion, I fought with everything I had. All I'd done for the past seven days was train. I hardly slept and I hardly ate. I thought, once I was the Keefe's champion, everything would be fine. I'd feel whole again.

"But I lost." Jade whispered. "I didn't even come close. I was knocked out of the fight in the first round. I ran in my shame. I'm still running. I cannot bring myself to be a champion like him. Part of me wonders if I'll ever be ready."

"How did—" Crow hesitated, listening to the sound of the sea, "how did he die?"

"He fell from his horse." Jade whispered. Her eyes were wide and distant, she looked younger than Crow had ever seen her. "Such a great man, and he died from a knock to the head. I think I would have preferred if he died in a Petty War, or...any other way really."

"I'm sorry." Crow mumbled.

Jade stiffened. "It's fine." She said, her regular hard demeanor returning. "Tell me, how did Kath die?"

Crow clenched his fists, banishing the memory of her standing in the field. "You were there."

"Tell me."

"Why?"

"Tell me. Make it real."

"She—she was killed by a centaur." The words hurt more than any strike from a blade.

"Aye. She was killed." Jade nodded; her voice soft.

"She was killed protecting her friends." Crow's vision blurred, and suddenly the deck appeared to be under the sea. He wiped away his tears.

Jade rested her hand on his shoulder. The act was unnatural coming from this hard woman, and Crow could feel her unease as thick as heat. Regardless, he took her comfort gratefully. He leaned into her, and he cried.

The rest of the journey went better. Kath still haunted Crow's dreams, but as the days passed, the pain lessened. Crow worked with the crew to keep himself busy under the blazing sun. He scrubbed the deck, learned sailor's knots, and even took up an oar. *I'm stronger than I used to be.* His muscles shifted beneath his skin with each push and pull of the water. Shadow flew beside the *Wave Song,* spitting ice into the hot air. The blast was so cold that they felt it from the deck, and the crewmen begged the dragon for another taste of the chill. The ice was a blessing from the sun's harsh rays.

One day, Tree joined Crow for his midday snack at the ship's prow. They both stared at the open horizon while eating a ripe bunch of purple grapes.

"I miss land dearly." Tree said, their skin a gray shade of green.

"I think we'll reach it soon, right?" Crow had lost track of how long they'd been on the sea.

Tree nodded. "We are close."

"Did nymphs ever live on the ocean?"

"Long ago, some dwelled on the shores, but most are suited to live in the trees." Tree said. "There are many songs dedicated to the power of the sea."

"Will you sing one?" Crow asked, popping another grape into his mouth.

Tree pondered for a moment. "I am quite sick of the ocean." They whispered, as if saying it aloud might anger the water beneath their feet. "But perhaps a song will flatter the waves and take us closer to shore." And so, their song began.

Shadow screamed and landed at Crow's side. She ruffled her scales like the feathers of a bird, and cocked her head to the side as she drank the nymph's swelling song. The song was a lot like Tree's other ones, Crow realized. The songs of the nymphs all held a sort of melancholy tone, slow and building and magnificent and beautiful. A sudden breeze ruffled Crow's hair. He looked up to the black sails, which billowed against the wind's call. The crew stopped their tasks to listen, until only Tree's voice rang throughout the ship.

Crow offered Tree a smile when the song reached its end. "I think the sea heard you." He said, looking back to the tight sails drinking up the wind. Tree smiled too.

"We land at dawn."

That night, the winds remained strong and the stars bright. Crow sharpened his sword, preparing for his evening training. Then, a shout from the crow's nest alerted the captain and crew. "The Isles!" The man called.

Jumping up, Crow raced to the ship's side.

There! Before them, out against the ink black waters, Crow spied tiny lights hovering over the sea. It was too dark to see much else, Frukjera's coast could be within reach and Crow wouldn't know. But the cluster of lights was the first hint of land they'd seen since sailing from Crescent Bay days ago.

"Crow!" The slap against his back nearly sent him tumbling into the ocean. Crow spun around, clenching his longsword before he saw it was just Captain Julio. "We dock at sunrise." Julio continued, ignoring Crow's reaction. Crow frowned, rubbing his shoulder. "Come dine with me tonight. Bring your dragon. Let's celebrate a journey of fine winds and waters!"

For as long as they'd been aboard the *Wave Song,* Crow had only sparingly spoke to her captain. That is not to say, however, that the man didn't attend to his docks. Quite the opposite. He was *everywhere.* It was impossible to find him. One moment, he'd be at the wheel, the next tying sails, suddenly on the oars, or even scrubbing the planks. "A man who doesn't clean his ship is no better than a flea on the back of a dog." He'd told Crow while on his hands and knees.

The dining quarters were small but elegant. A table made of fine white birch sat in the middle. Brass candle holders adorned the walls wrought as mermaids, and a woven rug covered the floor in colors of reds and yellows and greens. Crow marveled at the simple luxury of it. He knew without being told that it was an honor to be feasted here. They didn't even eat in this place on their first night at sea. Tree, Jade and Francia were already sitting at the table.

Shadow was quick to follow after them, landing upon the back of an empty chair. As Crow took his seat beneath her, a platter piled with colorful fruit was brought out for them. "It's customary to have a night of drinking and feasting before we dock." Julio explained. "Only the finest for the Northern Child and his friends!"

Crow reached for a slice of orange when Jade shot him an icy look. "Thank you for your hospitality." Crow said, before grabbing it and stuffing it into his mouth. The fruit burst on his tongue in an explosion of sweet citrus. The fruit in Griffin's Peak tasted of sand in comparison.

"It's been years since I've been to the Isles." Jade said. "Talio Rope-Ringer was a young king last time I was there."

"He's still king." Francia replied, grinning. "He has three daughters now. They'll love to see a dragon and nymph, surely."

"We're goin' to meet the king?" Crow swallowed.

"Of course." Lady Francia gasped. Julio let out a hardy laugh.

"This one doesn't trust royal blood; I can see it." He leaned on the table. "I don't blame you, the Arrowheads are a crude bunch, threatening another Petty War with every passing winter. The Rope-Ringers will fall over themselves begging for your company."

"Will they, now?" Jade seemed doubtful too.

Crow smelled their supper before it appeared. Lobsters as large as Crow's forearm were displayed on slices of lemon, bright red and sizzling with large crystals of sea salt sinking into the white flesh. Oysters rested on a bed of seaweed, flakes of red chili dusting the soft meat inside the shells. Crow's mouth watered at the sight of it all. He'd never had food this fancy before.

Captain Julio stood, grabbing a pitcher of dark liquid and pouring them each a small amount. Smiling, Francia kissed her captain upon the cheek as he poured for her, later squeezing an orange into the amber drink. Crow swirled his glass, holding it to his nose for a sniff. "Our Mother!" Tears sprang to his eyes, the strong stench wafted up his nose and punched up beneath his eyes. It was sweet and deep and *strong*. Everyone at the table laughed at his reaction, even Tree.

"This is the nectar of Vitania herself." Julio said, holding up his glass. "She made men not only to protect our women, but to make rum. And no one has perfected rum like those from the Crystal Isles." Julio raised his glass. Tree politely declined, asking for fresh water instead. Jade took a swig and nodded, praising the fine drink. Holding his own, Crow allowed a dribble to seep through his lips. It tasted like liquid fire. The room boomed with laughter, again, at Crow's aversion. Crow frowned. He took a deep breath and swallowed the rest of the drink down. His face felt hot as more was poured for him.

The night grew merry as they feasted and drank to a smooth journey. The lobster meat was sweet and juicy, the oysters tasted like the ocean and sang with fiery spices. Crow's usual feeling of unease was untangled by the rum, and he even sang a few verses of *Wanda the Wonder*, much to the amusement of Julio and Francia. "The songs of the Peak are such simple things." Francia laughed. She turned on Tree, her face glowing from the rum. "Now, yours, though," she said, "I am the most blessed woman in the world to have heard a nymph's song. Even our own songs in the Isles don't hold a candle to you."

"Thank you." Tree dipped their head. "I have not heard any of your songs, I should look forward to it when we arrive."

"Have you ever ventured to the Green Coast in all your winters?" Captain Julio asked, slurping an oyster.

"No. But I have seen the ocean to the east." Tree said.

The one against the Forgotten Forest, Crow knew.

"And you," Lady Francia looked to Crow, "you have never left your mountain kingdom before now?"

"Aye." Crow nodded, vision swimming. "I had a brother—another Lad—who was from the Crystal Isles, though. He'd talk about the clear water, the warm sea breeze and the fish. He said the fish looked like nothing I'd ever seen. Because of him, I always wanted to go to the Isles. His name was Shadow." The dragon at his back chirped. "Or at least, that's what we called 'im."

"He must have been a resourceful boy to make it up there." Julio allowed.

"He was." Crow smiled. "He had all sorts of stories to share. He talked about the foot knight who traveled the Boiling Sea and married a mermaid." He could nearly hear the boy inside the caves, digging at a vein with Crow and talking about the creatures of the deep. Somewhere in the darkness, Bones would say, *"what's so great 'bout a woman that's half a fish?"*

"Ah, yes!" Julio clapped. "The tales of Sir Yourel Sea-Chaser are well loved among the boys of our city."

"This Shadow, is he still digging in the mountains?" Francia asked softly.

"No." Crow's mood turned swiftly from the rum. The sadness swelled inside of him like a giant wave. He felt dizzy with grief, and tried to hold back the tears that sprung forth. "He's at the bottom of the Pond, I think." The silence that followed was louder than the crashing waves.

"To Shadow." Captain Julio held up his glass. "May his spirit have found rest in our Mother's arms!"

"To Shadow," Francia, Jade, and even Tree held up their glasses.

"To Shadow," Crow confirmed.

"And to Lady Kath." Jade raised her glass a second time. Her dark eyes connected with Crow's, and he brought his own glass back into the air.

"To Lady Kath." The rum burned, but the pain was good.

Seventeen

The Crystal Isles

The Crystal Isles were unlike any city Crow had ever seen. As a boy, he'd heard of the kingdom built upon the shallow sea, lashed together with wood and rope, only the tiniest slivers of sand islands anchoring the whole thing in place. But growing up in the dark caves and deep valleys of the Peak, his imagination could only stretch so far. This was like another world.

Like Griffin's Peak, the Isles had no wall to shield it from an attack. Instead, a horde of ships clung to the outer docks like swarming wasps. A wall in motion. A wall that could act as an offense. The fleet was a separate kingdom in its own right, black sails furled along tall wooden masts. And each captain a king. As they rowed in on their row boat, Captain Julio pointed out the ships crafted for attack. They were smaller than the fat trading cogs floating close by, and narrow with a deadly bowsprit sharpened and designed to split enemies' ships apart. "They're swifter than any steed, and can crack another kingdom's ship in two." He said. The ships swarmed around the outer ports, a silent threat.

"Has another king ever attacked the Isles?" Crow asked.

"Not since I was born." The captain shook his head. "But Seal Island thought they deserved to be independent from the

Rope-Ringers, and revolted seven winters ago." He laughed. "Foolish. They were smashed and beaten back to their rock within a fortnight."

"What happened to the duke?" Jade asked.

"King Talio, in his good grace, showed the duke mercy, and allowed him to keep his seat. The Wind-Surfers are an ancient and proud line, which saved their heads. The island must report every new ship it builds to the king, so that they can't try and rise up again."

Beyond the Isle's fleet, the other boats surrounding the city clouded the planked kingdom in colorful banners. Some sails were white, some red, purple and blue. Crow wondered how far they had come, and if they knew of the impending war on the mainland. Shadow was perched on the prow, she screamed, thrashing her tail as they drew closer. Crow stood up, shaking the boat back and forth. The Crystal Isles was marvelous.

The wooden city sprawled out like a great spider. In the middle, lay a sandy key larger than all the others, nestled in the breast of salt bleached wood. Tall thin trees with flaring leaves sprung up from the center. "Palm trees," Jade told Crow. Draw bridges—eight, Crow later learned—connected the green island to the rest of the floating city, and from those eight bridges, sprung the main docks—or roads—which branched off into smaller floating streets. The entire kingdom appeared to hover above the calm green waters, but as they drew closer, Crow could spy the wooden stilts balancing the whole city upon the planked docks. People traveled between channels in thin canoes and flat rafts. The streets were full of folk, dark skin standing out beautifully against light colorful fabric that blew from windows on the sea breeze. Laughter of children echoed in the channels, fishermen yelled from their rafts, and the cry of sea birds filled the air with a buzzing song of life. Crow hadn't seen so many people since he'd left the Peak, and almost forgot how bustling a true kingdom could be. He looked to Tree and Shadow. "They'll see us soon." He said. *And what will they think?* He'd find out soon enough.

News of the boy with the dragon had traveled fast. So fast that the royals were expecting them by the time they floated to the eastern port. The city guard held long spears taller than men. They wore sparkling shifts different from anything the guards from the Ridge wore. Chainmail that looked more like cloth than steel.

"What's that they're wearing?" Crow asked.

"Armor, boy." Julio laughed. "It's made special. Lighter than anything on the mainland. If we fall into the sea mid-battle, we don't intend to drown."

Crow knew he looked like a ragged thing as they rowed in, with his sun burnt face, ill-fitting clothes and sliced arms. Despite this, he tried his best to appear proud. The boat was easy to balance, and Crow didn't stumble as they docked. Shadow screamed their arrival. The guard could not hold back their surprise, they balked at the dragon glimmering black in the sunlight. And, though Crow was never excited to see a city guard, he was glad that they were there as the locals crowded around. People were held back easily with spears and harsh warnings. Among their welcoming party, a woman in glittering chainmail, chased with gold, stood tall and still as stone. Her spear was black as obsidian, and twice as tall as she. She watched them approach, with only a cursory glance at Tree and Shadow. Her black eyes found Crow and held him.

"Teresa Crab-Catcher." Captain Julio said. "The Rope-Ringer's champion. She boarded her first ship at eight winters old, and slew the pirate captain of the *Black Thief* at twelve."

By the time they roped in, the crowd around them had swollen to hundreds. The shouts consumed them. Crow could barely hear the champion as she spoke. "King Talio has heard of your coming. He would be honored to host you at his hearth and home." She said.

Crow didn't know if he could trust this king, but he saw little choice. The folk pushing against the guard were wildly excited, and he didn't know what would happen if they were left to the streets by themselves. "The nymph's Tree," Crow replied eventually, stepping from the bucking boat to the sturdy dock, "and the dragon's Shadow."

Teresa bowed her head. "Let's be off."

They were escorted through the kingdom along one of the main straights, lined with fish markets, apothecaries, inns and taverns. All were painted different bright colors: yellow, white, green, orange, and red peeling from the salt in the air. Light wood shown behind it. The water beneath their feet was clear as a looking glass, and Crow spied tiny fish flitting between docks. Women and children swam leisurely in the watered pathways, pointing up at Shadow in the sky. People hung out of large airy windows, where drapes of hundreds of colors danced in the gentle ocean breeze. The air smelled of salt and seaweed. *It's beautiful,* Crow marveled. The Isles were beyond anything Shadow could describe.

"The seasons do not touch here." Tree said at his side in amazement. Crow only nodded; his mind was far from the impending winter.

The castle was called the Gardens, Crow learned. As the bridge was lowered over the Ringer's Canal, it was easy to see why. The Gardens was less a palace and more a collection of breezy wooden temples. The structures were open to the lush gardens beyond, indoors and outdoors flowing together harmoniously. They stood upon white sand and tall grass, palm trees sprouted between outdoor arched halls, and bushes of pink and yellow flowers swarmed with winged insects that looked more like fabled fairies than bugs. Floral perfume and salt mixed in the warm air. A smile stretched Tree's face as they laid eyes on the abundance of foliage. A bronze statue of Vitania stood as a greeting, turned green from the salt in the air. The sight of her eased Crow's nerves. Hopefully the Rope-Ringers held hospitality in high regard.

"The Rope-Ringers are as ancient as the kingdom itself." Julio said, swaggering across the bridge as though he owned it. "They sailed to the Gardens and built here, expanding out to the surrounding keys."

"They've ruled since the Conquering Age?" Crow asked.

"Aye."

"That seems an exceedingly rare thing." Jade smirked.

They followed a path of white shell gravel to the largest and most decorative of the temples. It mirrored its kingdom, nestled in the middle of the Gardens, surrounded by its smaller cousins. Two large doors carved with mermaids and pirates and ships barred entry. Waves swirled with strange creatures jumping from their depths, krakens clung to sinking ships. If thunder carved the Roost, then Mother Vitania lovingly molded the wooden epics of these temples with her own hands. Royal guards stood sentry on either side.

Shadow landed on Crow's shoulders with a heavy thump. She barely fit now, and dug her claws painfully into his flesh as she clung to him. The guard opened the doors, Crow's heart pounded through his ribs.

The long hall had high vaulted ceilings. Tall windows lined the walls, white thin silky drapes twisted lazily in the wind. Natural light flooded inside, illuminating the dark wood. A patterned carpet woven in colors of sea greens and blues stretched the length of the room, Crow was afraid he'd dirty it with his sand and dirt caked feet. Chandeliers of black iron hung from the high beams, white pearls and dripping wax candles crusted their twisting limbs like snow. The pearls clicked softly with each gust of wind. At the other end of the hall was the throne.

Like in Griffin's Peak, the throne sat above everyone else, though it wasn't nearly as tall and foreboding. It topped a three-tiered platform. On the first tier a collection of simple benches held a group of men and women with sun-darkened skin and colorful clothing. *The council, probably,* Crow thought. The arrangement reminded him of the Roost. The only one who didn't sit with the council was a girl, maybe a winter or two older than Crow, wearing a simple white dress and standing off to the side. She held a silver harp in one hand, and her green eyes shone brilliantly against her deep complexion. Dark curls clustered like a halo around her pretty face. *A singer,* he ripped his eyes from her before she caught him staring.

The next platform held three girls in pillowed seats. They wore silky black gowns, beaded with white pearls and gleaming diamonds. Silver bands adorned their brows. *Princesses,* Crow guessed. One looked to be his age. The youngest couldn't have been more than five winters old. She stood at the sight of Shadow and pointed a chubby dark finger at him, shouting at her sisters to "Look! Look! Dragon!"

The king sat at the top, where his queen stood by his side. The throne of the Rope-Ringers was stark white limestone, carved just as delicately as the epic pictures on the doors. The stone looked like knots of white rope. Where the throne of Griffin's Peak was brute and blocky, this one was delicate and airy. King Talio Rope-Ringer sat on satin black cushions, wearing a black studded doublet cinched at the waist with a rope of spun gold. He was a tall and dark man. A crown of white ivory twisted in the shape of sailor's knots rested on top of his shaved head. His wife was a tall beauty beside him, willowy and delicate with a shock of blond hair that contrasted dramatically against her black skin. She matched the rest of her family, dressed in black and white and unquestioned wealth. Behind them a large banner hung, the sigil of the Rope-Ringers: a white knot on a black field.

Crow walked the length of the hall, behind Captain Julio and Teresa Crab-Catcher. Shadow's scales puffed up and she hissed. The council murmured among themselves, the princesses craned their necks, and the king and queen gave nothing away. Jade knelt first, and Crow quickly followed. Shadow launched from his shoulders into the air, landing in the wooden rafters. Tree stood to his right, but did not kneel.

"You may rise." King Talio said, voice deep as thunder.

"You are graced by the presence of King Talio and Queen Tyla Rope-Ringer, rulers of the Green Coast," a woman of the council announced, "along with their three daughters: Princess Talia, heir to the Crystal Isles, Princess Daria, and Princess Maria."

"When we heard of a boy with a dragon traveling with a nymph, we could hardly believe our ears." The king said. "The Mother has been kind to bring you before my eyes." He looked to Tree. "It's an honor to have you in our hall and home."

"Thank you." Tree nodded. Their chimed voice set the council to murmuring again.

"We are humbled by such guests." The queen smiled. "Captain Julio," the man bowed when she addressed him, "we must handsomely reward you for delivering such precious gifts to us." Her dark eyes shifted to Crow once more. "Please, your names?"

Crow opened his mouth, but Jade stepped forward. "This is Crow, born of Griffin's Peak, the proclaimed Northern Child by the unicorns." *There's a fancy title,* Crow raised his brows. "I am Lady Jade Threu of Good Land, and this is Tree, last of the nymphs as we know, of the Forgotten Forest."

The dragon screamed.

"And this is Shadow." Crow said as she plunged from the sky to land back on his shoulders. He winced but didn't stagger under her weight. "The ice dragon."

"Ice dragon..." the council grumbled. Crow found confidence in Shadow's icy blue eyes. Her energy was like a ball of lightning, and he felt it as though it were his own. *Go on,* he lifted his arm. She leapt back into the air, up and up back into the vaulted beams, and spat ice across the exposed wood. The cold blast wafted past them on the ground, and Crow grinned at the spectacle, looking back to the council and smirking. Princess Maria clapped and screamed. The king's regal expression was lost for a moment in quiet shock.

"Dragons are a common sight over the seas down here." King Talio explained. "But an ice dragon..." he smiled, "we are truly privileged to be witnessing such history before our very eyes. Lyla, you must write a song about this day."

"Yes, my liege." The girl with the harp replied.

"The honor is all ours." Jade said.

"Tell me," King Talio leaned forward, "what is your business here?"

Crow glanced at Jade, and she nodded. *"Make it to the Isles,"* Kath had said. *Do I tell him we're going to Glorygradus?* He wondered. King Talio didn't seem to wish them harm, but Crow held a natural distrust for the royals. And he wasn't ready to trust them just yet.

"The feln attacked Youngston." Crow began.

"Aye." Talio frowned and leaned back. "That is not all." He hesitated, but then leaned forward again. "They've taken Augustii as well."

The news came as a surprise to all of them. Jade was nearly landed by the king's words. "Augustii?" She asked. "How could that happen?"

"The barbarians came from the north." Talio's gaze shifted to Tree now. The nymph's expression was a mask, hard as oak. "Augustii had time to bar its gates, but fell in a few weeks. We didn't know it was under attack until a ship escaped and carried the message across the sea, and by then it was too late. We sent out a quarter of our fleet, but have heard nothing."

Crow was surprised the king would readily share this information with them. He looked up to the rafters, where Shadow was perched on a high beam. *A child with a dragon running from battle makes interesting gossip. But a man with a dragon, flying into battle, that is worthy of a song.*

"Our friend, a foot knight, died bringin'—bringing us here." Crow said, adjusting his posture. He stood tall, as tall as he could from the base of a throne. "I need training. Lady Jade does well, but I can't fight if I keep running." The more he spoke, the more he felt it was true. Crow wouldn't let Lady Kath die in vain. *Whether here or Man's Wall, I need to fight.* "If Frukjera's going to war. I want to fight for men." Crow's words tumbled from his mouth, confident and strong. "I want Shadow to fight for men."

King Talio smiled and stood. "Teresa, tell the servants to prepare the guest quarters." The champion bowed and walked off. "The Crystal Isles is glad to host you—what was it—Northern Child? Your companion was right to send you here. Our finest warriors will give you aid, and make a fine knight of you. Please, treat the Gardens as you would your home."

Jade raised her brows at him, but nodded. Tree wrung their cloak between delicate hands. Crow wanted to comfort them, to let them know that he still intended to go to Man's Wall as the unicorns wished. But he thought of Lady Gretchen, traveling to Youngston with nothing but her battle ax. And Lady Kath, shooting her last arrow into the skull of a monster. It was time for him to be brave.

It was time for him to join the fray.

Eighteen

The Gardens

The sun sat hot and thick atop Crow's skin like a wet rag. Not even the light silks and trousers that the Rope-Ringers had kindly given him could keep him cool. *Hard to believe it's nearly winter,* he thought as he walked across the sunbaked path. The only tell of the season was the setting sun, sinking earlier and earlier each night. Shadow flew lazily above his head. Crow was on his way to the library, where Tree was waiting for him.

One of the castle guards watched him walk by. They always kept a close eye on him here. He appreciated the royal family's hospitality, but he noticed that the household servants, guards and knights were never far from sight. He tried to ignore their prying eyes. *If I told Bones I'd been wined and dined by a king, he'd never believe me.* With the imminent danger of the roads behind him, Crow thought of the Lads even more often than before. Of the home he'd lost.

Shaking his head, he opened the library doors. The book-packed temple was located at the far end of the Gardens, shaded by a grove of palm trees. It seemed to be Tree's favorite place. The little nymph was fond of written words. "We do not write." They admitted to Crow one day. "But I find profound artistry in script."

Crow preferred to spend his time training in the yard. He was getting better. And the sword play distracted him from the anxiety that gnawed relentlessly at his stomach. It was Jade's idea that Crow must learn to read.

"If you're going to be among high born blood, you should learn to read and write." She insisted after a long day in the arms yard.

Crow groaned. "You goin' to teach me that too?'

"I can only stand to be around you so much." She pursed her lips.

"I will teach you." Tree's light voice injected. They were sitting on a patch of grass, stroking Shadow as she baked beside them. "The Rope-Ringers have an assortment of books. They even have books of felnish text. Are you familiar with felnish, Lady Jade?"

"No." Jade frowned. "There was never a reason."

"I think it would be wise for the Northern Child to be well versed in both."

Crow grunted. "I don't see much of a point. I had a brother, Gravel, who said readin's for people who don't know how to work."

"Knowledge is a privilege." Tree said. "But it can also be a weapon. Men and a few feln immortalized their knowledge on paper. It would be wise to know it."

"Yes." Jade smirked. "Take your lessons and learn to read like a good boy."

Crow glared at her. "I'm nearly a man now."

He'd noticed his growth shortly after settling into the Gardens. His chamber held a looking glass and Crow hardly knew the reflection staring back at him. His skin was browned and blotched red by the sun, and his face was sharper than ever before. Crow ran a hand across his square jaw, feeling the barest of hair starting to sprout, though he could hardly see it. His arms and chest had filled out as well, lean muscle from days of training. He'd always been a wiry kid, but now he looked like a proper growing young man. Had the solstice come and gone already? It was hard to tell time in a place where the seasons didn't change.

The shade from the palm grove was a welcome reprieve from the sun. The temple in front of him was small, with an even smaller stone statue of Mother Vitania standing before the door. She reminded Crow of the old weathered one in front of Garrett's door back in the Ridge. His mind wandered to Lady Gretchen. *Did she find Wanda?* He hoped she was still alive. But thinking of her always brought reminders of Kath. Crow frowned, expelling those thoughts. Kath would return to him in his dreams, he knew. A bow would be in her hand, and instead of a centaur running her down, it would be him—mounted on a giant white dragon.

Shoving the door open, Crow spotted Tree at one of the rounded wooden tables, with two tall waxy candles lit for light. Although it was daytime, the library remained dark because of the tall shelves casting deep sharp shadows. Shadow flew inside, landing atop one of the dusty stands.

"I have found an interesting book today." Tree said as Crow sat across from them. Their green skin showed almost gold in the firelight. The pages were crackly and yellowed, the print was tiny and ink faded. An old thing.

"You're not planning on making me read that, are you?" He asked.

"You should." Tree smiled.

"What's it about?"

"The dragons of the Boiling Sea. It could be useful."

"Shadow's an ice dragon. Do they have any books on those?"

"No. Oddly, I have found nothing about them, not even in fiction." Tree said. "Tell me, what do you know of the dragons of fire?"

"Not much." Crow admitted. "All I know is what Stone Teeth told me from songs and stories. They can't be tamed. They hunt whatever pleases them..." He looked up at Shadow, curled across loose papers and leather books. "They live on Dragon Island, where no one really goes. The ships that wander too close get attacked. Stone Teeth told me about an explorer who managed to land on the shore, but I can't remember his name."

"That is all?"

"I know that dragons destroyed the kingdom of Stone Yard. There's a song about it, *'Death from Above.'*" A dramatic tune. He knew it because there was a Lad whose parents were from Harold's Holding, a kingdom completely underground to avoid dragon flame.

"What happened?"

"During the Conquering Age, King Harold set out to find gold along Mermaid's Bay. He found it right at the tip and built Stone Yard, which grew into a city quickly because it was so rich. But the bigger it got, the fiercer the dragons became. They rained fire down and stole children from the streets, cattle from farms and horses on the roads. Then, one day, they all came." Crow struggled to remember the verse. "*'The clouds were feathers of black and red, a storm of beasts with rain that rivaled the sun.'* The king died, but his son led the remnants of his people to Harold's Holding."

"You should read this, once you are ready." Tree patted the book carefully. "From what you tell me, dragons are fire and death. But that is not all they are. They care for their young fiercely and bond for life, they are the regal children of Summer and Winter. And yes, are not to be tamed. This will help you understand Shadow as she grows larger."

*Shadow's different from them. But still...*it would be good to know all that he could. "I understand." He said slowly. "I've only heard the violent stuff about dragons. I should know more."

"Yes." Tree smiled.

Crow sighed and took the book. The script was small and tightly written, much harder to read than the big blocky words he'd been learning in children's books. "It's goin'—going to take me a while to get through this one, though."

"Perhaps we can finish this, Princess Maria has given it to me." The nymph produced a thinner book, with bright pictures of sea creatures swimming across the front. Crow grabbed it from them and pursed his lips. Looking over the title and raising an eyebrow.

"The Mer—Mermaid's Ock—Ockean? Ockean Friends?"

"*Ocean.*" Tree pointed to the word. "It is a mystery to me as well, but in men's written language, the *c* sounds like an *s* sometimes."

"The Mermaid's Ocean Friends."

Tree nodded. Crow sighed, embarrassed of the childish nature of the book, but opened it regardless. "I'd rather read something about battles." He mumbled. The thought of the little princess picking this out for him was nearly unbearable.

King Talio seemed keen on dining Crow with his three daughters. Although, he couldn't imagine why. Surely, he was too lowborn for there to be any motivation behind it. He certainly felt low born whenever he was with them. His manners were all wrong, he ate too fast and didn't speak properly. Crow might have a dragon, but at the end of the day, he was just another orphan from a different city. Their dinners were awkward. Crow had nothing in common with the three princesses. He knew tunnels, working, darkness and—more recently—running. The princesses knew servants, gowns, court affairs and feasts.

Talia, who shared his age of fourteen winters, clearly thought of him as a dirty peasant. She hardly offered conversation, instead paying more attention to her roasted fish. Meanwhile, Daria, of ten winters, seemed *too* interested. She'd stare at him with big ogling eyes, ask what he thought of her gowns, and once tried to show him her shell collection. The youngest, Maria, just wanted to know about Tree and Shadow. Crow actually liked her the best. As long as the subject wasn't him, he didn't mind. He was spared dinner with the princesses most nights, instead eating with Tree and Jade in their chambers. More recently, though, a fourth member began dining with them.

Lyla Mer-Song, the singer.

She'd taken to following Crow around the Gardens whenever their paths crossed. At first, Crow welcomed the attention. Lyla was beautiful, and he'd never had a beautiful girl's attention before. She'd watch him train with Jade, and Crow would try extra hard to show his skill. However, Crow soon realized that she wasn't interested in *him* exactly, but his story. He should start getting used to that.

"I will write this generation's greatest song." She told him, strumming her annoying harp. "Mother Vitania brought you here just for me. The Crystal Isles are so dull, it looks like my prayers have finally been answered."

Crow grew irritated with her presence at once.

"Are you going to write about my breakfast too?" He asked her one morning on his way to the kitchens.

"He held more passion to break his fast than he did for a pretty lass." She strummed.

He hated to admit that her voice was lovely. Luckily, she didn't bother sitting in on Crow's reading lessons, and Princess Talia often stole the singer away during the day anyway.

Crow finished the colorful book, Tree continued searching for important novels, and Shadow slept among the scrolls.

The temple door creaked open, and a shriveled old woman stepped inside. Crow recognized her as one of the council members. Her wiry hair had long since turned gray, and was knotted in thick braids tied up into a swirling point atop her head. She wore a gown of green silks that swirled around her shrunken form like kelp. Diamonds and sapphires crusted her ears and fingers. She gave the two a passing look, and then proceeded to walk through the shelves, as if searching for a book.

Crow tried not to glare at her. He didn't like the council members, they reminded him of the council from Griffin's Peak. They were of old blood; proud and above the common man. Crow could see it from their expressions: stern and angry and judgmental. They thought they were better than him. *Do they think I'm too stupid to know?* Everyone in the castle was watching him. From the servants to the council, maybe even Lyla. For a boy who'd grown up invisible, it was unsettling to have so many eyes on him.

Flipping a page of the dragon book, Crow waited for her dragging footsteps to leave.

"You notice how they watch us?" He whispered once it was safe. The nymph nodded. "I don't like it."

"You told them you would fight for them." Tree reminded him as they sat down.

"I know." Crow said. "But that doesn't mean they can spy on us. They should be glad I *want* to fight."

"The unicorns showed you Man's Wall. You cannot forget that message."

"I won't. But why shouldn't I fight along the way? It's what a hero would do. Even Jade agrees with me."

"I fear for you." Tree whispered.

Crow's heart skipped. He could see the worry deep in the nymph's green eyes. It swirled beneath the layer of sadness that was always there.

"You don't need to." Crow insisted. He smiled, leaning back in his chair. "I'm learning the way of the sword, and am better than the average man." Though still not good enough to land a hit on Jade. "And once Shadow is big enough, I'll have a dragon."

"Shadow is not a weapon." Tree quipped. It was rare that Tree showed anger, it took Crow aback. "If you treat her as such, she will disregard you as all dragons have disregarded men. I fear for your path. I do not want you to get lost. As you grow, men will flock to you, shower you with gifts and promises of glory. This is enough to blind even the greatest of heroes."

Crow bit the inside of his cheek. *They're worried I'll become some blood thirsty conqueror.* "I won't get lost." He promised. "But I *am* going to fight. I want to protect people. I want to protect people like Garrett and the Lads, Lady Gretchen, and you too."

"And you shall." Tree narrowed their eyes and leaned closer. "You are right not to trust the people here." They whispered. "Not all who have heard the song of the Northern Child will rejoice."

Crow frowned at that, but remembered Stone Teeth's warning—over a moon ago—and how King Arthur had ordered a manhunt for him. Did the king know something? Now King Talio watched his every step. Would King Arthur have let him leave the Roost if he knew Crow could hatch the egg?

"What would they have to worry about?" Crow asked. "I'm goin' to fight for men, obviously."

"And when the fighting is done, the people will sing of the man and the dragon who brought the unicorns and the nymphs back to the land." Tree said.

"That's a good thing." Crow frowned. "It's what we want."

"It is what *we* want. But, is it what *they* want?" Tree looked to the doors of the library, out the windows, and into the Gardens where the royals ruled and listened.

Nineteen

The Gardens

Jade's gait was swift by his side, her armored feet clunk against the temple floor like heavy horse steps. She had taken to wearing plate again after she was offered steel from the armory. The armor was well made, better than the mismatched steel she'd lost to the River of Song. Crow noted how she avoided anything enameled with the tied rope of the Crystal Isles. Next to her, Tree sounded like a ghost, bare feet patting against the floor in whispers, their silks just as silent. They still wore the cloak given to them from the *Wave Song*. Shadow crawled in front of them. She had grown remarkably since their arrival at the Gardens, finding fish aplenty and small creatures in the Ringer's Canal. She was too large to walk on her hind legs, and had to crawl awkwardly using her wings. Crow judged her to be a little smaller than a dog. *She's growing, and changing.* White tufts of feathers sprouted from between her scales and crept up from the tip of her tail and wings.

"Will she be covered one day?" Crow asked Tree as they lay beneath the beating sun one afternoon.

"Yes." Tree said. "All dragons are covered in feathers. They sprout their feathers as they mature. Another reason you must read that book I found for you."

She'll have horns soon too, Crow noticed. Two tiny nubs were protruding from the top of her skull, they were clear as glass. *Not glass, ice.*

The trio were summoned to King Talio's council. The past few days had been quiet, Crow trained with Jade at the sword, he learned writing with Tree in the library, and ate meals with the princesses when he had to. There was no doubt, he knew, that his movements were carefully watched by the castle folk. And though the Gardens were quiet, the same could not be said for the rest of Frukjera. The continent buzzed on the brink of war.

"It's a great honor to be called to a council meeting." Jade said. "Listen closely to what they say. This is how men rule."

When the guards bid them entry, they found King Talio sitting around a large round wooden table with his council. Unfurled in front of them was a large map of Frukjera inked on dried hide. Princess Talia was among the seated, staring at Shadow.

"Join us." King Talio motioned for them to sit. He wore a black woolen overcoat with a large silver knotted broach tied at his shoulder. *How can he wear such a thing?* Crow had been sweating through his silks all day.

Shadow curled beneath his chair once he sat down.

"You honor us." Crow rehearsed. "Thank you for callin'—calling us to council." If he'd learned anything from his time spent here, it was that the royals must be thanked for anything they did.

The king nodded. "It is only appropriate for the Northern Child to listen to Frukjera's happenings if he is going to fight for the righteous."

"Is it the feln?" Jade asked.

King Talio motioned to one of the council members, a small man with beady black eyes and a flat nose. His smooth dark skin melted from his bones; no hair grew from his thin scalp. His name was Grabiol Fish-Singer.

Grabiol shot Crow a quick dirty look before producing a rolled piece of parchment from under the table. "Youngston is lost."

The words were a spear through the belly.

"King Arthur Arrowhead writes to us from Griffin's Peak, asking for a formal alliance with the Crystal Isles. He's called all the boys and men from the Ridge to war." Grabiol rubbed his chin. "To have a kingdom fall to the feln…it is troubling news."

"Youngston was unprepared to hold against a proper siege." Teresa, the champion, said. "It always relied on the power of Griffin's Peak. With the centaurs running wild on the Roam, it was only a matter of time before the gates opened. By sieging the kingdom in secrecy, the enemy had an easy victory. Still…I've never heard of the feln to battle so efficiently."

"Perhaps they have learned from days of old." Tree said. The council was shocked by the nymph's revelation, but nodded solemnly.

"What of the Youngs? Any word about the queen?" King Talio asked.

Grabiol shook his head. "King Arrowhead doesn't mention them."

"Marching on Youngston would be a mistake." The old woman, Petunia, said. "Our power is in the sea."

"The feln must have huge numbers if they've been able to split and take both Youngston and Augustii. We should retake Augustii and then attack them on their island. Get rid of them as we should have generations ago." Teresa said.

"Did King Arthur mention anything about Fisher's Mark?" Jade asked.

"None, my lady." Grabiol replied. "Though it is safe to assume that Fisher's Mark simply kept its gates closed. The centaurs don't take sides, and it'd be foolish for the feln to test their luck by marching from Youngston when King Arthur is on the move."

"We have our own problems here." Petunia injected. "Let this king beg to another."

Crow held no love for King Arthur, but he thought of his brothers. They would all be called to war. They were off to fight a ruthless enemy while Crow sat with princesses at his evening meals. And what happened to Lady Gretchen with the battle ax at her side?

"We need to help." Crow said, his resolve hard as stone. Everyone looked at him in surprise. "I came to you ready to fight, now Griffin's Peak needs us. An entire kingdom fell. How can we sit here while innocent people are killed?" Shadow unfurled herself beneath him, chirping at his words. The council remained silent. Only Jade, Tree and Princess Talia paid him any mind.

"Griffin's Peak is strong." King Talio said. "As you should know. The king can handle Youngston's fall with his own men."

"You won't help your ally? You would rather leave them to fight the feln alone?"

Crow's remark left a bitter feeling in the air. Jade kicked him under the table. "Excuse him. He's not familiar with proper etiquette." She said.

"Clearly." Petunia hissed. Crow glared at her. Sensing his anger, Shadow climbed up the back of his chair, resting her large frame awkwardly at the head, she offered the old woman an icy look and hissed.

Grabiol quickly cleared his throat, producing another piece of parchment. "There is also the matter of this." He handed the paper to the king. Talio opened the letter and frowned deeply. "She has fashioned herself as their ruler. Calling herself a queen."

"She?" Crow asked.

"The feln never had queens." Tree said, puzzled. "Only warlords."

"Aye." Grabiol nodded. "But this is no feln. Somehow, a daughter of Vitania has brought the beasts to her cause. I assume she sent a letter out to all of the four kingdoms. *The Queen of Winter*, she calls herself."

King Talio looked over the letter and tossed the thing away. "A disgusting traitor. A peasant who wants a slice of power for herself. She's mad. She takes one kingdom and writes *terms?*" He laughed. Teresa picked up the letter and read it.

"*To the thieves who rule the five kingdoms, your time of reigning is done. You have grown comfortable in your stone castles, but you have crawled your way to power through lies. I know the truth. I am the truth. Strike your armies and crumble your walls. Nothing can stop the wrath of winter that will befall you. Surrender and I can keep the feln from ripping the continent to pieces. This is the long-awaited end to a war you started, and I have not forgotten.*

The Queen of Winter and the Feln.'"

Crow recalled the gruesome scene at the Jumping Trout. Innocent men slaughtered for no reason at all. Crow wouldn't bet that the small folk in Youngston were kept alive.

"We should have ripped out the feln from the root." Teresa said, flinging the letter away in disgust.

"We could never have guessed that they'd be used as an army. It has been two hundred winters since the filthy creatures returned." Petunia said.

Crow was growing tired of their talking. *They won't do anything.* He knew. *Not until the feln are in their oceans.*

"What of Augustii?" Jade asked, leaning an arm on the map. "It's also under attack. What do you plan to do about that?"

"I already sent a quarter of my fleet." King Talio said.

"We should fight for Augustii, take it back." Crow said at once. The princess regarded his words with a quiet nod, but said nothing. "If you won't help King Arthur, then help your people."

"We've already expended too many ships." Grabiol snapped. "Should the beasts decide to sail on the Isles with a proper army, we'll need all of our ships in port."

"Let the feln have Augustii for now." Petunia said. "We should evacuate Seal Island and Pointer. If the feln wish to test their luck there, let them find abandoned towns and empty ports. King Arthur will smash their northern army, and if they're stupid enough to try Seal Island, we will surround them and starve them out."

The council mumbled this plan over, with the king nodding his assent and eying the map. Crow could hardly believe his ears. He looked at Jade, who sat stiff and frowning, and Tree, who looked wildly uncomfortable. Shadow hissed.

"What about the people in Augustii? Are they not worthy of your action?" Crow seethed.

The council snapped at his insolence, but a stern hand from the king silenced them. "I already sent my men to Augustii, boy. Would you have me rip more fathers from their children than I already have? I will not send the people of my kingdom into a blind war."

"I came here 'cause I want to fight."

He gave a stiff nod. "Aye, and how will you fare with that hatchling of yours? Here is some council, boy: listen to those wiser than yourself. The heroes you worship are no more than characters in a song. Real war, real battles, are fought with strategy. I will not sit here and be chided by a peasant child who fancies himself the champion of right and wrong. Go on, march on the feln with no one behind you. We will not mourn you, and we will not sing of you. Leave my council at once, take your friends with you. You have nothing I wish to hear."

Crow expected to be assaulted by Jade's disapproval as they left the temple.

"What you said was stupid." Jade said. "But right. It is cowardly of him to abandon his people. When Gretchen, Kath and I went to King Arthur from Good Land, it was because the duke wanted more guards to defend the roads. But the king ignored us. Perhaps, if he listened, we would have learned of the felns' occupation before it truly began."

"We should leave this place." Tree whispered. "We should not stray from the vision the unicorns wanted. When the king decides to call all ships and men to the Isles, it will be impossible to escape."

Crow frowned, but he had a sinking feeling that Tree was right. "I don't want to wait out the war under palm trees while my brothers are made to fight. The unicorns showed me Man's Wall. There must be something there for me."

"Let's return to our chambers." Jade said quietly. "If we're lucky, we can hire a ship to take us across the Boiling Sea. Seal Island might even be mobilizing to defend Augustii. And if we make it before the king decides to evacuate, we can get another ship to the mainland."

"Who will take us?" Crow asked. "We have no coin." Though they looked like they did after getting pampered by the Rope-Ringers.

"We will find someone." Tree said. "Remember how they welcomed you on our arrival? The people are excited about the Northern Child, a sailor will be honored to carry you."

"Pack up immediately." Jade confirmed. "I don't want to linger here tonight; we must beat the king's summons."

They didn't have to pack much. Jade kept her armor and collected her sword. The River of Song had washed away their original gear. Crow replaced his light silks with tough black leather, stitched with white yarn. He strapped his longsword to his back. Tree carried their cloak and a soft pouch around their waist, which they stuffed with dried flowers and weeds that grew around the Gardens. The plants had healing properties; Tree had shown them to Crow one evening. The trio abandoned anything they couldn't carry.

Crow would miss the feel of a feather bed, but he was made of tougher stuff. Just as he was about to leave, a soft knock rapped against their door. Shadow chirped from her place upon the bed.

"Let me in, I demand it."

Jade frowned. "Who is that?"

"The princess." Crow gawked. He'd heard little of her voice, but he recognized it. "Princess Talia."

"What should we do?" Tree asked. They were staring at Crow, waiting for an answer.

"I said, let me in." Talia repeated. "I'm alone." She added quietly. Finding little advice from his companions, Crow opened the door. The princess regarded them coolly. If she were surprised to see them packed up, she didn't show it. "You're leaving. Are you running from the war?"

Crow pinched his brow. Should he tell her? Tree and Jade were leaving this up to him. *She listened to me at the council.* Crow had always been an observant lad, and he knew despite Talia's silence in council, she was sympathetic to his outburst. "No." Crow replied curtly. "Into it. We can't sit here waiting while the feln continue to attack Frukjera." *Now, what'll you do?* He hoped he was right about her.

Princess Talia's eyes lit up, and for the first time she looked at Crow how a maiden should at a proper young man.

"My father, he's a good man. But he's surrounded by old and selfish people. I think we should fight too. When I'm queen, I won't let an assault on the Green Coast go unpunished. Those people in Augustii will one day be *my* people. I can't abandon them."

"You will make a fine queen." Jade approved.

Talia smiled proudly. "Lyla Mer-Song will be waiting at the bridge over the canal. She knows of a ship headed to Seal Island. Go, Crow. Do what my father won't."

Crow wasn't thrilled with the singer's appearance as they left the Gardens. Servants watched them go but none dared interfere, not when the princess ordered them not to. Crow's dragon flew above his head like a winged shadow. Lyla wore a simple cream dress, tied and accentuating her waist with a thick rope. She had a pack on her back and a harp in her hand. "Today begins the greatest song in history."

"We'll be mobbed before we can make it to the docks." Jade frowned, looking at the bustling streets across the channel.

"We're not walking to the docks." Lyla laughed, descending towards the canal, where she waved down a man on a long thin boat. He parked just before the arched gateway that led into the Gardens. He blanched at Crow, Shadow and Tree, bowing. He'd love to carry the Northern Child around the kingdom.

"Take us to the Boiling Pier." Lyla said, jumping into the shallow boat and tossing the man a coin.

When they all got in, the pole boat crawled along the lazy current of the canals. Folk stopped to wave and point at Shadow in the sky. Stilted streets smelled of sizzling chilis and fish, salt and seaweed. Colored fabrics danced upon the winds, hanging from open windows. Some of the canals were so thin that the multistoried homes and taverns built upon the docks leaned forward and nearly touched at the top, shadowing the water. The waters were green in the sunlight, and seabirds filled the air with chatter. Crow couldn't help but glance behind him to see if anyone from the castle was following. The feeling reminded him of the road from Griffin's Peak. He swallowed the bitter taste of anxiety that rose to the back of his throat.

Lyla strummed her harp again. "I haven't been off of the Isles since I was a little girl." She mused.

"You're comin' with us?" Crow squinted. "The princess said you'd hire a ship to carry us off."

"I will." Lyla replied. "But how am I supposed to write the song of the Northern Child if I'm not *with* the Northern Child?"

"There is already a song for the Northern Child." Tree pointed out.

"A song for men, I mean." Lyla corrected. "Just think of it. A song of adventure, magic," she looked up to the sky, "and dragons."

TWENTY

THE BOILING SEA

They boarded *Mermaid's Kiss* quickly. The ship was roughly the same size as the *Wave Song,* with dark wood and black sails. At the ship's bow a crudely carved mermaid covered her lips with oiled hands—forever offering a blown kiss. The captain was a young man, slim and dark as the makings of his ship, with chestnut curly hair that bounced around his long face with every gust of wind.

"You think the king's going to chase after us?" Crow asked Jade as the city disappeared behind them.

"He won't be happy we left." Jade said. "But no one stopped us from leaving the Gardens, so it's hard to say."

Mermaid's Kiss was tied at the Isles' western most harbor, the Boiling Pier, named for the Boiling Sea that stretched out endlessly to the south and the west. *Somewhere out there is Dragon Island,* Crow thought. *And Mermaid's Bay,* where fish-women were heard to lure sailors to their deaths with songs sweet as honey.

"To Seal Island?" The captain, Lorenzo, gave them each a curious look at the start. He held Lyla's stare the longest, and Crow knew instantly that Lorenzo would take them wherever she wanted to go.

"Yes." Lyla touched his arm lightly. "The princess asked me to help them find passage, and you were the first captain I thought of." Crow watched as Lyla squeezed Lorenzo's bicep, and looked away flushed and smiling. Crow scoffed.

"You came to the right man." Lorenzo approved, face tinted with a blush. "Carrying the Northern Child across the sea is my pleasure! But not more than the pleasure of carrying you, my lady."

The sailing was smooth, as had been their luck with each pass across the sea. Crow couldn't help but grow restless on the deck as the days blended together. He was sick of ships and oceans. Once, he'd longed to see the ends of the world. From cramped mountain tunnels, it was impossible to imagine the open ocean. After a while, though, the oceans all looked the same.

Jade and Lyla were offered a separate cabin. But Crow and Tree slept in the crew's quarters. Crow slept restlessly on a swinging hammock that swayed with each wave.

His dreams were haunting him again. The man with the broken face made an appearance tonight, bursting from the ground and grabbing hold of his ankles. Crow reached for his longsword, but before he could grab it, an arrow sprouted from the man's chest, and he fell. In front of Crow stood Lady Kath. She nocked another arrow and aimed it at him, pulling the string taut.

"Who do you fight for?" She asked him.

Crow's eyes watered at the sight of her. "I'm sorry." He murmured, reaching out a hand.

Her eyes hardened. *She's going to shoot me,* Crow realized, and suddenly a great white beast rose from behind his back. It was a dragon the size of a castle with gleaming white feathers, spiraling horns glittering like deadly icicles, and piercing blue eyes. *Shadow,* Crow knew. She pulled her lips back into a fearsome snarl, and before he could stop her, she opened her mouth wide to blast Kath in a blinding blizzard of white.

He woke screaming with Shadow sleeping soundly on his chest.

Crow was grumpy as he nibbled his morning meal of thin bread spread with salted fish paste. He sat on the deck as Shadow flew above the boat, searching the green waters for fish. Tree sat with him, nursing a cup of warmed fresh water. Crow was thankful that the little nymph was content to sit in silence. *They must hear me yell every night,* along with the crew. Tree said nothing about it and Crow hoped it stayed that way.

"Good morning." Lyla appeared, barefoot and in her nightgown, a piece of bread in hand rather than her harp.

"Morning." Crow muttered, crunching on his breakfast. Lyla spent the majority of their ride with the captain, smiling and playing songs for the crew at dinner. Captain Lorenzo doted on her, but Crow could see the falseness in her smiles. *She doesn't care for Lorenzo as much as he thinks,* Crow knew. Each time the young captain turned his back, Lyla rolled her eyes and picked idly at her beloved harp.

"It's a beautiful day, isn't it?" She held her face up to the blue sky, letting her skin soak in the sun. Crow's own skin had turned red and peeling since his visit to the Isles.

"It is pleasant." Tree agreed, despite the obvious sick tinge to their skin.

"Lorenzo tells me we'll reach Seal Island this afternoon, when the sun is at the highest point in the sky."

It was the best news Crow had heard. "Good. I've had enough sailing."

"Truly?" Lyla seemed surprised, but then laughed. "You are from the mainland, I suppose."

"What's that supposed to mean?"

"Nothing." Lyla shrugged. "The people of the Ridge belong to the mountains, the people of the Roam to their tall grasses. But I am from the Green Coast, and we belong to the sea, and the sea is always moving."

Crow quietly chewed on that. "My brother from the Isles was like that. After years with us, he wanted to keep traveling." He eventually said.

"Sounds about right." Lyla replied proudly. "Where did he go?"

"Back to the sea."

As the sun rose higher, the crew prepared for docking. Crow saw Seal Island on the horizon—a small dark hump over the water—and wondered what they would find there. His black leathers cooked in the sun, but the pleasant breeze kept most of the heat at bay. Shadow sat up in the crow's nest, where a crewmember stood. Lyla had on her white flowing gown, and Jade put on her sword.

"Will they welcome us?" Crow asked.

Shadow screamed, and launched from the tower. The crewman yelled a word down to the decks, and the rest of the men exploded into life. As they drew closer, Crow spotted a single ship between themselves and the growing island. It was larger than theirs, narrow with a stem sharpened into a deadly point.

"That's one of the king's ships." Lyla said.

Captain Lorenzo ran up to them, a spyglass in one hand. His face was ashen, eyes wide with fear.

"Tell us what's happening." Jade demanded.

They heard a long loud boom of a horn, carried across the waters from the other ship. Somehow, Crow knew it wasn't a sign of greeting.

"This is madness..." Lorenzo stuttered.

"Tell us!" Lyla urged, her own confidence shattering.

"It's—it's one of the king's ships, aye." Lorenzo whimpered. The crew emerged from below decks wearing toughened leather and carrying extra oars. "But—but the crew..."

Crow already knew, even before Jade snatched the glass from Lorenzo's hand and stood at the front.

"The crew are feln." She said. "And they've seen us."

Twenty-One

The Boiling Sea

Their crew were few. Only two of the men wore the lightweight armor of the Isles, the rest were in tough working leathers. They only had a handful of rusted swords and spears customarily kept on deck to ward off thieving ships, but nothing appropriate to take on an army. Oars, poles and ropes were sought by those with nothing. Lyla was tossed a pole and caught it in trembling hands. Her usual easy confidence leaked away, leaving a scared girl in her place.

As the captain, Lorenzo had the best weapon: a spear long and sharp and pointed. He tried to keep his demeanor calm. His word was law on this ship. *He's never been in danger like this.* Crow felt afraid, his heart pounded and his palms sweat, but his mind was oddly clear. The crew looked to Lorenzo for guidance.

"We—we must try to outrun them." His voice cracked.

The lines were tugged, sails spun and oars dipped. The ship turned, churning up foaming water. Crow saw the folly in their flee. *We're not fast enough, and we've got nowhere to go.* The king's ship had already seen them, and was gaining.

"Have you never seen a king's ship?" Lyla voiced, frantic. "We won't make it." Her hands shook. "They'll catch up. Oh, our Mother, keep us safe..."

The horn sounded again.

Jade held her sword, Tree stood by Crow's side, and Shadow was thrashing her wings up in the crow's nest, screaming her response.

"What do you think?" He asked them quietly, holding his own sword in two hands.

"I think the gods want the Northern Child to fight." Tree said sadly. "The waves brought us here."

"Lyla is right, that ship will catch us." Jade whispered. "For all we know, it could be lightly held. But look at the crew and the captain. See their faces. They're afraid."

"We're all afraid." Crow whispered back.

"Aye, but their captain has already given up. The feln will catch us, and each of these men know it. We will need everyone to fight when they sail us down."

Shadow screamed again; the wind rose. He could feel her eagerness, covering his own fear like a blanket. She knew they were being hunted and was angry about it. He let her anger smolder in his belly.

"Dragons do not run." Tree whispered. "Nothing hunts a dragon."

"Lorenzo has already failed." Jade murmured, shaking her head. "We need to fight. You're ready, better than the men on this ship. Lead them, Crow. I could turn them, but it must be you." Their ship was nearly turned around, but their enemy was already gaining on them.

"Lorenzo," Crow shouted, "tell your men to take up their oars and prepare to ram the ship." He made sure everyone could hear him.

The captain looked at him like he'd grown two heads. "Are you mad?"

"No. I just want to live." Crow swallowed and tried to look brave. "The feln will catch us, and if that ship hits us first, which it will, we will sink to the bottom of the sea like stones. We're *men*. We don't run from nothin—anything." Crow's words turned a few heads. "If they're going to catch us, let *us* hit *them*. Let's crack that ship in two and take them down with us!"

"Aye!" Jade raised her sword. A few of the crew nodded as well, feeling shamed by the bravery of a boy and a woman.

"These are feln in your waters." Crow added. Perhaps it was Shadow's anticipation he felt, or the invincibility of youth, but he was nearly drunk from the prospect of battle and glory. This was no game of war he'd played with his brothers, pickaxes and torches in hand. He held steel now. "We pushed the feln to their island winters ago. And now they think that we'll run from them. We should remind them—remind them who we are!"

"Aye!" The crew raised their weapons.

"A-aye." Lorenzo swallowed.

"We are Vitania's children!" Jade cried. "Our Mother will protect us from these goddess-less beasts!"

"Aye!"

"We have a dragon!" Crow thrusted up his sword. Shadow launched herself from the crow's nest, swooping down and unlocking her jaws to blast ice so cold that the tips of Crow's hair frosted in white. The sight of her sent the crew into a frenzy. The ship was his.

"Here's a song for you." Jade smirked, knocking Lyla on the shoulder. She stood stock still and ashen.

The ship was turned again. The green waters churned beneath them, the winds began to rise, and clouds gray as mountains rolled into the sky. Tree looked up at them, and held up their hands. "The gods will give us the wind." They said, and began to sing.

Their voice lifted as the wind howled. The black sails filled with air and thrust them forward. Crow's hair blew wildly about his face.

The sea frothed from green to gray, mirroring the sky's angry complexion. Seal Island lay in the distance, growing larger with each gust of wind, a green and black beacon among a graying world. King Talio's stolen ship foamed in the water, the black sails snapped in the wind, the oars dipped into the water to try and turn her, but the feln were working against the gale. Crow could see them now, their armor dark and burnished as they ran about the deck. *These are no sailors.* Crow heard their voices yelling in a gruff ugly language. A language that had been unheard for generations. King Talio's ship was crafted to slice effortlessly through the water, but it floundered in the hands of an uncoordinated crew.

The men on *Mermaid's Kiss* worked in unison, drunk on the same elixir of glory and fear.

"Brace for impact!" Lorenzo shouted.

Lyla clutched her pole and began to pray, Tree held the rail but continued to sing, Shadow spun around in the air—her eagerness nearly intoxicating.

"Crow," Jade said, grasping her sword and kneeling. Crow followed her lead, ready for collision. "Remember, you hold a two-handed weapon. You don't have a shield. Be conservative with your strokes, let them come at you, dodge and wait for an opening. When you see it, make sure your hit is the only one you need."

He nodded, unable to find words.

Crow heard the impact before he felt it. Like lightning coming from the sky to smash them all. The jolt nearly knocked him to the ground, shaking his frame and pounding through his bones. Like a landslide that hit too close, the entire world seemed to shake before settling into a stomach-churning sway of ocean spray and wind. They'd done it. They'd slipped around the side of the ship and smashed into her midsection. Both ships were locked in a deadly tangle of splintered wood. *Mermaid's Kiss* took most of the damage. They needed to abandon her before she slipped beneath the sea.

Jade was first to her feet. "Good Land!" She cried.

"Crystal Isles!" The older men regained themselves and followed her, but Crow's joints seemed locked in place.

Tree ran past him, pulling Lyla to her feet. "Come," the little nymph told the crying singer, "the ocean will swallow this boat."

"We're dead..." She whimpered.

"Our song does not end today." Tree locked eyes with Crow, the world continuing to sway.

No, it doesn't. Standing, with Shadow swooping above his head, he charged.

King Talio's ship was in chaos.

Feln ran around on the swaying boat. But in their armor, they looked almost like men. A few were sprawled about the deck, taken unawares from Lorenzo's retaliation. There weren't as many as Crow had feared, but most were properly armed and armored in their oily black garb. Crow's eyes darted around the scene: there was a feln among the splintered wood lying still and bloody, a man was already dead, and Crow caught sight of Jade dodging a curved felnish sword before driving her own deep into the enemy's belly.

The pounding of approaching steps matched the rhythm of his heart. Crow whirled around and brought his sword up just in time to block a deadly downward blow. It was a female. Her helm was lost, blood soaked through her stringy white hair and ran down her pointed ears. Crow's mind went blank, and his body began to dance to the song of steel.

He thrust her sword away, remembering Jade's advice and letting the feln try at him again. Dodging right, he allowed her another go before hopping out of the short sword's reach. Crow and the feln were the only two creatures in the world. The swaying of ships, Jade, Tree and Lyla, Shadow, all of it disappeared. The dance of life and death *was* his world—always had been—and he dodged her blows again and again. One wrong step and he was dead. His leather was tough, but not tough enough to guard against a sharp weapon.

Finally, an opening. *Square your feet, now.* He aimed his blade for her chest, but she clumsily parried it away. *Again, while she's off balance.* He feinted right, she struggled to regain her footing and dodge, but he caught her. Grunting, Crow shifted his weight and brought his sword up from the left, the blade buried itself in her neck. She slid to the ground, staining his steel red. Crow had no time to celebrate his victory before another feln was on him, and he began the dance again.

This one was easier; his opponent was tired and wore tough leathers instead of armor. Crow's sword burst through the feln's chest like tender meat. Time for another.

At one point Crow felt like his limbs were moving on their own. He laughed as the high of battle pumped through his veins.

The next feln had his back turned, his dagger buried in the eye socket of one of their crewmen. Crow's sword sliced the enemy nearly in two.

How long has it been? Did time still turn? As the blood fever continued, Crow's senses stayed tangled on the edge of his blade. Blood was slick between his fingers, causing his grip to slip. It was on his face as well, and ran warm down his arms.

A blunt oar smashed Crow upside the head. Falling, he caught himself on the deck and rolled just in time to avoid a skull cracking blow. His massive sword slipped from his grasp, and he was too busy avoiding the smashing oar to pick it back up. No longer was he the bringer of death, but instead a boy rolling on a blood-soaked ship, scrambling for his life. Another corpse blocked his way as he shuffled to the right. *Lorenzo.* The captain stared up at him blank and unseeing. The feln picked up Crow's discarded sword and raised it.

The roar halted everything.

"Shadow!" Crow screamed.

He'd been so bloodthirsty that the dragon had slipped his mind. Maybe she'd stayed out of the fray, but now she came down; fierce and lustful.

The feln had been yelling to each other in their ugly language since the ships had collided. But this word, it seemed, was the same in both felnish and Frukjeran. "Dragon!" They yelled, and the feln above Crow's head paused to stare up at the sky with eyes the size of chicken's eggs. Shadow bolted out of the sky; jaws wide open. Crow shielded himself from the frozen blast, but the feln wasn't quick enough. The enemy blocked the brunt of her attack with a bronze-clad arm—which froze solid as a block of ice, white and frosted and permanently shielding his face.

Jumping to his feet, Crow pried the blade from the feln's frozen fingers. Shadow's wingbeats fluffed the hair around his face as he kicked the feln down, cracking the other's fingers open. It took all of Crow's strength to wrench the hilt from the feln's grasp as the creature writhed on the ground and screamed. Without hesitation, Crow brought the sword down on the feln's arm, and it burst into hundreds of shards like it was made of glass. The meat from the jagged stump left behind was already black and dead. Shadow landed upon the feln's chest and ripped out his throat.

Crow stumbled away. Bile spewed from the back of his throat and onto the deck.

The dance of battle left his mind foggy. The fighting continued around him in slow motion, his ears felt clogged. Did he hear a trumpet in the distance under all this suffering?

The dark wood of the deck swayed beneath his feet. The deep brown planks were awash red with blood, poured from corpses littering the ship. Shadow was at his feet, guzzling the dead feln's throat. Lorenzo next to him, six puncture wounds marred the captain's chest. Crow didn't let himself linger on Lorenzo long. Turning, he saw a ragged chunk of the ship had splintered off into the churning open sea. *Mermaid's Kiss* was gone, swallowed by the deep ocean as gray as the rolling clouds above them. *I'm exhausted,* he realized as he brought his sword back up.

Many of the crew were dead, but the few that still stood were now armed with the looted weapons of their enemies. *We're outnumbered,* Crow despaired. There were three feln for every man. Some were rooted in place after seeing Shadow's savage attack. But Crow saw hatred in their ugly red eyes.

The clouds continued to roll above them, stirring up the ocean into spiked waves of gray and white. The black sails of Talio's stolen ship were expanding full of air, following the howling will of the wind.

To his relief, he spotted Tree and Lyla, who stood between two crewmen brandishing spears. Lyla's green eyes stared back at him in horror—her white gown spattered red. Jade was near the rail, covered in blood and smashing two feln at the same time. *I have to keep fighting,* Crow thought as he watched her. Jade's sword flashed through the air, touching flesh in a deadly kiss.

"Shadow!" Crow called. "Go to Tree and Lyla!" He was exhausted and he would need her, but he needed to know his friends were okay too. Shadow eyed him with a red snout but understood. She launched herself from the dead thing's chest. *I've sent these men to die, I can't let them die for nothing.* With Shadow aiding his friends, he joined the fray again.

Before, it had felt like Vitania was controlling his limbs herself, but now every stroke was a struggle weighed down by stones. Each thrust left his muscles screaming. His heavy sword required a price for each swipe, and the price was his strength. The glory he'd found just moments ago had left him. At one point, he stepped the wrong way, and would have been shortened a head if not for one of the crew stabbing a dagger through his combatant's back.

Crow heard the clash of steel from where Jade fought. She had slain one of the feln and still danced with the other. It was another female holding a short sword and shield. She blocked each of Jade's taps with ease and was pushing Jade back with every step. Jade kept herself on the defense, conserving her strength and allowing herself to be goaded toward the shattered rail. It would mean death to fall over the side, but she allowed the feln to push her. Crow didn't understand what she was doing, until at the last minute, Jade released all of her strength.

Jade had lulled the feln into false security. She drove her sword into the other's side, not to slice through armor and flesh, but to push the slender female with a force strong enough to switch Jade's precarious position off the rail. The feln smacked Jade in the face with her shield as she scrambled for purchase along the torn wooden planks. Jade reeled back, dropping her sword, blood spurting from her nose. Crow started forward, but Jade recovered fast—grabbing the feln's shield as she teetered off balance and shoving it with the force of her anger. The felnish female fell...but not before grasping at Jade's ankle on the way down. The enemy slipped and disappeared over the side, taking Jade with her.

Jade hit the deck with a hard smack before sliding over the edge, her hands scrambling for something to hold.

She would have been swallowed by the sea if Crow hadn't reached her in time. Diving, the deck flew up to meet his chest but he hardly felt it. Instead, the pain ripped through his arms as he caught Jade's wrist. She would have dragged him down too if it weren't for a body giving his legs something to grip. *She's too heavy!*

Beneath Jade the water was a foaming beast, hungry for blood. She scrambled for any kind of purchase on the ship's slick side but found nothing. Her dark eyes were full of fear, and for once she looked like a young woman rather than a battle tested ragged foot knight. Crow screamed; the muscles of his arms felt like they were ripping from the bone.

"Let go!" She screamed, despite the fear etched in her expression. "Let go! You'll kill us both!"

I won't! He didn't have the strength to speak. Jade swung beneath him; she rotated her wrist in his grip. *She's going to make me let go!*

Footsteps pounded the deck behind him, a trumpet sounded somewhere, and a blast of icy air laid across his back like a frozen blanket. A feln fell to his right, face blue and swollen. Crow's hands were wet with salt water, and Jade was slipping.

"Let go!" She yelled again. Were those tears in her eyes? Or just the ocean?

Then, someone grabbed his middle and heaved him back onto the ship. His screamed rivaled Shadow's as his arms carried Jade's weight with him, and dragged her back onto the deck as well.

It was one of the oarsmen from *Mermaid's Kiss.* He offered Crow a curt nod before picking back up his stolen sword and running off. Crow didn't have the energy to get to his feet. With Jade back on the boat, his strength ran dry, and even the thought of picking up a sword seemed impossible.

That trumpet again, he thought through the haze of exhaustion. Its shrill shriek pierced the air. Shadow wheeled above his head against the gray sky. The ship was a bloodbath, filled with dead white feln and dark men of the Isles. Lyla and Tree were running for him, a dirk in the singer's hand and an oar in the nymph's. Jade had regained her footing, and the few feln remaining yelled to each other in their strange tongue.

Then he saw them.

Sails black as night coming onto the starboard side. Trumpets and drums sounded, and flags flapped wildly in the wind. *Green,* he saw, *green and blue, with a black seal in the middle.*

The crewmen cheered, Lyla looked ready to faint, and Jade took up her sword in a victorious battle cry.

The feln saw their cause was lost. These were not allies of theirs. Crow saw one feln shove a sword in his own belly, and another two jumped into the sea. Shadow landed next to him, her few white feathers tipped red with blood. She stood tall on her hind legs and roared.

Seal Island had come to their aid.

Twenty-Two

Seal Island

The ride to Seal Island was a blur. With the fever of battle leaving Crow's body, details were hard to recall. He remembered men and women swarming him, pressing bandages to wounds he didn't feel. Tree and Lyla were at his side, receiving the same treatment. Lyla's white garments were spattered red, and her face was ashen from shock. Tree sat silent, staring at the rising island with melancholy eyes. *The violence upsets them,* Crow knew. He wanted to reach out and take Tree's hand in comfort, but his arms hurt too much to move. *Does the violence upset me?* Crow wondered. He stared down at his bloodied hands, too exhausted to feel anything. Meanwhile, Jade held a cloth to her bleeding nose, explaining what happened to the captain. She seemed to be the only one in her right mind.

Seal Island was a mass of black rocks carpeted in green moss. Thin grassy plants slipped through the cracks in the dark stones. The difference between this harsh island and the Isles was night and day. The Crystal Isles held soft sand beaches, rainbow flowers and tall palm trees, while Seal Island stood before them as a mass of black sharp rock and roaring angry waves. An ancient volcano gave birth to this island, Crow heard someone say, and the stones themselves still held that ancient heat. Seals as large as horses baked themselves upon the coastal cliffs. The beasts raised their great gelatinous heads and barked at them as they sailed in.

The edges of the island were speckled with fishing huts and farms holding chickens and goats. The castle sat on top of a tall jagged cliff that shot high into the sky like the blade of a black knife. It was a modest stone castle, with three stout towers spattered with bird droppings and lichen. The colorful flags of the Wind-Surfers snapped in the wind from the towers' crowns. It was a steep climb to the castle, and the journey reminded Crow of the carved paths and stairways of Griffin's Peak. The island's main port clung under the castle's shadow, crowded with trading posts, inns and shops. Only a few of the structures were built from wood, most were crudely piled rocks. Crow's eyes darted around the empty port. "Where is everyone?" He asked Lyla. The singer shrugged.

Walking to the castle was as hazy as the ship ride. They were offered donkeys to carry them up. Crow managed to offer his own donkey a thankful pat, his arm smarting in pain. At first Shadow frightened the donkeys, but once they sensed she was no threat the ascent went smoothly. Their practiced hooves had traveled this path a thousand times before, which was for the best since Crow's arms still hung like limp weeds. He wouldn't have been able to properly steer the animal if he'd tried.

"Duke Willemio saw you coming." One of their escorts said. "He'll want to feast you, but would like to see you well rested and cleaned first. He's heard of you, but didn't think you'd come to the island."

Crow breathed in a salty sigh of relief. The last thing he wanted was another meeting with the nobles.

The keep of the Wind-Surfers was humble but well provisioned. Rather than getting dragged to the duke's company, they were given to their chambers where a fire was started in the modest hearth and a bath was brought up. Crow's room was the largest, he learned, holding a double bed, reading table and large window facing the eastern sea. A carpet of spotted seal skin covered the stone floor, and tall wax candles were lit upon the wall sconces. A worn copy of *The Written Word* rested beside the bed. Lady Jade and Lyla were given the room next to his to share, and Tree's was further down. Even the crewmen were offered hospitality as befit their service for battling the felnish ship.

A serving boy brought up Crow's bath with steaming pails of hot water. The salty breeze left the room lofty and cool. The boy gawked at Shadow, who sat in the open window like a black and white gargoyle. "If-if it would please you, sir, let us wash the blood from you." He said.

"I'm no sir." Crow huffed. The idea of someone else washing him felt awkward too, so he had the boy leave and thanked him for the bath.

The water soaked his skin and joints like a soothing warm blanket. Crow leaned into the tub and groaned, throwing his head back and allowing the tension to leak out of his joints. After several seconds he reluctantly took up the rag. Crow ran it over his new scratches, grinding his teeth at some of the more sensitive parts. *I don't remember getting sliced so much.* Soon the water ran brown and red.

"Come here, Shadow." He called. Shadow glided over and perched on the basin's side, chirping and ruffling her feathers as Crow ran the cloth over her to wipe away the mess. The soft feathers had continued to crawl up her body and wings. A ring of snow now bloomed around her eyes. Her horns—which used to be small clear nubs—already appeared sharper and as long as Crow's pointer finger.

Pink and clean, Crow dried himself with a towel when he heard a knock on the door. Before he could answer, Lyla made her way in.

Their eyes met for a heartbeat before Crow tossed his towel at her; mortified.

"Get out!" He screeched, face burning hot.

Lyla, who had only caught a glimpse, quickly shut the door. "Sorry." He heard her murmur. "I can come back."

"No, it's fine..." Crow grabbed the underclothes left for him and pulled them on. They were soft and plain, a welcome respite from the tough leathers he'd taken from the Gardens. He let his heart rate calm and tried to wipe the blush from his cheeks. Clearing his throat, he called out, "You can come in now."

She entered almost shyly, a bizarre contrast to how she usually appeared. She wore a simple green gown with large blue pins lining the middle torso. It hugged her frame tighter than her usual white garb. *Her eyes look nice,* Crow thought before looking away. He folded his towel at the end of the bed.

"Does Jade want me?" He asked.

"No. She's bathing."

"Oh. Tree, then?"

"No."

Crow frowned, and Lyla sighed, eying his dirty bath water before plopping down on his bed.

"You going to write 'bout—about my bath water?" He asked.

"No." She didn't take her gaze from it, though. Suddenly, tears sprung from her eyes. "I don't want to write about that." And then she was crying.

Crow watched from where he stood, muscles tight. He didn't know what to do. He'd never comforted someone before...let alone a woman. All he could do was stand in place and watch as tears ran down her cheeks and snot dribbled from her nose. His palms sweat. Crow's eyes darted to the door. Should he leave?

"He's dead because of me." She whimpered. "I knew he'd take us; I knew he'd take *me.* I just wanted to write a song. I wanted to make something, but all I've done is make a ghost."

"Lorenzo." Crow breathed.

Lyla nodded. "If—If I didn't convince him to take us here, he'd still be alive. Him and all those men..."

Crow sighed, he sat down on the bed, far from her, feeling too strange to reach out. He knew how she felt. "You can't—you can't think like that." Jade's words from before, and now he was wielding them.

"It's easy for you to say that." She wiped her eyes.

"I'm the one who wanted us to attack the ship." He offered.

"Don't try that." Lyla shook her head. "It would have come to battle either way. Even I saw that. It's my fault..."

"I know that's how you feel." Crow swallowed. "I know exactly how you feel. But you—you have to accept what happened. Lorenzo was killed." Lyla flinched but he continued. "He died honorably." *That's what Jade would say.* "You didn't shove the sword in his chest or nothing."

"I might as well have." She looked to him now, eyes glassy like fresh due upon a field of grass. Crow thought of Kath making her last stand as the centaur ran at her. "You really suck at this." She added, wiping at her tears.

Crow's ears burned in embarrassment. "This isn't some stupid song, it's real life. You should've expected people to die." He snapped.

The fire crackled in the hearth.

Lyla sprung up. Bright flames of anger burning in her eyes. Crow looked away, immediately feeling rotten.

"I don't think Lorenzo *expected* to die." She spat, getting up to leave. "Forget it. I came in here thinking you'd understand." She wiped furiously at her face. "But all you care about is yourself."

Crow scrambled up, beating Lyla to the door and blocking her way. A large chunk of him wanted to let her go. Why should he have to comfort her?

But he remembered how alone he felt on the *Wind Song*. He'd isolated himself, and would have been swallowed by the dark guilt that threatened to drown him if Jade hadn't pulled him out. Growing up in the Lads, Crow and his brothers rarely shared how they felt to one another. They buried their abandonment in the caves they worked. Only now was Crow beginning to realize how that had blinded him from understanding other people.

"No—look, I'm sorry. I shouldn't have said that." Crow said quickly, halting Lyla in her tracks. He looked anywhere but her face. "I do suck at this."

"You do." She crossed her arms.

"I meant it when I said I know how you feel." Crow told her Kath's story. He almost started to cry too, but managed to hold back his tears. He told her of the centaurs, of how he turned and ran before he saw her die. Of how he blamed himself. "If it weren't for me, she'd still be alive too." He whispered. "I don't know what to tell you to make it better. But don't let the thought of Lorenzo bury you, otherwise his death will be for nothing."

Lyla swallowed. "I'm sorry that happened to you." She whispered.

"Kath told us to sing for her before she died." Crow murmured, gazing at the floor. "After, all I wanted was to be alone and suffer for what I thought I did. Most nights, I dream of her. But each day, I think she fades a little." He looked into Lyla's eyes. "Lorenzo's dead, aye, but you can make him immortal. You're a singer. So, sing for him too."

Lyla stood quietly for a long moment. Shadow flew to the window, watching birds race across the clearing sky. The bath grew colder, and the fire crackled idly in the hearth.

"How long will it take to get easier?" She sighed.

"I don't know." Crow replied honestly.

The servants gave Crow proper clothes to wear: a black tunic with a deep blue over shirt, and a pair of black trousers with blue waves sewn onto the pant hems. The clothes were a bit snug, but seemed presentable enough. *They love to dress me in their colors.* They also brought him a plate of goat cheese, hard bread and seal blubber. The blubber looked like a greasy pad of butter. Crow wrinkled his nose at it, but ate it anyway. It was fatty and slid down his throat like slime, but added a richness to the bread. Once he was finished, the servant told him that Duke Willemio had summoned Crow and the others to his private chambers.

The door to the duke's study looked like every other in the castle: simple driftwood with a brass knob in the shape of a seal. Inside, Duke Willemio sat at a round oak table, surrounded by shelves of scrolls and tall waxy candles melted from use. The study was small compared to those in the Gardens, it was no larger than Crow's own room, but it felt elegant with the hanging tapestries of sailors lining the walls and rugs of silver seal hide carpeting the floor. The study smelled like old paper and salt. The duke was older than Crow expected, with weathered dark skin and graying hair shaved short. His eyes were silver like the close-cropped beard that clung around his full lips. Old as he seemed in his ornate green and blue robes, his eyes were alert and sparkled with wit. He sat with his champion, who wore the light armor that Crow had come to expect from the men of the Green Coast. A strapping youth only a few winters older than Crow. He reminded Crow of Shadow.

"No dragon?" Duke Willemio raised a brow. "And here I was so eager to see it for myself."

"She's hungry, so she's out over the sea hunting." Crow said. Shadow stayed behind at his open window, and Crow knew she was eager to find food. Even now, he felt connected to her, and didn't worry about her whereabouts. She'd return to his chambers once she had a full belly.

The duke nodded. "We're familiar with dragons here, they roam over the Boiling Sea and can often be seen on the horizon. Their island isn't far, although I must say, ice dragons are something entirely new." He stood. "But I see you brought the next best thing: a nymph! It's an honor to house you. I'm sure you're used to men gawking at you by now."

"I have never felt more impressive." Tree shrugged. That brought a smile to the man's lips. He offered them a seat.

"As you know, I'm Duke Willemio Wind-Surfer. This is my champion, Sir Juan Harpoon-Wielder. And you, I've heard, are Crow the Northern Child, his knight Jade Threu of Good Land, Tree the nymph, and..." He looked at Lyla with a raised brow.

"I am Lyla Mer-Song. A singer from the Crystal Isles." Lyla straightened her back proudly.

"A singer." Duke Willemio seemed pleased. "Good, we shall need a good singer for the celebration on the morrow. We will get to that later though, please, please take a seat."

"How do you know so much about us?" Crow asked as he sat.

"Rumor spreads fast from sailors. But," the duke said, "I also received a letter. Only our Mother knows how the riders and ships were able to deliver them, what with the current climate of things. Juan, bring it here." The champion handed Crow a folded piece of parchment, weathered and yellow. Thankful for his lessons, Crow began to read it.

War is upon us. Glorygradus has joined forces with Griffin's Peak in mobilizing against the feln. Let us show this self-styled queen what happens when men join kingdoms as they did in the Conquering Age.

We are made in the Mother's image, and thus, Mother Vitania has offered us a gift in this fight: The Northern Child. A boy with a dragon. The knight who smuggled Queen Charlotte across the Pond of Serpents told us about him. She traveled with the Northern Child and his champions for a time. As queen of Glorygradus and the West, I implore each duke and king to deliver Crow to us. Let us rally the largest army in Frukjera with the goddess's Chosen as our warrior. Deliver Crow to us, and we will end this war before it can truly begin.

Queen Joanna Usario, Protector of Glorygradus and the West.

Crow's hands were shaking near the end of the letter. He handed it off to Jade, who took it eagerly. "She's alive," Jade breathed, "safe and alive."

"Aye." Duke Willemio said. "We received another letter from Lady Gretchen giving us more detail of you, and we've been able to corroborate it with the accounts from sailors and traders alike. Rumors spread like fire. You're the talk of the world."

She made it. "Be brave and keep that cloak nice for me." She'd said. Jade read the letter with a toothy grin; it wasn't often that Crow saw her so happy. Even Tree, who often seemed so detached from the emotions of men, broke into a smile.

"I'm sure Lady Gretchen has some insight on this traitor queen." Duke Willemio continued. "Last we heard she'd taken up residence in Youngston. Queen Joanna may be keeping some things close to her chest. Tell me, what have you seen on the mainland?"

Crow glanced at Jade, and he replied with the scant information he had. The disappearances on the roads of the Ridge, the corpses in the Jumping Trout, and King Arthur's call for banners.

"It seems like your king wants to stay out of it." Jade said.

"Aye." Duke Willemio's eyes narrowed. "The feln have taken our sister city and he's sitting in his Gardens with his tail between his legs. You saw how the feln sailed around here; we took down one of their scouting ships not long ago, but not without heavily damaging our own. With King Talio's decree to limit my fleet, I don't have many ships to spare."

He doesn't care for his king, Crow thought. "That's why we're here." He said. "We want to fight for you, for Augustii and Youngston."

"I'm surprised King Talio sent you here." The duke said.

"We sent ourselves." Crow gambled.

"Did you?" The duke folded his hands. "And should the king order your return?"

"Knowing Talio," it was Lyla who spoke now, "he will." She crossed her arms. "But he will not force your hand. Even losing Augustii wasn't enough to rouse him from his seat. It was his daughter and heir, Princess Talia, who bid us leave to help her people."

"Princess Talia is not the king; he may look negatively on us should he call forth for you." The duke said. Lyla pursed her lips and sat back.

"She's not the king." Lyla allowed. "But she will come into her kingdom and remember how Seal Island once stood up for her people. In fact," she leaned close, *this is like a game to her,* "the rest of Frukjera will remember. King Talio's in no position to fight with his own duke.

He sent his men to Augustii and lost. He will not risk wasting more men."

It was what the duke wanted to hear.

"I see." Willemio leaned back, rubbing his stubbled chin. "Queen Joanna summons you. But she is no queen of mine. King Talio will write to me in due time, hoping you are here...tell me, Crow, what do you want to do?"

"You are willing to ignore your king?" Jade cut in.

"Bugger the king." Duke Willemio spat. "He taxes my island and bans my ability to build ships. And in exchange for what? Protection? I don't even have that. But you, you've proven your bravery to me. So, I don't care what Talio wants. Tell me, what is it that *you* want to do?"

Crow already knew. Lady Gretchen awaited them in Glorygradus and the queen in the West wanted to fight. The vision of Man's Wall returned to him, stronger than ever.

"We're going to Glorygradus to join the battle. I am fighting for men." For Kath, for Greg and Paul, for Garrett and his daughter Wanda, and for Lorenzo too.

Duke Willemio smiled. "Then Seal Island will stand behind you."

A feast was in order. On the morrow, Duke Willemio announced a celebratory banquet in honor of Crow and the crew for defeating the feln in their waters. The dining hall was prepared for the guests, while tables and stands were set up for the commons outside the castle. Word traveled fast through the small island, and already folks were flocking the docks and lower courtyard. Crow opened the window, watching them mill about outside. The duke was right, a feast seemed to boost the morale of the people. The streets were clogged with folk in preparation, and the island looked more alive now than it did when they'd arrived.

Shadow chirped from the feather bed. Crow smiled and joined her. Stretching her serpent-like neck, she placed her head in his lap. Her feathers were soft as down. *She'll be white by spring,* he suddenly felt foolish for naming her Shadow.

The fish had been feeding her well. It never ceased to amaze Crow how large she'd grown. Her horns were quickly turning to sharp deadly icicles. Crow wrapped his palm around one, half expecting it to melt. In a flurry of motion, Shadow shook his hand off and snapped her jaws. Her teeth missed his fingers by a hair.

"Hey!" Crow yelled. "No!"

Shadow pulled back her lips in a spitting hiss. Curling into a tight ball, she turned away from him. She was angry too. Shadow had always been proud, although now that she was getting bigger...*I should read that book that Tree took.* Crow was confident in his reading, though writing was still hard and his lettering was atrocious. It helped that Tree was a patient teacher.

Crow felt that he should visit the little nymph, he'd hardly seen Tree since the battle. It already felt like it was days ago, rather than just hours. Tree always remained quiet in their meetings with the noble bloods. *What do they think of all this?* Crow hopped out of bed, ignoring Shadow's sulking form.

Tree's chambers were close by. Crow walked down the hall, rounding a corner before almost smacking into Jade's chest.

"Sorry." He grunted, staring at the pitcher in her hand.

Jade flushed. "It's good to drink after a victory." She muttered, sloshing the pitcher of wine.

Crow could feel the unspoken words passing between them. Jade's gaze darted anywhere but his face. "I was actually about to come find you." She said.

Crow felt her embarrassment like it was his own. "You don't have to thank—"

"What you did was stupid." Jade hissed. She caught herself scowling and quickly adjusted her expression. She sighed, crumbling for a moment, "But...also brave. Thank you, regardless. You saved my life, Crow, and I owe that to you."

"You saved me from the River of Song. Just consider us even." Crow replied, offering her an awkward smile. She smirked at that.

"I remember. Listen," Jade's face was suddenly serious, "you're a good lad. And I- I couldn't ask for a better friend to fight by my side."

"Friend." Crow repeated. It was the first time he'd ever heard Jade call him that. He felt a giddy glow in his belly.

Jade smiled, raising her flagon of wine in a mock toast. "Care to join?"

"I was actually looking for Tree." Crow said. He felt embarrassed. Receiving compliments from Jade felt like witnessing a goat fly. Weird. Jade nodded.

"I'll leave you to it." She seemed almost relieved. "I think Lyla needs this wine more than I do."

Crow found Tree in their chambers, wearing the red cloak that was gifted to them from the Wind-Songs. Tree's room was much smaller than his own, but still held a nice feathered bed and tall candles for reading. The window was narrow, built less for a view and more for defense. Regardless, Tree was enjoying the fresh air, their hair ruffled in the salty breeze. Tree's few belongings were sitting on a small corner table: the book of dragons and their pouch filled with dried plants.

"Hello." Tree greeted.

Crow nodded. "I might need to start reading that dragon book."

"Oh?" Tree cocked their head. "What happened?"

Crow told them about Shadow. To his surprise, Tree laughed, a light lilting sound—like bells chiming.

"Perhaps you should." Tree said, taking up the book in their hands.

"What if she gets out of control? She's growing bigger, I need to learn how to train her."

"That is part of the problem." Tree shook their head. "That is why men never learned dragons. They cannot be trained. They are not dogs or horses. They are equal to you. You must respect her with dignity if you wish for her to respect you. There is something in your blood that binds you together, but if you raise your hand to her as a man would another beast, she will not work with you."

"And it says all that in the book?"

"Somewhat." Tree opened it delicately. "Although most is just observation on natural behavior—still useful. The nymphs that lived close to dragons knew their songs the best. Some of their knowledge lies in this book as well."

"Did you ever talk to the nymphs from the south?" Crow asked.

"No. They were chased away or killed by the feln."

"What do you think about the war?" *War.* The word frightened him, but filled him with giddy excitement as well. "That woman calling herself the Queen of Winter, why would she say that?" Crow was more troubled by her title than anyone else seemed to be.

"I think that this is a war that never truly ended. This queen seems strange to me as well, I am not sure why she would want to align herself with the feln. But men have always enjoyed ruling over others." Tree shrugged. "I do not understand the blood lust that plagues so many creatures of this world. But I will fight with you, Crow. The gods have chosen you, and I am glad they did. But you must not lose sight of yourself, or what the unicorns have in store for you. The blood and greed will cloud your vision, you have to remember the unicorns."

"Man's Wall. They showed it to me. It must be because they want me to join Queen Joanna." Crow resolved. *Why else?* Tree seemed unsure, but even they had to agree their next move laid in the West.

Twenty-Three

Seal Island

The day tapered into a quiet evening. Crow supped with Tree in their chambers. Shadow was out at sea—a black and white ghost against the darkness, and Jade and Lyla kept to their own quarters. Crow's dinner was a juicy piece of goat thigh drowned in butter and spices, paired with a side of salty sea greens. He'd missed the taste of goat, it brought him back to the dining hall of the Lads. Tree drank from a glass jug of spring-fed water and ate some dried sea nuts. They spent the night talking by candlelight about dragons and unicorns. Tree had Crow practice reading out loud from the dragon book, but he could barely string a paragraph together. Eventually, Shadow returned with a full belly and scales slick with sea spray. She greeted Tree and Crow with a chirp, and Crow knew that their short spat from earlier in the day was all forgiven.

Gray clouds and a chill wind swirled in the morning sky. *For once, it feels like winter is coming,* Crow thought as he sat up. His serving boy brought him boiled eggs and salted sardines for breakfast. He ate them thankfully. It was still strange to be waited on. The rest of the morning carried on with little word from the duke. Crow wandered the castle with Lyla. She was excited to sing at the feast, and though her eyes were still haunted, Crow knew she'd be okay.

He was shoved back to his bedroom as the feast grew closer. By that time, the entire castle bustled with people and the scent of roasting meat and frying fish was heavy in the air. Crow paced his room, excitement and anxiety buzzing through his body and mind.

"Will your dragon be there?" His servant asked, laying clothes for Crow on the bed. "Folks have seen her hunting in the sky. They run from their homes and watch the whole thing. We've seen dragons here sometimes, but never ice dragons."

"Yes, I'll have her with me." Crow said. He'd seen the entrance hall of the castle where the celebration would happen, and though it was small in comparison to the Roost or the Gardens, Shadow would fit fine in the tall lumber rafters. He wanted the noble blooded and small folk to see him with Shadow by his side. Then maybe he'd look like a proper warrior instead of a growing boy.

Crow's outfit was laid across the soft mattress. "The duke had these quickly altered for you." On the bed were pants white as snow, they flared out at the calves. A belt of soft black leather with a silver clasp wrought as a dragon was looped through the top. Black boots matched the belt, and the servant unfolded a shirt soft as silk, white as the pants and reminiscent of the flowing loose tops of those worn in the Crystal Isles. Snowflakes were sewn with bright blue thread across the puffed sleeves, joining together at the collar. The boy then gave Crow a sash of the same shade of blue to put across his shoulder, and then was told to buckle his longsword to his back. Crow had his servant leave to get dressed, too awkward to let the younger boy do it. He ran a boar hair brush through his hair, pulling the wild strands out of his face when he was done. *My hair's almost to my shoulders,* Crow noticed when he saw his reflection. He looked almost like a prince. Reaching out, Crow lightly touched the noble boy staring back at him. His fingers shook.

"Who made these clothes?" Crow asked his servant when he came back in.

"Duchess Teresa. When she heard you were here, she was up all night with thread and needle."

I'll have to thank her. Crow nodded, stood up straight and swallowed the knot in his throat.

The common folk were already celebrating in the castle's courtyard. Wine and ale flowed freely, bread was given out by the loaf, and fatty seal steaks, fried fish and boiled seaweed were filling their bellies. Crow could hear the songs and laughter from his window. His heart thumped with excitement. He'd never been invited to a true celebration before.

He was escorted with Jade, Lyla, Tree and the remaining of Lorenzo's crew. Shadow flew with them, hovering low over their heads, lazily circling the length of the hallway. Jade was back in steel; she'd polished it last night. Her sword clung to her back, silver pommel gleaming in the firelight. Tree looked like a bright flower in the drowned hall, their hair fluffy and yellow, bronze clips in the shapes of palms kept the bangs away from their large green eyes. Under their bright red cloak, they wore golden small clothes, plain but elegant. Lyla returned to her usual gown of white, synched this time with a thick belt of black rope. Her pile of curly hair was collected into a thick bun atop her head. She held her silver harp.

"Crow," She said when she'd seen him, "you look quite handsome." She smiled. "You'll make all the ladies swoon at the sight of you." Crow blushed in reply.

The music, smells, and voices intensified as they walked. "Everyone is already in attendance." Their escort said. "Duke Willemio wanted the Northern Child to arrive later so everyone could see the dragon fly in." The double-doors that lead to the castle's great hall were nearly bursting from the sound of lute, drums and singing. Muffled laughter knocked against the door. The smell of food and smoke seeped from the cracks. Crow's heart thumped in time with the music. Shadow came soaring from behind.

"Open the doors." Crow said.

Shadow burst in before them. The hall grew silent for a brief moment, every eye upon the dragon in the rafters. Then, in a wave as deep as thunder, the crowd roared. Cheers rang, drinks slammed on the table, and hands pointed in wonder to the ceiling. Shadow screamed; Crow felt her excitement like a buzzing current through his veins. She landed high in the wooden beams, her tail lashing the smoke that collected up there. Torches and candles steamed the hall; men and women clogged the benches sitting side by side. The doors at the entrance were opened, and filled with more people scrambling to see the spectacle inside. Despite the chilly weather, the cool wind that blew in from the opened doors was a welcome respite from the heat of the packed hall.

When Crow entered the cheers started anew. "Smile." Lyla said at his side, and he did. There were so many faces, Crow didn't know where to focus. But when he lifted his arm to wave, the people screamed again.

"Hero!"

"Dragon tamer!"

"Feln slayer!"

It was almost absurd. *They're screaming for an orphaned boy.* Crow wanted to laugh.

The duke stood and all grew quiet. He was at the center of the long table, his champion sat to his left, and to his right his lady wife. The seats next to her were empty.

"Our Mother above used the sea to bring this warrior to our island." Duke Willemio said. He introduced them with theatrical gusto, telling an exciting story of the felnish ship going down, ice encasing the splintered wood as Shadow tore at feln and Crow plunged his sword into the enemy captain.

"That is not what happened." Tree whispered.

"Let the man embellish the details." Lyla whispered back. "The crowd loves it."

Jade set her mouth in a hard line. "Lyla's right. It's not the truth, but people will rally harder for a more exciting tale."

Men and women were going wild, knocking their cups against the tables with each thrilling detail. As Crow and his friends were escorted to their seats, the duke held up his cup in a toast. Crow brought his own up, and knew he was expected to say something. He let Shadow's excitement blanket his own anxiety. Closing his eyes, he felt the heat from the hall collecting in the rafters, the smell of sizzling meat and live prey outside, and an insurmountable amount of pride that *he* was prey to nothing. When he opened his eyes again, he stood proudly.

"I'm not fighting for a king, or a queen, or a kingdom. I'm fighting for you!" Crow looked to the rest of the folk outside. "They may have dressed me up like some noble lad, but I won't forget who I am, and who I want to fight for! The feln think they can take what is ours, but I am the Northern Child! And I say we shall take what is *theirs!*" Shadow flew from the rafters and landed on the back of his chair. She was almost large enough to topple it over, and barely fit upon the arched back. Stretching out her wings, she roared.

The hall went wild. Crow felt like he was on top of the world. *They're cheering for me.* He drank deep from his cup. The ale slid thick and bitter down his throat.

Food and drink flowed liberally. As Crow drank, he found that the ale didn't taste so bad after all, and that he quite liked it. It heated his cheeks and left him feeling giddy. Food was brought out on giant platters; Crow had never eaten so well in all of his life. First, they were served salted oysters still in their shells over a bed of salt and seaweed, then came lamb steaks soft as butter, grilled red fish flaking from the bone, and seal belly so fatty that Crow thought he'd start sweating blubber. Shadow sat in the rafters above the smoke of torches and candles. Sitting to his left was Tree, who had grown a taste for the sweet red wine favored among the women. "Men make better drink than songs." They hiccupped. "But Lyla does have a wonderful voice."

It was true. The singer had joined the rest of the musicians at the left of the duke's high table. Lyla sang songs to match the merry mood. Songs like *The Mermaid's Lover*, *Sailing the Boiling Blue* (Crow liked that one most), and *Salty Mateo*. All charming and upbeat, the men and women of the hall sang along in drunken bliss. Crow wished she knew *Wanda the Wonder*, perhaps then he could sing along as well.

To his right sat the Duchess Teresa. Dressed in green and blue, she appeared like a dark mermaid. Her coiled black hair was oiled and tied in thick box braids that ran to her shoulders, woven with pearls and seashells. Her hair clicked with each turn of the head. With some ale in his belly for bravery, Crow thanked her for the lovely outfit.

"The thanks should be coming from me." She said, sipping her wine. "We've been a scared and desolate place as of recently. The feln were in our waters and our pleas to the king fell upon deaf ears. You've given us hope again. You, your nymph and your dragon."

"The dragon and nymph aren't *mine*." Crow corrected. "They're my friends." He looked to Tree, who was chatting with Jade.

"Either way," she nodded at the merry folk below them, "they will tell their children of this day for years. 'The day the Northern Child came,' they'll say. You should have your singer friend write that. She has a lovely voice."

Lyla gained attention from a lot of the young men in the hall. Crow even noticed Duke Willemio's champion staring, only to look away flushed when she caught his eye.

Crow drank some ale. "I'm glad Seal Island understands. We were...nervous after King Talio." *The ale's making me talk too much. Be careful around these lot.*

"Aye." Duchess Teresa pursed her lips. "I'm sure my husband let you know how he feels about that."

Crow nodded.

"I'm from Augustii myself. My father was on the small council of Duchess Fahlia Palm-Weaver's father. It's a beautiful port town. The houses are pink, yellow and blue. Roofs are tiled with sea shells. Palm trees drop coconuts on the beaches, and the grasses are tall and full of tiny lizards." She smiled; eyes lost in her old home. "Augustii is a formidable stronghold, the northern wall is strong as most, but the people of the Green Coast are not made to battle upon the land. The feln came in the night; it's said, from the shadowed forest in the north. I was not surprised to find out Augustii fell."

"The king said he sent ships."

"He did." She allowed. "We saw them off here. We even offered some of our own, as is expected." The duchess nursed her wine. "I don't know if the feln have some kind of godless magic, but the ships never returned. The ships that *have* were captained by feln. Our messages for help have gone unanswered, until you arrived."

Crow remembered hearing how Seal Island had once risen against the Rope-Ringers. "It's not right for the king to leave you defenseless." Crow muttered. He thought of Greg and Paul, *"This is my queen."* Greg said about his boat. *"And Young's River is my king."* Respect for the royals didn't run deep among the commons. But could he blame them? Crow certainly didn't hold any love for the Arrowheads. They only called on their people to start another Petty War for more territory. Crow had lived in Griffin's Peak all his life, and only saw the king once. *And when I did, I back-talked him and got a bruise for it.* Stone Teeth was the one to raise a hand to him, but even then, King Arthur chose not to reward them. Stone Teeth's ominous words that night rang in his head. Crow found himself wondering again what the leader of the Lads had meant.

The pounding drums and lilting fiddles stopped. Their silence was replaced by the lyrical melody of Lyla's harp. The talking of the hall quieted to a bubbling murmur. The music was sweet and slow and echoed off the stone walls. Lyla began to sing. Her voice sounded sad and haunting, as enticing as sirens lost at sea.

> *"Young and strapping boy of mine,*
> *To sea he dances the waves so fine.*
> *I held his face as he said to me,*
> *'Wait on the shores,*
> *My dearest.*
> *I will be back on the tide of the moon,*
> *Do not weep, I will be home soon.*
> *I am an adventurer*
> *My shield is my youth.*
> *Do not weep, my dearest.*
> *I am an adventurer*
> *My shield is my youth.*
> *Do not weep, my dearest.*
> *O' Captain my sweet I bid thee farewell,*
> *Your last journey awaits*
> *On this ocean's swell.*

O' Captain my sweet please return to me,
I'll meet you again
On the open sea."

Lyla's eyes were glassy with tears, as were Tree's and half the women in the great hall. The singer bowed, and the folk applauded.

"Lovely." The duchess whispered.

Crow caught Lyla's eye, and raised his glass to her, offering her a smile and nod.

Duke Willemio seized the moment of silence. He stood up, clanging a dagger against his horn of ale.

"As we know," he began, "the feln have taken Augustii, and run a rampant plague across Frukjera's mainland." Hisses and jeers followed the news. "Our king sits a coward in his flowery keep, as his women and children burn!" Men thumped their horns against the table, the common folk outside screaming their agreement. Crow felt lightheaded from the ale, but the severity of the duke's words still weighed him down. People in Griffin's Peak could get their tongues ripped out for speaking slander against the king. Duke Willemio's words were borderline treasonous. Tree seemed intrigued by the man's speech, and Jade sat rigid by the nymph's side, careful not to show her thoughts. "It will not be said that Seal Island sat idly while our brothers and sisters were slaughtered! If our king will not help his people, then we will follow someone who will! Stand, Crow, Northern Child."

Crow rose to his feet.

"Unsheathe your sword."

Reaching behind his back, Crow scraped his long sword from his scabbard. It showed off the torchlight and was heavy in his grip. The duke waved him over, and they stood in front of the long table so they could be seen by the masses. Crow's heart jumped in his throat.

"Queen Joanna Usario is raising her army of the West to flatten the feln to the ground. Seal Island will join her, and deliver the Northern Child to the front!" The cheers nearly shook the walls. It was then that Crow knew what was about to happen. He'd dreamed about such things long ago when he was young and stupid in the darkest tunnels of the Peak. "Kneel before me, Crow, and give me your sword." He felt as though his body were controlled by a puppet master. He had to savor every moment. *I'm kneeling a boy.* The tip of his longsword tapped on his shoulder as Duke Willemio Wind-Surfer said the words, bringing the point over his head and to the other. "Before our Mother Vitania, and the people of my stronghold, you have knelt a young man of Griffin's Peak. Now, rise as a knight. Rise as Sir Crow, the Dragon-Tamer!"

He rose.

Twenty-Four

Cregan's Mark

A moon had come and gone since Crow was knighted in the long hall of Seal Island. He stood at the bow of *Sweet Melody,* Duke Willemio's prized ship, as the wind tore at his hair with harsh chilled fingers. It was cold despite the warming waters of the Boiling Sea. *Winter at last,* he thought. Cregan's Mark rose to meet them against the green waters. It had taken them a fortnight to reach it. Crow's previous luck with smooth sailing finally ran out. Their journey was plagued by storms and ripping winds. They set out with seven ships; the most Duke Willemio could afford without leaving his island defenseless. It'd taken them fourteen days to prepare to leave. Men and boys old enough to fight were mobilized to pack the decks. Crow trained harder than ever, and sat in on council with Willemio and his most trusted knights. Crow liked the Wave-Surfers. Willemio cared deeply for his people, sending left-overs from feasts to the commons and filling his council with men and women from all walks of life.

"As much as I wish to rush Augustii, we do not have the men, not without the Isles." The duke said. "Our priority will be to connect with Queen Joanna."

"Aye." Sir Juan Shell-Cracker, a grizzled old knight with tight black skin and silver hair, agreed. "With our forces combined, we will squash this felnish uprising before it can truly begin. They'll be forced to abandon Augustii before winter's end."

"What of you, our duke?" Sir Taeto Swift-Dancer, a strapping youth who held a spear like a singer held a harp, wondered. "Will you be joining us?" His features were soft but held an edge that only wit could hone. His hair bounced around his head in loose light brown curls.

"No." Willemio frowned. "Though I wish I could, I'm not as strong as I once was. The remaining people here will need their leader. And should we receive word that Augustii is ours once more, I would like to sail there myself with my lady wife to take it back."

Not in the name of the king, though, Crow thought.

Their plan was straightforward. Queen Joanna was assembling her army of the West in Glorygradus, behind the impenetrable Man's Wall. Seal Island would meet her there, sailing to Cregan's Mark and traveling north to Riverset, where the waters of the Blue Vein would carry them. They decided to leave as soon as possible, though there was more preparation to be made. Duke Willemio already received two messengers from King Talio, asking for the whereabouts of the Northern Child. Not only that, but the men of the Bay—the lands of Harold's Holding—were also ready to march. They were waiting for Seal Island's small army and the "dragon warrior" to join them.

The war plans were exciting. Perhaps it was inexperience, or youthful stupidity, but Crow itched to be on the road to battle. The road to glory. He expressed as much to Tree in his chambers one night.

"I wish we'd sail now." He said. "I want to see the knights in shining armor and giant war horses with streaming banners. I'll be on the front lines I bet, with Shadow by my side and we'll kill every feln we see."

"Do not forget what the unicorns have shown you." Tree said.

"I know, I know. They showed me Man's Wall, and that's where we're headed. This is what they want me to do." He insisted. Tree's solemn words dampened his mood, but Crow made sure to listen to the nymph.

Sir Crow, he tested the name on the night before their departure. Shadow was curled at his side, nearly taking up the entire feather mattress. She was almost the length of Crow now, though most of her was neck and tail. *I'm a proper knight.* His younger self would be proud of who he'd become. Crow thought about Bones, of his brother who'd also never stopped dreaming. He wished he could return to him now, and tell him everything that's happened. *When this is over,* his lids slid closed, *I'll find him when this is over.*

That night his dreams carried him high above Griffin's Peak in the wooden mining baskets that crossed the city's sky. The kingdom lay beneath him, quiet and peaceful in the night, flames flickered in every window. Asleep.

Then he heard the roar.

The dragon descended on it like a white demon. Huge. The great snowy wings swallowed the stars as it passed overhead, before sinking great crystal claws into one of the stone griffins of the Roost. The dragon was so large that it dominated the summit of the Great Claw like a feathered avalanche. It roared again, shaking the mountains. Crow struggled to hold onto his basket as it bucked wildly. "No!" He screamed, spotting a small figure on the beast's back. Their armor was white and polished so fine that it shone like the moon in the night. Raising an arm, the figure pointed to the sleeping city below. The dragon opened its jaw, and bathed the kingdom in ice.

Crow woke to his servant shaking him.

The dream still haunted him, even as they arrived at Cregan's Mark two weeks later.

"I have had enough ships for a lifetime." Tree said at his side. Crow smiled at that. This ship was much larger than the others they'd sailed on, with multiple cabins and oarsmen, but that didn't make it any easier for the little nymph.

"Me too." Crow admitted.

Cregan's Mark was the northernmost stronghold of the Bay, the territory of the Harold family. The Bay was a small chunk of land, nearly an island. A thin natural land bridge connected it to the mainland of Frukjera. Crow watched the bridge grow before them, a great cliff of stone with swirling waves beneath. Cregan's Mark sat atop like jagged scales across a lizard's back. It was the only other city of the Bay. Towns around here tended to fall prey to dragon flame. Dragon Island lay not far to the south. In fact, they'd seen a dragon a few days into their journey.

Crow was called up from his cabin early that morning and shown a tiny speck flying across the southern horizon. The captain gave him a spyglass to see what it was. Through the glass, Crow glimpsed a snake, with feathers red as crimson. For a moment, Crow was afraid that Shadow would race out to meet it. To his relief, she stuck closer to the boat that day.

"She is no fool." Tree said. "Dragons of ice and fire are as different as the seasons, and neither wish to mingle."

Shadow flew along the water's surface now, just a hair's breadth above the salty waves searching for prey. Her white feathers ate up the entirety of the black scales on her wings, tail and snout. Splashes of obsidian still remained on the ridge of her back and flank. Spanning the length from tip to tip, she was larger than most dogs, and looked a formidable predator. Crow watched as she dove beneath the waves, disappearing for no more than a few seconds before she burst back into the sky with a fat silver fish in her jaws.

"So that's Cregan's Mark." Lyla joined them, arriving from below after hearing that they were landing soon. "I've never been on the mainland before. It'll be strange to be away from the sea."

Crow nodded. "When I first left the Peak, I'd never seen an open sky. It seemed to stretch on forever." He said.

"There's so much mystery out there. Seems like a waste to never leave our corners of the world."

"There was a time when I thought I was meant to stay hidden away in the mountains." Crow murmured, staring out at the churning waters. "I can't imagine that anymore."

Lady Jade and the others were soon upon the deck. She seemed to enjoy the company of the knights that Duke Willemio sent along, even if Sir Juan started out a little stiff toward the woman. He'd watch her and Crow spar with harsh skepticism. "It's not right for Vitania's daughters to be swung at by a man." He'd say to Crow privately. But he softened when he heard of Crow and Jade's travels, and the bravery of Lady Kath. Sir Taeto Swift-Danger was less concerned with Jade's gender and more with her skill. Being of age with one another, he looked forward to having a new companion to duel. The two couldn't have been more different. Built like a brick wall, Jade's fighting stance relied on devastating two-handed blows. Meanwhile, Taeto was slender and fluid as he danced around, poking here and slashing there. The two were surprisingly evenly matched. Jade paid great attention to Taeto's movements, and would block each stroke before waiting for a mistake so she could rush in past his spear's point. Sometimes she made it, other times Taeto was too fast and would have killed her two times over. He reminded Crow of the man from the champion melee all those years ago. Crow expressed as much to him after a day of sparring.

"It doesn't surprise me that such a man won." Taeto said proudly, as if it were him. "A spear is the perfect weapon, and preferred by those of us from the Green Coast."

"A spear is only as good as its wielder." Jade quipped, she turned to Crow. "Remember, if you wield a spear, you better hope your enemy doesn't get past the tip. Once they do, you're a dead man."

Jade took Crow by the shoulder now. "I'm sure the duke will want to meet with us to call a council. Make sure you're ready."

"Another council." Crow gagged. "I'm ready."

Docking at Cregan's Mark was a challenge due to the wild waves that ate away at the rock, but the crew on all the ships were experts and managed the landing well enough. As expected, the port was bursting with people who had heard news of the arrival of the Northern Child. Crow waved at them, feeling only slightly awkward as they cheered and pointed to Shadow in the sky. He was escorted with the others from their boats by a collection of guards to keep the crowd at bay.

Jade wasn't wrong about her predictions. The duke requested their council immediately. Cregan's Mark was a narrow city, made of black and gray stone and cobbled streets. A brisk breeze blew through that smelled of sea salt. The city was walled in from the north and south gates. If someone wanted to pass from the West to the Bay, they'd have to move through Cregan's Mark first. The duke's keep nestled in the center, ringed in with another thick wall black as night. The castle itself was squat and thick, made up of four round towers. The Boiling Sea and the wild Foam Water clashed beneath the city.

They were brought directly to the council chambers. Shadow stayed outside, flying around the castle's towers. "Should we call her in?" A guard asked Crow.

"No." He felt her hesitation, and knew she didn't want to be squeezed into a narrow hall or chamber. "She'll find my room when we're done. She won't wander off."

There were much more castle folk here than Seal Island, and Crow soon learned why.

When they entered the council room of Duke Cregan III O'Mark, they found him sitting closely with another man almost twice his age. Duke Cregan was still young at twenty-five winters, he had thick brown hair and a matching beard. He wore a gray tunic with a sewn seagull spreading its wings on the right shoulder. Crow recognized the white seagull on a gray field from all the flags that flapped outside. Surprisingly, the duke wasn't sitting at the head of the table, but instead to the right of an older man.

The man at the head was dressed in shining mail. A sandy brown cloak streamed from his shoulders clamped with golden rings. A clenched fist was hammered into the breastplate of his armor. He was thick of shoulder and neck, with yellow hair, streaked silver, tied in a long braid down his back. Sparkling blue eyes snapped up to regard Crow with a curious gaze. Crow's party kneeled immediately. Crow followed after them in a clumsy fashion, his heart nearly jumping into his throat. *Of course,* he thought, glancing up and spying a simple golden band across the man's brow. *The king of Harold's Holding.* He couldn't recall the name because he didn't really know the name of any of the royals, but the band was as much a giveaway as anything.

Crow bit the inside of his cheek. He didn't seem to have a great track record with the kings.

"You may rise." The king said, and they did. The only one who hadn't kneeled was Tree.

"We have the pleasure of hosting King Arnold Harold of Harold's Holding. We thank the Mother for bringing you here safely." The duke rose and bowed, offering them each a seat at the large round table. Maps and handwritten letters littered its surface. A few men and women occupied the other chairs, council members and champions.

"It's an honor." Crow parroted, sitting between Jade and Tree. The obligatory introductions were said around the table. Special attention was paid to Tree, as expected, but other than that, there was not a moment to waste.

"We apologize for bringing you straight here." King Arnold said. "I'm sure the journey left you weary, but war doesn't wait." The word hung in the air

"We're surprised to find you here, sire." Sir Juan said.

"We made an alliance with Glorygradus. I'm sure you saw how packed Cregan's Mark is, we are marching up to join the queen's army, and I wanted to march with my men. Harold's Holding is in the trusted hands of my daughter and heir."

"A noble thing." Taeto nodded.

What a true king would do, Crow thought, his mind wandering to King Talio sitting in his Gardens.

"We have news from the Roam." The duke said. "We thought it best to share with you while it's still fresh." He wore a grave expression. Crow waited with baited breath. The last he had heard; King Arthur was marching on Youngston. "King Arthur reached Youngston only to find it abandoned and ruined. The feln...they put the entire kingdom to the torch. *'Only ashes and bones remain,'* he wrote. The feln must have learned that Griffin's Peak was coming for them, and that they couldn't win. The king reported that he'd managed to capture a few prisoners, but the self-styled Queen of Winter wasn't among them."

"Were they put to questioning?" Jade asked.

"Aye. But they gave nothing away. King Arthur took the kingdom back and plans to camp there before his next move."

Crow wondered what had happened to Wanda.

"There's also the matter of Fisher's Mark." King Arnold said. "The farms around the stronghold fell to the centaurs. The centaurs have grown bold since the feln invasion. We have no proof that they are in alliance, but it cannot be ruled out as of yet. Luckily, the beasts cannot swim, and most of the men and women that escaped behind Fisher's Mark's walls are safe. Right now, the Roam is in ruin, but with the feln retreating back to their island, it will not take us long to gain it back."

"Any word from this queen?" Sir Juan asked.

Duke Cregan nodded, and King Arnold shook his head in anger.

"Foul woman, traitor." King Arnold spat. "She wrote to my daughter shortly after we marched. *'A new Conquering Age begins,'* she wrote. As far as we can tell, she's a cowardly woman who kills innocents and runs back to that ruined island once the true warriors appear. She may think she has won one battle, but the feln do not strategize, and a war isn't won by raising a kingdom to the ground and leaving behind the ashes. My people have fought dragons, we can fight these creatures as well. Nymph, or Tree as you are called, do you know more than us about these beasts?"

"I am surprised by this human queen's leadership of the feln. The feln of old had no royalty, but instead warlords who won their title by brute violence." Tree said.

"All this is known, yes."

"But we cannot assume the feln will fall. I have not seen a feln in many winters, and do not know what has happened to them on their island. Accepting a human leader means they will think more like you do. It is a dangerous thing."

"If you stick an animal in a cage and do not tend to it, is it surprising when it turns feral?" Sir Juan injected.

"They seem to follow the queen blindly." The duke said. "Even when put to...less savory questioning, the prisoners refused to give any whereabouts of her. It appears this woman knows her history. The siege of Youngston and Augustii, they're using our ways to fight against us."

"We should have rid them from the world the first time." King Harold muttered. "You, lad, you've been quiet."

Crow balled his hands into fists. "There was a man whose daughter lived in Youngston during the siege. He asked me if I could find her and tell her to write to him. When do we fight these monsters?"

King Arnold laughed and Duke Cregan smiled.

"Ready for blood, this one." Taeto smirked.

"We march at dawn." The king said. "Which is another reason we brought you straight here. I'll want you and your companions with me towards the front of the march, it'll be good for the men to see you."

March with the king? Crow may have shuddered at that in the past, but he was a knight now. He belonged at the king's side. Crow nodded.

"I was hoping to see your dragon with you." King Arnold confessed.

"She's outside the castle. Every day she grows larger, small places make her uncomfortable."

"She won't wander?" The king asked.

"No." Crow said with certainty.

"Good." King Arnold smiled. "With our Mother's grace, I hope she keeps growing. And raises an appetite for feln."

TWENTY-FIVE

THE WEST

Crow was shaken awake as the sun peeked over the horizon. They'd march after their first meal. The night before, he'd been feasted again. *I'm getting good at riling men up,* he thought as he remembered raising up his glass as the Northern Child last night. The great hall was filled with soldiers rather than nobles, and Crow liked their rowdy company much more.

He put on his tough black leather underclothes and had a serving boy help with his armor. The armor was heavy and uncomfortable to wear. He didn't understand how Jade basically lived in it, and yearned for the light flowing chainmail of the Crystal Isles.

Boiled eggs, fried bread and five thick slices of bacon swimming in grease awaited him at breakfast. He dined with Tree, Jade and Lyla in his chambers. Once they were done, they'd get rushed off.

Crow's appetite had left him, but he forced the food down his throat.

"It's amazing that we're marching with the king." Lyla said excitedly. She'd traded her white gown for brown riding clothes. Crow thought she looked quite nice despite how plain they were. "Imagine it: rugged men who've kissed their wife goodbye for the last time. They'll carry small drawings of their daughters in their armor." She sighed.

Jade rolled her eyes. "I'm surprised you're coming."

"Of course." Lyla replied, seeming offended. "This is my song and I must see how it ends."

Tree nibbled at an assortment of mushrooms and nuts. "I am just glad that we may walk on land."

Crow, Tree, Jade and Lyla departed Cregan's Mark with a blessing from the duke and a priestess before they were ushered towards the front of the column with the king and his escort. They were mounted on horseback with countless other knights and soldiers surrounding them. The most common men marched behind on foot, a never-ending sea of folk who cheered and roared whenever Shadow passed above. At first, the young dragon spooked their horses to near frenzy, but Tree sang a pretty song and the horses soon calmed. The mounted soldiers praised the little nymph, calling them Vitania's gift. Tree accepted the praise awkwardly.

They left Cregan's Mark by the north gate; the land of the West stretched out before them.

Crow never learned how to ride properly, save for his short time upon Little Traveler's back. He was given a beautiful white gelding with a flowing mane gray as smoke. The saddle helped him keep his balance, and the gelding followed along the other horses without need of direction. Crow let the horse walk where it wanted. Shadow soared above. Crow could feel the dragon's anticipation mixed with his own. There was a sense of adventure in the column. New lands, and for Shadow, new prey. *One day I'll ride her,* Crow hoped, *and I'll see the world like I did from the heights of Griffin's Peak.* His heart fluttered in his chest.

The road from Cregan's Mark split in two, one led further west to the cliff-edged coast, where the city of Crab's Cliff braced against the rolling Foam Water, and the other led inland north, to Riverset and the great river called the Blue Vein. The roads were paved with neatly cut stone and wide enough for ten horses to walk side-by-side. "This is the biggest road I've ever seen." Crow marveled.

"Welcome to the West." Jade said from her black stallion. "These are the richest and oldest lands conquered by men. The other kings of Frukjera control no more than three strongholds, while Queen Joanna rules over five." It was true, even at the other side of the continent, the lowly boys of the Underground Lads knew about the splendor of the West. Glorygradus was the crown jewel of it all.

The road to Riverset reminded Crow of the Roam, with fields of tall grass, wild flowers, and wheat. The sky above them rolled with dark gray clouds, and a chilling wind blew in from the north. The great road was dotted with empty hunting shacks, and far-off farms with baron fields and abandoned paddocks. *The farmers have run,* Crow thought with a chill. Ahead of them, the king rode with his champion and guards in heavy armor and brown cloth banners. Crow and the chosen from Seal Island were just behind, with an endless stream of men at their tail. There were riders sent ahead to scout, Crow knew, and he wished he could be one of them. He wanted to see the land first, without a massive crowd in front of him. He looked up to Shadow again.

"I will get to see the world from a dragon's back." He murmured.

"You may want to learn how to properly sit a horse first." Jade jested.

Crow frowned. Shadow screeched and flew off ahead of them. "She's hungry."

"She'll need more than fish to fill her belly now." Jade said warily.

Watching the dragon's pale shape sink over the fields of wheat and grass, Crow thought of his dreams. The giant white beast that swallowed cities in ice.

Tree reined up beside the two knights. "Winter will touch us soon. The wind sings of the seasons to the north." Tree's words rang true, another harsh wind whipped at the sides of Crow's face.

Their march continued through the afternoon. The clouds stayed thick, and the weather grew colder. Crow's stomach growled loudly as his horse plodded on. He felt Shadow's return before he saw her, and knew the dragon had found prey somewhere in the abandoned fields. The men cheered at her arrival. As they marched, the grass grew brown and dry, long passes of uninterrupted plains slowly changed to a landscape smattered with tall pines and oaks. Small hills humped across the horizon and trees punched into the sky like long guardsmen. The pines were still green, but the others had long lost their leaves and now stood bare.

With the sun hidden by the clouds, evening rushed up to meet them, and the boom of trumpets sounded through the lines to let everyone know it was time to make camp. Crow kicked his horse to follow as the front of the column disbanded from the road to set up a short way off. His stomach rang hollow, his body ached from riding in heavy armor, and he wanted nothing more than to sleep. He'd never marched in a war column, though, and rest was far from his grasp. The king's tent, more a canvas castle in truth, was erected—a large sprawling thing that would be protected by the groups of tents surrounding it. Due to their rank, Crow's tent wasn't too far, and mingled with that of the high knights and champions. Tree tended to their horses as they dismounted, and their companions from Seal Island began to assemble the black canvas shelter they'd call home until Riverset.

Lyla stood with Tree, brushing her white mare and complaining of her sore legs.

"A soldier's camp is no place for a woman." Grumbled Sir Juan as he threw a few wooden rods in Crow's direction. Crow caught them with arms that felt like stones.

"That so?" Jade asked from where she'd already erected her own small tent.

"You don't count." The old man spat, and Crow laughed.

By the time they set up their sleeping arrangements and had a fire going, it was well into the night. Tree helped Crow out of his armor. He settled in a dark woolen cloak with silver thread trimming. The fire and heavy clothes helped keep the chill at bay, but as his breath puffed from his lips, Crow was reminded that winter was here. "A few weeks out of Griffin's Peak and I've become weak." He joked to Tree. He shivered, patting Shadow's cool head from where she rested on his lap. The dragon had come down to coil around him once the camp settled down.

A thin broth of onion and carrot boiled atop their flames. The camp buzzed like a great hive. Fires blinked in the darkness as far as Crow could see. Different smells wafted through the air, and men talked loudly. The whole thing was exciting. Crow felt a warm glow of brotherhood between each man, a feeling he thought he'd lost when he ran through the gates of Griffin's Peak.

A boy came around with chunks of beef for their simple broth. After separating some broth for Tree, Crow added it and waited for the meat to cook and tenderize.

The soup was greasy and hot, and filled Crow's belly with some much-needed heat. He listened as Sir Juan told them about how he'd nearly drowned when Seal Island rebelled against the Crystal Isles. "I made the mistake of wearing heavy armor, even though the battle took place on the slippery decks of ships." He said. "That's the stupidity of youth for you, lads. I thought there was no way I'd slip beneath the waves, and it nearly killed me."

"You wore heavy armor on a warship?" Taeto laughed.

"Now listen here," Juan fumed, "I've fought in a hundred melees, boy, and a Petty War besides." He sighed. "But, aye, it's true. It was ignorant of me. King Talio was but a young pup when he took the throne, and the Wind-Surfers were done being controlled by a king from some far away isle. That's why Seal Island rose, we'd seen the kings upon our shores maybe once every ten winters. Why should we be ruled by someone who never sees his people? Our true ruler was Duke Willemio Wind-Surfer. Let King Talio Rope-Ringer have Pointer and even Augustii if he must, but Seal Island is its own.

"We knew the king would send ships after us, and we were prepared with our own, we lured the king's larger boats to the thrashing cliffs bordering the island. I felt nearly drunk on the prospect of war. 'Our Mother's on our side,' one of my companions said. The day was warm and cloudless, but the sea was thrashing as it usually did. The king's ships came over the horizon, and we waited."

"Was it the crash of the ship, or a man that did you in?" Taeto asked.

"Some lad half my age. I shoved my spear in his belly, but the fool actually pushed further into it to knock me off! No one is half as strong as a dying man; don't you forget it. Right before Vitania takes us home, she gives us a taste of her immortal power."

"So then, who pulled you from the water?" Crow asked.

"Sir Rieko Fish-Finger and a few lads under his command. He died last winter, that old grizzled bastard." Juan shook his head, but still smiled at the memory. Crow thought it strange to laugh at nearly drowning. He remembered nearly drowning in the River of Song and never wanted to experience it again. "I sank like a stone when the water met me. For a moment, I tried to swim but it was useless. By the time I thought of unstrapping my armor, I was nearly at the bottom. Have you ever imagined your lungs catch fire? I imagine it feels the same as drowning. I can remember the first swallow of sea water... I gasped for air, and the ocean felt like molten lava in my throat. I don't remember the second swallow or the third...our Mother is kind and took those memories from me. The next thing I knew, I woke on the sand, Sir Rieko beside me with three other men. Our ships were smashed against the rocks and the beach, we underestimated the king's response."

"One of my brothers from the Isles said the king was kind to allow the Wind-Surfers to rule after that." Crow said.

"Aye." It was Taeto who spat now. "But they took away our ships. The Rope-Ringers have always been cowards. They knew that if the Wind-Surfers were stripped of power, the whole island would rise again."

"The Rope-Ringers are an ancient and noble family." Lyla defended.

"They would rather hide in their Gardens than fight for their people."

"Princess Talia sent us here." Lyla said. "She cares for her people. She will make a brilliant queen."

"A queen over the Crystal Isles, but not Seal Island. Why must we continue to follow these ancient kings who stay hidden from their people?" Taeto glanced at Crow.

Crow nodded. "They never did much for me." He agreed.

Lyla huffed. "I'm going to bed."

The rest of them stayed near the fire for another few moments before also retreating to their sacks. "We resume training tomorrow, but today, we'll rest." Jade said as she stood from the fire. Crow sat with Tree and Shadow until the flames burned to embers and the light of distant campfires were blotted out.

The warmth from the soup and liveliness of camp left as well, and Crow felt chilled to the bones. "I'm surprised you're still up." He said to Tree.

"And I you." The little nymph replied. "It is cold, but I want to sleep beneath the open sky tonight, to be with the gods."

Crow looked up to the sky.

"Does it feel strange for you to be on the march to war?" Crow asked. "Nymphs are so peaceful. Even when the feln started burning the woods, you didn't fight them."

"It weighs heavy on my heart, yes." Tree said. "I do not wish to see so much bloodshed. But," Tree frowned, "my people's inactions have led to the end of the unicorns, weakening the gods. I do not agree with war, but I also do not agree with what we have allowed to pass."

"We'll be fighting against the feln soon, I think." Crow said.

"Yes. But the unicorns chose you. We are marching to Man's Wall, as they have shown you. It gives me comfort that we have not lost their vision."

Crow idly stroked Shadow's glistening feathers. "I still don't understand why they chose me. But I know I'm meant for this. I can feel it." As he said the words, he knew they were true. He was never supposed to stay plugged up in those mines.

"There is something special about you." Tree whispered. Crow scoffed, leaning back on his palms. He dragged his gaze from the sky to Tree's face.

"I guess." He said, his face hot. "But, how did the unicorns know?"

"Unicorns are not the same as us. They are messengers of the gods."

"Until they were killed." Crow frowned.

"Yes. They hold magic unknown to all of us, but they can still be killed. Anything can be killed."

Another icy wind rolled from the sky, and it sent another chill down Crow's limbs.

"Do you think it has something to do with my parents?" Crow was thinking out loud now, speaking not only to Tree, but to the thoughts in his head. "I never knew them. I was dropped off with the Lads before I was five winters old." He continued. "Bones and I used to pretend our parents were heroes traveling distant lands. Or maybe a king who dropped us off to keep us secret. Bones was abandoned really young too. It was easy to make stuff up, because why else would someone abandon their son? As we got older, I realized it was dumb to wait for someone who'd never come. But now..." Crow sighed, and his breath left his lips in a mist of moist air. "...what if they were hiding me? What if they knew? I know it might be stupid, but what are the odds that I found Shadow's egg?

"I don't want to hope, but what if my parents are out there? What if they hear about a boy with a dragon and know it's me?"

He felt Tree's hand rest on his shoulders.

"It is not stupid to hope." The wind rustled Tree's hair. "Sometimes hope is all we have."

Twenty-Six

The West

The days grew colder as their army crept north. A trumpet woke the men at dawn to begin their march. Crow's legs had grown tough from the long days on horseback, they always ached less than the night before. Three days into their march, he'd been invited to a meeting with the king. There was no news from the Queen of Winter, but they'd be reaching Riverset within six days' ride. "I hope that dragon of yours is hungry for feln." King Arnold said. "Our scouts have reported scorched farms and corpses rotting in their homes. They've been ravaging the West's country-side."

"I want to scout with your outriders." Crow said, standing up. He wanted to escape the clustered war column, where he felt useless. He wanted to see the West unmarred. The king and council seemed skeptical.

"Is that wise, your highness?" A shrewd man asked. "We've encountered no feln as of yet, but it could be risky to allow this boy to ride out alone."

"I won't be alone." Crow flared. "I'll take Lady Jade with me. And if I may remind you, good sir, I'm a knight in my own right. I fought the feln on Seal Island's waters and was dubbed by the duke."

King Arnold laughed. "A fierce lad, this one is. Aye, ride out, but see that you take the appropriate men with you."

"I will." Crow smiled.

Snow fell gently as he and Jade trotted out before the column. Shadow flew overhead, a white serpent in the air. Her feathers had grown in, appearing white as virgin snow. The land stretched out before them, unmarked by horses and men. The trees were bare and black against the gray sky, grasses and wild flowers had long died as autumn slipped into winter. The air was crisp and cold. Jade and Crow took the eastern flank. The West's land rose and fell in lazy swooping hills, topped with trees and lakes, deep valleys and fields that clung to the easing slopes. Crow thought of the Ridge, and how jagged and harsh it seemed in comparison. It was no surprise that men settled this place so long ago.

"It's nice to break from camp." Jade said from her stallion's back. "I've missed the Western country."

"You've been here before?" Crow asked.

"Aye." A sad smile touched her lips. "With Lady Kath and Gretchen. There was a merchant from Augustii carrying rare sea shells to sell up in Hudson. We escorted him as protection." She rolled her eyes. "One of us would have been enough, but men are stupid, and he thought it would take the three of us to fight someone off. He was cheap too, and paid us as though we *were* one man."

"I don't know much about your life before." Crow realized.

"You never asked." Jade smirked.

"I guess not."

"I was knighted by Duke Milfred Keefe at sixteen winters." Shadow chirped and disappeared among the trees. "I already told you what happened after my father died." She murmured. "I had trouble finding work on the road because of my womanhood. I had as much skill as the boys my age, but no one wanted my sword. After moons of petty work, I came across Lady Gretchen in Youngston, who'd been knighted by the queen. There was a lot of work in the Roam for us, since folk often wanted protection from centaurs, though Gretchen tried to stay out of it as much as possible."

"Did you ever find any centaurs?"

"No. Once we saw a herd far off, but that was all."

Crow shivered, pushing the memory away. "When did you meet Kath?" He whispered.

Jade smiled. "Lady Gretchen and I stayed at a small inn called the Green Sea Witch. We were exhausted after giving chase to a trader's runaway crewman. But as it would have it, there'd be no rest for us. A brawl broke out in the tavern, so loud it made the floorboards shake. I went down to break the fight myself, dagger in hand, and that's where I met Lady Kath, standing over a bruised man and drinking a tankard of ale. She'd been with us ever since.

"It will be nice to see Gretchen again." Jade said as the trees swayed in the wind.

"We'll have to tell her that Kath died." Crow's hands tightened on the reins; the thought nearly unbearable.

"We will." Jade frowned. "Listen here Crow, as a foot knight, there's an unspoken understanding between us. A knight does not live long, especially a foot knight. Death follows close behind us every day. You must accept it, or might as well renounce the title."

"I don't like thinking of my friends that way." Crow said stubbornly.

"Then you are in the wrong company, and in the wrong war, for that matter."

Before he could respond, Crow was taken by a sudden sense of anxiety. *Something's happened,* he knew. He turned his gelding around, and Shadow reappeared above them, hovering and chirping. Crow knew she'd seen something.

"Is it feln?" Jade asked, grabbing for her sword.

"I think so." Crow replied.

They heard the hoofbeats of the scout before they saw him. It was Taeto, Crow realized. The man reined up beside them on a horse slick with sweat. "They captured a feln." He said breathlessly. "Come!"

Crow's riding was put to the test as he galloped back to the column. Shadow stayed close behind as Jade and Taeto inevitably ran ahead. The war column looked like a long snake made of men, horses and smoke. All were clustered against the western road as far as the eyes could see. Colors of brown, white, and green and blue dotted the snake like scales.

They were greeted by the others. Tree and Lyla were the first to arrive. Crow quickly jumped off his horse and handed it over to a young boy. Men were packed together, squabbling with one another and pushing at a ring of king's men to get a glimpse of the enemy. *They'll rip the feln to shreds if they get the chance,* the aggression was nearly intoxicating. A tent had quickly been erected in the middle of the guards. Shadow landed on top of it, perching above the gray fist of the Harolds. She roared, a blast of ice smoking from her jaws. The crowd grew silent before bursting into cheers. *It's in the tent.*

Tree clung to Crow's side, nearly getting swallowed by the sweating crowd around them. He was shoved in front of an armored guard; the man's face was pale beneath his helm. "Let us pass." Crow said, standing tall and puffing his chest.

The guard looked him up and down. "No one's allowed 'cross this point."

"I'm the Northern Child. I've sat in council with the king." Crow said.

"I said, no one's allowed 'cross this point, boy. I have orders."

"Sir. Don't call me boy." Crow bristled.

"Is the king in that tent?" Jade asked, towering over most of the men.

"None of your concern, my lady."

"I believe it's all of our concern." Jade said. The crowd yelled in agreement.

"The enemy is being questioned." He said, unrelenting. "I am under strict orders to keep everyone out. A dead feln is of no use to us."

Crow looked past the guard to the flap of the canvas tent. An older man Crow recognized as a knight of the king emerged. Captain Roy Milligan, a hard old man who sat in King Arnold's council and weighed in on war and battle. Thick as an anvil and bald, Crow rarely saw him outside of his armor. A war hammer hung on his hip. His brow was creased, he said something quietly to one of the guards stationed outside the entrance, shaking his head.

Lyla's green eyes sparkled beside Crow. She suddenly grabbed hold of Tree's arm, and yelled for the councilor. "Oi!" She screamed, voice rising above the rest. She shook Tree's arm like they were a child's doll. Crow grabbed her shoulder.

"What are you doing?" He spat.

"Getting us inside." She hissed back. "Oi! The nymph speaks feln!"

The captain looked up. Roy crossed his hands behind his back and walked over.

"You speak the language of these savages?" He asked Tree.

"Yes." Tree nodded, pulling their arm free. "We speak every language designed by the gods."

"Then come with us." Roy turned without looking behind him.

Crow made to follow but was halted. "The nymph is allowed, not you." The guard said.

Crow frowned, about to speak when Tree turned back.

"I wish for my friends to join me."

Captain Roy narrowed his gaze. He looked Crow, Lyla and Jade up and down. Shadow flapped down from the tent's peak, circling above Crow's head and causing some of the men around them to duck out of the way.

"Let the feln see me." Crow said. "Let it see that we have a dragon on our side. Maybe she'll scare it."

Roy offered them nothing in the form of words, but gave a curt nod to the guard holding them back. Their armored wall opened, and Crow was able to squeeze his way into the pavilion with Jade and Lyla. Soldiers yelled behind them.

"Feed the beast! Feed the beast!"

The ground beneath their feet was all mud and horse dung. Crow wondered what the feln thought of the sour smell of camp, and hoped it was afraid. His heart beat heavily in his chest as the tent's flaps were moved aside. Shadow, much too large for his shoulders now, landed and prowled through the mud. Her white feathers spattered with flecks of brown as she crept behind him like a white shadow.

Inside, the air was warm from the bodies of men and burning lanterns. The tent had been erected quickly; the usual furnishings were still packed away in chests outside. A large bear skin was thrown over the ground, a hulking crate shoved off to the side served as a table holding a flagon of wine and bread. King Arnold stood over it holding a glass of red with Sir Charles Campbell—his champion—and three councilors who had joined him on the march to war: Griff Gulden, Jensen Crecknyle and Captain Roy–who now reached for some bread.

The king paid them little mind.

"The singer says the nymph can speak to it." Roy said between mouthfuls of hard bread.

"That so?" King Arnold raised an exhausted brow. His yellow hair was frayed, and the lines of his face showed starkly against his white skin. "We have been civilized with the creature, perhaps you can get through to it." King Arnold's gaze flickered to Shadow. "If not, we'll move to different tactics."

Sir Charles moved his hand to the dagger at his side.

"I still say we slit its throat and be done with it." Griff grumbled; he was thin as a spear with a mop of black hair. "We've beat these savages before. It has no information we need."

Crow's gaze crept to the center of the tent, where a thick wooden rod stood straight, holding the canvas high above their heads. That's where the feln was, tied like a captured deer and thrown unceremoniously on the floor. Skin slick and white, hair long and white and plastered to his face, the feln stared back at Crow with eyes red as blood. His teeth were as pointed as his ears. The feln took a long look at Crow and pulled back his lips and hissed. Crow swallowed hard. He could suddenly taste salt water and smell blood soaking into splintered wood.

A hand on his shoulder pulled him back. Crow turned. *Jade.* She nodded at him before he turned back to the feln.

The creature's attention had drifted from Crow to Shadow. The feln's face lost what color it had, appearing almost blue. Crow's bravery returned to him. "I'm the Northern Child." He said. Shadow's tail swished from side to side, her feathers ruffled and stood on end, puffing up to make her look larger than she was. "Can you speak?" Crow asked.

The feln didn't regard him.

"No." King Arnold said, sipping at a glass of wine. "Or it's playing dumb."

Crow turned to Tree, who was lingering behind with Jade. The little nymph's expression gave nothing away. They appeared calm, save for the melancholy that always lingered in their eyes. "Tree, can you ask what it knows?" Crow asked.

"Ask about this queen of theirs." Said Sir Charles.

Tree glanced at Crow before proceeding. They stepped forward, only when they stood over the feln did the creature take his eyes from Shadow. He uttered his first word since capture. *"Saarcoskii."* The feln spat. An ugly word. *A curse,* Crow knew.

The insult rolled through the air, silencing the men in the tent. It was the first time the men heard the voice of a feln. A sound that belonged to memories of blood, to generations passed.

Without much pause, Tree spoke.

Felnish sounded alien coming from the gentle nymph. The language of the nymphs was soft and lyrical, more of a melody with no beginning and no end. The feln's own tongue was sharp, prickly and harsh.

The feln spit a glob of red saliva at Tree's feet.

Griff slammed his fists together. "Tell the foul feln if it doesn't find its tongue, I will rip it out!"

Tree relayed the message after a nod from Crow.

The feln began to speak again.

"'I will eat my tongue before telling you anything.'" Tree relayed. "'This is all I shall say. The cold winds are rising. Ice will burn as hot as fire, so says the Queen of Winter. Join her, or get buried by the storm.'"

"Cold winds are rising, aye." Crow stepped forward, taking Tree's place. He let Shadow's simmering anger settle inside him. "Your winter queen is false. I'll show you the real queen." Shadow slunk from behind his legs. She prowled like the large mountain cats from the

Peak, her horns sparkled clear and deadly in the firelight, her lips were pulled back in a silent snarl. Smoke seeped from the cracks between her teeth. Ice that burned as harsh as fire. When Crow looked at this creature's face, he imagined the bloated bodies of the Jumping Trout, a helpless father looking for his children. Anger boiled his blood and a cold confidence spread through his mind.

"Where is your queen now?" Crow whispered. Shadow pulled back her head and blasted the feln with a shock of ice. A bone-chilling wind ripped through the tent, and along with it came the screams. White crystal exploded from the frozen rope. The feln's skin turned from white to blue to purple to black.

"Control your beast, boy!" Griff yelled among the cries.

"Shadow, get back." Crow shooed her away. The creeping aggression that had taken over him was gone. The feln's face was completely disfigured. Eyes swollen shut, cheeks bloated from cold, his tongue had blackened and the tip of it chipped off. The sight of it turned Crow's stomach. He heard Lyla twist and leave the tent. The feln continued writhing on the floor.

"Put an end to it." King Arnold said, his voice grave and tired.

Sir Charles grabbed for his sword, but Crow stopped him, reaching for his own on his back. "I'll do it."

Sir Charles glanced at the king, who nodded.

The scrape of the sword from the scabbard was nearly as deafening as the screams. "Make it quick." Jade said from behind. Crow held the long-sword up over his head, he didn't let himself look away as he brought the point down on the flesh of the feln's neck. He remembered Lorenzo and the crew members that had sailed bravely to their end, and put his hatred into the swing. The screams stopped.

"There goes our lead." Griff hissed.

"You need a better handle on your pet." Captain Roy said.

"She's no pet." Crow snapped. "He wouldn't have talked."

"Your pride cost us information." Griff bristled. A few of the men inside the tent nodded, brows furrowed.

King Arnold raised a hand. "The child's right. The feln are savage beasts known to die before giving anything away. That being said," he took another drink, "you acted out of turn, Crow. You may be a knight, and you may have a dragon, but you are of common blood. You have been raised higher by those of nobler birth around you. You need to remember your place in this."

"And where is that?" Crow asked, the end of his sword was red with blood.

King Arnold put his glass down. "To the side, until more is asked of you." He regarded the blackened corpse on the ground. "If there's one feln, it must mean they're scouting. Alert the camp to keep on guard, there may be an army of them not too far from here. We'll hasten our pace so as not to be caught on the road. The faster we make it to Riverset the better. Everyone, out."

Crow was greeted by cheers and slaps on the back as he made his way back into the column. The men outside had heard the feln's suffering, and took to calling Shadow "Feln Eater" and "Vitania's Vengeance".

"It was good of you to kill it yourself." Jade approved.

"It was easy." Was all Crow said.

Twenty-Seven

The West

C row spotted the smoke before the charred ruins came into view.

The sky was slate gray, a thin layer of snow crusted the ground, and smoke struck into the air like an ugly black fist. It'd been days since Crow killed the feln. So far, the creatures slipped the grasp of the outriders. Instead, the column came across the felns' marks on the West. Burnt fields, dead cattle and shacks left in shambles. Crow and Jade found a man left to rot in a small outcropping of trees, the man had been stripped of everything. Animals ate away most of his flesh. The ground was too hard to bury him, so Crow and Jade laid him to rest as best they could. They left him covered in sticks and leaves and rocks.

"He's with our Mother now." Jade lamented.

With each corpse and ruined farm discovered, Crow's resolve against the feln hardened. He dreaded to think of what they would do to a place like the Forgotten Forest, or even Griffin's Peak.

"I hope we fall on them soon." Crow said to Jade from his gelding. "I'll show them the true power of winter."

As the black smoke billowed into the sky, Crow wondered if he'd get his wish today.

The king sent three of his knights to scout the fire before the column approached. "Nothing left." One panted. "We'll need more men before we deem it safe, but it appears the feln have fled."

After waiting on additional scouts, the column was allowed to close in. Shadow screamed from the sky, swooping down to the black skeleton of the village below. *It smells like death,* Crow's stomach rolled. The horses spooked at the charred stench that hung in the air, burnt and sour.

The king ordered a stop, urging those mounted off their horses. "We bury the dead." He commanded, face grim.

The village had been small, nothing more than a collection of hovels. Crow guessed it'd been used as a rest stop for those traveling the West. In the ruined center was the remnant of an inn, cinders still glowed from the collapsed thatch roof. The firepit in the middle was blacker than a moonless night. Ruined hovels were crowded around it, likely belonging to the people who worked inside. Falling snow gently drifted over the black remains. *Winter is burying them.*

Twenty bodies were found, most of which were women and young boys. There were only two men of fighting age, perhaps knights or foot knights. Their weapons and armor had been taken, leaving their bodies naked against the elements. The frigid air preserved the dead, their mortal wounds were black with crusted blood, and fear marred their expressions in frozen dread.

Shadow perched on the blackened spire of the inn. Crow could sense her unease. Even the crows wheeling above refused to scavenge their remains.

"Women and children." Sir Juan spat. The rest of the column made work to secure the town as they dug. "I pray our Mother lets me get my hands around a feln. I will rip the heart out of its chest."

"I doubt they even have hearts." Sir Taeto replied grimly.

Crow frowned as he stabbed at the dirt. "The feln die just like men do. Heart or not." They continued on silently.

Lyla sang *Into Her Arms,* a long somber song for those newly departed from this world. Crow knew the song well, as did most. Stone Teeth would sing it for the boys who'd succumb to the elements or sickness. He even sang it on the edges of mountains where boys had crawled into the caves and never crawled out. The song was about the soul's journey back to Mother Vitania, who would welcome all of her children back with open arms to be cared for all eternity. Crow hoped it was true.

Lyla's voice was beautiful and haunting. Her dark skin had a shallow wash of paleness since the march. She didn't say anything when she was done, stepping aside to where Tree stood among the men. She'd been quiet since Shadow and Crow froze the feln. Crow stared at her, but she refused to meet his gaze. *I should talk to her.*

Instead, Crow helped the knights of Seal Island set up camp. King Harold announced a halt for the night. They'd reach Riverset the next day, and the shell of the town provided comfort from the frigid weather. Crow set his tent up against a waist high cobblestone wall. The knights wandered off for firewood, and Crow unstrapped his sword from his back, the relief from the weight made him groan. He started to awkwardly unstrap his armor when Tree approached.

The little nymph was silent, no louder than a ghost. Crow only knew they were coming from Shadow's chirp from her place on the wall. Crow smiled, despite the subdued mood of camp.

"Need help?" Tree asked.

Crow nodded, raising a brow as Tree lifted their hands to work at Crow's shoulder straps. *Tree looks smaller.* Crow wondered if he'd grown a few inches since traveling the road.

"Did the feln do this to the nymphs last time they were here?" Crow asked, glancing over his shoulder to where fresh graves now marred the dirt like scars.

"Yes." Tree replied, moving to Crow's other shoulder as the armor clanged to the ground. "Though we were not easy to find. The feln killed their way across the land. No creature was spared their cruelty. They ripped up trees, burned fields, and hunted until entire forests were laid bare. Nowhere could sustain them long. For the feln are hungry creatures, and their appetites are never satisfied.

"We would hide in our trees and sing to the gods, praying that the feln would not find our woods. We never stood a chance against their brutality. They were unlike any creature we ever knew. Even the centaurs feared them."

Crow frowned at the mention of the centaurs. He would never forget what they did to his friend.

"The feln will not stop." Tree murmured.

"We've killed them before." Crow said, shrugging out of his breast plate and helping Tree ease it to the ground. He took a seat, the ground cold and hard beneath him.

"They did not have a queen before." Tree frowned.

"They only have one." Crow shrugged. "We have five. Kings and queens both."

"Five." Tree mimicked, holding up their hand, five thin fingers splayed apart. They closed it into a fist. "One."

Shadow hissed from her perch above their heads, and a frozen breeze cut deep into Crow's bones.

The fires were blazing by the time the sun sank below the horizon, filling the town with fluttering fallen stars. Crow wore dark woolen clothing to keep the worst of the frost at bay. He sat in a circle around the fire as a black pot of water boiled with onion, carrot and potato.

As always, Crow separated a portion for Tree before someone came with a chunk of meat that was offered to the higher-ranking members of the war camp. Snow fell from the starless sky in thick flakes, melting upon men's shoulders.

Crow watched as Lyla idly chatted to Taeto, wrapped in a cloak trimmed with white fox. The fox collar reminded Crow of Bones. Crow's belly was warmed from dinner, and he was content to sit around the fire with Shadow coiled at his side.

The great sword hit the ground with a clang as it landed in front of him, still sheathed in the shoulder strap. Crow's eyes whipped up to meet Jade standing above him, her own magnificent sword unsheathed.

"Now?" Crow already felt his joints whining.

"Yes. Now." Jade said.

"It's snowing." Crow protested.

"Aye." Jade poked him with the toe of her boot. "If you are so hungry to find a feln, then you must have an appetite to train."

"Go on, Crow," Taeto snickered, "we could use some entertainment tonight." The others around their fire nodded and whooped in agreement.

"Right." Crow grumbled and stood, holding his sword in a half-hearted grip. He and Jade had been slipping on their daily training, the march took too much of the life out of them. But he couldn't say no. Crow knew he must keep training.

It was hard to see in the snow, and the light from the fires made confusing flickering shadows of every shape. Crow squinted past them. The distractions only served to make him better.

Jade lunged first.

Crow played defense, aware of the sharp edge of Jade's blade as it slashed through snow and air like a silver claw. He blocked her with ease, predicting her next movement from the placement of her feet, the flit of her eyes and the shift in her weight. She feinted left, but Crow called her bluff and brought his sword down, blocking a slice at his right hip. "Good." She breathed.

They danced, their swords clanging with the song of battle. Crow defended, thrusting every now and then with a swipe. He decided to bide his time for now. It was too hard for him to see, and Jade had the advantage on him as the better swordsman. *Let her tire herself out, she'll get sloppy.* He had to count on it.

Men abandoned their fires to watch them spar. They roared at each of Jade's attacks. Some yelled strategies out to Crow, and soon there was cheering on both sides. Crow smiled to himself, marveling at the attention. *Ah!* His sword glanced off Jade's just in time, the last-minute parry nearly knocked him off his feet. It took several steps for him to find his balance again.

"Pay attention." Jade scolded, earning a hounding boom from the crowd.

She was coming at Crow less frequently, forcing him to make the attacks. *She's not tired,* Crow knew, *she predicted my plan.* So, he'd have to bite.

Crow came at her, but remained conservative in his attack. She took him easily. The crowd fell away, and all Crow thought about was his next move, her next move, and the ones after that.

The chill was chased away as they danced. Sweat ran down Crow's sides in cool sheets. He allowed Jade to make an attack, and waited for her confidence to reign. *There!* She planted her foot, ready to style a savage side swipe. Crow could easily block it; she'd then force his sword up and see where it took her from there. Or...

Crow dove, dropping his sword briefly as he rolled to the side, right under Jade's blade. It whistled as it cut through the air. He picked his sword back up the moment his feet were under him again, popping up and spinning to her side. His sword swung to bury itself into her rib cage. He stopped it just before it bit into her jacket.

Jade froze. The men around their ring froze. Not even Shadow moved from where she watched.

Then the soldiers cheered. A few grumbled and dug into their pockets, relieving some coppers into their companion's hands.

Jade dropped her sword in the dirt. Pulling his own away, Crow could only stare. He'd done it. He'd beat her.

"Well done," she smiled, "Sir."

The king's men forced them back to their tents, citing an early morning. Crow laid in his furs, Shadow a feathery heap beside him. He stared into the blackness before closing his eyes, the nightmares didn't come. Instead, his head rang with the song of swords.

Morning was white and bright. A layer of snow hid the ugly massacre that had happened here. The town was behind them soon enough, and eventually the road reached the mighty Blue Vein, the river that fed the West. It was three times wider than the River of Song, the eastern bank seemed impossibly far away. Swimming this river would be impossible, not even a pole boat could securely get across. Crow didn't even know that rivers could get so large.

"Magnificent." Tree gasped, bowing their head to the river. The roar was a constant thunder in their ears. A beast that rivaled the sea.

The clouds parted at midday, and the sun began to slip lower until their shadows trailed behind them like black ink. Crow thought they'd have another day of marching before the horn sounded from the front of the column.

They'd reached Riverset at last.

Twenty-Eight

Riverset

Riverset seemed nearly a kingdom in its own right. It sat upon the mighty bank of the Blue Vein. The walls were high and slick with moss, covering the outer wall in a great living carpet. It stood like a large green ring against a landscape encased in winter's throng. A tall, two-towered castle stood at its middle. Crow could see the top of it from beyond the wall, flat like a drum with colorful flags of orange and gold whipping in the wind. A large iron drawbridge lay open across a great churning moat carved from the river itself.

Smoke rose from inside the walls; the first signs of life Crow had seen since they'd begun their travels this way. Even as they walked through the village that led to the safety of Riverset's walls, the houses stood empty as tombs.

"The duchess has pulled her people inside the walls." Jade explained. "She's protecting them."

The duchess was waiting for them atop a black stallion, two knights on either side of her at the open gates. Crow couldn't see much of her from his place in the column. She wore an outrageous orange overcoat and cape, covering herself and her stallion's hind quarters in a bright flame of cloth. The king rode out to meet her with his guard. She bowed her head but did not dismount. Afterall, King Arnold was no king of hers. Crow was too far to hear what was said, but they must have kept the pleasantries brief, for soon they were riding back into the city.

We're wasting no time, Crow thought as he strode down Riverset's castle hall. Despite the chill outside, it was warm inside. Torches blazed on their sconces, baking Crow's face. He was exhausted from the march and barely had time to get out of his armor before getting dragged to an urgent meeting with the king and duchess. Only Tree accompanied him. Shadow, Lyla and Jade were resting in their shared apartments.

Their arrival was bleaker than Crow expected. No waves and shouts of joy were sung from the folk here. Many blanched at the sight of Shadow soaring in the sky. A few children managed a squeal of delight, but the men and women seemed weary. There were monsters at their doorstep, and Crow bet that many of the folk crowding the streets were those who lived outside the walls, forced to flee their farms and hovels from the threat of the feln. Crow hoped the West had something like the Underground Lads. He saw a lot of boys that reminded Crow of himself. They watched from rooftops, clustered together and thin, gazing at Shadow with curious eyes. A voice inside Crow whispered that he should be among them. He *belonged* among them.

Instead, he opened the door to Duchess Wanda Cullimore's council chamber, and took a seat saved for him next to Captain Roy. The man barely acknowledged him, which was fine. Crow planned on keeping his mouth shut. He was invited as a kind gesture, at this point the boy with the dragon was on the mouth of every bard in Frukjera.

"Thank you for joining me." Wanda said. She was much younger than Crow expected. Maybe only a couple winters older than himself, and younger than Jade. She'd been wearing tan riding leathers under her orange cloak; a broach of golden wheat was pinned above her heart. Though her brown skin was bright and smooth with youth, her slanted dark eyes showed wisdom beyond her years. Her hair was black as pitch, straight and left unbound to fall over her shoulders. Crow thought of Wanda the Wonder from the songs, and though this woman bore no resemblance to her, she was beautiful all the same. "Riverset would like to formally welcome you, King Arnold. My father hosted you many winters ago, I was just a babe and fear I don't remember. But he always spoke highly of you, despite fighting the Bay in the last Petty War."

King Arnold smiled, a memory glinting in his eye. "It's been a long time since we've come West." His expression turned serious. "But it's not good news that brings us here."

"No." She agreed, barely glancing at Crow and Tree. "I needed your company right away. We have news from the king of Griffin's Peak." Crow's heart stuttered in his chest. He audibly swallowed, balling his hands into nervous fists in his lap. *Don't show fear.*

"Last we heard the king took Youngston back." Roy replied.

"Aye. He erased the scourge of feln from the Roam, and took the lands around Fisher's Mark back from the centaurs as well. Once a true army arrived, the centaurs fled. It doesn't look like they are in league with the feln. The few straggling feln they found were wild, and willing to slit their own throats rather than surrender. The king allowed no mercy, and couldn't torture any answers out of them. We still do not know where the bulk marched off to." Wanda reported.

"Perhaps back to their hole on their island." Roy said. "They were lucky to capture Youngston by surprise, but cannot hope to win the war they started."

"We can't underestimate them, or this queen of theirs." Griff argued. "They have sacked Youngston, and no one knows what has become of Augustii to the south. If they are able to split their forces so wide, they must have alarming numbers."

"Even more dangerous," King Arnold said, his hands folded in front of his face, "they are fanatic. Willing to die for their queen. They will not turn against her."

"We know they're here." Wanda said. "The scouts we send out never return. I've sent messages to Crab's Cliff, Fork's Rest, Albashell and Hudson, but have heard nothing. It's a miracle from the Mother that we've received King Arthur's messages at all."

"What kind of madness..." Roy mumbled.

"Do we have further word from their queen?" Griff asked.

Wanda shook her head. "She abandoned Youngston, but not before ripping the banners from the Lodge and burning them. It's said the word 'thieves' was written in blood across the great hall's walls." Her gaze flickered to Crow. "The feln hold her as a goddess, spewing that she is winter incarnate. Destruction of life." Wanda regarded Crow for the first time. "What do you think of that?"

"I think they'll find true winter when we meet on the field." Crow said.

Though the news was dire, and the West was holding its breath, a feast was still in order. Afterall, a king was staying behind Riverset's walls. It would be an insult not to wine and dine him. Crow could have gone without the feast, he lamented from his seat at the edge of the long table. Shadow sat quietly in the rafters, seeming as bored as he. *She's sick of this too.* He'd rather be among the men clustered at the lesser tables beneath them, or even with the soldiers eating outside around their fires, camped around the castle. He found his appetite lacking, but Crow had gone too many hungry nights to waste what he was given. Picking up a dripping duck leg, Crow bit into it, chewing and tasting nothing.

Lyla joined him after opening the feast with a couple of songs. She didn't have a seat saved, but by the time she perched on the table's edge, the folk were drunk enough not to notice. Crow's own head swam from the ale he'd been drinking.

"How's your song coming along?" He asked her, noting how her dark skin glowed in the torchlight. Lyla pursed her lips.

"I can't decide the tone of it." She hummed. "Shall it be a crowd pleaser for drunks in a tavern? Maybe an adventure that will have folks on the edge of their seats…" She smiled, but it didn't quite reach her green eyes. "Or maybe it'll be melancholy, and women will tear off their clothes and weep just to hear it."

Crow frowned. "Don't make it sad."

"I guess it depends on how this all ends," Lyla shrugged, staring up at Shadow twisted in the wooden beams, "then I can decide." She was quiet, despite the chatter around them. Crow noticed the dark circles under her eyes, and she seemed thinner than before. He bit the inside of his cheek.

"Do you regret coming?" He asked her.

"No." Lyla replied at once. "Ever since I was a little girl, I wanted to write the greatest song ever made. I was like you. My parents were lost to me a long time ago. They were fishing folk. I lived on the outer docks and decks of ships more than solid ground. One morning, my mother went out to catch something from the deep waters. The sky was blue as your eyes, not a cloud in sight. The storm seemed to come out of nowhere, it crept over the horizon like a black demon. My father and a couple of men went out to find her. No one returned." Lyla shrugged, as though the memory had lost its pain. "There was nowhere for me to go. But I always had my voice. I used it the same way you and Jade use your swords, sharpening it until I found myself as the Rope-Ringer's singer."

"I had no idea." Crow gasped. He always thought she was high born. He'd never guess that she'd been orphaned like him. If Crow didn't have the Lads, he had no idea where he'd be now. His parents left him when he was still a babe. Crow would probably be dead.

"I know." Lyla smiled. "And I like it that way. But being the singer to a king isn't enough." She balled her hands into tight fists. "I need to be the best. I need to be legendary."

Crow stared out at the men below them. He spotted Jade and the knights from Seal Island clanking their tankards together. Sir Juan was chattering while Taeto muttered things to Jade every now and again. Crow longed to join them. He felt out of place up here. "Legendary huh..." He muttered. "...seems a bit much."

"Easy for you to say. You don't know how lucky you are. You've got a perfect story wrapped up and handed to you." Lyla sighed.

Crow took a drink of ale. "Lucky me." He muttered. "What's the deal with you, then? Why do you want to be 'legendary'?"

"Doesn't everybody?" Lyla jested. When Crow didn't answer, she sighed. "I—I want to be worthy of Princess Talia." Her cheeks colored a light blush after she said the princess's name. For another rare moment, Lyla looked almost shy, fumbling with the loose fabric of her skirts.

Crow swallowed the lump in his throat. What would possess someone to leave all they'd ever known? *Only one thing,* as the songs would have it.

"Why do you need to be worthy of her?" He asked, though he felt he already knew the answer.

"I love her." Lyla said simply, releasing a breath. "We've always been close. But she could never be with a girl like me. A singer brought off the docks isn't fit for a future queen. But the legendary bard who wrote the epic ballad of the Northern Child? Well, *she* could have a chance. I'm so jealous of you. The king practically threw you at his daughters when you arrived at the Isles. Not all of us are lucky enough to have a dragon at the royals' disposal."

Crow ignored the small seed of disappointment in his belly. *It all makes sense now.* At first, he'd thought it was Lyla's ego that brought her this far. "Well, the royals are stupid to think they're so much higher than us." He said quietly. "I think you're worthy of Talia as you are now." He downed the rest of his ale; the bottom was thick with yeast. Lyla smiled at him, placing a delicate hand on his shoulder.

"Thank you, Crow." She smirked. "You need to be careful with that mouth of yours. As much as you hate it," she motioned to the soldiers feasting beneath them, "you'll never be one of them again."

The light of morning filtered through the ice crusted glass, white and bright. Fluffy pieces of snow blanketed Riverset below. Shadow was crammed on the window's narrow sill, scratching and hissing to get out. Crow got up from his feathered bed, shivered, and pushed the window panes open. Icy air blasted his face, but he welcomed the chill, for it woke him up. Shadow leapt into the sky, and Crow watched her fly up and away, wishing he could join her.

Crow met with the others in one of the castle's small dining chambers. They were given smoked salmon on a bed of fried sweet reeds.

"The duchess sent a ship at dawn for Glorygradus announcing our arrival. Hopefully it will reach the queen." Jade said.

"How long are we going to stay here?" Crow asked.

Jade shrugged. "Either until we hear from Queen Joanna, or King Arnold decides to march again."

Crow flaked a chunk of salmon from the steak, the fish was tender, melting on his tongue. He wondered what the men of the camp were eating this morning. "I want to get to Glorygradus." He mumbled. He felt Man's Wall tugging at him, the vision the unicorns had shown him seemed to dance before his eyelids each time he closed them. Whatever the unicorns wanted must be close. *I feel like I could reach out and touch it.* Something was coming. It had to be.

"So do I." Lyla sighed. "It's the first kingdom of the continent, our crowning achievement." She spoke as though she'd built the city by her own hand. "I've always wanted to see it."

"My brother Bones always wanted to see Man's Wall." Crow said. His fish suddenly tasted of nothing. He pushed his plate away. *My brother,* he frowned. Bones felt like he belonged to another lifetime. Was it really just a few moons ago that Crow was eating breakfast with him and the other Lads?

"And he can." Tree said, drawing Crow back to the present. "Once we follow the unicorn's message you can always go back to him." The little nymph smiled. They were trying to cheer him up. But Tree didn't know that Crow's last interaction with Bones was a childish fight. Would Bones even want to see Crow again?

Jade's wooden chair squealed against the stone floors as she stood. "I'm going to the yard. Care to join me?"

Crow made to stand, he felt like hitting something, but Tree grabbed his woolen sleeves.

"Actually, I believe it would be beneficial to review your letters." The nymph said. "When have you last read?"

Jade and Lyla both smirked. Crow narrowed his eyes. "I don't think I have much need for reading lately."

"The mind is just as important as the blade." Tree rebutted. Jade laughed, nodding her agreement.

"You're sitting with kings now, Crow." She said. "Best not to sound like a bumbling fool in front of your new company."

Crow frowned, but ultimately decided they were right, and ended up following Tree to the castle's library.

Riverset's castle was a simple thing, despite the vastness of the city itself. It was built of gray river stone, and its simplicity spoke to its age. The West was the first part of Frukjera settled by men. This castle was double the age of anything built along the Green Coast. What the castle lacked in fancy architecture, it made up for in artwork. Colorful tapestries swung from the walls, draping the stone from ceiling to floor. It bathed the otherwise gray interior in yellows and oranges, greens and reds...Scenes of the West's rolling hills, leafy trees, and fertile lands were sewn into rich fabrics, depicting the settlement along the Blue Vein.

They passed the castle's chapel. A moon was carved above the wooden door. Two priestesses stood outside in robes dyed the deep purple of night. *I wonder if I should stop to pray,* Crow thought. He felt that he'd need Vitania's favor for the inevitable moment he collided with the feln. He looked the priestesses up and down, cowled in the shadows of their robes. One lifted her head, and he saw striking blue eyes beyond her cloak's shadows.

Crow shivered and looked away, nodding awkwardly as he followed Tree. *I'll just pray on the battlefield.* If it came to that.

The library was simple. A large window facing the east let in the sun's rays, bathing the rectangular room in glowing light and floating dust. A perfume of stale paper filled the air. A large canvas map hung on the opposite wall behind rows of wooden shelves. Crow found himself standing in front of it, eying the letters next to the marked cities. He found Riverset, huddled against the Blue Vein's thick inked line. He followed it downward, his eyes roaming over the hills, seas, forests, rivers, mountains, until they found Griffin's Peak. It sat on the north eastern tipped peninsula among jagged drawings of crashing waves and spiked mountains. Great serpents were illustrated in the surrounding waters. Crow reached out and brushed his fingers against the rough canvas of the Pond. He saw the large island in the middle, blank of detail. *Feln* was scratched lazily at its center.

"What does it say, up there?" Tree said, suddenly at his side. Crow flinched, "You scared me." He hissed.

"What does it say?" Tree asked again, ignoring his fright.

"What does what say?"

"That island there... North of the Pond, above Glorygradus."

Crow frowned. High above Glorygradus, up into the waves of the Wild Sea was a tiny island, slender and thin, butted up against another that was slightly larger and covered in pine trees. Crow frowned at the script, working at the name in his head. Maybe it *had* been too long since he'd reviewed his letters. But after a moment, he said aloud, "Isle of Birth."

"Do you know why it is called that?"

"It's where men came from." Crow shrugged. "They sailed to Glorygradus, built the wall, and then decided to conquer the rest."

"Why conquer the rest, when the feln were running the land red with blood?" Tree asked him.

"I don't know." Crow didn't understand why the nymph was asking him, he was pretty sure Tree knew more. "Power, I guess."

"It is important to know. It is your story." Tree produced a heavy leather tome. Crow hadn't seen them grab it from the shelves. Tree shoved it into Crow's hands, the leather was cracked, the pages stained deep yellow from age. *The Mother's Womb, an Observation of the Isle; by Priestess Amara.*

"It's not *my* story." Crow mumbled, wishing that he was out in the yard with Jade.

"But it is." Tree led him to a small table tucked away in the corner. "I have told you that the song of the Northern Child has been sung before."

"If there was a man with an ice dragon, we'd have heard of him." Crow said, cracking open the book.

"Yes, I would think so." Tree pondered. "Yet, here we are." They motioned a slim green hand at the book in Crow's hands. "Go on, let us hear about the Isle of Birth."

The Isle of Birth was now a desolate place, cold and hard as the first men it bred. Little remained on the island, windblown and wintry as it was, save for the cracked shells of ancient homes. It hugged the western shore of a much larger island, thought to be uninhabited due to the harsh conditions. And though the Isle of Birth was a dismal place, it was said to be where Mother Vitania gave birth to men, and so was held in holy regard. Priestesses and missionaries were the only souls who braved the Wild Sea for reflection and holy relics. Crow struggled through the read. Reading out loud was always much harder than in his head, and it didn't help that Priestess Amara had an incredibly dry tone. He barely paid attention to the words he was choppily saying, but Tree listened with great intent, pausing and helping Crow when a particularly challenging word showed up in the narrative.

"How can this continue on?" Crow complained, flipping through the pages. "There's nothing up there. Even Amara wrote that a storm blew the whole place to bits."

Tree grabbed the book, briefly skimming a couple of pages in the middle. "It seems this priestess is very reflective in the coming chapters."

"Great." Crow muttered.

"I believe this is still worth reading." Tree pushed the book back to him.

"I'd rather go hit something." Crow made to stand, but Tree grabbed his wrist and pulled him back down.

"You are sitting with rulers now." Tree whispered. "Do you believe that these men stayed in power with blades alone?" Crow didn't answer, instead he just blinked in reply. "It would be wise for you to remember the company you keep now."

Tree let go of Crow's hand, straightening up as though they hadn't just chastised him like a child.

"Now." Tree said. "Continue."

Twenty-Nine

Riverset

*E*yes *blue as steel.*

Blood.

Blackness.

Crow shot up, sweat sticking to his skin like a soggy blanket despite the chill from the open window. His heart beat erratically in his chest, threatening to break through his ribs. "Shadow…" He called, his voice cracking. "Shadow!" The dream had left him panicked.

He'd been standing in the snow, his feet frozen to the ground as a shadow approached from the horizon. He'd been unable to move. Instead, he held a sword, Jade's sword. He had no choice but to raise it, to fight the impossible force that approached him…

"Shadow!" The dragon burst through his window, screaming. She flapped around his chambers once before landing on top of him in a mass of feathers and claws. She was hysterical, nipping at his arms, screeching loud enough to make his ears ring.

Crow felt no relief from waking up. Shadow raised her head, releasing an icy blast that frosted the ceiling in spikes of glass. Shooting up from bed, Crow knew what was happening before the warnings sounded.

The shouts and booming horns were blaring in full by the time he dressed and Jade burst through his door.

"The feln," she said, "they're here."

THIRTY

RIVERSET

It's cold, Crow thought as the air left his lungs in gusts of smoke. Though in truth, the winter's chill didn't touch him. Not with the promise of killing on the horizon. A fire of fear and excitement had settled in Crow's belly, keeping him warm in the armor that covered his limbs. The stars blinked overhead like the torches that lined Riverset's walls. Mother Vitania had granted them a night clear as glass. From Crow's vantage upon the wall, he saw the flicker of enemy fire dancing against the Blue Vein's black waters. The feln were no larger than a speck at this distance, but they promised impending violence. A watcher confirmed through his looking glass, the pale shapes of the feln manned the ships. Ships from Augustii, traveling up from the Green Coast to smash Riverset in the early darkness of morning.

Shadow screamed from her perch on the crenelated stone. She resembled a white ghost in the night, fearsome as a living gargoyle. Crow squeezed his bow in anticipation. The sight of Shadow upon the walls gave the soldiers spirit. Those who'd marched with them from Cregan's Mark called her Feln Eater, and those who kept to Riverset's walls called her Vitania's Gift.

Crow sighed, flexing his fingers around his bow and shifting his feet. He'd never practiced shooting before.

"Don't hold the arrows too long." Jade's voice was grim beside him. "Do you remember how Kath would shoot?"

"Barely." Crow answered honestly, his eyes remained glued to the fire far away.

"Once she had her target, she'd loose." Jade pulled an arrow from the quiver at her waist to demonstrate, but before letting the arrow go, she pointed the bow to the ground, releasing the pressure from the string. "Trust your eye more than your hand. If you leave it to your hand too long, you'll shift and miss your target." She paused, inhaling the night air. "Though from up here, I'd say aim isn't much of a worry. Just shoot the arrows as fast as you can, and with any luck, we won't need to use the swords on our backs."

Tree stood to Crow's left, looking almost ridiculous with the massive bow in their small soft hands. The wind ruffled their hair, making it dance around their pretty face. *They look more sad than usual,* Crow thought.

"Do you know how to use that?" Crow asked them.

"I will not need this." Tree said. "When the time comes, I will sing to the gods."

"We should all sing to our gods." A man next to them said. He wore plain armor, a breastplate adorned with a bundle of wheat from Riverset. "Sing to them now, nymph. We'll sing to our Mother to vanquish this evil on our shores."

"Mother maid please hold us tight, see us through this darkest night." Jade's voice was low, but carried on the wind. Others soon picked up the prayer. Crow found himself joining, though he didn't think Vitania heard him much. *If ever there was a time,* Crow thought, *hear me now, and keep my friends safe.* Before long, the entire wall was collected in song.

"Deliver us through pain and fright,

Bless us now and give us light.
Your faithful children
to you we pray,
Grant us dawn of the next day.
Mother maid please hold us tight,
See us through this darkest night."

Another long *woooo* from the horn blared through the night, scrambling those still not in position. The prayer left Crow giddy, and he wondered how Lyla felt in the castle's cellars; hidden away with the children and women. *She's probably singing the same song down there.* Though he knew it would sound much better than theirs.

"Lovely prayers, men!" Sir Charles called. He strode the walls in his gleaming armor, a cloak embroidered with the punching fist of the Harolds hung from his shoulders. He looked a proper champion, pacing behind the archers in the torchlight. "But tonight, we will need more than prayer for us to see the dawn. Our Mother granted us steel so that we may wield it against our enemies! Against the faithless! Tonight, we'll give her the color red. The blood of her enemies who think they can harm her children!"

The waters churned beneath them as the river ships were released. They formed the first line of defense, while smaller swifter crafts followed behind to slip through the bulky river ships and attack on offense. The Blue Vein was so mighty that a proper battle could be fought in her current with multiple ships as though it were a battle on the sea. Crow knew the men of Seal Island were down there, manning one of the swift river speeders. The king also walked the deck of Riverset's largest ship, *Sunset Traveler. "Do not say I am not a king of the people. A king who does not fight for his men is a sorry excuse."* He'd said.

I want to be with them, Crow lamented. He'd said as much in the chaos of the early night, when men were running about the keep, ordering groups where to go.

"It is a fool who runs into battle with no experience." Duchess Wanda had chastised. "I'm sure you're fine with that sword of yours, but I'd prefer to produce the Northern Child to Queen Joanna whole, with his dragon. You'll stay on the walls."

The duchess was with Lyla and the others in the belly of the castle. She was the last of her line, and it wouldn't do to lose her in battle. The king's champion was also loath to stay on the walls while his king went to board, but orders were orders.

So, Crow watched as the feln sailed beneath the star-studded sky towards them. His heart beat in tune with the thrumming drums. First, the ships would collide on the river, then any stragglers would have to pull up against the wall, where a rain of arrows, boulders and oil would topple over their heads. *And ice,* Crow thought, looking to Shadow. Her tail whipped back and forth, frozen steam leaked from her teeth. He reached out, stroking her soft cool feathers. She chirped, rubbing her snout along his arm. "Show them winter." He whispered. She roared, and leapt from the crenelated wall. Crow wished he could sit upon her back.

'The ships from Augustii were clustered together, with no real form unlike the straight line of ships that were crawling to meet them. However, Crow could see that in the back of the jumbled feln's offense, a ship larger than the rest lagged behind with sails white as snow shining in the starlight. Crow squinted. *Could the Queen of Winter be aboard that ship?*

The first of the river boats clashed.

The sound of splintering wood sliced through the air like lightning. The current foamed an angry white as the smaller ships smashed together. Crow could just make out the ropes being tossed from one deck to another. Men and pale feln clambered toward one another, fire bright and orange sprung from arrows and hungrily ate the sails of whichever ship they caught. Crow's heart beat heavily in his chest as he watched. He held his bow so tightly that the string threatened to snap his fingers in two. Then the screams began. It was impossible to tell which side was bleeding more. Shadow plummeted upon the carnage like a white wraith from the sky. Crow saw her icy blasts against the fire's growing glow. He felt her anger and her hunger. His mouth watered at the promise of biting into flesh. He smelled the blood upon the decks, felt the wind rustle through his feathers, and relished in the sweet fear that poured through the feln's skin before he opened his mouth to freeze the flesh off his...

"Nock your arrows, lads!"

Crow flinched, nearly dropping his bow.

"Are you alright?" Tree murmured.

"Yes." Crow swallowed, grabbing an arrow and tugging it back. The string was taut, and his bicep felt like it'd rip from the bone if he held it tight for too long. He focused down on the collided ships. Most of the scouting ones were locked up now, some no more than burning husks already sinking into the river's hungry waters. A few from Augustii were starting to slip through.

"Loose!"

They pointed their arrows at a slight upward angle, before letting go and watching them rain down. Crow couldn't track whether they hit anything before Sir Charles cried again from somewhere on the wall. "Nock!"

Nock.

"Loose!"

Loose.

"Nock!"

Nock.

"Loose!"

Loose.

The pattern continued until Crow's arm felt numb. Flames danced upon the river. Crow's arrows fell from the sky, striking nothing, striking someone, striking something, he didn't know. Shadow circled the carnage like a hungry eagle, and ships continued forward. From where Crow stood, it looked like the feln were losing. The Augustii ships were sinking like stones, but the large one still persisted. Riverset's smaller scouting ships were too small to take it, and it looked heavily crewed. Arrows rained from her deck onto anyone that dared sail too close.

A boy ran by atop the wall to refill their arrows.

"Hold!" Charles yelled.

Two of the chunkier defensive ships left the barricade to take on their larger opponent. The felnish scouting ships were all burnt to ruin, and the stragglers still afloat were locked up in combat. *Once the ships collide, this'll be over.* Crow thought.

Shadow screeched, turning back towards the wall. Crow knit his brows together.

Sunset Traveler raised her oars towards the fray. The other two of Duchess Wanda's ships were almost there. The feln put up no resistance to the larger ships. The smaller ones scrambled out of the way, and Crow even saw pale bodies abandoning the deck once Wanda's fleet grew close enough to toss the ropes.

"Are they surrendering?" Crow said in disbelief.

"Feln do not surrender." Tree replied.

Shadow reached the wall. Blood stained the edges of her feathers and snout. She landed on the crenelated stone and turned her serpentine neck back to stare at the waters. Crow's stomach grew cold.

"Get down–"

The blast turned night into day.

The shockwave nearly blew Crow off the wall. He covered his eyes against the impossible brightness of it all. In an instant, the large Augustii ship was gone in a flurry of swirling flame, and the fires from her belly reached out and consumed all of those around her. The sound was akin to a mountain being blown apart, a landslide, an impossible thunder. Crow felt the warmth of its kiss against his skin. When he dared peek at the carnage, the fires were bright enough to blot out the stars.

The ship from Augustii was gone, a pile of splintering kindling remained in its place. One of Wanda's galleys was little better, Crow could hear it crackling like a hearth, the sails were walls of flames reaching towards the sky. The other already had fires spreading on her deck, eating up wood and rope and canvas. Nearly all of the boats, even the smaller scouting ships, were fighting fire. And they were losing.

It was a trap.

Goosebumps prickled Crow's skin, despite the heat wafting from the river below. Luckily, *Sunset Traveler* was far enough to avoid the blast, and was retreating fast.

Mother, Crow prayed, *please let the men from Seal Island be alive.* But he felt his hope turn to dust as he again looked to the carnage on the Blue Vein. A river now turning red and bright as the sun.

Tree's voice rose above the cries from below. They raised their palms towards the sky. Folk upon the wall looked at them with uneasy expressions, but Crow nodded to them in reassurance. A cool breeze ruffled through their hair, and the clouds rolled in from the western sky. The water churned angrily, unable to eat the flames fast enough. The clouds roamed closer as Tree's haunting song continued. And with them, *there*, Crow had to squint to see, *snow.*

"Keep it up!" Sir Charles yelled. "You see this, men? The nymph sings to our Mother to put out the fires!"

"Breach!" The cry ripped through the wind sharper than a knife through flesh. Crow's chest felt as icy as the heavy snow now pelting his hair. A soldier nearly collided with Sir Charles, his helm missing and face splattered with sweat and blood. "The northern gate," he gasped, "an attack from the inside. The northern gate is under as-sault—"

"Oi!" Charles tried to keep the wall under control, but men were already scrambling from their position. Whether to run, or to fight, Crow didn't know. But he *did* know that he wasn't going to stand up here while Riverset was being attacked below.

The snow came down in bursts of frozen sleet. Tree continued to sing as though they felt nothing. The fires on the river were fighting it, and the previously crisp night was swallowed in gray darkness. Crow dropped his bow, hoisting his great sword from his shoulder. "I'm going down to fight."

Jade stood beside him; her hair plastered to her face. She nodded, sword already in hand.

"Sir Charles!" Crow called, spotting the grizzled champion through the snow. The champion managed to gain order once again, parceling men out to help the northern assault, keeping the smaller and younger soldiers on their current portion on the wall. Charles turned and scowled. "Protect Tree." Crow ordered. "The snow—"

"Aye. It'll obstruct the enemy." Charles growled. "I have orders from my king and the duchess to keep you from the worst of it."

Crow clenched his jaw, preparing to shove his way through if need be.

"I'll keep him alive." Jade said with cool confidence. Sir Charles scoffed, but his gaze drifted to Shadow, where she sat perched on the wall, upright and ready to take wing.

"Show us you're worth following, Sir." Sir Charles said. He turned back to the folk on the wall.

Crow and Jade shared a quick glance before taking off. Shadow ripped into the air with an angry cry.

The quickest way to the northern gate was to stay atop Riverset's outer wall, snaking around the city's perimeter from above. Like most strongholds, Riverset had two walls. The second wrapped securely around the castle. Crow hoped that those outside the castle's inner wall had time to run before the feln reached them.

"How'd they manage to open the gate?" Crow huffed.

"I don't know." Jade slowed as they approached a clump of men dropping their bows for swords and spears. Their fires were a dull orange beacon in the blizzard.

"Northern Child!" They called, clapping Crow on the shoulder and praising Shadow as she flew above. Crow heard it now, the clang of steel on steel. The song of life and death. The clouds had blotted out the stars, their torches flickered and struggled to stay alight. A slender man pushed through the crowd to reach them. A slit in his helm revealed dark brown eyes.

"The gate was let down after the blast." He said, catching them to speed. "A spy, we think. The bastard killed five men."

"Did you catch him?"

"No. The feln rushed in like demons. They haven't made it far, though, but most of our men are stationed on the walls, it's a scramble to get enough people on the ground. We're trying to close the gate, but the fighting's too heavy. If we can close it off and trap the feln inside before too many get in, we can survive this."

"Let's get to it, then." Crow said.

They reached a watch tower on the wall, and jammed inside to take the stone steps down to the bottom. Crow enjoyed the respite from the snow while it lasted. The torches were warm on his face, the scent of sweat and smoke hung heavy in the air, and his limbs burned to kill something.

"Crow," Jade said, her voice nearly a whisper, "remember, don't be a fool out there. You must keep yourself alive."

"I thought *you* were supposed to keep me alive." He smirked.

She glared at him. "I will. But don't do anything stupid, like back on the boat to Seal Island." Her expression was hard. "Don't sacrifice yourself for anyone."

Crow frowned. "I don't see why—"

"It would have been for nothing if you died." Jade continued. "The ones who died to get you here, they would have died for nothing. Don't be a fool."

"I won't." Crow growled. "You planning to die on me?"

Jade smiled. "You'll need a champion when all this is over, I think."

Crow smiled at her. "I can't think of anyone better."

He channeled his mind back to blood. He knew Shadow was in the sky close by, he could taste her lust for blood on his tongue. His boots hit the ground, the narrow doorway opened up, and Crow ran forward into battle.

THIRTY-ONE

RIVERSET

Blood sprayed across Crow's face, warm, unlike the snow that continued falling from the black sky. The feln fell, dead before it hit the ground, a red slash opened the creature's throat. Crow barely looked the body over before swiveling around, parrying a vicious downward strike. He quickly adjusted his footing, waiting for the right moment...*there.* The feln raised her arm, but Crow's blade plunged through her armpit. He tugged it out, the feln dropped her weapon and lurched forward. Crow slashed again, nearly chopping her head in two. Shadow spat ice from above, cooking Crow's enemies with cold. Crow was winter incarnate. Death. He had no future and no past. In battle, there was only the present.

He'd lost Jade a while ago. The drawbridge had been opened as expected, and the northern gate was chaos of fighting men and feln. Arrows and stones rained from the wall above, trying to quell the feln crossing from the river. It was too dark to see beyond the arch. Crow had no idea how many more feln waited for them. Fires caught along the bridge, but nothing burned thanks to the heavy snow. The feln that slipped through wore bits of armor, some iron and crude. Others wore pieces with familiar symbols, fish from Youngston or a palm leaf from Augustii. Crow even came across feln that wore nothing at all, attacking men and picking up weapons from the ground like feral beasts.

The air reeked of burning pitch, iron, and the sweet stench of death. The sky was turning from black to bruised gray as dawn approached. *Has it been that long?* Crow watched a feln fall, face blackened by Shadow's ice. Something bumped against his back. Crow whirled, only to find a boy not much older than him holding a spear. The boy nodded before running to meet another foe. Crow didn't see who fell before turning as a dagger missed his neck by inches. He killed the feln like those before. Running for shelter, Crow let the snow melt and wash the blood from his face. *Protect your back.* He slammed against the stone wall of a small apothecary. The windows were broken in, the door ripped from the hinges. The inside was bright with flames.

With stone at his back, Crow looked himself over for injuries. His armor had kept him safe for the most part, but he suddenly felt pain blaze from his left elbow. His left forearm was running red with blood. *My blood.*

The screams and curses turned to cheers. Crow looked up in the brightening dawn to see the bridge groaning to life as it slowly rose from the angry river's current. Men and feln alike fell from the slick wood to their death as it ascended. Crow cheered with the others, spying a familiar face up by the winch.

Jade stood with a handful of knights. They'd retaken the gate, and within moments it was fully shut.

The men on the walls allowed a quick moment of victorious cheering. Crow didn't let his relief last too long; he still didn't know what was waiting for them beyond the walls. Riverset might last the night, but who knew how long the feln could keep this up. "Focus on killing the ones in here." Crow said out loud. He held up his sword, ready for the blood lust to take him again.

But then the blizzard stopped. Like a switch had been pulled. The snow fell to the ground and the world stilled.

Abrupt. Unnatural.

"Tree!" Crow's stomach dropped. He spun to run for the southern wall, the battle forgotten. But then fear, slick and slimy, froze him in place. It was a fear Crow had never felt before. Not even when he'd left Griffin's Peak. He was frozen, utterly afraid.

The fear was not his own.

Shadow screamed, it nearly sounded human, before darting away into the graying sky. Her fear was infectious and locked him into place.

Only the roar broke the spell. Men screamed for cover. A few brave souls shot arrows up. Crow nearly fell to his knees when he saw it. A descending mass of horns and feathers. The dragon roared again. It was the size of a war horse, and blended perfectly with the gray dawn. Its feathers were gray as storm clouds, but its horns were sharp and clear, like melting icicles. And when it opened its great jaws, winter came for them all. Crow watched men freeze in their armor before they had a chance to duck. They fell from the walls like children's toys, smashing onto the concrete and shattering into pieces. The dragon landed above the gate. On its back, two riders.

"Hold fire!" Someone cried desperately. "She has the duchess!"

When the dragon lowered its head, Crow saw Duchess Wanda bound and gagged; a knife held to her bare throat. The dragon's rider clung to the duchess's back, using her as a human shield. Crow couldn't see much of the rider. She had long black hair dancing erratically in the wind. He thought he saw spires of a sparkling crown poking from her head.

"The Queen of Winter." He murmured. The battling on the ground ceased. Every eye was glued to the beast clinging to the battlements, icy steam rose from between its teeth.

"Bring me your Northern Child!" The rider screamed. She sound-ed young, perhaps the same age as Jade. Her voice carried across the field with all of the authority of a ruler. "If he lies dead, then bring me his corpse so I may look upon him!" She shook Wanda. "Bring him to me and I will deliver your duchess back to you, and the bloodshed will stop! Refuse, and I will strike her down with the entire city!"

Crow's heart sank. A few soldiers furtively glanced in his direc-tion. He thought of Lyla and the others unable to fight. They were supposed to be safe with the duchess. His stomach lurched. His eyes found Jade up on the wall. She met his gaze and quickly shook her head. *Don't,* she said. He thought of Tree, and bile coated the back of his throat. He thought of Shadow, wherever she was. She must have fled after sensing the larger dragon. *If Shadow survives, if Tree or Jade or even Lyla survives. She'll find them.* He swallowed his fear. *I won't let these people die for me.* He had enough blood on his hands. *"Sing for me."* Kath had said. *Someone will. Just not me.*

Crow looked down at his hands, counting his fingers. They shook wildly.

Sheathing his sword, he stepped away from the burning shop. The sky was now overcast in the morning. The air was bone chilling, but after the heat of battle he barely felt it.

"It's me!" He called up. The dragon growled. The silence was loud as the Queen of Winter forced Wanda back down and kicked her dragon forward. Men flung themselves out of the way as the dragon landed before him, feathers gray as steel, and eyes blue as ice. Blue as his own. The queen continued to use Wanda as a shield. The duchess was afraid. She'd seemed so hard in council, but right now she looked like any other young girl.

Wrenching a fistful of Wanda's hair back, the queen exposed her throat further, and looked over the duchess's shoulder to behold the boy who stood before her dragon. She wore beautiful steel armor stolen from Youngston, probably from the queen based off of the engravings on the breastplate. Her hair was black as ink, skin pale as snow, and eyes...*bright blue.* Her features were sharper than soft, lending her a harsh appearance, like the jagged edges of her crown. The crown was fashioned from bone-white bark, resting atop her long flowing hair. She had a wild and feral look. Yet, her face was familiar somehow.

Their eyes met, and a cruel smile graced her thin lips. "Yes." She breathed, a wild elation fraying her tone. "You look just like her."

Her dragon rose its head like a snake about to strike. *Shadow,* Crow called with his mind. He reached for his sword, he knew it'd do nothing against the beast in front of him, but it gave him comfort.

"Where is your dragon?" The Queen of Winter asked, still hiding behind Wanda's bared throat. It didn't take long for her to grow impatient. Wanda grunted through her gag in pain when the queen wrenched at her hair in frustration. "No matter." With a wordless command, her dragon peeled back its lips.

The fear uncoiled from his stomach then.

But it was not his.

Shadow plummeted from the sky. She did not utter a sound as her hind talons shot forward like an eagle's. She fell and raked at the Queen of Winter's skull. Crow saw a flash of red, and heard the woman screech. Her own dragon whipped around, snapping at Shadow, forcing the two riders on its back to fall. Shadow screamed; her smaller size kept her from the larger dragon's jaws. She twisted away from the beast as it leapt up into the sky after her.

Chaos erupted.

The duchess was thrown aside. Still bound and gagged, Wanda thumped onto the blood-soaked ground like a sack of stones. The queen rolled before standing back up. Her crown had fallen from her head, and blood leaked down her face from her tattered scalp. Her eyes were frenzied with anger. With a grunt, she unsheathed two cruel swords from scabbards on each hip. Crow barely had time to register what just happened before she lunged at him.

He'd never fought against dual weapons like this. Crow quickly realized he was outmatched. It was all he could do to block every blow. She came at him at record speed.

The dragons roared from above. Blasts of ice cooled his skin from the battle in the sky. He heard the song of steel ring again as the remaining feln and men on the ground took up their arms. Crow heard arrows whiz passed, uncaring of their target.

"Such a weak thing!" The queen laughed, her smile bordering on mad. She spun again, Crow blocked her right swing, but her left cut at his side. The blade bounced off his armor, knocking him to the right. Crow nearly stumbled over Wanda, still on the ground and struggling to free herself. He leapt over her, and prayed for the Mother's forgiveness as he kicked her forward into the queen's legs. Wanda grunted in pain, but the queen didn't see the duchess until it was too late.

She fell forward, dropping one of her swords and quickly bringing the other up to parry Crow's blow to her face. But Crow's sword was bigger, and he hadn't spent himself with wild attacks. The sword flew from her hand. For a moment, fear dominated her blue eyes, and Crow reveled in it as he raised his blade to kill.

"I'm the one who killed your mother." The queen spat.

Crow hesitated.

That's all it took.

She plowed forward, knocking him on his back. He'd lost his weapon. The queen reached behind her, pulling out a dagger that had been kept against her lower back. Crow's arm shot up to stop the blow, but the dagger was too long. The point plunged into his left eye. Half the world went dark before the pain came. His screams were all he heard as he pushed against her, desperately trying to keep the knife from plunging further. The steel was cold, lancing through his head unlike anything he'd felt before. His blood ran hot down his cheeks, and spurted the blade red. He'd forgotten everything outside of the pain. His mind screamed. *Survive!*

The Queen of Winter was lithe and slim, Crow managed to savagely kick her off, and her knife slipped from his eye with a sickening *squelch*. A new lance of pain shot through his head, nearly knocking him over again. Arrows rained from the sky; one plunged into the queen's shoulder. She screamed, falling to her knees and gritting her teeth. A wall of gray feathers landed behind her as she stood back up. With a cry of anguish, she leapt onto her dragon's back. Its feathers were tipped with blood. Her arm hung limply at her side. *Shadow,* Crow thought as he struggled to sit up. The queen smiled then from her perch. A victor.

"Tell her hello." The queen gasped.

Her dragon's mouth opened wide. White smoke rolled from the back of its throat, surging forward like an avalanche.

Jade's sword took the beast in the face. A blow like that would have cleaved any other creature in two. The dragon stumbled to the side, blood gushing from its sliced jowl. It turned its head and blasted Jade where she stood.

Crow screamed in horror. The pain forgotten. The queen's dragon stumbled again, shaking its head from the blow. Blood ran freely down Crow's face, and over his armor, dripping down onto his hands as he lurched to Jade. He could feel the cold wafting off of her. Points of black dotted the edges of his remaining vision as his bloodied hand grabbed her leg. It was so cold it burned. His skin stuck to her, ripping away from his palms as he hit against her frozen armor.

"Glorygradus!" Someone yelled from above. "Glorygradus!"

Crow wretched, his vomit freezing to Jade's chest. His blood sizzled and froze from where it stained her. His vision swam, he felt the wind of wingbeats, he smelled sweet frozen flesh cooked by ice. The world began to spin. His vision darkened faster than the winter sky. He needed to see her face. He needed to *see*.

A fresh gush of blood pulsed from his ruined face, and Crow fell forward onto her chest. His body screamed as Jade's frozen armor burned at his cheek. *Shadow...* Crow thought, struggling to stay above ground.

But the darkness took him.

Thirty-Two

The Blue Vein

Crow felt his body sway gently back and forth. For a moment, he thought he was dead and cradled in the arms of Mother Vitania. But then the smell hit him, waste and fetid wounds clotted the stuffy air. And then the pain hit him too. The left side of his head felt like it was filled with stones, dully aching and pulsing in tune with his rocking body.

Jade, a wave of nausea hit him then. Crow turned over, his good eye snapping open as he heaved over the side of his hammock. Clear bile spilled onto the cabin floor; his stomach had nothing to give. *I'm on a ship.* He reached up to his pounding head, cloth bandages covered the left side of his face. The slightest touch made him wince, the skin on the other side was tender, like it was burned.

Shadow chirped from beside him.

"Hey." Crow rasped in relief. He reached for her. Shadow sat at his bedside like a loyal hound. She was tall enough to lay her head on his chest. He stroked her white snout, trying to ignore the waves of grief rolling towards him, threatening to sweep him away.

"Thank the Mother."

Flinching, Crow turned over. Lyla and Tree sat at his blind side. He released a strangled sound of relief when he saw them. They looked tired, and Tree looked sick as they usually did on boats, but otherwise, they looked unharmed. "You're okay." Crow croaked. "I was afraid when the blizzard stopped..." He wanted to reach out to them too, but it hurt too much. The little nymph offered Crow a bowl of fresh water. After struggling to sit up, he took it.

As suspected, they were in the underbelly of a ship. It was fairly large, filled with four other hammocks, three of which were occupied. Crow soon realized why their cabin smelled so unpleasant. The other occupants were covered in bandages similar to his own. Their edges were frayed with yellowed pus and dried blood. One man groaned, turning over, his leg was tied up at an awkward angle. Crow saw Sir Taeto, sleeping, his limbs all wrapped up and oozing some kind of sweet-smelling dressing. Crow was glad to see that the young knight was still alive.

"He's the only one from the island." Lyla murmured. "The rest..." She swallowed, unable to finish.

Crow's mouth grew dry. He fisted up a bunch of Shadow's feathers for support. "And Jade?" His words were little more than a whisper.

Tree lent Crow their hand before sadly shaking their head. Crow waited for the tears to come, for the sobs to wrack at his chest, but he felt nothing. The silence lasted an eternity.

"The Queen of Winter retreated after the Usario's river fleet was spotted coming down the Blue Vein." Lyla continued. "With the gates closed and her dragon injured, she turned and ran. Her army followed, and those left behind were slaughtered. They say Jade's sword turned the battle, after seeing the dragon stumble, men started fighting twice as hard. Duchess Wanda survived, and is declaring you both heroes."

The news did little to cheer Crow. Being deemed a hero wouldn't bring Jade back. "Then what?" He asked dully.

"Queen Joanna's men and the survivors secured Riverset. King Arnold collected survivors from the river," she glanced at Taeto, "but there weren't many. The brazen attack on the West has the Usarios ready for blood. Once it was deemed safe to travel, we set sail on one of her ships for Glorygradus. There's to be a war council. All of the royals from Frukjera will be there."

Crow frowned and laid back, another wave of exhaustion sweeping over him. "How long until we get there?"

"Just a few more days." Lyla said. "You've been in and out for a long time. Tree's been ladling water into your mouth like a doting mother." She smirked.

Crow knew he should talk more to his friends, he was grateful they were still alive, but he just didn't have the energy. Half of his world was now dark.

"Wake me up when we reach the wall." He mumbled, and closed his eye to go back to sleep.

Tree was the one to shake him awake. The cabin was pitch black, the only point of light a small lantern that Tree held to his face. Lyla was gone, and one glance at Taeto's hammock told him that the knight was too. Crow briefly wondered how long he'd been out.

Shadow followed them up to the deck. She stretched her wings and took off into the dawning sky. The crisp winter air bit at his skin, and snow covered the far away banks in blankets of pretty white. Winter was here. Tree led him to the rail, where the sun was rising from the east, illuminating Man's Wall in reds and yellows and oranges. It was a thick band of white, sparkling in the morning across the horizon. They were still miles and miles away, lending creed to the sheer size of it. Even from this far away, it was breathtaking.

Yet Crow found little beauty in it.

"The Queen of Winter said she killed my mother." Crow whispered. "She looks like me. Her hair is black, her eyes are blue." He turned to Tree. "She has an ice dragon. Did you know there were more?"

"No." Tree replied honestly.

"Do you think I'm not—"

"You are." Tree turned to regard the wall. "I know you are the Northern Child. I have seen the unicorns choose you with my own eyes. And even if I did not," Tree's eyes were as deep and green as spring, "I would know. You are worth following." Tree swallowed. "And you are worth dying for as well."

Crow wasn't sure he believed that. He stared across the waters to whatever awaited them beyond the wall.

Epilogue

Standing atop Man's Wall reminded Crow of the high-roped baskets from Griffin's Peak. He let the frozen air swirl around him as he looked down on the wintry countryside of the West to the frozen waters of the Pond of Serpents. It was the shortest day of the year. *I'm another winter older,* the light would die soon. The hills rolled like frozen waves. Bare trees dotted the land like gnarled hands. The Pond stretched out to the western horizon, nearly as endless as the sea. But Crow knew Griffin's Peak was on the other side. And somewhere out there was the desolate island that held the feln.

His body suddenly felt warmed by the hatred brewing in his belly. *On that island is the Queen of Winter.* She nor the feln had been seen on the continent recently. It was assumed that she'd turned and ran back to the island because her dragon was injured. Augustii was left burned and ruined. Duke Willemio wrote to them promising revenge. Soon enough, the royals from all over the continent would be here to decide their next move.

Crow fingered the bark crown in his grasp. It'd been recovered and given to him shortly before their arrival. Tree smuggled it away. And with it, the numbness in Crow's heart came alive with the heat of a promise.

"I will be the one to kill the queen." He said out loud, staring at the gray waters.

"Only if you don't let me get to her first." Lady Gretchen said from behind him. A new battle ax hung from her hip, a gift from Queen Charlotte of Youngston. Gretchen had taken up the position as Crow's guard after their bittersweet reunion upon the docks of Glorygradus. Crow could barely stand to look at her when he'd arrived.

Gretchen had put the puzzle together when she saw Kath and Jade weren't with him. She'd pulled Crow into a hug, and he'd stood still as stone.

"Did you find Wanda?" He'd asked her.

"She didn't make it." Gretchen whispered, tears rolling down her cheeks. Crow's resolve only hardened.

Shadow landed beside them on top of the wall; her snout red from a fresh kill. Crow reached out to pat her head, fingers tracing up her long twisting horns. "Soon she'll be big enough to ride," he said, staring into the endless gray, "and then, nothing will stop me."

END OF BOOK I

ABOUT THE AUTHOR

Ashley Cullen lives in Perth, Australia. As a fantasy reader, she often escapes to worlds crafted by others. More recently, she's been escaping to one of her own. Her other hobbies include painting, drawing, and taking care of her two lovely bunnies.